LETHAL KISSES

LETHAL KISSES

19 Stories of Sex, Horror and Revenge

Edited by Ellen Datlow

MILLENNIUM

An Orion Book
London

This edition first published
in 1996 by
Orion Books Ltd
Orion House, 5 Upper St Martin's Lane
London WC2H 9EA

A CIP catalogue record for this book is available
from the British Library

ISBN: 1 85798 480 3 (cased)
ISBN: 1 85798 481 1 (trade paperback)

Typeset at The Spartan Press Ltd,
Lymington, Hants

Printed and bound in Great Britain by
Clays Ltd, St Ives plc

For Pat Cadigan

*I would like to thank Merrilee Heifetz,
Caroline Oakley, and Lucius Shepard
for helping to make this anthology possible.*

CONTENTS

INTRODUCTION

You're walking down the street and the one who broke your heart walks by. You feel feverish, your heart starts beating faster, and your stomach clenches. You see that person step off the kerb and in your mind's eye you see a bus barrelling down the street, running down and squishing him (or her) like a bug on the windshield. And you smile.

Or perhaps you lose the promotion *you* earned at work to some jerk you can't stand and know only beat you out because she sucked up to the boss or is related to someone higher up. And you have to see this person daily. You feel angry and resentful and imagine poisoning her coffee at the next weekly meeting. Even though the passion, the fury, the disappointment will fade with time, initially you find yourself obsessing about getting back at those who wronged you. But most likely you won't, at least not in a particularly destructive way – because that's what keeps us civilised. Francis Bacon acknowledges this by saying 'Revenge is a kind of wild justice, which the more man's nature runs to, the more ought law to weed it out.' Civilisation teaches humans not to act on these and the other dark, roiling passions residing within, for if each of us did, society would collapse.

But we can still imagine. Perhaps that's why revenge, one of the great motivators of life, is as naturally one of the great themes in literature, particularly in dark suspense and horror literature. From William Shakespeare, John Steinbeck and William Faulkner to Edgar Allan Poe, Joyce Carol Oates, Ruth Rendell and Stephen King, revenge – for actual or imagined slights and deeds – has been a compelling motive in storytelling along with vengeance, the active complement – the punishment inflicted on the recipient of the revenge.

When I approached writers, I asked them to employ intriguing motivations for their characters' furies in addition to unusual methods/actions in which this payback would be dispensed, and I think the nineteen stories in this anthology reflect this dictum better than I had hoped. The motivations range from romantic failures or slights (intended and unintended) and professional envy, to unacknowledged racism, self-hatred and the desire to shake up the status quo. And the methods range from the down-to-earth direct approach of physical violence to the more subtle and occasionally supernatural.

The contributors are a varied lot, but most have one thing in common – they are cross-genre writers; they ignore genre boundaries. And I believe it's this impulse to write *what* they want in whatever genre works that makes for a strong brew of powerful and effective stories.

Vengeance doesn't have to be ugly, but one thing seems crucial – a diminishment of the other party in some way. Even in humorous stories someone must be defeated, either physically or emotionally. So we have A. R. Morlan's grisly little opener set against the rock and roll business, David Schow's dialogue between two ex-friends in Hollywood, Pat Cadigan's SF story about a woman convinced she's been robbed at the end of a bad relationship, Michael Cadnum's first-person turn about a man abducted by aliens, Pat Murphy's paean to chaos, Joyce Carol Oates's story of a woman who just wants to be left alone, and Christopher Fowler's treatment of London as a living entity. Ghosts, a traditional vehicle for vengeance, play a part in at least six of the stories in this anthology.

Whatever you personally may believe about revenge – that it demands an eye for an eye, that it is sweet, that it is a dish best served cold – you will probably find it addressed here.

Perhaps these tales will persuade you that if vengeance *could* be yours, it might be best just to go on living well.

. . . WARMER

by

A. R. Morlan

A. R. Morlan lives in Wisconsin. Her short fiction has been published in magazines such as *Night Cry, The Twilight Zone, Weird Tales, Worlds of Fantasy and Horror, The Horror Show, Phantasm,* and in the anthologies *Cold Shocks, Obsessions, Women of the West, The Ultimate Zombie, Love in Vein, Deadly After Dark: The Hot Blood Series, Sinestre, Night Screams* and *Twists of the Tale: An Anthology of Cat Horror.* They have been reprinted in *The Year's Best Fantasy and Horror.* She has published two novels, *The Amulet* and *Dark Journey,* and has recently finished a third.

Morlan is a flexible and talented stylist. Here she takes a poke at the sometimes sleazy world of rock and roll, in a story that, belying its title, gives the reader quite a chill.

. . . WARMER

Before Edan Westmisley faxed his summons to my agent, my only legitimate (as in you could see my face) claim to semi-demi-fame was the Steppe Syster's 'Love Victim' video where I licked the tattoo off the chest of their lead guitarist, Cody Towers.

Yeah, that was me. Not that anyone makes the connection between the big-hair, tits-swaying-in-a-bikini-top, thong-bottomed retro pre-AIDS bimboid slithering up the paint-drizzled riser towards Cody's semi-desirable, love-handled bare torso, tongue out and lashing against candy-apple lips, just before he notices me, slings his Stratocaster behind his pimply back and hoists me up by the armpits, so I can lovingly slurp off his licorice-icing tattoo (painted on over his Dermablend-smeared real phoenix-in-flames tattoo by a bandanna-covered bald-pated tattoo artist) in slo-mo close up, and what I am now, thanks to Edan Westmisley and his once-in-a-career offer –

– the offer he didn't share with my agent, or with anyone employed in his hidden/not hidden studio; the offer which held out the promise of me becoming something far more spectacular and memorable than just a tattoo-devouring bimbo . . .

'Thaaat's riiight, kiddo, Edan Westmisley, Gran' Poo-bah -supremo at Genius Productions, as in get your mini-skirted bum down to his office, pronto –'

It wasn't unusual for my agent Gerhard Berbary to speak in italics, but for him to even come close to swearing (he was Canadian, which made 'bum' synonymous with 'ass' or worse), something much bigger than just another metal video shoot or frontal nude body-doubling part was at stake here, especially as far as Gerhard's cut was concerned. And at this point in my 'career', considering how few videos, walk-ons and tit-'n'-ass insert shots he'd been able to round up for me, I knew that he would've sold my corpse for morgue gape shots if it would've netted him a commission . . .

Not that being dead could've made me feel any less uneasy than Gerhard's wake-up call about Westmisley wanting me to come to his studio early that afternoon; while I didn't consider myself an 'insider' when it came to the music scene, I did have subscriptions to *Billboard*, *Variety*, *Rolling Stone and Spin* . . . and with all my free time, especially after the 'Love Victim' shoot, I'd had the opportunity to learn more than I actually cared to about Mr Westmisley, formerly of the sixties Fluxus movement (a well-to-do group of what Gerhard dubbed 'art-farts' which included Yoko Ono and her bare-buttocks-in-a-row film, really classy shit like that), and currently sole owner, stockholder, president and producer-in-residence at Genius Productions Ltd, a record company that produced hard-core industrial, techno, alternative and speed metal acts (like Steppe Syster), almost none of which ever charted higher than 150 on the *Billboard* Album Chart, but which were killers on the college charts – all the more ironic because Westmisley had supposedly (if the unauthorised bios reviewed in *Rolling Stone* could be believed) been all-but-bodily-thrown out of every university in Europe and the East Coast, for a little more than simply flunking out or missing dorm curfew –

(– as in things even pay-to-say journalists like Kitty Kelly were afraid to reveal after one unauthorised bio writer turned up belly-bloated on the Nantucket shoreline after interviewing some ex-Vassar co-ed in her nursing home bed . . . the bed she'd been confined to after dating soon-to-be-ex-Harvard alumni Westmisley –

– one of the same universities he'd later endow with trifles like libraries, gymnasiums and radio stations during the early eighties, after he'd finished the last round of chemo-and-radiation for his near-fatal bout with skin cancer.

He'd contracted said skin cancer during a two-year round-the-world junket in his favorite yacht in the mid-seventies, when he was on his collecting binge . . . and he'd sped home across two oceans with close to a dozen countries breathing down his burnt-to-jerky neck, threatening legal action for whatever illegal/endangered baubles he'd 'bought' . . .)

And now Edan Westmisley wanted me to drive to his office, for a reason even my agent didn't know –

I asked Gerhard twice, 'You mean to meet *with* him, like face-to-face?' and both times, his answer was the same . . . and as maddeningly vague:

'You want me to *read* you his fax? Here it is: "Ger*hard*, please send your client from the Steppe Syster 'Love Victim' shoot to my office for a private meeting, noon to*day*." *Hear* that, dear*heart*? The man said "Pl*ease*" . . . '

'He didn't mention me by name,' I'd countered both times, as the phone cord wrapped itself around my wrist like a curly python, but Gerhard was adamant – I was his only client to appear in a Steppe Syster video.

'But Ger, Westmisley only produces records, as in musicians . . . his *people* handle videos, he just oversees what they come up with.' As I pleaded with him, I squeezed the receiver anxiously, my skin crawling under the remembered pressure of Westmisley's smoke-glass-shielded eyes.

I suppose people who saw the 'Love Victim' video assumed that my tattoo-slurping cameo was morphed, but that wasn't 'Edan's *style*.' Or so said Kenny, the director, while everyone waited for Mr Bandanna to finish embellishing Cody's chest as he stretched out like a fallen Christ on the drum riser, bitching about how much the black paint-thin icing tickled as the glumly sweating tattoo guy spent an hour of studio time painting faux needlework between Cody's nipples. There was only so much butt-wiggling for Kenny to do in that hour, so eventually he confided, 'Great Scarface's into sen*sat*ion, albeit visually simulated sen*sat*ions . . . *he* can't feel a damn thing any more.' Kenny whispered in his irresistible Capote-esque drawl, glancing towards the rear of the studio, past the terminator of on-set lights, between every word. After the third or fourth glance, I looked back towards what he was staring at . . . Edan Westmisley, or some of him. He was a featureless, dark slice of shadow against the murky studio shadows, with only the plump, convex ovals of his sunglass lenses reflecting the arc-light glare.

'Looks like roadkill before it's run over,' I whispered in Kenny's hoop-lobed ear; he whispered in my thrice-pierced ear, 'Oh no, Edan's not roadkill . . . he's an immobile, hulking *beast* that smashes and twists grillwork, before sending your car into the fucking *ditch*,' just as the suspended-in-darkness lenses drifted away to the *clup-clup* of his retreating lizard-skin boots. Once Kenny seemed sure that he was out of range in the huge studio, he added, 'I've developed "shoulder eyes" while working for him . . . all Edan has to do is stare at me, and my skin *writhes* . . . like getting a sunburn while staying dead-fish-*white*.'

I thought Kenny was just blissfully melodramatic, but once Bandanna-Guy was finished, and Kenny started flat-clapping his hands, begging for '*Qui*-et,' as he cued the lights and the assistant director set the electronic clapboard, I heard that steady, rhythmic *clup-clup* echoing in the far reaches of studio, a staccato wooden-heeled counterpoint to the fuzzed-out tape the band was syncing to . . . and while I could barely see those disembodied shimmering discs of reflected light hovering behind Kenny's muscular, T-shirted back, they began to bore down on my exposed skin, the way light rays exert a trace of real weight – an unseen, yet measurable pressure. If Kenny endured 'shoulder eyes', *I* endured 'body eyes' . . . and by the time I snake-slithered up that riser, and tiny splinters dug into my exposed midriff, my skin felt as if it were being smothered, each pore screaming for air, and once Cody's sweating, call-oused hands hoisted me up for my tattoo-tonguing close-up – Kenny barked orders at the Steady-cam operator, but his voice seemed filtered, as if unable to penetrate Edan's suffocating stare – I forgot Kenny's directions about keeping my eyes open, and began furiously lapping and slurping up bitter black icing, not caring where or how furiously I licked, until Cody jerked back, yelping, 'Hey! Watch the nipple ring, wouldja?' after my left incisor snagged the gold ring jutting out from his raisin-like nipple, and Kenny soothed, '*Go* with it, Co*deee*, make it *work* for you,' but all the while I couldn't shake that hand-firm pressure all over me, as if Westmisley's eyes were doing a King Kong on my Fay Wray skin, so I wound up licking Cody's Adam's apple before Kenny burbled, 'Cut! *Per*-fect . . . it's a wrap. *Hon* . . . Hon*ey*, time to get up –'

Only, I didn't want to get up, not with Edan still there, behind Kenny; I stayed on my knees until Cody hoisted me up by the armpits, roughly, and whispered, 'Get lost, wouldja?' then stalked off for his dressing room, whining to Kenny, 'She almost yanked my ring out, man.' I still couldn't open my eyes, though, until Kenny shot back, 'Just as long as it wasn't in your dick . . . not that *that's* big enough *to* pierce,' and under those playfully drawled words, I heard the ever-more-distant *clup-clup* of Edan's boot heels, as he left the studio.

'Don't mind that pimpled *twit*, dear, he'll never stop you from working,' Kenny began as I opened my eyes, as if it was Cody I was so obviously scared of; not wanting to spoil Kenny's fantasy about Edan being hung up on him, I just smiled, nodded, and took the hand-down he offered me, before stepping off that riser and out of the studio, into the fading-but-*real* touch of sunlight on my oxygen-starved flesh.

'– listen, *kid*do, do *I* question Edan West*mis*ley and still expect to make any more deals in *this* charming burg? If he faxed me a request that I *per*sonally swab out his private vomi*tor*ium with my *ton*gue, I'd glaaadly *do* so – am I speaking *Eng*lish to you, or am I jabbering in fucking *Greek*?'

Privately replying, '*No, Gerhard, you'd gladly* do *him if he'd stoop to dropping his pants for a third-rate wanna-be-like* you,' I mumbled, 'English, Ger,' before asking (even as my brain protested), 'When did he want me there?'

'*Noon* . . . do you realise that any *other* of my clients would already be *at* Westmisley's as I speak, doing the knee-dance under his *desk* in gratitude? And swallowing every damn *drop*? If he hadn't of asked for *you* in particular, I'd have called one of my other clients . . . what's the matter, you scared of the *sto*ries about him?'

Even though he had no way of seeing me, I shook my head of would-be-video-queen big-hair *No*; crazy producer stories were as commonplace as urban legends – didn't Tina Turner once see Phil Spector pick up an apple core coated with cigarette ash out of a tray and eat it? The quirks and foibles of producers were the stuff of *Rolling Stone*'s 'Random Notes' column, weren't they? But the underground zines, the grungy hand-Xeroxed jobbies sold at the bigger book stores, they had the real, fresh dirt on No-Eyes Westmisley: the over-lord attitude with his engineers; the sudden, blackball firings; the kinky stuff his ex-lovers only hinted at; the way he circumvented customs with whatever fetishes or artifacts he'd glommed on to during that cancer-causing last jaunt of his; and how he'd beaten said cancer by going to Third World doctors who'd try anything, from whatever source, to heal what should never be healed . . . yet, despite all the weirdness he'd indulged in from the sixties on (long past the time when his fellow Fluxus members went respectable – like when Yoko made huggy-kissy with McCartney at the Rock and Roll Hall of Fame induction), Edan Westmisley was the original Teflon Dude, and never mind Ronbo Reagan.

No union could touch him. No woman – no matter what bed or cell or worse she occupied – could blackmail him. Whether it was out of fear, or because he was so well insulated (old money rich, from a peerage in England), no one knew for sure, save for knowing that Edan Westmisley was about as close to a god as a man could be and still need to shake his dick after pissing (or so Kenny advised me during a chance meeting outside of Spago).

Yet, as powerful as Westmisley was, he'd said 'Please' to the cut-rate agent of a would-be actress . . . someone who couldn't do a tattoo-licking shot without almost removing a guy's nipple ring the hard way.

To get a 'Please' from Westmisley was far rarer than gobs of manna dripping on the Walk of Fame . . . a courtesy he wasn't obliged to give to anyone, for anything. But as Gerhard gave me directions to Westmisley's office-cum-studio, I wondered just what sort of price-tag – be it actual or something less tangible – was attached to that unexpected show of civility . . .

Now, I realise that Edan's adding 'Please' to that fax had nothing to do with politeness, or any normal human civility, but was perhaps meant only to forestall suspicion.

Genius Productions Ltd was located out in the Hills, or almost past them, to be exact; to this day, I can't find the spot on any map. But then again, since I've never driven near the place again, let's just say it's Out There. Anyhow, if you were to drive past it unknowingly, you'd never realise that you'd just whizzed past the entire complex – not that the building was hidden by trees or by a fence (Edan detested the obvious, in all things). It was just that the place was so unassuming that it barely registered. Oyster-white stucco exterior, minimal smoke-tinted windows, three squat storeys, flat tile roof, superbly earthquake-proof in that there was nothing to break off (and reinforced from within by double-strength I-beams, as Edan proudly informed me), with only a bizarre metal sculpture adorning the brownish stubble of grass directly in front of the entrance to indicate that it wasn't a warehouse or sweatshop garment factory.

Yet, the sculpture itself was the key to both the identity of the building and the mentality of the man who designed and built it; from every angle but one, it resembled randomly staked Christian and Coptic crosses, of varying heights and widths, fanned out in a crescent shape across the lawn. But once a car was almost past the entire building, if you happened to look just *so* in the rearview mirror, the assemblage would suddenly meld together into a concave, seemingly smooth unbroken surface – save for the open spaces which read (in reverse, since it was *meant* to be read in a mirror):

GENIUS PRODUCTIONS LTD.

It was so perfectly executed it was chilling; even if a motorist noticed the solid version of the sculpture (including the squared-off words), it only remained solid-looking long enough to barely register the words before dissolving into a scattering of haphazard steel as soon as the car sped forward.

But I didn't feel privileged to have caught on to Edan's single-glimpse-only sign, as I backed my Escort up and then drove into the nearly empty parking lot to the east of the building; the *selectiveness* inherent in the design of that sculpture/sign galled me, perhaps because it gave no concession to unavoidable, human things like an eyelash getting in one's eye, or someone blinking at that exact second, or something going wrong with the car, or with traffic. Happen to miss that fraction of a second of the sign's wholeness, and a person might spend hours combing the freeway, searching for the elusive edifice just passed.

But the true pre-eminence of Edan Westmisley was waiting

to be revealed to me; the double-paned smoked doors in front of the building were operated by a sensor, like those in a store, so that in itself didn't spook me . . . but the lack of anyone – security guards, receptionists, cleaning men with big sloppy galvanised metal buckets, wanna-be recording artists hoping to get *past* the non-existent receptionists – I-mean-*any*one, inside that stucco, steel and glass edifice did get to me. In a major way . . .

All I saw was a quarter mile of empty hallway, carpeted in the sort of plushy beige carpeting that mats down if you sneeze at it, extending in a straight line from where I stood to the back of the building. Which culminated in another door, this one industrial-steel-with-pneumatic-hinges (the emergency-only type usually seen in the rear of by-the-highway chain stores), and surmounted by a red-lit 'EXIT' sign.

'You're quite cold, yaw'know, just standing there.'

The voice was without a definable source; just simply *there*. But I was clued in enough to realise that it was Westmisley's languid, English-accented upper-class-twit voice (I'd seen that MTV interview Kurt Loder did with him just before he'd gone on that ill-advised yacht voyage and brought home a little more than a hold full of illegal goodies), and nervy enough not to want him to realise how badly he'd frightened me, so I drew myself up to my full five nine plus heels, smiled my toothiest should've-been-a-model smile, and forced myself to purr (didn't Gerhard tell me how *lucky* I was to *be* here?), 'And I don't like being cold –'

'Start moving and you'll begin to warm up –' At least the disembodied voice had a slight hint of warmth in it by then. When he stopped speaking, he began humming, a tuneless, one-note drone that allowed me to figure out that he'd planted speakers in the walls, ceiling, even *under* the carpeting . . . which made me feel as if I was walking down his throat. As I walked, casually swinging my arms with each step (even though I would've rather hugged myself by then, purely for the security of it) down that diffusely lit hallway – recessed fluorescents that cast less than forty watts per fixture – I noticed there were doors set into the cream-coloured lucite walls; the pin-thin outlines were unmistakable . . . as was the lack of knobs.

Twenty steps down that runner of carpeting.

'Warmer.'

Ten more steps, slowing down near each door outline.

'*Much* warmer –'

Glance up, but still no cameras visible. *Maybe in the fixtures?*

'*Waaarrrmmm*ah –' The humming became a throaty growl.

Two steps forward. Then one back. *There.* Just like with the statue outside, I didn't see the unadorned embossed lettering over the one doorway until I'd almost passed by:

'*Timeo Danaos et dona ferentes*' – Virgil

I might've been only a model-without-portfolio, an ass-or-boobs-for-hire body-double for straight to video flicks whose sole claim to semi-fame came during the increasingly infrequent airings of the 'Love Victim' video, but I didn't consider myself an uneducated bimbo, no matter what Gerhard thought. I'd finished high school, top third of my class, and had done a year and a half of college, too. I couldn't read Greek, but I'd heard of Virgil – not that I was ready to let Westmisley know *that* much about me yet.

'*Verrry waaarm* –' I moved a foot sideways, to the right.

'*Hot* –' The door slid open before me, gliding into the wall with a muted *schwoosh* of lucite rubbing lucite. Beyond me was yet more unmatted plush carpet, culminating in another blank cream wall. *Smartass bastard.* I trotted up to the unopened pocket door so fast Westmisley barely had time to blurt out 'Boiling!' as the door opened, and I strode through the newly revealed opening –

– into what looked, felt, and even smelled like a pit, like a droppings-piled bat cave, or some ransacked ancient tomb still swirling with the dust of disturbed mummified remains . . . the contrast between creamy-bright *nothingness* and prodigal *fullness* finally smashed the last shards of my pseudo-hip LA woman veneer; I stopped so abruptly I almost fell forward on to the swirling arabesques of his Persian/Oriental carpet from the built-up momentum.

As I steadied myself, I became aware of –

– Eyes. Everywhere around me. Square-and-triangle Kachina doll eyes, tight-lidded slits in the faces of African fertility figurines whose bodies were little more than knee-to-chin engorged vaginal lips. Glass and plastic orbs set in the nappy heads of mounted game animals, more than a few of them from extinct or endangered species. Pin-prick gargoyle eyes, unblinking in their stony intensity. Wrinkled, fine-lashed lids drawn tight over the sunken orbs of several shrunken heads which hung by frazzled, beaded topknots. Bland concave pupilless eyes in chipped Grecian and Roman statuary fragments. Frosting-bright sockets in Mexican sugar skulls. And peepholes set in the gold and silver irises of the rows of gold and platinum records which formed dividing lines between the shelved antiquities and oddities covering the walls of Westmisley's office.

And reigning supreme in that silent, frozen freak show was Edan Westmisley himself, his purple-wattled, burst-capillary red and mottled-greyish tan full moon of a face suspended over a bridge of semi-clawed, tortuously linked fingers under his ill-defined chin, his eyes protected with those oval smoky glasses, his carefully brushed and dry-sprayed greying hair (a wig, perhaps?) a glowing nimbus over his ruined features . . . but despite the almost heavenly way his neatly side-parted hair seemed lit from within, the effect wasn't angelic in the least.

His immaculate grey Italian silk suit, starched-till-it-shone white shirt, and burnished pewter-tone tie didn't register on my consciousness until a few disoriented seconds had passed (I did know his boots were lizard skin, as Kenny had claimed); precious seconds during which he was able to survey and . . . *catalogue* me with those near-hidden, impartial, *appraising* eyes of his. As if I was yet another *item* he could buy, then mount on those cluttered walls of his . . .

That much I realised when he smiled; not a friendly, glad-to-meet-ya smile, but a stiff rictus of those purple-tinged lips, which parted to reveal a fence-like double row of white, flat surfaced teeth . . . seeing that pseudo-smile, I knew that whatever words came through those bloated lips, past those hard-edged, perfect teeth, wouldn't convey one iota of whatever a jaded, world-weary man like Westmisley might still be capable of *feeling*, if, indeed, he felt anything for anyone at all.

I think I smiled in reply; I don't recall much besides him

pointing out a chair, and me easing into its spongy depths, unable to speak . . . unable to *think*, actually. Drumming his blunt-tipped, crescent-clawed fingers (each ridged nail perfectly manicured, save for the tip of the left forefinger, which was missing above the last joint) on top of his empty, black-wood-surfaced desk, Westmisley said without preamble:

'Lovely . . . how you licked away that buffoon's tattoo . . . I could almost hear the uppermost layers of flesh parting from his chest . . . an exquisitely painful moment, especially the way the chap winced until his eyes fairly *watered* –'

'I snagged his nipple ring with my incisor,' I blurted out, my face flushing at the memory. 'Kenny said he'd edit it out, but –'

'But he didn't . . . I assume you can figure out why.' There was no question mark punctuating his voice, as if positing that I should know such a thing. Directly behind his left shoulder, a particularly rabid-looking Indonesian carved mask leered at me until I felt incredibly exposed, vulnerable, and found myself babbling, 'Not really . . . Cody seemed to be so piss–upset about it, I just figured Kenny *would* edit it out –'

'As he intended to do, until I told him not to. That flash of pain in the guitarist's eyes was precisely what I wanted. The object, as it were, of the entire tattoo-removing scene. The act leading up to it was only a means to a most specific end . . . after all,' he added, his Twit-of-the-Year tone growing softer, yet darker, with each carefully enunciated syllable, 'I could have had that sequence morphed in less than half the time it took that tattoo *artiste* to embellish that blubbery fool's epidermis with frosting, and probably at a comparable expense. The resulting faux tattoo, and you as well, were fungible . . . all I ever had in mind was seeing that unfeigned twinge of agony in the chap's eyes, accompanied by an unrehearsed grimace of pain about the lips. Nothing more than what might've been accomplished by a swift, clean thrust to the uncupped groin . . . but via a more aesthetic route. A small tid-bit for the visually jaded.'

His short speech finished, Westmisley laced bent fingers into a fleshy shield before his lower chest, and stared at me until I could almost make out his eyes behind the infernally reflecting lenses . . . slow-blinking, turtle-wattled eyes, small shiny balls set in a webbing of crinkled, oddly shiny skin. Those eyes were so unnaturally bland, so removed from pain or any sort of inner suffering, I wondered if they were cosmetic contact lenses, perhaps to cover sun-induced discoloration or disease; no one who had gone through such indisputably painful treatments for cancer should've possessed such calm, untroubled eyes.

Oh, I'd heard of people with no threshold of pain, who never felt as much as a headache, but that was a rare condition; what could the odds have been of such a rich, worldly man also being blessed with freedom from external or internal agony? Yet, for him to intentionally inflict pain on another –

'But it was an accident . . . I didn't mean to hurt him,' I countered, as I shifted around in the chair, trying to assume a more upright position, but the chair (a modernistic, nubby-surfaced marshmallow perched on a stem-like base) seemed to have no internal framework . . . just layer upon layer of spongy softness, with no hard core to pull myself up on. So there I sat, legs slightly splayed, arms loosely akimbo, head just barely supported by the high back of the stupid seat, yet still trying to hang on to whatever dignity I possessed.

'All the better for the desired effect . . . why do you think I told Kenny to hire a woman to devour Cody's tattoo? All the members of the group were similarly embellished, some with more pleasing designs . . . but only he sported pierced nipples. And the nipple is such a sensitive area of the anatomy . . . much more so than the earlobe, don't yew think?' He stared at my ears, with their trio of studs per lobe, and I reflexively pawed my hair over my ears before replying, 'Yeah . . . I don't know how anyone could have that done –'

'Getting your ears pierced didn't hurt?' Behind those shining lenses, something flickered for a second in his pale eyes, something eager, hungry –

'No – wait, I mean, yeah, it hurt, y'know, but it wasn't a major thing . . . not enough to stop me from having more holes put in. But an earlobe isn't a nipple –'

'No, no, it isn't,' he agreed, in a surprisingly regretful-sounding tone. Then shifting his voice from wistfulness to its former briskness, he went on, 'You probably realise I didn't ask you here to discuss body piercing and tattoo-removal . . . listen carefully to this, would you?' Nearly smiling for real, he unlaced his fingers and reached over to his left, where he pressed a slightly recessed portion of the desk-top. A few seconds of hissing static followed, the sound coming out of every wall as well as the ceiling; white noise amplified and captured on ferrous oxide, then came this almost-familiar looped sample, its tune nearly buried in industrial drum-beats and fuzzed-out electric techno synths, with additional layers of reverb and redubs –

'Is that the intro to Fleetwood Mac's "Tusk"?' I ventured timidly, having decided that Westmisley got off on whatever information he could glom on to from people; in reply, he said softly, 'Luke-warm . . . it's the drum-line from "Goody-Two Shoes", Adam Ant's solo effort – but *wait* –' With his right, whole index finger, he motioned for me to lean forward. Despite the squishiness of the chair, I *leaned* –

– and a fraction of a second later, this . . . *voice* cut through the beat, redubs and reverb; just a single sustained note that somehow grew stronger, louder and *needier* by the minute. When it seemed that no set of lungs could power a note for that long, that *energetic* a period of time, the voice swooped down to a shivery whisper, droning on and on in a rhythmic, chant-keen-*prowl* melody without actual words . . . definitely not house, not quite speed metal caterwauling, nor thrash, and certainly not a grunge growl, but whatever this . . . *sound* was, it was definitely hard-core. And miles beyond any alternative music I'd heard before . . .

More like . . . *elemental*. Pre-primitive, but with a hybrid industrial/thrash/techno back-beat swooping in and around every flutter and trill of that incredible, inexhaustible set of pipes.

And as I listened, I felt myself wanting, needing to *move*, to just free whatever it was that made me *alive* in my body, to shake flesh and bones and pulsing blood to that impossibly fast over 140 beats per minute melody . . . I can't remember getting up, but a couple of minutes into the song, I *was* up and dancing around the cluttered, musty-aired room, my limbs jerking from places deep within me, my head rolling sinuously on my neck, my eyes almost but not quite closed, as if I'd just dropped a cocktail of smart drugs, or 'E' –

– but when I found myself face to face with one of *them*, it was like a switch had been shut off in my brain, leaving me frozen in unblinking place before the wall opposite Westmisley's ebony desk.

I was virtually eye to eye with a trio of the most gawdawful *ugly* . . . constructions I'd ever seen anywhere, be I sober or stoned, and as I gazed at their oddly slick and slightly moist-looking surfaces, I wondered how their owner could bear to look at them while sitting serenely behind his desk, especially since their lidless eyes were all but locked on his shielded ones.

They were about twenty-some inches tall, like baby dolls, only no kid would've taken one of *those* things to bed with her. Big bald heads, the skulls ivory-pale with nary a hint of hair stubble, just filmy-thin shiny flesh, with gelid glassy eyes set into the sockets, and open jaws filled with glistening over-sized ivory teeth. No hint of flesh on the exposed arms; just finely carved bones attached to each other with some sinewy-looking waxy amber threads. The rest of the bodies were wrapped in quasi-mummy-style linen bandages, culminating in a blunted point where the feet should've been. Repulsive as they were, I couldn't stop staring at them; whoever fashioned these images did an ingenious job of waxing or varnishing or . . . wetting the surfaces to make everything glisten in a not-sunny-but-it-*should*-be-manner, so that the skulls and their pencil-thin arm bones shone like they were resting under clear, clean water instead of being exposed to the drying, polluted LA air.

Just then, the song died away, culminating in a fevered, intense whisper before the final triumphant *whoop*, and I was able to speak once more, now that the song had released my body and mouth.

'Wha . . . what *are* those things?'

'What do you think they might be?' That same cold toying voice I'd heard upon entering the building. Not wishing to be suckered in again by the sheer power of his ability to possess things, to manipulate that which was just beyond his reach, I concentrated on the middle figure, taking in the gelid yet hazy tan-irised eyes, and began, 'Uhm . . . representations of dead people –'

'Warm,' he conceded.

'Or . . . life after death, like spirits?' After the intense work-out I'd just experienced, I still had trouble organising my thoughts.

'Waaarmer . . . '

'Really *old* spirits,' I ventured, to which he replied in a terse whisper, 'Hot . . . they're *Kakodiamones*. Ancient Greek for evil spirits. Very rare representations . . . I acquired them three years ago or so –'

Without needing for him to explain further, I realised he was talking about his final yacht voyage; within months of return-ing home, he'd haunted every cancer clinic in the world, trying to halt the fast-spreading, disfiguring melanomas which threatened to all but rot the flesh off his carcass – the indy zines and even Loder on MTV attributed it to too much time spent lounging in equatorial and Mediterranean sunlight, and not enough time spent smearing on sunblock. As my gaze cautiously roamed his corrugated flesh, while I tried to appear as if I were maintaining polite eye contact, I was struck by the irony of such a powerful, old-money dude not bothering to shell out a few bucks for a case of SFP 32 sunscreen, but then again, if what I'd read in those same indy rags was true, parts of his body which didn't show in polite company were still . . . viable, according to those ex-mistresses who were willing or able to say anything at all about him.

After taking in every ridge, wattle and unexpected contour of his face, I realised that the subject of his repulsive, spit-shined figurines might hit too close to home, make him uncomfort-able (or possibly invoke his legendary, quirky temper), so I took a conversational side-step and asked, 'Isn't that inscription over your outer door Greek too?' in an over-confident voice which made me cringe in retrospect, for Westmisley's puce-mottled shining lips jerked into a chilly smile. 'Just warmish, if that. Actually, it's from the Latin . . . Virgil was a Roman, after all. It means, "I fear the Greeks even when they offer gifts."'

Glancing back at the stiff trio, I remarked, 'Considering what *they* look like, no wonder Virgil said –'

The puckered skin of his lips twisted into a full *moué* as he answered in a slightly peevish tone, 'I'm certain that Virgil wasn't referring to Katharine, Kerenze and Kristine here –' Noting my puzzled expression, he elaborated with a crêpe-lidded wink. 'I've found the best way of dealing with the unknown and the frightening is trivialisation . . . condescending pet names, inappropriately silly –'

'"Silly",' I found myself echoing with a dumb nod of my head, until Westmisley's expression shifted from indulgent to irritated; then, with a flick of his clawed hand, he indicated the concealed tape deck in his desk-top and asked, 'Well, what do you think of this?'

Giving Westmisley my most sincere would-be model smile, I began slowly, while making my way back to that impossibly pneumatic chair, 'The singer . . . god, she's *fabulous*. Just incredible . . .' Then, remembering that Westmisley had actually composed music, back in his Fluxus art-fart days, I backtracked, '. . . I mean the music itself was fantastic, but that *voice* . . . to sing like that, she must've been opera-trained, like Pat Benatar, or Linda –'

At that, Westmisley again pursed his lips into a crooked *moué*, as if I'd insulted his newest musical acquisition in an unknown way, so I quickly added, while trying to lean forward, 'But she blows them away, no contest. I'd *love* to see the reaction of the first rave crowd who hears her –'

It was then, for just a fraction of a second, that he let down his guard – or at least allowed whatever it was that he was thinking or feeling to change his expression; no sooner had I uttered those last words than his features softened, as his eyes (through the tinted lenses) grew wistful, their surfaces sheened with unmistakable moisture, and, for a moment, he once again resembled the fairly-good-looking-in-a-snooty-British-fop-way producer he'd been before the low-hanging Mediterranean sun made his skin go supernova. It was like this song, this singer, meant so incredibly *much* to him; the pride he felt at that moment was all but palpable –

– and, watching his ruined features melt with inner warmth, something went slightly soft and vulnerable in me; looking back on it, I can only describe what happened to me as being like that . . . momentum thing which occurs when you lift up one of those hanging steel balls and let it strike the rest of the balls suspended from that rack of five or six balls, when the moment of impact causes the last ball in line to fly free of its fellow balls. You'd think the last ball in line moved in sympathy with the first ball, rather than it being a controlled, impersonal reaction. His changed expression was that first ball. And my feelings were free-flying far from reality when my eyes registered those shifting features . . .

There was a beat of silence as I let my voice trail off, then, while I still flew high and loose, words tumbled out of my mouth.

'I've been to a few raves, but nothing they played matched *this* . . . it's . . . it's like you tapped *into* her, and put all of her there *is* on to a master tape . . . it's life, in a song. Something that sweeps you into it and doesn't let go until it's done with you –'

Cutting off my stream of babble with one slicing motion of his curved right hand, Westmisley leaned forward ever so slightly, and asked softly, his voice teasing in its insouciance, 'What do you suppose she looks like, while singing?' Then, as if sensing that I'd need prompting in order to answer him, he thumbed on the tape player, albeit at a lower volume. I concentrated as I listened, letting my mind paint an image to match the voice before I spoke again.

'Wild . . . jerking like Janis Joplin, not holding back at all . . . sweating, she's *dripping* . . . hair's all spiked where she's run her hands through it as she sings . . . I see her dripping with chains, little rings digging into her skin between them . . . if she's wearing anything, it's mostly ripped off from all her flailing around . . . ribcage is heaving, the hollow of her throat is fluttering . . . she's just sweating and gleaming there –'

The silence which followed that wordless melody was painfully loud and echoing in my ears. I slumped back against the billowing padding of my chair, eyes half closed, and finished, more to myself than to him, '– then she just collapses in a shiny heap, panting softly. That's . . . that's what I see when I hear her . . . '

'I suppose that's one way of picturing her,' Westmisley reflected in a tone which somehow suggested that his mental image was far, far different from mine – but also one he was disinclined to share.

Before I could ponder his words (as I've done so, *so* many times since), he smiled again, then added, 'How would you like to . . . act out what you've just described to me?'

That time, I needed no time to reflect on his words – or their implicit meaning. I'd been knocking around LA and the fringes of the music scene long enough to recognise his pitch for what it was, as my mind scolded me *What else did you think he'd want from you? Did you think you had any* talent *he could exploit?*

He was talking C & C Music Factory, Black Box, even Milli Vanilli time. As if I was some hick bitch who'd just stepped off the Greyhound from Bible-Belt, USA in search of instant fame-'n'-fortune.

'I won't lip-synch,' I said tersely, remembering all the negative press those video body-doubles had accumulated so quickly – and so permanently. I was about to get up and leave when Edan replied softly, his voice almost seductive in its faux warmth, 'But I know what you *do* do . . . you wait in an overpriced, undersized apartment, waiting for your barely-in-the-loop agent to come through with yet another crotch shot or back-of-the-stage-only video shoot. Between each ever-more-infrequent gig, you wait. Growing a little older, a little less firm, a little less "in" and a lot more desperate. I've checked your . . . resumé. You've tumbled from B-flick body-doubling to Euro-market crotch-grinds for US made-for-TV films. And despite what our sweet friend Kenny assured you, that nipple-sore guitar god *has* spread the word about that wicked incisor of yours –'

'But it was what you had in mind when – you *used* me –'

'Shouldn't one use what is bought? And if so, isn't re-using it up to the owner, too?'

I stood up, ready to head for that Open Sesame door . . . knowing that what waited for me beyond that endless, empty plush-floored hallway was just as barren – and without any potential surprises lurking behind those paper-cut-edged doors. I knew I was meat . . . which meant being devoured or left to rot. I sat down again, biting my lips to keep quiet, while Westmisley purred, 'Thought you'd agree . . . now, how limber are you? I expect more than a mere mouthing . . . *my* divas dance,' he added with a spittle-flying burst of emphasis that made *this* slab of meat begin squirming on the plate, as if I'd been cut into steak but not yet placed on the sizzling grill –

Trying to remember if Genius Productions Ltd's client roster boasted any other high-profile diva types, I decided to buy mental sorting-out time by asking, in an off-hand tone, 'Poor thing . . . she must be terribly fat, or homely, for you to go through all this trouble . . . I've seen how the press eats performers alive when word gets out about them doubling for a singer . . . but with a voice like hers, could she really be *that* bad-looking?'

Once the words were out of my mouth, I regretted them, for surely I didn't have enough clout to get away with a taunt like that with someone as hideous-looking as Edan Westmisley . . . but his reaction proved to be far more frightening than an unleashed flood of curses or show of temper could've been –

– he simply leaned back in his chair, laced his talon-like fingers behind the back of his had-to-be-wigged head . . . and began laughing, a deep, bubbling-from-his-toes chuckle that soon brought pearl-like tears to his shielded eyes, and exposed both rows of teeth back to the first molars. He rode his swivel chair like a bronco, while the laughter erupted from his heaving chest, as if he were mentally replaying Monty Python's 'Killing joke' skit, prior to him keeling over in a spent heap of ruined flesh – then he simultaneously stopped rocking back and forth and placed his tight-skinned curved hands on the desk before him, while regarding me with a sly, I-know-something-*you*-don't smile.

'How bad do you sup*pose* she looks?'

Like you, *prick*, my mind raged, while I forced my lips to smile prettily before replying tentatively, as if this *were* simply another mind-game, 'Oh, overweight, no tan . . . couch potato city –'

'Brrr . . . cold, cold, *cold*,' he teased in a voice that carried no hint of humour, while his eyes danced and glittered behind the dark convex glass.

Remembering some article in *Spin* mentioning that the only artists signed to his label were bands, all male bands –

(my *divas dance*)

– I shrugged my shoulders and tried, 'Stringy hair and skin like the inside of an English muffin,' not caring how he'd react; true, he may've just been referring to divas in general before, but that 'my' was far too possessive to be figurative . . .

'Hmmm . . . warmish, but not very.' He still half-smiled.

Glancing at his wall-ensconced trophies for inspiration, I ventured, 'Bug-eyed, or cross-eyed?' while staring at that Indonesian mask, and was rewarded with 'Warmer . . .'

Wishing that this guy *was* into harmless quirks like chomping down on ash-breaded apple cores, I laced my fingers in front of my waist before suggesting, 'Too skinny . . . like she'd make Kate Moss look like a blimp?'

'Uuummm, *waaarm –*'

Mentally tallying my 'warm' score, I formed a mind-picture that looked teasingly familiar . . . even if it was too impossibly ugly to be seriously considered. *He has to be playing another Genius mind-game . . . like that sign outside. I'm just seeing pieces . . . all I have to do is step back a few paces to get it –*

Shifting slightly in that pillow-like chair, I looked around at walls that stared back at me, and asked, 'Is it true that this studio is called "Genius" in honour of your IQ score when you were a boy in England? I've read that in a couple of articles –'

'Which means more than one person has bollocked it up, doesn't it?' Westmisley's smile was a lop-sided smirk, underscoring the peevishness of his voice, as he went on, 'It's yet another reference to the Romans, *like* Virgil . . . they believed that just as each woman had her Juno, so a man had his Genius. A spirit which gives each person his or her being, a sort of . . . guardian angel, protecting them throughout their lives. Although sometimes said protection is very limited indeed,' Edan mused, as his stub of a finger caressed one cratered cheek, 'forcing the person to seek out other forms of protection.'

'You're really in*to* ancient cultures, aren't you,' I asked as brightly and wide-eyed-video-queenly as possible; hoping that he'd dropped the 'warmer' game for good. I thought that if I could pull his attention back to himself, to *his* all-consuming needs, he'd forget that I'd been gauche enough to ask *why* my services would be needed by him . . . especially after he'd taken such pains to remind me exactly why I couldn't turn down his offer . . .

But I'd forgotten that meat shouldn't think or hope at all.

'"*In*to ancient cultures,"' he echoed softly, each syllable eating into the room's silence like a drop of acid, leaning forward slightly and adding in that same stinging, biting whisper, 'All of us, me, you, that spotty lout with the edible body ornament, my lovely friend Kenneth, every man-Jack of us, is the result *of* ancient culture. Nothing's new, *nothing*. No artwork, no song, no work of literature . . . nothing at *all*. Different configurations, that's all. Took me a long time to realise that, starting in the sixties, back when all my co-conspirators in artistic challenge were trying to set this bloody sphere of water and mud on its arse. Only then, I was content to haul out what was very old, and try to pass it off as new by changing bits of it around. Music as art form, or some self-deluding *rot* like that.

'But I wasn't any more profound than Yoko was with her bare bum – which included my vertical smile, by the way, before I broke free of the whole Fluxus movement. No one realised how far back I'd been digging for my work . . . probably because I didn't go back *far* enough. Nothing I'd done was old enough to be new. Which was *so* frustrating. The kind of frustrating one needs to get out of one's system in any way, any form . . . When I couldn't do what I needed to do, I switched gears, went the "those-who-can't-do-teach" route, only for musicians, "can't do" becomes "can produce" . . .

'*That* gave me credibility, additional power . . . as if I really needed more,' he added, with an icy-toothed grin.

'Yet I never got over my love of what was old, what was exotic simply because it *was* old enough to be forgotten. Quite an addiction, actually. A bigger rush than the usual hands-on power games I'd played since I was in short pants . . . and if one can do that ferreting into the forgotten times, forgotten places, all on one's lonesome, *quite* unlike a curly-headed tot, that rush can be intoxicating. Better than dropping Ecstacy, or listening to derivative house-techno-thrash gibberish,' he admitted with a self-deprecating wave of his hands.

'Although this last time around, I quite outdid myself . . . I certainly outstayed my welcome in the Mediterranean, at least as far as that curly-haired, cherubic former tot was concerned . . . But,' he confided with a wink in my too-confused-to-react direction, 'the fact that my personal Genius chose that time to go on temporary holiday was outweighed by what I brought back with me – aside from my obvious "gift" from Apollo, of course . . . you *do* realise that Apollo was the Greek sun god, no?'

'I'm not dumb,' I whispered. 'I've been to college –'

'So have I, so have I . . . tons of them. I suppose it was what I learned there that put me in this fix –' again he tapped his lopped-off finger against his flesh, producing a drunk-like leathery *thonk* that turned my stomach and guts to mush – 'all those tales Thomas Bullfinch and Edith Hamilton translated from the Greek . . . all those marvellous creatures with un-believable, fantastic attributes. What I wouldn't have given to have heard the melody of Pan's pipes, or the song of the Sirens luring sailors to their doom – can you imagine how captivat-ing, how alluring, their voices must've been, for men to risk all, forsake all, just to continue listening to that deadly melody under that lethal sun? And think, not one of *them* lived long enough to find out what sort of throat produced such bewitch-ing arias, alas –'

Unsuccessfully trying to sit upright in that adiopocere-squishy chair, I flicked a strand of hair out of my eyes and said, 'But none of them died . . . the Sirens were just a myth, like the Cyclops and the witch who turned men into pigs and dogs, so nobody missed –'

All he did was smile at that, but the genuine nature of that smile, the eye-crinkling *completeness* of it, shut me up faster than a back-handed smack across the lips.

And think, not a one of them *lived long enough* –

My agent wasn't the only man in LA who literally spoke in italics . . . but Edan was no closet-queen, like Gerhard, or sweet, gentlemanly Kenny. Westmisley used his verbal italics most sparingly . . . most pointedly –

And as he continued to smile at me, his vaguely reptilian

flesh merrily crinkled around those dancing eyes (my *divas dance*), I felt that burning pressure on my exposed back and shoulders, as if a steady gaze was being aimed my way, only Kenny's appellation 'shoulder eyes' didn't cut it at *all* – what I felt was more like 'shoulder daggers' –

Hundreds of painted, carved and inlaid eyes watched me impassively as I gracelessly clawed my way out of that cupped fleshy palm of a chair, dropping unceremoniously to my knees before I was able to regain my footing and make for that closed pocket door, my hands extended before me like those of the newly blind, as I tried to walk while peering through cast-down lids and capri-shell lashes, so as not to see those shiny-raw *things* Edan had so playfully named after collecting them – if, indeed, he'd merely *obtained* them at all – but just before Westmisley obligingly opened that sealed lucite door, and it *shwicked* aside in a rush of sterile, unscented displaced air, I heard his soft, soft whisper behind me.

'*Much* waaarmer . . . '

Edan Westmisley's latest diva, capriciously dubbed 'Cer-een', made her first and last appearance at a rave held in an abandoned warehouse on the outskirts of Santa Monica a few weeks later. And while the cops blamed what happened on some bad 'E' which was passed out that evening and early morning, the fact that all the people who died were men more than told *me* what had really gone down. From what those who survived had to say to *Spin* and *Circus*, or (at much greater length, and in gorier detail) to the tabloids, Edan had actually listened to me that afternoon, in as far as what I'd said about what the singer looked like. Whoever the lip-syncher was, she'd been far more desprate than I was – word was she was pierced in places no sane person should allow themselves to be pierced, and that her black spiked hair resembled bits of wire shoved in her scalp. Nobody mentioned how well she moved; after she opened her mouth behind the headset microphone, things like writhing and being limber didn't matter at all. But what went down in that strobe-lit warehouse didn't derail Westmisley's latest diva; he merely sidestepped the issue by using that *voice* as an uncredited sound-bite on other Genius records . . . which is probably what he meant to do all along. Or what he should've done, if he hadn't been consumed by his twisted need for revenge, after his own flesh went nova . . . the price paid for living through what no man before him had survived.

The press almost found him out after one dance-mix engineer decided to isolate the voice from the rest of a bootleg tape made during the Santa Monica rave, but when his wife found him dead in his home studio, word was she only played so much of the tape before setting fire to it, and the studio itself.

Even that episode did nothing to stop Edan from blowing his own horn one last time . . . Just as he'd predicted, I was sitting in my overpriced, too-small apartment, watching my expanding waistline in my hall closet mirror and not really caring one iota about my increasing girth, when the Express Mail package came. There wasn't much in it, just a cassette, some photos in a plain manila envelope, and a self-taped video. No note, no last verbal jab . . . although once I heard that naked, raw voice on the tape, torn free of the lulling, masking overdubbed music, and thumbed the eight by ten inch black and white photos out of the envelope, I couldn't bring myself to watch whatever it was he'd videotaped, for I knew I wasn't nearly insane enough to live with myself after watching it. The way Edan was, or had become after his last voyage in the land of the Sirens. And before he'd turned the tables on them in memory of every other man they'd managed to kill.

I've since burned the photos, but removing the images from my mind isn't as easy as licking off a tattoo the hard way. He'd kept them as they originally were for a time, long enough to photograph them. Aside from being small, delicate, they were more or less human looking. Before he flayed them, taping their voices as he did so. But only above the waist; after they finally died, and were preserved with whatever it was he used to render them glassy-hard above, it was obvious from the lone shot of the unwrapped one that he'd taken pains to keep the flesh of the legs and what was between them soft enough to keep enjoying, perhaps in honour of those who'd died before being able to enjoy *them*.

After all, word was that the skin cancer didn't ruin all of *his* skin . . .

But, despite my own flabby body, and my descent into crotch shots, despite *all* that Westmisley did to ruin me, I've never needed or wanted personally to verify that rumour . . .

ANAMORPHOSIS

by

Caitlín R. Kiernan

Caitlín R. Kiernan was born near Dublin, Ireland, the year Brendan Behan died, but has lived most of her life in the south-eastern US. She holds degrees in philosophy and anthropology, and has worked as a palaeontologist, a newspaper columnist, and an exotic dancer. In 1992, she began pursuing fiction writing full time. Her short stories have sold to a number of anthologies and magazines, including *Book of the Dead 4, Love in Vein 2, Darkside: Horror for the Next Millennium*, and *Sandman: Book of Dreams*. Her first novel, *The Five of Cups*, was published in 1996. Her second novel, *Silk*, is forthcoming. She lives in Athens, Georgia.

Kiernan says, 'Music is *extremely* important to my fiction. I absolutely cannot write in silence. And every story winds up with two or three albums that absolutely define the "exact" tone of the piece. With "Anamorphosis" it was Nine Inch Nails' *The Downward Spiral* (1994), Tool's *Undertow* (1993), and October Project's self-titled début (1993). For me, that's the "soundtrack" for this story, that particular mix of industrial discord and ambient sadness. Also, the liner artwork for *The Downward Spiral* was a major inspiration (Russell Mills and David Buckland), and the fairy rings got stuck in my head because of a particularly fabulous photograph that Cindy Palmano did for Tori Amos's *Under the Pink* (1994).'

ANAMORPHOSIS

Deacon was walking, ragged boots slapping concrete, not even noticing cracks or a quarter someone dropped. *Just keep walking*, marching, letting the red shit behind his eyes bleed off with the *Atlanta* April heat, *and what's that Mr Eliot? Sorry, man, no lilacs*, just bus fart diesel and the shitty sweet stink of kudzu. In the east, the sky had bruised down to dull indigo and there was still orange towards downtown, and Deacon, pressed in twilight.

He didn't want to go back to his apartment, one sweaty room and a thrift store Zenith, always the same snowy channel because the knob broke off. Didn't want to stop walking and have a beer, two beers, even though he still had the twenty Hammond had shoved into his hand when no one was looking. No way he wanted to eat. Might never want to eat again.

'Yeah, well, Lieutenant Hammond says this one's different,' the greasy cop with the neck like a dead chicken had said as they climbed the fire stairs, seven flights because the elevator was busted. And the stairwell choking black because the lights must have been busted too, and Deacon had just kept his hand on the rail and followed the cop's voice and the tattoo of his shiny policeman shoes.

This one's different, and he almost stepped in front of a big ugly Pontiac, bondo and some paint on its shark snout the colour of pus. The horn blared and behind the wheel the driver jabbed one brown finger at heaven. And Deacon stepped back up on to the kerb, *This one's different, Deke, OK?*

They had stood in the long hall, yellowy incandescence and scrubby green carpet, Hammond looking old and sick, hatchet-faced and yesterday's stubble sandpapering his cheeks. Deacon had shaken his head, *Yeah, man, whatever*, didn't know what else he was supposed to do, say, but Hammond really looked like cold turds and he'd said, almost whispered, *Just be cool, man, it's real rough in there, but just be cool.*

Deacon watched the Pontiac until it turned and headed down Edgewood. The streetlights along Hilliard buzzed like giant bugs and faded on.

Hammond had opened the door and there'd been other voices inside, other cops, muttering navy shapes past the detective's wide shoulders. The air that spilled out into the hall had been cool and smelled the way hands do after handling pennies or old keys, meat and metal, and Deacon had known that there weren't going to be any handkerchiefs or dog-eared snapshots this time, no pacing back and forth over a weedy, glass-crunchy vacant lot where someone had said the missing husband or girlfriend or daughter had last been seen. Once Hammond had even made him hold a tongue some old lady had found in her garbage can, a dried, shrivelled tongue like beef jerky or some Viet Cong's misplaced trophy, and *Aren't you getting anything, Deke?* but this one was going to be different.

Just stay cool, Deke.

He was alone on the street now, except for the sound of cars on other roads and low voices through the opened door of a bar with its rusty sign that read Parliament Club, Ladies Always Welcome. Deacon walked on past the bar, dark in there, little pools of neon and someone laughed, deep and threatening enough that he didn't turn his head to look.

Hammond had looked at him one more time, apologetic, before they'd stepped through the unnumbered door and Deacon had slipped, skidded and would have gone down on his ass if chicken neck hadn't been back there, caught him under the arms. *Christ, man, what the,* but by then he could see for himself. The carpet had ended at the threshold and the floor was just hardwood and something on it that looked like Karo syrup. Except that it wasn't, and *What the hell, Hammond. I don't need this kind of shit.* But the door had clicked shut behind them, safety bar snug down across his lap and the rickety little train was already rattling into the fun house.

The apartment had been bigger than his, cavernous studio and a kitchen off to one side, a hallway that probably led to a bedroom. One wall entirely of dirty awning windows, hand-cranked open, like that was gonna help the smell. He'd wanted to cross the room and stand there, stare out at the city rooftops and catch mouthfuls of clean air, not look at the syrupy maroon floors or the brighter smears down the plaster walls. But instead he had just stood there, staring, tasting the acid ghost of the diner eggs and hash browns from breakfast hanging at the back of his throat and waiting for Hammond to say something, anything that would make sense of this.

You OK, Deke? I know, Christ I know, man, but . . .

Deacon had done his hangover morning counting trick, backwards from twenty-five, and the room, impossible Jackson Pollock nightmare, shreds and things hanging, ugly things, draped from furniture and lampshades. Disembowelled sofa cushions and crisp slivers of shattered glass.

Just tell me if you feel anything, anything at all.

I feel sick. And he'd gagged, covered his mouth with the back of his hand.

Hammond's frown had deepened, careless thumb gouges in wet clay, and to chicken neck, *Cummins, why don't you see if you can find Mr Silvey a glass of water*, and Deacon had raised one hand and shook his head to stop Cummins, hadn't dared open his mouth again to speak. Breakfast and bitter bile tang and the room, getting in past clenched lips, slipping through his nostrils.

Deacon had closed his eyes, swallowed, and when he opened them it had all still been there, and Hammond, running fingers through his thinning hair.

He looked up from the sidewalk, disoriented, no street signs in sight and for a moment the buildings, the billboards, meant nothing. And the slippery certainty that if this amnesia could be generalised, made complete, but then the world tilted back; vicious recognition, a derelict beauty salon, windows and door plywood scabbed and bandaged with movie ads and election bullshit. Almost full dark, and there were better neighbourhoods.

What do you want me to do? as he'd taken one step towards the centre of the room, the gutted sofa and belly-up coffee table, shoes smacking like cola-sticky theatre floors.

Anything you got, Deke, as he'd lit a cigarette, one of his stinking menthol Kools, exhaled grey-white smoke, and even that hadn't disguised the red smell. *Do that voodoo you do*, and to chicken-necked Cummins, lingering somewhere too close, *I want to know the second forensics shows up down there, you understand, the absolute second.*

Deacon had looked up at the high ceilings, just bare concrete and exposed plumbing, hovering fluorescent fixtures on taut chains. Jagged butt-ends of shattered tubes. And ropy garland loops dripping thick blood and shitty spatterings below. The video tape, glossy brown in the morning sun and shadows, had reached down to the floor like streamers.

Who was this, Hammond?

He hadn't felt the breeze through the open windows, but the lights had swayed a little, rust creak and whine, and the tape had rustled like dead leaves.

Small-time porn operator, and the detective had sucked at his cigarette, *guy named Grambs.* Pause as the smoke whistled out of him and Hammond had inhaled loudly, chewed at his lower lip; eyes cloudy with the familiar indecision that Deacon knew meant he was weighing how much to say.

Anyway, looks like Mr Grambs had bigger enemies than us, so that was all he was getting today, but really Deacon hadn't given a shit. His head had begun to throb, rubber band winding itself up at the base of his skull and dull sinus burn. And hadn't he read something somewhere about poison fumes from broken fluorescent bulbs? Mercury gas. Neuro-toxins. Mad as a fucking hatter.

Deacon sat down on the metal bench inside the plexiglass bus shelter, alone, and here the tubes were shielded behind dirty plastic and hummed like a drowsy memory of wasps, electrons danced and he blinked in the ugly, greenish light.

I don't want this one, he'd said to the detective, but that had been later, after he'd stepped over or around crimson rags and the expensive-looking chair toppled over on its side, after he'd noticed all the mean little gouges in the dark wood. And there behind the sofa, hiding in plain sight, such perfect circumference, an architect's anal retentive circle traced in tattle-tale grey and argent feathers, eggshell, sharp teeth and the pencil shafts of small, bleached bones. And the mushroom clumps, fishbelly toadstools and fleshy orange caps, sprouting from the varnished floor.

Maybe five feet across, and nothing inside except the fat

pinkish slug of the penis, the scrotal lump, a crinkly bit of blond pubic hair.

Slow seconds had passed, time seep, and no sound but a garbage truck loud down on the street and the Cellophane crackle of a police walkie-talkie.

I don't want this one, Hammond. Go find yourself another head monkey, but maybe he hadn't said the words aloud, because no one had seemed to hear and his mouth had been so dry, tongue and palate snagging at each other like worn-out Velcro.

In the bus stop, Deacon closed his eyes, shut out the shitty light and the translucent reflection of himself in the plexiglass, tried to swallow, and his throat felt twice as dry as it had in the dead man's apartment. But, hey kiddies, we got a cure for that, yes sir, that's something we can most definitely fix.

Hammond had been suddenly swearing at everyone then, for not having seen, for not being able to find their navy blue assholes with a flashlight and a roll of Charmin, and Deacon had sat down on the edge of the sofa, not minding the stains, the wet that had soaked right through his threadbare jeans.

Nobody fuckin' touch it! Hammond had growled. *Don't even fuckin' breathe on it!* He'd shouted for Cummins, but Cummins had already been talking, had stopped and started over again.

Forensics is downstairs, sir. They're probably already on their way . . .

But Hammond had interrupted, *Take Mr Silvey out the way you brought him in,* and then, *If I need to talk, Deke, I want to be able to find you;* he hadn't taken his eyes off the thing on the floor, the thing within a thing. And he'd pushed the palm-sweaty, crumpled bill into Deacon's hand.

And try to stay half-way sober.

Then Cummins had led him back across the room to the door, ride over, this way, please, and watch your step, hadn't said a word as they'd followed the darkened spiral of the stairwell back down to the sun-bright street.

Deacon had the job at the laundromat thanks to Hammond, and Tuesdays and Thursdays and weekends he sat on the wobbly bar stool behind the counter, watched street lunatics and traffic through the fly-specked windows. Read the paperbacks he picked up at the Salvation Army or Goodwill for a quarter apiece and tried to ignore the incessant drone of washers and dryers. Just make sure no one steals anything or writes on the walls or craps on the floor. Sometimes the machine that sold detergent and bleach would break down, or one of the Maytags would stop running and he'd have to make an out-of-order sign, red magic marker on ripped-up Tide boxes or pages torn from the phone book.

Late Saturday morning, and the hangover had faded to the dimmest brown pulse of pain in his head, but things could be worse, he thought, the handy credo of the damned, but true nonetheless. The laundromat could have been full of the fat ladies in their dust-stained pink house shoes, every drier roaring, tumbling loads of towels and boxer shorts like cotton blend agates. The hangover could have had a little more backbone, could have done the dead soldiers proud.

There was a Ben Bova space opera beneath the counter, and a coverless collection of Faulkner short stories, but the eleven-thirty sun hurt his eyes too much for reading. Deacon pushed his sunglasses tight against his face, sipped at a warming 7-Up.

When the pay phone began to ring, he moaned, glared through his tinted drugstore lenses at the shrill metal box stuck up below the sign that read 'The Management Assumes No Responsibility . . . ' Thought about slipping out until it stopped, maybe going across the street for a fresh soda. Or perhaps he could just stay put and stare the fucker down.

Fifth ring, and the only customer in the laundromat, a Cuban girl in overalls and a Braves cap, looked at him. 'You gonna get your phone,' she said, not quite a question and before he could answer it rang again. She shook her head and went back to her magazine.

Deacon lifted the receiver half way through the next ring, held the cool plastic to his ear.

'Yeah,' he said, and realised that he was actually sweating, had all but crossed his fingers.

'Jesus, Deke. Does Henessy know you answer his phone like that?' The detective's voice was too big, too friendly; behind Hammond, Deacon could hear the station house mutter, the clatter of tongues and typewriter keys.

'Hey,' and Deacon wanted to sit down, knew that the cord wasn't long enough for him to reach his stool. He leaned against the wall, tried not to notice that the Cuban girl was watching him.

'We gotta talk, bubba,' Hammond said, and Deacon could hear him lighting a cigarette, hear the smoke exhaled and hanging thick around the detective's head.

'I think,' pause, and so quick then that the words seemed to come from someone else, 'I think I'm gonna sit this one out. Yeah, man, I think I'd rather sit this one out.'

Heavy silence pushing through the phone and a woman's faint laughter, Deacon's heart and sweat and the dark eyes of the girl across the laundromat. And when Hammond spoke again, his voice had lost its big, crayon-yellow sun cheeriness.

'I thought we had an understanding, Deke,' then more silence, skilfully measured and strung like glinting loops of razor wire against his resolve. And he wanted to ask when there'd ever been an understanding, what Hammond could possibly think he understood, how much understanding you could buy for the odd twenty bucks and this shitty job.

Instead, he stared back at the Cuban girl, waited for the silence to end.

'Well look. I don't want to get into this over the phone, bubba, so how about we get together after your shift, somewhere we can talk.'

The girl looked away and Deacon closed his eyes, focused on the not-quite dark, the after-images swimming there like phosphorescent fish.

'Yeah, sure,' he said, finally, 'whatever,' imagined the cautious edges of Hammond's smile slinking back. 'I'm here until six, unless Wendel's late again.' And of course, the first bar he named was OK, and certainly, six-thirty was perfectly fine, calculated concessions now that any pretence at resistance had been put down.

Deacon set the receiver back, and when he opened his eyes the girl was gone.

Deacon wanted more than the beer he'd nursed since six thirty-five, wanted more than anything else, even the amber burn of the scotch and crystal clarity of the vodka lined up pretty behind the bar, to just get up and walk out. Almost half an hour and no sign of Hammond, and he was still sitting in the smoky gloom, obedient, sober. He sipped at his flat beer and watched the glowing Budweiser clock over the door, tiny Clydesdales poised for ever in midtrot, promised himself that at seven he was out of there.

Just what exactly is it that's got you so fucking spooked anyway, Deke? the purling, sexless voice inside his head asked again, something he pictured from a cartoon, angel white wings and a barracuda grin perched on his shoulder. *A little goo and a couple of 'shrooms? Afraid whatever chewed up poor ol' Mr Grambs and sprayed him back out is gonna come lookin' for you?* Deacon watched the clock, the door, concentrated on tearing his cocktail napkin into soggy confetti.

Think the boogeyman wants your balls, too, Deke?

And the door opened, still so much brighter out there, and for a moment the street sounds were louder than the jukebox disco, for a moment Hammond stood framed in the fading day, silhouetted absurdly like some Hollywood bad ass. Then the door eased itself so slowly shut behind him and Deacon was blinking past the light trapped inside his eyes, the detective moving through the murmuring happy-hour crowd toward the corner booth.

'I'm late,' he said, like Deacon wouldn't have noticed on his own. And the waitress, swooping in like a harpy with a tray and a soppy bar rag; Hammond had pointed at Deacon's almost empty mug, held up two fingers for her to see. She took the mug away, left Deacon staring at the ring of condensation on the table between them. Wet raised around something scratched into the wood.

'Look, before you even say a word, I gotta apologise for dragging you up there the other day,' and he fished the green pack of cigarettes from his coat pocket, tapped it hard against his wrist and a single filtered-tip slid smoothly out; the Kools made Deacon think of burning cough drops, and he wondered if there was a word for that, for being reminded of an odour you'd never actually smelled.

'Sick fuckin' shit, Deke, but I just wanted you to see it, you know. I needed you to be there, stand there and . . . '

'It's all right,' but he didn't look up, didn't dare meet Hammond's eyes when he said that, 'I'm all right.'

'Yeah, well, you had me worried, bubba. On the phone, you had me thinking I'd scared you off.' And before Deacon could respond, the big kraft envelope was lying in front of him, nothing on the outside but a coffee stain and he really didn't want to know what might be inside.

'There's some stuff in there I need you to take a look at, Deke,' and then the waitress was back with their beers, set them roughly down and was gone again. 'Just tell me if you get anything. And then we'll talk.'

Deacon picked up the envelope, carefully folded back the brass-coloured clasps, reached inside and pulled out several sheets of heavy paper; a child's drawings in coloured pencils, one done in the sort of pastels that smear and stain your fingers if you touch the finished page. Stiffer, slick paper underneath, and he knew without looking that those would be glossy black and whites. He put it all back on the table, took a long swallow from the fresh beer, dry cold, and Hammond sipped at his own, watched every move.

'Just the drawings for now,' the detective said, 'and then we'll go over the photographs, afterwards.'

Deacon studied each piece, each as unremarkable as the last, depthless stick figures outside stick houses, an animal that might have been a horse or a brown dragon, another that he was pretty sure was supposed to be a giraffe. Simple green and blue and red, violet, and everything traced in heavy black lines that bracketed the primaries. The last actually a page torn from a colouring book, and he recognised Winnie the Pooh and Eeyore. Lots of messy smudges, as if someone had handled these with dirty hands, and even the smudges held inside dark borders.

He chose the giraffe, random pick or maybe it seemed like the one that must have taken the most work, the most time, each brown spot divided from yellow with that bold black. Deacon followed the outlining with his fingertips and waited for the gentle vertigo, for the taste like licorice and the first twinge of the migraine that would swell and dog him for days. Index finger past indistinct shoulders and up the long neck, and here was another of the smudges, hovering to the left of the giraffe's head.

Glasses clinked loud behind the bar and stitched into the din of voices, an old Rolling Stones song blaring from the jukebox, people talking louder to be heard. Deacon tried to shut it out, tried to focus on the rough grain of the paper beneath the whorl of his fingerprint. He lingered a moment longer on the head, goblin parody of a giraffe's head, both eyes on the same side and the knobby little horns looking more like a television antenna, rabbit ears. Long tongue lolling from the corner of its mouth.

But like sitting on the crapper, five days and no BM, or the maddening name or word or thought just out of reach, tip of your tongue but nothing, grasping at shadows at the corner of your vision. Nothing.

Almost ten minutes spent staring before, finally, 'I'm sorry,' although Deacon didn't feel sorry, felt vague relief and reluctant embarrassment, a need to escape the smell of stale beer and the detective's smoke, the pounding mesh of conversation and rock and roll. To escape this thing that was being asked and the memories of that eighth-floor abattoir, fungus and copper, the growing certainty that Thursday morning had only been window dressing.

'Shit,' and Hammond crushed out his cigarette, grey wisp curling from the ashtray, drained his glass. 'Then that's all she wrote, hmmm?'

'Maybe if I knew something, man, if I knew *anything*, maybe then . . .'

'Maybe then you could just tell me what I want to hear, right, Deke? Maybe then you could be wrong and I'd go the fuck away, get out of your face and let you get back to the booze, right?'

Deacon didn't answer, stared at the giraffe, the smudge carefully bordered. Waited for Hammond to be finished.

'Look, you think I like getting messed up in all this hocus-pocus? Christ, Deacon you know how much flak I caught over the Broder case? And if IA finds out I had you up there the other day my ass is gonna sizzle for a month.'

The waitress rushed past, balancing empty mugs and cocktail glasses, stopped long enough to ask them if there'd be anything else.

'No ma'am, I think we're finished,' cold, slamming finality in the statement, words like fishhooks, and Hammond took out his wallet, laid down money for them both and a fat tip besides.

Deacon returned the giraffe drawing to the stack, pulled the photos from underneath. On top, surprise, not crime scene *noir*, but a colour portrait of a small girl, seven or maybe eight, cheesy K-Mart pose in front of a flat winter backdrop. Red and spruce green dress and she'd smiled for the camera, wide and gap-toothed, plastic holly in her gingery hair.

'Did she do the drawings?'

'Yeah, she did them.'

'And Grambs, he was into children.'

'Yeah, Kreskin, Mr Freddie Grambs was a grade-A, first-class sicko,' exhaustion, exasperation thinning his voice, sharpening its edges, 'and he liked to take dirty pictures of little girls. Made a lot of money selling them to other sickos.'

'And she's missing, isn't she.' *Or dead*, and he knew, more than ever, that he didn't want any part of this, but the hot barbs, Hammond's twisting guilt needles, were in his flesh now. Flensing resolve, backing him into submission, lightless cul-de-sac, and the barracuda jaws laughed and yammered, *So close, Deke, so goddamned close, and you don't even give a shit, just too fucking yellow to say no.*

The detective said nothing out loud, nodded slowly.

Deacon laid the smiling child on top of the giraffe, her giraffe, and there was the thing from behind the couch, the methodical arrangement of bone and feather, and the corpulent fungi, spongy organs from ruptured floorboards, *but, something's different, what?* And *yes*, the next shot, wider angle this time, and it wasn't Grambs' apartment at all, some place smaller, seedier, one room and no evidence of a window. Ruined walls that might have been papered, pinstripe ghosts of darker and lighter greys within the splatter.

'Those were taken the day before, over in Midtown,' pause, then, 'Grambs had a partner.'

Deacon didn't look at the lump inside the ring, been there, seen that shit. He rubbed his smokesore eyes, began to put the drawings, the photos, back the way he'd found them, stuffed it all back into the envelope.

'Look, bubba, do you see now? Do you see *why* I'm going outside the department for help on this?' Hammond was speaking quietly, calmly measuring his words, his tone, making Deacon feel like a fish straining at the end of an invisible line, the big one, easy does it, a little slack, don't let him get away.

'*Two* of these and we're stumping around with our thumbs up our butts. Forensics has been over both scenes with tweezers and goddamned microscopes and they don't have a fuckin' clue what happened to those SOBs.'

Deacon closed his eyes, smoothed the envelope flat with the palms of both hands.

'What do you want from me?' he asked, and that was the white flag, wasn't it, 'I tried, honestly, I tried and I didn't get anything.'

'Those things on the floor, the circles, is that some sort of cult symbol or what?'

'I don't have any idea,' and the basement smell, musty cloy, rushed suddenly back at him. 'Sometimes mushrooms grow like that, you know, toadstools, in the woods. Fairy rings.'

Hammond sighed, rapped the table once with his knuckles.

'Well, hang on to the pictures, Deke. Keep trying. Maybe something will come to you later.'

Deacon opened his eyes and Hammond was standing now, straightening his tie, rubbing at wrinkles in his white shirt.

'You think she might still be alive, don't you, the girl who did the drawings.'

'Hell, bubba, I can hope, right?' and he laid a twenty and a crumpled ten on the table. 'Eat something, OK? Call if you come up with anything.'

After the detective had gone, Deacon signalled the waitress, ordered a pitcher and a double shot of oily, bar-brand vodka. When she brought the drinks, he gave her the ten, pretty much wasted the bill, crammed his change and the twenty into the front pocket of his jeans. And then he sat for a while, breathing other people's cigarettes, and watched the yellow-brown envelope.

Deacon woke up, dragged slowly, by degrees, back to fuzzy consciousness by the noise next door, men shouting and the hot smack of flesh against flesh. He'd dozed off sitting on the old army hospital bed, his back against the cast-iron headboard and wall, sheetrock washed the blue of swimming-pool concrete. Rumpled blanket and the lost girl's art scattered carelessly across his lap like fallen leaves. His bladder ached and his back hurt, dull drum between his shoulder blades, neck stiff and slime on his lips, his stubbled chin, coagulating slug trail of his own saliva. Dark outside, eleven-fourteen by the clock radio on the floor, still playing public radio jazz.

Through the thin plasterboard, androgynous weeping, and 'You suck dick like a woman, sissy,' the man said, 'You suck dick just like a goddamned lousy fish.' Deacon brushed the drawings aside and stood, waited out the vertigo before risking the long walk across the room to the toilet.

His urine was dark, the colour of apple juice or rum, and after he'd flushed it away, he went back to sit on the squeaky edge of the bed. His mouth still tasted like stale beer and the greasy fried egg and sausage sandwich he'd picked up on his way home from the bar, keeping promises. He briefly considered another trip to the bathroom to brush his teeth, picked up the envelope instead and dumped its contents across the foot of the bed.

And there was the girl, Sarah M. in black felt tip on the back, and so she had a name, and a birthday beneath, 2/23/87, so it was eight after all.

'Sarah,' he said, and turned the Kodak paper back over. Next door, something hit the wall and shattered, and the crying faded down to ragged sobs. A door slammed and Deacon listened to heavy footsteps pass his door.

And then she came, no effort, swept inside him in a choking swirl of orange peel and dirty river water, and Deacon dug his fingers into the mattress, gripping cotton-swathed springs like a lover's flesh,

and Sarah's on another bed, green pencil in her hand making grass for a giraffe that floats in construction paper nothingness until she lays her streaky lawn beneath its bulbous feet

the scalding chills and nausea, the sinking, folding himself into her, into himself; Deacon held on to the bedding, held on to her.

the pencil scratches the paper like a claw, and something moves, flutters past her face and she smiles, more teeth than in the portrait, swats it playfully away, but it's right back, whirlwind around her head, whipping curls and shimmering strands of blackness, glimpses of mockingbird grey wings and a dry clatter like jackstraws falling

'Oh,' that single, empty syllable drawn out of him again and again, '*Oh,*' and Deacon knew better, knew to stay put and ride it out, but the pain at the base of his skull leapfrogged past migraine, past anything he'd ever imagined, and he tried to stand, panic and legs like taffy, blind to everything now but Sarah, Sarah M. and her goddamned mutant giraffe and the whirlwind racing itself around her red hair.

As he fell, feet tangling in lamp cord and old magazines, as gravity sucked him toward the floor, his perspective shifted, falling past the girl, past the edge of her bed and its gaudy pink Barbie bedspread

and the whirling thing settles on her shoulder, snuggles itself into her hair, and from this fleeting vantage the blur solidifies, light curdling into substance,

as Deacon landed hard, hard enough to knock the wind out of him, leave him gasping, tasting blood,

wings spread wide, kite-boned and iridescent butterfly scales, gristle twigs,

clinging madly to the floor, sensing there was further to fall. He opened his mouth to scream and felt the warm rise, indisputable acid gush from his lips,

leering jaws, lipless, eyes like indigo berries sunk deep in puckered skin and it sees him, hides its impossible face in her hair.

And Sarah laughs.

And the sunlight through her window, the tempera sky, goes out, and here it is cold, slime dank, and beneath his fingers bare stone. A dark past the simple absence of light, can't see, but he can hear, metal clink and scrape and her breath, laboured; the sweet-sour ammonia stink of piss, shitty rich pungence, mould. Distant traffic and the steady drip of water from somewhere high overhead.

Wet hiss, air drawn hard across clenched teeth, or escaping steam, and

she was gone, and nothing left under him but the floor of his own apartment, his face cushioned in cooling vomit and umber shag. He did not open his eyes, already strained painfully wide, but the darkness had begun to pale, thinning itself to a pasty, transparent charcoal as the world faded leisurely in neat Polaroid trick.

Deacon blinked at the huge and sombre dust bunnies massed beneath his bed, an old Schlitz can back there just out of reach. And then the straggling headache reached him, slammed home, and he turned over on to his back, stared helplessly into the electric white sun screwed inside its bug-filled globe, crisped little Icaruses; he knew that feeling, passing too fucking close to something hot enough, black enough, to boil your blood and brains and leave behind a hollow parchment husk.

Deacon lay very still, hands fisted, and waited for the pain to ease off enough that he could move without puking again or passing out, until the phantom smells faded and finally there was only the vomit reek, the kinder mustiness of his room. And then he crawled the five feet to the telephone and dialled Hammond's number.

Hammond had sent a car for him, and the two officers had complained about the Olympics while Deacon stared silently out at the lighted, empty streets, at the bright cluster of office towers and high-rise real estate raised against the night sky. If there'd been stars out, they'd been hidden safely behind the soft, Dreamsicle orange curtain, the glow of thousand sodium-vapour bulbs. The envelope with Sarah M.'s drawings and the photos had ridden on the seat next to him.

Now it sat marooned in the wild clutter of the detective's desk, concealing the art history textbook he'd spent fifteen minutes rummaging for in cardboard boxes and on the sagging shelves he'd built out of alley-found boards and concrete blocks. Deacon sipped scalding, sugary coffee from a styrofoam cup and waited for Hammond, waited to say words that sounded just as insane no matter how many times he pulled them apart and stuck them back together, polished absurdities, arranged and rearranged in his head like worn and finger-worried Scrabble tiles.

Just show him everything, let him connect the dots for himself. If he can see this on his own . . .

The office door slammed open, banged loud against the wall, and Hammond seemed pulled through by the slipstream, threaded into the disorder. More than exhaustion on his face, haggard, around his guarded eyes not sleep, but sleep forestalled, sleep purposefully misplaced. The eyes of someone who might not want to sleep ever again. For a moment Hammond stared at him, as if he hadn't expected to find Deacon sitting there, anyone else either, as if he'd been escaping, fleeing into this sanctuary of manila folders and overflowing ashtrays and had encountered an obstacle, had been caught.

'Deacon,' he said, shut the door more carefully behind him, but the way he said it, Deacon hardly recognised his own name. 'So what you got for me, bubba?' and the words sighed out, hushed of their intended tone, sieved raw.

Deacon chewed at his lower lip, toying with a ragged piece of skin there, his eyes drawn past the impatient envelope to the dusty grey streaking the detective's suit, unwashed hands stained with rust and dirt.

'C'mon, Deke. You even look sober, man. Something's up,' and still that brittleness, picture-perfect likeness of Hammond's bluster, but cold porcelain cast and maybe already broken. Sharp and scattered edges waiting to slice.

Deacon set down his coffee cup, no clear spot on the desk, so he put it on the floor a safe distance from his feet. And then he slid the big, green book from beneath the envelope, *Art Through the Ages* and Matisse's five dancing maidens on the cover, imperfect ring, left hand to right to left; began to flip through dog-eared pages as he spoke fast, nearly stuttering, before he lost his nerve.

'Remember when you said that it didn't matter whether or not you believed, if *I* even believed, that the only thing that mattered to you was whether or not it worked? You said that, the first time . . . '

'I remember what I said, Deacon.'

'It's important this time,' and he wandered past Hieronymus Bosch and the St Anne altarpiece and into pages of baroque architecture; couldn't recall the page number, but this was certainly too far, and so he began to search more slowly backwards. 'It's important, or else you're gonna throw me out on my ass before I'm finished.'

And there, the top two-thirds of page sixty-ninety, and he turned the book around so Hammond could see, bent across the desk; caught the musty smell clinging to the detective beneath ubiquitous stale menthol, faint dampness, mould and iron rot.

'This was done by a sixteenth-century German painter named Hans Holbein,' and he pointed at the two men in the painting, standing, neat-trimmed beards and sombre faces, before an emerald curtain, arms resting on the tall side-table between them.

'They were French ambassadors to England. You have to understand, this thing is fucking meticulous. Look at the stuff on the table,' and he jabbed his finger, first at a globe, then a compass, astronomical and navigational instruments he knew no names for. 'The realism is incredible. He got every detail, the numbers on the sundial, the broken string on the lute, and the perspective is flawless. But here,' and Deacon moved his finger down towards the men's shadowed feet, 'there,' and the grey-black slash across the bottom of the painting. 'What do you see there?'

Hammond took the book from him, shrugged, stared a moment longer before shaking his head.

'Now, move your face a little closer to the book, and look *across* the painting from an angle, towards the upper right-hand corner.'

Hammond hesitated, mouth drawn taut and sincerest *I-have-no-intention-of-humouring-you-much-longer* cast in his eyes, but then he obeyed, leaned close and tilted his head, stared at *The Ambassadors*, eyes narrowed, almost squinting.

'Do you see it?' Deacon said, nearly a whisper.

Hammond shook his head again, his cheek almost touching the paper now, then, 'Yeah, OK, it's a skull,' he said, 'but it's still distorted, all stretched out.'

'That's because Holbein meant it to be viewed through a cylinder-shaped mirror. Now,' and he reached for the envelope, noticed how his hands had begun to tremble, 'look at this.' Deacon pulled out the giraffe drawing and laid it inside the open book. 'The smudge up next to the head. Try the same thing, except this time, look out of the corner of your eye, straight down from the top edge of the paper.'

Hammond paused, then set aside the textbook and lifted the drawing, flat across both palms, to eye level. Turned his head away so that he seemed to be watching a row of filing cabinets across the office instead. Then, lips parted slightly and not exactly a sigh, but lungs emptying, breath across ivory-yellowed teeth and nothing drawn in to replace the expelled air.

'It's there on every one of them, more than once on some,' Deacon said, and waited for a response. Hammond said nothing, laid the drawing on the desk and continued to stare at the filing cabinets.

But Deacon knew what he'd seen, knew what Sarah M. had carefully scrawled there in the same deliberate hand as she'd decorated the giraffe. Knobby arc of wings and the ridiculous, needle-toothed grin, the spidery arms and legs, too many joints, ending in the stiletto intimation of claws. Pupiless eyes like poisonous blue-black berries.

'Ok, bubba,' Hammond said quietly, some time later, after he'd finally returned the giraffe to the envelope and closed *Art Through the Ages*, 'now it's my turn.'

Deacon and the detective sat alone in the darkened conference room, their faces lit by a shifting salt and pepper blizzard of electronic snow; Hammond had hit the mute button even before the tape began and now, past the three and a half minutes salvaged from Gramb's apartment, the voiceless storm raged across the screen.

'The optics guys thought maybe it was a flaw in the camera lens,' Hammond said; he made no move to turn the lights back up or shut off the television.

Deacon concentrated furiously on the writhing static, but saw nothing past the last seconds, the last scratched frames of tape. Final, brutal close-up of Sarah's face, harsh light and tears and something indistinct moving rapidly across the shot. And then the VCR had clicked itself off, rewind whirr, and this, white and grey and black and him talking, the things he'd seen in his apartment when he'd held the giraffe, the darting blur and the piss-stinking place. Playing the proper psychic and describing every sound, the traffic, the dripping water, every vague, half-assed excuse for an impression he could recall.

And Hammond nodded, took out a Kool but didn't light it, held the cigarette tight between his fingers and stared down at the dull glimmer from the television reflected in his shoes.

'Yeah, bubba,' he said, 'well, we've been there. We tracked down a realtor friend of Mr Grambs this evening and he was nice enough to show us a basement over on Butler,' and Hammond coughed, cleared his throat, too loud in the dark room. 'Shit, Deke, those guys had their own little Hollywood crammed into a hole about the size of the men's crapper down the hall'

'No,' Deacon said,' the place I saw was nothing like that.'

'They were keeping her in a sub-basement, Deke. Christ, there are old cellars and tunnels down there that go all the way back to the friggin' Civil War. Nobody has any fucking idea . . . ' and Deacon turned, his chair grating on the tile; the detective looked like an old man, time-sick, every line, every wrinkle deepened, bleeding shadow.

'We found the trapdoor under a throw rug, right there in the middle of the basement. Brand new Yale padlock on it, big enough to choke a goddamn horse,' and he held up his fist to demonstrate.

'I climbed down first, this rickety-shit ladder, you know. Guess it went down twenty or twenty-five feet, and the floor was just cobblestones. It was like crawling into the sewers, man, the smell . . . ' And Deacon looked away, didn't care for the sudden age masking Hammond's face, clouding his eyes.

'That kid's been missing since *February*, Deke.'

'She was dead?'

'Dead? Hell, she wasn't even *there*. I stepped off that ladder right into a bunch of those goddamn mushrooms, *huge* things, high as my ankle and big around as dinner plates. I shone a flashlight around, hardly ten feet square, and it was just like before. Not a soul, just this perfect circle of those things. And the bones, pokin' up out of all those toadstools. And this.'

Hammond removed something from the pocket of his jacket, handed it to Deacon. Slippery, cool plastic, an evidence bag, already numbered, and inside, something he had to hold up into the flickering light to see clearly. Four, maybe five ginger strands of hair.

'Listen, bubba. I'm telling you this because if I don't tell someone . . . but it doesn't leave this room, do you understand?'

'Who would I tell, Hammond?'

'I picked those up right at the centre, before anyone else came down the ladder. And I swear before the saints and angels and Holy Jesus, they weren't just laying there, Deke, they were sticking up out of those old cobbles. I had to break them off.'

Deacon passed the bag back to the detective and for a little while they sat, not speaking, only their breathing, and footsteps coming and going in the hallway outside, muffled conversation from other rooms.

'I'm not going to be able to help you any more,' Deacon said, and he stood up. Hammond remained seated, had gone back to staring at his shoes.

'I'm sorry,' he said, 'I truly am sorry about that, bubba, but after this shit, I guess it's fair enough. You take care of yourself, Deacon Silvey.'

'Yeah, you too,' and then Deacon walked to the door, slow, stepping cautiously around other chairs, invisible in the dark and the flittering red and white after-images from the television screen. The doorknob was cold, almost as cold as the fluorescent light that flooded in through the open door, keen and sterile light that could cut like scalpel steel if you looked directly at it long enough.

He shut the door behind him.

> Come away, O human child!
> To the waters and the wild
> With a faery, hand in hand,
> For the world's more full of weeping than you can understand.'
>
> W. B. Yeats, 'The Stolen Child' (1886)

With thanks to Brian Froud and Trent Reznor.

AFTERWORD

According to Kiernan she set out to write a story about the Cottingley fairy photographs, a series of photographs allegedly taken in 1917 by a ten-year-old girl named Frances Griffiths in Cottingley, England. The photographs, pretty obviously fakes, got all tangled up in the spiritualism movement and Arthur Conan Doyle, who thought them genuine, wrote a book about the whole mess called *The Coming of the Fairies*. (A parody of the book, called *Lady Cottington's Pressed Fairy Book* was created by Brian Froud and Terry Jones a couple of years ago.) At some point, the concept ceased to be an idea for a period piece and went sort of goth-noir. The story was originally intended for Dean Wesley Smith's never-to-be-realised *Splatterfairies* anthology.

A GRUB STREET TALE

by

Thomas Tessier

Thomas Tessier is the author of several novels of terror and suspense, including *The Nightwalker*, *Phantom*, *Finishing Touches*, and *Rapture*. His short fiction has been published in numerous anthologies, including *Best New Horror* and *The Year's Best Fantasy and Horror*. He lives in Connecticut and is working on a new novel.

'A Grub Street Tale' cuts rather close to the bone – it's about the relationship between a writer and his editor. The editor is the ultimate critic – of necessity perhaps *more* critical and even more important to the witer than anyone else – because it is the editor who chooses to buy or not to buy that story/novel.

A GRUB STREET TALE

'I still don't think he was that good,' Geoffrey Wilson said as he charred the tip of a pantella. 'Obviously he had a talent, but the fact is he never knew quite what to do with it.'

'He's being compared to Hawthorne now.'

'Ridiculous, isn't it.' Geoffrey smiled and shook his head. 'The same people who say that wouldn't deign to review his novels if he were still alive.'

Judith Stockmann nodded hesitantly, as if she almost agreed with him. Geoffrey rather liked her, this dark-haired dark-eyed young beauty. The perfect companion for a lovely summer evening. They were sitting on the terrace of a pub in Chiswick, discussing the short life and varying literary works of Patrick Hamm.

'You think he's overrated?'

'Oh yes, of course.' Geoffrey flicked his lighter again and puffed until the cigar was properly lit. 'No question.'

'What was he like as a person?'

'He had a certain charm. We had some good times together in Soho, early on. He drank too much, needless to say.'

'Especially in the last year?'

Geoffrey considered that. 'All along the line, really. It did get worse towards the end, I suppose, but by that time Patrick and I saw very little of each other. Alas.'

A sore point, that falling-out, but one that could hardly be avoided. It was a part of the unfortunate history. Geoffrey was reluctant to discuss Patrick Hamm with anybody and at first he'd tried to fend off Judith Stockmann. But she had persisted, with notes or phone calls every week. Geoffrey eventually realised he couldn't put her off for ever.

So he had agreed to this meeting on neutral ground. Dredge up a few moth-eaten tidbits for her critical biography of Patrick

Hamm and try to cast things in a positive light. Geoffrey didn't care about her project, but why not see what Judith Stockmann was like in the flesh? So far, she seemed fair and objective. Quite attractive, as well.

'Were the two of you friends before –'

'No, it was strictly business at first. Our friendship grew out of our work together, over the course of time. I had serious hopes for Patrick and I genuinely liked him as a person. When he wandered off-track I did my best to help him right himself. But it's difficult for an editor and an author to hang together when there are serious disagreements.'

Judith nodded again. 'Commerce and creativity?'

'That was one part of it, yes,' Geoffrey replied, 'but there were other problems. Patrick could never bring himself to decide exactly what kind of writer he wanted to be.'

'Don't most writers work through that?'

'It isn't easy to market an author who jumps from one genre to another and mixes them together. Booksellers have a hard time dealing with that, and so do readers.'

'But the consensus now seems to be that Hamm found his true voice towards the end, with *The Lime-Kiln* and *The Varna Schooner*.' Judith sipped her wine. 'He was only forty-one, you could say he was just hitting his stride when –'

'I know, I know,' Geoffrey cut in. 'Everybody seems to love those two books, and of course it's all very tragic, the way that it ended. But I thought at the time that those books were really very pretentious, and I honestly still do.'

'You prefer his earlier work?'

'Yes, I do. *Our Lady of Heavenly Pain* and *Nightmare in Silk* are my two favourites. I published them both, and I believed that Patrick was on to something new. It was brilliant erotica, it was elegant and stylish. It used elements of the thriller and horror fiction to good effect. I loved it, and I can remember thinking, he can't miss.' Geoffrey shrugged sadly. 'But he did.'

'Critics now tend to see those works as potboilers,' Judith said. 'Efficient, but limited. Finger exercises, part of Hamm's mastering the craft of fiction.'

Wilson scowled. 'They would, wouldn't they.'

'After the first two books –'

'That's when he started to drift,' Geoffrey answered before he heard the rest of the question. 'He wrote that ill-conceived family gothic, *The Weybright Curse*. God, I hated that. I'd just moved up to Pell House then and I was eager to bring Patrick with me. But I couldn't accept that book. He stayed at Bingley, they published it, and it promptly sank like a rock.'

'Were there hard feelings?'

'Some, yes.' Geoffrey reflected for a moment. 'But I still wanted to publish Patrick, so I encouraged him to get on with the next novel. *Ill-Met by Gaslight*, which I did publish. It was an odd book, a modern murder mystery with time travel, but it worked in some bizarre way, and he was back with me.'

'Was that about the time he turned to short fiction?'

She had an exquisite neck, Geoffrey noted. Honeyish tanned skin set off by a brilliant white blouse and tiny pearls.

'Yes, and it was infuriating. Nasty little stories, full of disagreeable people doing disagreeable things. He put together a volume called *Micronovels of the Dead*, and that was soon followed by a second one, *Tales of Extreme Panic*. But nobody would touch them. Patrick eventually lost his agent over that short fiction. No one knew it at the time, sad to say, but he was well into his final phase by then.'

'Now those stories are highly regarded.'

'Patrick would appreciate the joke.'

'Did he discuss the last two novels with you?'

'Oh yes, and I advised him as best I could. But there were some serious problems to overcome.' Geoffrey put his cigar down on the ashtray. 'You see, by that time his name and sales record in the book business meant nothing. He'd frittered away whatever identity he had managed to create for himself. He was getting to be old goods, a maverick, and nobody cared. Career-wise, Patrick was in big trouble.'

She had gorgeous legs, long and slender. Geoffrey could see and enjoy them properly, now that Judith was leaning back on the sofa in his sitting room. They'd had a couple of polite drinks at the pub, and then she accepted his invitation to dinner. He took pride in his cooking ability and he intended to broil two superb Wiltshire steaks – assuming they got around to food.

He could dole out boring old Patrick Hamm anecdotes for days if that would keep her happy. Days, nights. First, he dug out a file of old letters from Patrick. Harmless stuff, often amusing, none of the final anger and anguish. Judith scanned them quickly and murmured with delight at certain passages. She gave Geoffrey a warm smile when he offered to make copies for her.

She knew the books quite well, but not the man's life. Her knowledge of personal details was limited to the kind of material that had appeared often in the press. Geoffrey was the first of Hamm's personal acquaintances that Judith had approached – so he had clear sailing and could set the tone. They had more wine as he talked and she listened.

The Soho clubs, Hamm's assorted and equally hopeless lovers, a brief stint working in an East End soup kitchen, Hamm's writing habits, his appalling taste in food, his uninformed love of music and art – Geoffrey told Judith all sorts of odd details as they came to mind. It might not be significantly illuminating of the man's work, but it certainly had the authentic feel of first-hand experience. Geoffrey could see that Judith was loving every word of it, and that pleased him.

'To get back to his books,' she said. 'He did stop writing the short stories and started a new novel, *The Lime-Kiln*. And he showed it to you as he was working on it, didn't he?'

'Yes, that's right,' Wilson replied. 'I thought it started off in very promising fashion, but at about two-thirds of the way through it Patrick lost the thread. I don't think he liked his own characters. He killed them all off, every one of them, which resulted in a book that ended as a damp misfire. What was it all supposed to be about, and who cared anyhow?'

'What did he do then?'

'He went back over it from scratch, just as I suggested. It wasn't the plot so much as the characters, the heart of the book. And the ending, of course.'

'But that first version is essentially the same one that has since been published and acclaimed everywhere.'

'Oh yes, yes.' Wilson still ground his teeth at the notion. 'After his suicide, all that gloom and despair no doubt seemed more convincing. You could say it gave him literary credibility. I know that must sound awfully cynical, but that's how the world works sometimes. If Patrick had remained here in the land of the living, the living would have continued to ignore him.'

It was sickening, really. Three years after Patrick's death *The Lime-Kiln* was published to sudden acclaim. A year later, *The Varna Schooner* followed to an equally enthusiastic response. The collected stories. and the literary community embraced a corpse, made a fallen hero of him. To Geoffrey it was all so hypocritical and crass. Trading on the dead. Sickening.

Patrick's suicide had occurred a decade ago, and the bubble had diminished somewhat in recent years. It was bound to subside even more in time, Geoffrey was convinced. Patrick's writing was often interesting, striking and disturbing, but it was not great. Not truly classic. No matter what anyone said.

'You didn't publish the second version either,' Judith said. 'Can you tell me about that?'

'It was no better,' Geoffrey replied promptly. 'And in some ways it was actually worse. Revision was never Patrick's strong suit, and he was almost relieved when I suggested that he set *The Lime-Kiln* aside for a while and start something new.'

'*The Varna Schooner.*'

'Yes, and a great idea it was. The full-length treatment of an episode merely hinted at in *Dracula*. What went on aboard that ship carrying Dracula's coffin to England? What if there were a few passengers, as well as the crew? I loved the idea. But once again, Patrick had problems. He had a very hard time getting the period atmosphere right. He wouldn't do the research, he had no interest in the kind of details that would make a book like that convincing. Instead, there was more of that fancy philosopical talk, endless pretentious babble. The same thing that I believed was the cause of all the trouble in *The Lime-Kiln*. It got in the way of the story, just totally flattened it.' Geoffrey continued quickly. 'Now, I know what you're thinking. That what I disliked is exactly what people now praise in those books, it's what makes them so good. Right?'

Judith smiled. 'Well, that is true.'

'Yes, it is.' Geoffrey turned his hands palms-up and gave a helpless shrug. 'What can I say? Perhaps I was wrong. Mistakes do happen in the book business. Eighteen publishers rejected *The Day of the Jackal*. Everybody knows de Gaulle wasn't assassinated, so who cares? Twenty publishers rejected *Watership*

Down. Nobody wants to read about a bunch of bloody rabbits.'
Judith laughed. 'So, those things do happen.'

'And that was when the two of you had your final break?' she
asked cautiously.

Geoffrey nodded tightly. 'It was an honest disagreement. I
told Patrick that his characters weren't real enough. He was too
interested in using them as ideas, as symbols. That and the lack
of attention to period atmosphere ruined both books.'

'For you.'

'For me, yes,' he agreed reasonably. 'If I could just give you my
capsule view of Patrick's last two novels, I honestly feel that
they fall between two stools. They're too sophisticated and good
for the commercial market, category fiction, but they're not
quite brilliant enough for literary acceptance.'

'Hmn.' Judith appeared to consider that.

'Patrick didn't care whether he was a commercial success and
made a lot of money, or achieved literary stature. But he wanted
one or the other, and that's the sad part. He never experienced
either of them in his lifetime.'

'That's certainly true.'

They were in Geoffrey's study. He had remembered a box of old
photographs from his days at Bingley and he knew that several
of them showed Patrick. The Thursday afternoons when some
of the house authors would drop by and the booze flowed, the
fierce talk about literature and the book trade. Great times.
Unheard of in this new era, with the business driven by
accountants.

Judith loved the snapshots and thought one of them might be
reproduced satisfactorily in her eventual book. Geoffrey agreed,
happy to please her. It might never happen, anyway. Most books
died before they reached hardcovers, and he was far from certain
that there was enough event in Patrick's gloomy life to justify a
proper critical biography. But why discourage her?

Geoffrey sat close to her on the sofa in his study, looking
down her blouse while he explained who people were in each
photo. Very minor writers, most of them, sorted out and
silenced by the marketplace over the years. Decent folks, and
they all had their two or three published volumes, now
yellowing on a shelf at home, to comfort them in the genteel

failure of their advancing years. Even one forgotten book – is still something.

'Did he –'

'Enough,' Geoffrey interrupted softly. He took the box of photographs and set them on the coffee table. 'I think I've done enough talking for one session. We can always return to Patrick Hamm another time. I'd like to hear more about you now.'

'You would?'

'Yes.'

Judith smiled. 'But should I tell you?'

'Yes, you should.'

Geoffrey caressed her cheek with the back of his fingers, and she liked it. She didn't do anything but he could see it in her eyes, and he suddenly thought: she may be in love with a dead man but she will sleep with me tonight. Judith smiled at him, rested her head on his shoulder and then gazed absently at the wine glass that she still held on her lap.

'Where to start?'

'It's your story. Anywhere you like.'

He felt her laugh silently and managed to use that moment to slip an arm around her shoulder. Geoffrey thought he noticed her body respond by settling closer against his.

'We came from Russia. It was quite an adventure, actually,' Judith said. 'But at the time it was very frightening.'

'Is that so?'

'Oh, yes. Our family name was Bronstein but my father took the name Stockmann, from Ibsen's *An Enemy of the People*. He was opposed to the government, he wrote pamphlets and tracts, he went to prison twice, they beat him. We lived in constant fear, never knowing when the police might come. But father was a man of real integrity. He was an anarchist, in the truest sense of the term. An idealist, really.'

'A Russian anarchist,' Geoffrey mused. 'Fantastic.'

'Anyhow, the regime was very shaky,' Judith continued. 'My father believed that real change, revolution, was bound to happen soon. Perhaps my father went too far in his papers and speeches, or it was just another crackdown. The Tsar's secret police had my father's name on a list of people to be arrested, and everyone knew that this time the accused would never come back from prison alive. So we had to flee the country.'

'Good Lord.' Still, something was not right there.

'There was no time to spare. We left everything behind, and had to sneak out of Moscow in the middle of the night.'

'And you made it, thank God.'

Geoffrey stroked her neck lightly, tracing lines down towards the collar of her blouse. The Tsar? She meant the KGB, clearly, but this was not the time to play editor.

'Only just,' Judith said, 'and not all of us. We managed to get across the border, into Romania, and then on to Bulgaria, but police agents stayed on our trail. We had a couple of very close escapes along the way.'

'Of course the Romanians and Bulgarians would co-operate with the Russians, wouldn't they?'

'Or at least look the other way, yes. But we made it to the coast and my father had enough money to bribe an official and buy passage for us on a cargo ship to England.'

'Aha. Very good.'

'Can you guess where we sailed from?'

'I have no idea.' Geoffrey laughed at himself. 'In fact, I didn't even know Bulgaria had a coast.'

'It's on the Black Sea.'

'Yes, yes, of course. The Black Sea, the Caspian. They're all somewhere in that neck of the woods, aren't they.'

'We sailed from the port of Varna.'

'Va – you're joking.' With his free hand he took Judith's chin and turned her face so that she was looking at him. She was smiling, but not as if she'd made a joke. 'You weren't serious, were you? Varna? Really?'

'Yes,' she said simply. 'It really happened. I know it's incredible, but it is the truth.'

'Incredible? Not half. Ah, now I understand it,' Geoffrey went on. 'You grew up here in England. Later, you saw Patrick's book, *The Varna Schooner*, and so you read it because you'd passed through Varna. That's how you first came to know Patrick's work, you fell in love with it, and and – here we are.'

'That's not entirely wrong.'

'What do you mean?'

'You're right – here we are.'

God, sometimes he was bloody slow on the uptake. There she was, lips parted, eyes half shut, offering herself to him, and he was still trying to carry on a conversation. Nitwit! He quickly pulled Judith closer and kissed her. It was long, slow, deep and utterly wonderful. Geoffrey's hand slipped inside her blouse and touched skin that felt like warm silk, like some rare gold liquid that seemed to welcome and embrace his own flesh. Her whole body seemed to melt into his and that somehow made him feel profoundly alive, vastly more aroused.

Her tongue – no, a tooth, surely – entered his tongue, and it was like smooth sex, a painless, exhilarating penetration. He was puzzled and startled by it, however. He opened his eyes as he tried to pull back a couple of inches – and he couldn't move. It was as if Judith held him by the tongue, with some part of her mouth. Her eyes were locked on him, but she didn't appear to see him. His tongue throbbed, but not unpleasantly. Geoffrey had an odd sense of his mind slipping out of focus, drifting hazily. It was difficult to form thoughts, they seemed to keep falling beyond his grasp. He didn't mind. Much easier to drift, to float along in a delicious fog. It was so comforting.

He didn't hurt, but he felt weak. He was still on the sofa in his study, but now he was lying flat on his back. Judith sat on the floor beside him. The golden glow of her cheeks was now suffused with a faint pink blush. He felt so tired. He smiled, glad she was still there with him, though he wasn't exactly sure what had happened between them.

'You never even read *The Varna Schooner*,' she said almost in a tone of regret. 'You thought *The Lime-Kiln* was a waste and you were sure *The Varna Schooner* would be just as bad.'

'No, I read it.' Now he knew something was wrong.

'You didn't even remember my name,' Judith told him.

'Years ago. Ten, at least. More.'

'Patrick gave me life,' she continued. 'He created me, and at the end of the book he saved my life. I lost my entire family on the schooner *Demeter*, and the crew died as well. Patrick gave them all to Dracula, who came out of his coffin in the hold. But Patrick allowed one person to survive, a child, a little girl. I escaped ashore at Whitby.'

'Mad.'

'But there's a price to pay for life,' Judith went on. 'Any form of life. Patrick made me one of those who live for ever. He was a good man, strong in many ways, but hopeless at dealing with the outside world. Hopeless at career-building. He trusted you, in spite of the times you let him down. And when you had no use for him or his last two books, he finally gave up. He knew he'd done his best work, but he had no hope left for it.'

'He was a baby.'

Geoffrey felt good saying that. It took all his strength to get the words out. He could barely move.

'I won't take all of your blood. That would be too easy. I can keep you this way for days.' Judith smiled at him. 'Days on end. Until you eventually die of hunger. Like Patrick.'

'Compound organ failure,' Geoffrey corrected stubbornly.

'Brought on by malnutrition. Starvation. When Patrick died in that awful flat in Hackney, he had no money, nothing.'

'It was a Simone Weil stunt,' Geoffrey railed angrily. 'The ultimate career move. He had friends he could have gone to, he'd done so many times before. And he had money.'

The exertion nearly knocked him out.

'Friends?' Judith said. 'You were the only one, and you let him down. Money? He had seventeen pounds, that's all.'

'Enough to eat. To work, to live another day.' He tried to push himself up on one hand. He was shaky, but he thought he was beginning to regain some of his strength. 'He didn't have to die the way he did.'

'No, he didn't.'

'He had friends. I told you. He had money.'

'Yes, Geoffrey.' Judith smiled again as she leaned forward, her mouth approaching his. 'And I'm sure you do, too.'

BACK IN THE DUNES

by

Terry Lamsley

Terry Lamsley spent most of his childhood in the south of England. He has been living in Buxton, in Derbyshire, where many of his stories are set, for seventeen years. For some time he's been employed by social services, working with disturbed adolescents and their families. He has recently had stories published in *All Hallows, Ghosts & Scholars, Dark Terrors: The Gollancz Book of Horror, Shivers for Christmas, Year's Best Horror, Best New Horror,* and *The Year's Best Fantasy and Horror.* His self-published collection, *Under the Crust,* was nominated for the World Fantasy Award and the title novella won the award in 1994. The book, out of print before the award was given, will be reprinted in a new limited edition by Ash-Tree Press. His second collection, *Conference With the Dead,* was recently published by the same press. A third collection of tales should be complete by 1997 and Lamsley is currently finishing his novel *Dominion of Dust.*

A trip to the seaside would seem like the perfect way to spend a vacation in peace . . .

BACK IN THE DUNES

———

Nathan was on the lookout for the woman most of the time now. She didn't turn up while he was eating his late breakfast on the front steps of the caravan but after he washed the dishes, he saw her sitting on the sea wall, with her legs dangling over the edge. He watched her for a while through the cracked window that overlooked the beach. She was so *still*. He wanted her to turn round and look for him, to see if he was there. If she didn't want to see him, to talk to him, why did she come and sit so close? No one else lived in the caravan. He was the only tenant.

He glanced at his watch and saw it was after ten. He had to go out to buy food soon. The little shop at the back of the dunes was only open for a couple of hours in the morning, and he couldn't remember if it closed at eleven or twelve. If he missed it, it meant a long walk to the nearest village with a grocery store, and he didn't feel like venturing far that day. He planned to sit in the sun as much as he could. In little more than a couple of weeks he'd have to return to work: nearly a third of that time had already passed – had slipped by almost unnoticed.

He knocked on the window with his knuckle to see if the girl would respond. She was only about ten yards away, so she must have heard him. As far as he could tell, she didn't even twitch. He took a coin out of his pocket and tapped the edge of it hard against the glass, but to no effect.

He returned to the back of the caravan and shaved quickly. Even on holiday, he didn't like stubble on his face. The jeans he'd washed last night and hung to dry out of the shower-room window were not quite dry, but he put them on anyway. They felt cold and uncomfortable at the waist and crotch at first, but they soon warmed up. He checked his hair in the mirror, stuffed paper money in his pocket, thrust his arms and head through the holes in a T-shirt, and sauntered out to speak to the girl.

He looked down at her, with the smile he thought women found most appealing ready on his face, in case she should turn to him.

The sun-bleached denim jacket she always wore (she'd been hanging around for the last three days) was rubbed thin at the cuffs and elbows. Under it she had on an equally faded knee-length floral dress. She looked like a waif, except that her face was too old for the part. It was her posture and the way she moved, when she moved, that made her seem young.

'Another good day,' he said, squinting up towards the sun as he sat down beside her.

'They are all good days,' she said, without looking at him, or moving anything except her jaw.

'All yours might be. Some of mine aren't.'

'You've been lucky so far.'

'The weather's been OK,' Nathan admitted.

'What more do you want?'

'I don't know. Company? This is a lonely place.' He wondered if she'd take the hint.

She didn't. She said, 'Surely you knew that before you came?'

No: he'd had no idea what to expect when he'd hired the caravan four days earlier. He'd seen it advertised in a local newspaper someone had left in a picnic spot just outside the town, when he'd pulled in to eat a sandwich. Whoever it was had dropped the paper on the bench closest to him as he'd climbed out of his car, and had driven off at once. Nathan had picked it up out of curiosity when he'd finished his snack, flicked idly through it, and seen the advertisement for a holiday caravan for hire, made conspicuous by the paper's previous owner, presumably, with a surrounding square of heavily drawn blue felt tip. Nathan had decided it was just what he wanted and needed. The description of the accommodation offered seemed good enough, and he decided to go for it at once, if the person who had marked the paper had not beaten him to it.

It had been late in the day and he'd desperately needed somewhere comfortable to sleep. The previous two nights he'd spent sprawled uncomfortably along the back seat of his car, and that had not done his back any good. The pain in his spine had lasted all day.

And, after all, he was supposed to be on some kind of a vacation!

He told himself he'd been touring, but drifting was a better word to describe his passage up the west coast into Wales and away from the wreckage of his umpteenth relationship. He'd been in no hurry, because he had no specific destination, and had stopped off at various towns along the way for hours on end, aimlessly snooping around the strange and unfamiliar streets. Nowhere had taken his fancy particularly, and he wandered on until, at last, partly because whatever compulsion had driven him on had exhausted itself, he'd come to a stop.

And the caravan was still available, he had been told when he'd dialled the number given in the advertisement. The man at the other end of the line had seemed surprised by the enquiry, as though he'd half forgotten the caravan existed. Nathan would have to leave his car in the town, the man had explained apologetically, because there was nowhere to park among the dunes close to the site, but that hadn't troubled Nathan. He hadn't given the matter another thought. He'd taken the caravan until the end of the week, with an option to stay longer if he wished.

At first, he'd been content enough. The town, he'd soon discovered, wasn't up to much, but was curiously familiar: to his surprise he felt almost at home there, and seemed, instinctively, to know his way about. As he'd explored the streets, he kept turning corners he seemed to have turned before, which was disconcerting. But he supposed most small towns along that stretch of coast had a lot in common, and he had vague memories of spending time in that part of Wales as a child.

'I didn't even bother to look the place up on the map,' he explained to the woman in the denim jacket. 'I needed somewhere to flop, and this seemed as good a place to stay as any.' From his tone, however, it was obvious he was not entirely happy with his present situation.

She moved then; turned her face towards him slightly. 'You're disappointed?'

'Well . . . ' He shrugged, and decided to try again. 'To tell the truth, it's a while since I was on my own for any length of time.'

'And you don't like it?'

'No. It seems not. Not any longer. It makes me uneasy. How about you? You like solitude?'

'I can put up with it.'

He almost asked her why she felt she had to, when he was around, but instead he said, 'I'll be moving on in a couple of days, I guess.'

He got the impression she found this remark amusing for some reason. He thought she smiled. It was the first time he'd seen her do that.

'You live here, I suppose,' he observed.

'Not exactly.'

'But close by? You've been here some time.'

'Some time,' she agreed, and turned away to look out to sea, as though she didn't want him to pursue that line of enquiry. After a moment, though, she added, 'Long enough.' She made it sound like too long. She took one of her narrow hands out of the pocket of her jacket and reached for a pebble among the dozens on the ground beside her. Then she said, 'I'll be going away myself, very soon. I'll be leaving you to it.'

There was something that struck him as slightly odd about her last sentence, but she was a peculiar girl. Or woman, he reminded himself. There was nothing youthful about the way she spoke, either: she had a weary voice.

'Well, I'm OK here for a while,' he said. 'It's a change. It's nothing like home, that's for sure.'

Most people, he reflected, would have asked him about himself, and where home was. If she had, he'd have been pleased to tell her, because he wanted to talk about the self he had been alone with recently. But she didn't react the way he'd hoped she would. She never did. She said nothing.

She rolled the pebble she'd picked up on her palm, then closed her hand over it. The frayed sleeve of her jacket fell back to reveal her pale, thin wrist, which reminded Nathan of dried-out driftwood, as she held back her arm and hurled the stone out across the empty beach in front of her. Then she stared out towards the distant sea again, pointedly ignoring him.

Piqued, he jumped forward off the wall and dropped on to the beach. 'I have to get food from the shop,' he said, trying to make it sound as though he was about to set out on an interesting expedition. 'The cupboard's bare. Want to come along?'

'No thanks,' she said.

'It's not far.'

'I know.'

'I shan't be long. Will you be here when I get back?'

'Maybe. I won't be far away.'

He looked up at her. Her thin face, wedged between her hunched shoulders, was mostly hidden behind her fine, long, wind-blown hair that fluttered across her face like a curtain in an open window. All he could see of her features was the tip of her nose and her wide, wry, slightly down-twisted mouth. He couldn't be sure if he found her attractive or not. He wasn't sure about this one.

'Christ,' he thought, '*maybe!* Where else has she got to go? I'm wasting my time: she's not interested. It's not me she comes to see. She must have some other reason for hanging round the caravan.'

He murmured 'See ya,' and walked away quickly along the beach towards the footpath that led to the shop.

The way took him past a number of the other widely spaced caravans and chalets that were scattered along the sea-front. Most of them were empty, but some were occupied. The family in the chalet next door were setting up wind breaks and laying down towels in preparation for a day's sunbathing. The father, who was moving about energetically in spite of being over-weight, was about Nathan's age, and the oldest of the three children must have been ten or more. The sight of them made him feel he was missing out on something. The children, who were noisy but otherwise unobjectionable, recognised him, and greeted him when they saw him. Their mother, a figure in cut-off denims and nothing else, waved lazily at him too. He waved back and smiled, then quickly looked away when he realised he was staring at her small, sugar-white breasts.

As he walked on he thought, 'Why don't I have a wife and kids like that? Or a wife at all?'

But he'd never really wanted children, though he'd had wives and scores of lovers. And lost or run out on every one of them.

At last he turned sharp right off the beach, on to the path that wound its way inland between high sand dunes. Sparse, scruffy, yellowish grass sprouted from the top of these mounds, like hairs on an old woman's chin. Sand got in his trainers so he took them off, joined the laces, hung them round his neck and waded on barefoot, looking out for shards of broken glass. This part of the beach was ugly with litter: from picnics, he assumed, earlier in the season. Nobody was in among the dunes now, however, except for a bunch of kids he could hear but not see, somewhere just in front of him. Their jeering, taunting voices depressed him slightly with their edge of unkindness.

He was relieved to find the shop open. It was little more than a large shack, with a green-painted corrugated iron roof and a flap at the front through which were sold tea, soft drinks and sandwiches. The proprietor, a flabby man in a full-length grey overall, was crouching low down outside the shack, scratching at some scrawled black graffiti with a pan scourer. His position made it impossible for Nathan to enter without interrupting him. To attract his attention, since his feet had made no sound in the sand, Nathan said, 'Glad I caught you open,' fairly loudly.

The man stiffened, half turned, and squinted at Nathan, who was standing between him and the glare of the sun. Nathan grinned down at the man's unhandsome, unhappy face and said, 'Need a few things. Won't take a minute. Don't bother to get up.'

If the proprietor heard this remark, he chose to ignore it. He stuck the scourer into his pocket with an irritable gesture and pulled himself clumsily upright by reaching hand over hand up the edge of the door frame. When he was vertical he gave Nathan another glance, without registering recognition, though Nathan had visited the shop twice before during the previous days, then stomped into the hut and stood behind the little counter. He had an obstinate look, like a man standing his ground under difficult circumstances. On the shelves around him were piled tins and packets of instant food. As Nathan, reaching out on either side of the shopkeeper, made his selection from this store, he said, 'Having a bit of trouble out there, I see.'

The man didn't answer.

'Bloody kids,' Nathan said provocatively, and shook his head. 'Do they give you a lot of problems?'

'They don't bother me,' the man said. 'They don't come in here.'

Nathan wondered who bought the ice creams and the soft

drinks in that case. 'You wouldn't get adults scribbling like that on the walls though, would you?' he observed.

'Who said anything about adults?'

Nathan stooped down to inspect some boxes of shrivelled oranges and bananas. He chose a small bunch of the latter, and dumped them on the counter alongside his other purchases. He added some tins of Coke to his hoard, and reached in his pocket for money. 'Anyway, there's a bunch of kids up to something out there, back in the dunes,' he said. 'Fighting, I should think. They're making quite a racket.'

'They're always at it,' the shopkeeper said.

'Perhaps they're the ones who have been writing on your wall?' Nathan suggested.

The man straightened up and looked Nathan in the eye for the first time, but only for a second. Then he reached out quickly for the twenty-pound note Nathan was offering him, and said, 'Comes to eight pound thirty-nine. Have you nothing smaller?'

'Sorry, no.'

'Well, I can't change that.'

Nathan could see that apart from a few more twenty notes, a couple of ten-pence pieces and some copper, the till drawer was empty. He suspected some kind of scam, and felt slightly annoyed. He said, 'Can you trust me to pay next time I come – tomorrow, maybe?'

The man gave him an astonished look. 'No, I can't.'

'Well, perhaps you can give me my change tomorrow?'

'Could do, I suppose.'

Nathan frowned, to let the man know he wasn't a fool who was easily duped, and said, 'I'd like a bag for these then, please.'

The shopkeeper slapped a flimsy plastic carrier on the counter, stowed the twenty-pound note away in the till, then followed Nathan to the door.

It was comparatively dark inside the shop, and Nathan stumbled against a display of dusty beach games as he moved towards the door. He tripped and half-fell out of the shack so didn't get more than a momentary glimpse of the figure he had disturbed by the noise he had made, that scurried away round the side of the hut as he exited. Whoever it was was dressed in some kind of loose, dark, flapping top; probably a baggy T-shirt.

'There you are, I told you: kids,' he said, as the proprietor emerged into the sunlight. Nathan pointed to some new graffiti on the wall just above that which the man had been trying to eradicate earlier.

The shopkeeper muttered something sharp under his breath, pulled the scourer from the pocket of his overall and, before Nathan could read what, if anything, was written there, rubbed angrily at this new evidence of hooliganism.

'If I see them on the way back, I'll have a word with them about this,' Nathan said, but the man, obsessively scrubbing, was ignoring him again.

Nathan set off back the way he'd come. He soon heard the harsh bickering voices again, away to his left. He looked over in that direction but the hunched dunes, crested with quivering quills of primitive grass, appeared deserted as far as he could see. To get a better view of the surrounding landscape he climbed up the nearest hummock of sand, but found the only advantage he had gained was a glimpse of the distant sea and the tips of the roofs of some of the nearest caravans. The hollows among the dunes close by were all empty of life, though he could still hear rowdy voices not far away, and, once, what he thought was the sound of breaking glass.

Rather than go back along the path, he decided to make his way diagonally across the tops of the dunes towards his caravan. He'd not gone far when something flew through the air behind him and landed at his feet. It hadn't missed him by much. At first he thought it was a large pebble, but closer inspection revealed it to be a chunk of badly burnt meat containing a number of small bones. He reached down to prod it with his finger, got a whiff of the way it smelled, then, with his hand over hs nose, quickly stepped back to breathe some fresher air.

Someone close by laughed. A high, loutish voice cackled derisively, as though at something contemptible. Nathan spun round towards the sound that came from his left, but he couldn't see anyone anywhere. The dunes were still uninhabited as far as he could see.

He scampered a few paces to his left, towards what he perceived to be the source of the sound, and stumbled and almost fell. Something cold in the sand touched his right foot and slid up round the back of his ankle. He experienced no pain on the instant, and only realised he had been cut when he felt the blood begin to flow. He looked down behind him and saw the neck-end of a broken Coke bottle sticking up out of the sand.

Nathan swore, flopped down on his backside and drew his bare foot round to get a good look at his injury. It looked bad, with a six-inch vertical gash up the back of his leg that started under the sole of his foot. A sliver of skin bulged up under a cushion of oozing blood. He cursed, grabbed his foot, and wondered what to do next. He wasn't used to being hurt and couldn't remember the last time he so much as stubbed his toe. Even as a child he'd managed to avoid breaking an arm or leg, unlike most of his contemporaries, because he'd never shared their delight in risk-taking and adventure. And, being a hypochondriac, he was immediately out of his depth when his body presented him with any kind of problem.

Anyway, there wasn't a great deal of pain; nowhere near as much as he would have expected.

He gritted his teeth and sat and watched as what looked like quite a lot of blood dripped off his heel. With vague, first-aidish thoughts about the necessity for some kind of tourniquet, he tied his handkerchief tight round his leg just above the wound, and nervously got to his feet again. He found there was less pain if he kept his foot pulled up at an angle towards his leg, with his toes curled under. He tried half hopping along like this for a few yards, but it wasn't easy or comfortable in the uneven, shifting sand, and he soon found he had to put the front of his injured foot back in contact with the ground, to enable him to keep his balance. Perhaps he looked ridiculous then, as he hobbled off, because behind him there was more laughter.

The sound chilled him now, rather than annoyed him. There was unkindness, even cruelty in the voices (there was more than one person amused by his predicament, it seemed) and no humour that he could detect. Realising he was almost defence-less, and sensing he was possibly threatened – at risk, even, of being attacked, though he had no idea why – he stumbled on without turning to look at his tormentors. He couldn't be sure, from their voices, if they were merely children: suddenly, they sounded more like stupid, or even drunk or demented, youths, he thought.

He had to stop at last, to catch his breath and because he was beginning to hyperventilate, or so he imagined. Apart from his own panicky gasps, it had gone very quiet. There was no sound of pursuit. Without really intending to, he risked a glance over his shoulder. He caught just a glimpse of two figures, some yards back, as they must have ducked down behind the dunes closest to them. To Nathan, whose eyelids and lashes were soaked in sweat, they seemed to flicker and fall away to nothing, like dark, extinguished flames. He thought they must both have been dressed in extra-large and probably torn black T-shirts and narrow jeans. He got an impression that their limbs were short, but skinny. And he was sure they were wearing dark masks of some kind, or woollen helmets, over their heads.

He thought, 'Christ – what *is* this?' then shouted, 'What the bloody hell do you think you're doing?'

It was not a wise question to ask, and one that rarely receives a satisfactory answer, so he wasn't surprised when he got no response.

Except, perhaps, for a stifled snigger from somewhere round ahead of him, a long way from the spot where he had seen the two figures. He began to be concerned that he was being surrounded.

The pain from his cut was worse now, and spreading up his leg. He had been standing in the same spot for just a few seconds but there was a pool of blood seeping away into the sand under his foot. After trying but failing to tighten the handkerchief round his calf, he hobbled on again, faster than before, driven on by fear that felt like an acute disorder of the stomach.

He was pleased when, at last, he could see the roof of his caravan, but not by how far away it looked. He realised he had somehow managed to hang on to his heavy bag of provisions, and decided to throw it down to enable him to go faster, and because its contents might create a diversion to delay his pursuers. He dropped the lot, then forced himself, with one last burst of energy, to cover the descending stretch of ground between him and what he hoped would be a place of safety, running on both feet now, since he was sure his wound was full of sand anyway.

Half way down the final slope he stumbled again, lost his balance and rolled, arms and legs flailing ignominiously, ten feet down the steep side of the dune closest to the back of his caravan. Dazed, he lay still for a moment, then got to his feet, astonished he was able to do so easily – that he had not, at last, snapped a limb.

The pain in his foot as he made his way towards the door of the trailer, reminded him of the injury which he had momentarily forgotten. He groaned aloud, and swore vehemently.

The woman was still there, more or less where he had left her. She was standing now, and, for once, had her back to the sea. She was looking towards him, her long hair swirling behind her in the off-shore breeze. Her face was almost expressionless, with just a hint of what he hoped was concern, but that could have been mere curiosity, suggested by her slightly raised eyebrows. He remembered his final fall, and his subsequent tumble, and suddenly felt foolish. And he remembered how afraid he had been. His stomach was still queasy. He looked back the way he had come, but there was no sign of those who had been following him, if, in fact, they had still been in pursuit during the final stretch.

Perhaps in an attempt to regain a little dignity, he gestured down towards his bloody foot and fixed a brave smile on his face. When the woman failed to respond, he said, 'Had a bit of an accident,' and hobbled nearer to her to give her the advantage of a closer look at his injury. 'Cut myself on a broken bottle,' he explained.

She glanced at his foot, but didn't look concerned or impressed in any way.

Peering down himself, he realised the cut didn't seem so long and deep any more, and that the blood had almost stopped flowing. He must have plugged it with sand.

'I'm not a nurse,' the woman said. 'I can't help you.'

'Well, *thanks*,' he thought, and said, 'It may sound crazy, but I think I was almost mugged just now, back there among the dunes.'

'Surely not,' she said dismissively. 'That's most unlikely.'

'Maybe,' Nathan agreed, 'but it nearly happened.'

'Why should anyone bother?' she said. 'Dressed like that, you don't look worth the trouble. You obviously aren't carrying anything worth stealing.'

'There was a gang of – well, they were little more than boys – back there, and they seemed to have it in for me. Don't ask me why.'

This did have some effect. The woman's face registered a small measure of interest.

'How many boys?'

At first Nathan didn't want to admit, just two, or maybe three, but in the end he did.

'What did they look like?'

He described them as best he could. 'I think they were masked, or hooded,' he said, to explain his inability to provide any information that might identify them, 'and there was nothing special about the way they were dressed.'

Nevertheless, the woman seemed satisfied with what he had told her, and he felt she believed his account of what had occurred. Her readiness, now, to accept his story led him to ask, 'You don't have any idea who they might have been, I suppose?'

The woman shrugged and said nothing.

However, Nathan got a distinct impression she was pleased with the scant information he had given her, as though she had been half expecting it, or even hoping to hear it. Could it be that these were the people she had been waiting for in her vigils outside his caravan? Perhaps they were her own children, even, and she had been waiting for them to return?

But, no: she certainly didn't look old enough to be the mother of three teenagers, and there was nothing maternal about her response to his story. Just the satisfaction of someone enjoying the confirmation of some expectation; a pleasure he felt she was attempting, for some reason, to conceal.

The woman turned away to continue her contemplation of the sea. Nathan hauled himself into his caravan. There was a first-aid kit above the sink, containing a tiny bottle of disinfectant. He filled a bucket with water, put it out on the steps, sat behind it, and prepared to bathe his foot. He poured disinfectant into the bucket and stirred his foot around in the mixture. The sand fell away from his cut, and wisps of blood issued from the wound. There were bandages in the first-aid kit, too, most of which he wrapped inexpertly round his ankle. Then he forced his foot into one of his trainers, after removing the lace, because it seemed like a sensible idea. And it worked: he felt more comfortable at once.

While he had been tending his wound, the woman had wandered off among the dunes. He could see the top half of her body above him, as though she were partly buried in the sand. She was gazing inland, looking for someone, he thought.

A couple of hours later Nathan ventured cautiously out of the caravan, where he had been dozing. There was no sign of the woman.

Hungry, he was thinking about the food he had so hastily thrown away. He decided to go to see if it was still there, because, apart from half a loaf of stale bread, he had nothing to eat. Walking slowly and carefully, and keeping an eye out for anyone who might be nearby, he made his way towards the place where he had flung down the contents of his bag. He found the stuff easily, and nothing had been taken.

This fact made him feel small and stupid, and he wondered at the foolish panic he had felt earlier. Had it all been for nothing? Had he imagined the whole thing? He was beginning to think so when he saw footprints among his scattered groceries: his own, of course, but also other people's. The surface of most of the sand was smooth, so he could clearly see where he had been earlier by his lop-sided prints, but there were two other sets almost parallel with his own, heading in the same direction, and these looked equally peculiar, in their way.

They were definitely shoe prints, but they were oddly misshapen, with uneven outlines, as though the shoes had been badly damaged, or were falling apart. One of them seemed to have no toes at all on the left foot.

He wondered for a moment if he was confused; if they were in fact *his* prints, but was soon sure they were not. Nothing like. His were the reverse – toe without heel, that he'd tried to keep from touching the ground – and of course, he'd injured his *right* foot. The sight of these shoe prints depressed him for some reason, and he began to feel uneasy again, and to glance nervously about at the dunes around him.

The two other tracks wound away from the route he had taken, not far from where he was standing. Following them for twenty yards or so, he found they led him to what he at first assumed was the site of a bonfire or the remains of an ambitious beach party, perhaps, that had got out of hand. Limping slightly, he walked on to the bed of ashes, through which the harsh grass and a few determined yellow-flowering weeds were sprouting. It was an old fire, therefore, and probably from the previous summer. As he strolled further on he realised the area affected was greater than he had originally thought. He began to suspect he had come across the remains of a building, and quite a large one at that, that had burned down. He found the brick foundations of what must have been wooden walls, and the charred remains of a door. He scraped away some of the ashes and realised there were concrete floors under the impacted mess in the centre of the affected area. The fact stirred something at the back of his mind: a fragment of something almost totally forgotten surfaced there to tantalise him, then fell back down into the chaos of his past. Frustrated by this lack of access to his own recollections, he stood still, with his eyes half shut, and tried to take his memory by storm, and force it to recall whatever it was that eluded him – but without success.

There was an unexpected motion some yards ahead of him. Nathan tensed, opened his eyes wide, then relaxed. A freak breeze had flung a handful of ashes up into a rising spiral that sneaked towards him, like the fanatical soul of a whirling dervish. Travelling swiftly, it nevertheless seemed to pick its way among the heaps of burned rubbish almost fastidiously as it drew closer.

At the last moment, just before it reached him, it flickered away to one side and drifted off towards the sea, but Nathan was already on his way out of there because all around him, in three or four places, people were laughing at him again, or making sounds like forced, joyless laughter.

Invisible people. He was reminded of the staccato bursts of strained 'canned' laughter behind the action in dismal, unfunny TV sitcoms.

He forced himself to stoop and recover his discarded food as he passed the spot where he'd flung it down. The ugly, scornful sounds did not have quite the same effect on him this time, and did not unnerve him as much as they had done previously. They had not been completely unexpected, and, he reasoned, if anyone did intend him harm, they'd had ample opportunity to attack him while he had been wandering about in the ruin. If those who were taunting him were so reluctant to show themselves, it could be they had good cause to remain concealed. Perhaps they were not as dangerous as they would have him believe? He had no doubt they *intended* to scare him for whatever reason, but he was beginning to suspect they were less of a threat than he had feared.

He even turned back, because it occurred to him to shout something in defiance at them – to call them cowardly something-or-others – but he discovered he hadn't confidence enough for that. He sneered, though, showing his teeth, and spat back in the direction he had come, towards the continuing sounds.

Later, sitting in the sun eating warmed-over tinned stew, he wished he hadn't done that. He thought of himself as a mild man – a lover, not a fighter. His actions had been completely out of character.

And, in retrospect, seemed unnecessarily provocative.

When the heat got too much for him he went back inside his caravan, feeling lethargic, goofy, and half drowned in sunlight. He flipped the top of one of the tins of Coke he'd recovered, which he'd left cooling in the sink, and sat on the bed.

There was no TV or radio and he was beginning to realise he was not good at entertaining himself. That was one thing he'd learned during the last few days: he was not as independent as he'd imagined; he needed people around him. Especially, he needed female company, of almost any kind. He grew bored easily away from the distractions of the city, where he had his work and his women, and he didn't know what to do with his time.

Time! Time seemed to be stretching out, or shrinking. It was rubbery stuff. He was constantly surprised, when he looked at his watch, to discover how far off he was in his estimation of what time of day it was, and he seemed to have been away from home (well, not *his* home, but the home of the girl he'd been living with until their final bust-up) for a very long time.

And he couldn't remember much about the argument which had brought about the split that had sent him on his travels, or about the girl he'd deserted, even when he made an effort. There had been so many girls like her in his life over the last few years.

And, fuck: what day of the week was it? He wasn't sure. Christ! His brain must be rotting away.

Looking around for some distraction, he saw the newspaper he'd found, that contained the advertisement for the caravan. It was the only reading matter he had with him. He picked it up, sat back on his bed and began to read the first thing he laid eyes on. It happened to be the TV page. He read down the columns of programmes listed, noting those he might have wanted to watch, if he'd had the chance, until he came to a little feature about one of the soaps he followed. It previewed events in the lives of the characters that had happened ages ago, in episodes he was sure were not being repeated at that time.

He looked at the date at the top of the page, and was astonished to see it said August 18th!

No way!

He dropped the paper, leaned back, and forced himself to calculate the day's date. He did it a couple of times, and came up with the same answer. It was August 17th – there was no doubt about it, so what was going on?

He looked again at the date on the paper and read – August 18th 1994.

But it was *1995*.

Then he laughed at his own confusion, because the bloody rag was out of date by three hundred and sixty-four days! It was last year's news. No wonder the person who had had it previously had thrown it away. He or she (he was pretty sure it had been a woman) had found it at the picnic spot, discovered it was out of date, and flung it down again. Prior to that, it had probably lain there, unnoticed, for the last twelve months.

But no: if it *had* been there that long, the weather would have turned it to pulp long ago, and it was like new, just off the press, except that it had been marked and folded.

He opened the paper again, at the front page, and saw big headlines proclaiming the bare facts about some now ancient local tragedy. Bad news! He didn't want to read that stuff.

Almost angrily, he screwed the whole thing up. He got off the bed and thrust the crumpled paper into the swing-bin under the sink. The rubbish in there was beginning to stink, so he hauled the bulging bin-liner out, took it to the waste-disposal point nearby, and dumped it.

On the way back, he saw a figure up among the dunes. It was the woman in the denim jacket. She was talking to someone: he saw her lips move, and clearly heard her voice, though not what she was saying. Once, he thought he heard another woman's voice, but she appeared to be alone – he could see nobody with her.

So – she was crazy?

That would explain a lot. Why she was able to resist his charm, for instance. Nathan smiled at his own conceit. He was sure no sane woman would have turned him down.

He ate again, and fell asleep. It was late evening when he suddenly woke up. The light was fading deep into dusk.

Noises outside the caravan had disturbed him, and they were still going on. Scuffling sounds, of someone moving about in the sand, and scratching noises from over near the closed, but unlocked, door. At first he thought someone was trying to get in but, if so, they didn't know what the handle was for – all they had to do was turn it.

He sat up and looked at the door, half expecting someone to walk in. There was a series of bumps then, and a number of objects scraped along the sides of the caravan. The caravan rocked a little. At that point someone laughed, and another person joined in. Nathan knew at once where he'd heard those voices before.

He leapt up, turned the key in the door with an excess of energy that hurt his thumb, stumbled over to the window nearest to it, and stared out.

Four crouching figures were running away from the caravan, scrambling awkwardly up in the loose sand on the sides of the dunes. They were gawky, scrawny and oddly shaped, and their shabby clothing flapped wildly around them like black washing drying on a line in a gale. From what he could see, they were dressed in the dirty remnants of stylish teenage designer fashions, but they didn't move like young people. They hauled themselves up the slopes like desperate old men, digging their hands into the sand to help them along. They moved as though they were in pain, or agony, even.

But they were still laughing: through the open window he could hear their cruel, unremitting cackles, which sounded almost hysterical now.

To his relief, they scuttled very quickly over the crests of the dunes and out of sight. The sound of their laughter died away.

Nathan drank two tins of Coke, adding quite a lot of rum from a bottle he had picked up on his travels, before he felt like venturing outside. He eased open the door quietly, lowered himself cautiously down the two steps on to the sand, and took a look around.

Graffiti messages had been scrawled along the sides of the caravan in huge letters. To Nathan, they didn't make much sense, but that didn't matter. They scared the shit out of him. One read:

WELCOM BACK WERE GOWIN TO GET YOU FUCKER

another:

GOT YOU *NOW* WE GOT YOU GOT YOU

another:

SMELL THE SMOKE THATS US YOU BASTERD

There were others similar. They'd been written in something like thick black chalk, as were the scrawls that had appeared on the sides of the shop he'd visited earlier, which hadn't made any sense either.

He opened his last tin of Coke, slopped some rum in, but found he dared not drink it. If he so much as sipped it, he knew it would make him throw up.

He found that he felt safer outside the caravan than in, so he went for a stroll along the beach. He walked a good way out on to the sands, away from the dunes, and looked back into the increasing darkness behind him every few moments to make sure he wasn't being followed.

After about ten minutes a rocky area, full of pools and slippery weed, forced him to abandon the beach and step up on to the crumbling, battered concrete promenade that led into the town. Apart from a couple walking a dog and a single figure leaning against a handrail ahead of him, he had the promenade to himself as far as he could see. Nevertheless, the sight of the solitary person gave him a feeling of unease that increased as he drew nearer. For some reason, when the figure turned, gave him a tiny wave, and started to run towards him, when it was still some ten yards away, he almost expected it. His first impulse was to turn and run himself, and he probably would have done so if the person approaching him had not been so obviously female. He could see her silhouette against the lights of the fun fair in the town behind her: she was slim, young and, he saw when she was very close, attractive.

He was not even surprised when she flung herself into his arms and kissed him wildly all over his face: in the last few seconds he had known it was going to happen. He responded in kind.

At last she said, 'Where have you been? You're so late, I'd almost given up hope you'd come.'

'I fell asleep,' he admitted, quite honestly. 'I'm sorry.'

'Never mind,' she said, 'never mind,' and began kissing him all over again.

Nathan readily submitted to this treatment. He assumed he was benefiting from a case of mistaken identity, and in no time at all he'd decided to take advantage of the situation. The girl was obviously infatuated by whoever she thought he was, and the evening was beginning to look promising. Already she was leading him off the promenade, into the dunes.

And she really was a wonderful girl: the sort he went for most, when he got the chance, which had been very often. It occurred to him that he might, in fact, know her, or may have done once. Perhaps she was one of the many of her kind he'd had affairs with, who'd recognised him, though he'd forgotten her?

'Not that it matters, one way or the other,' he thought, as the girl impatiently pulled him down into a dip in the dunes and stretched out beside him. Very soon they were both naked, and Nathan had given up all speculation about the identity of the girl and lost himself in the action of the moment.

Or almost lost himself. After a little while, he became distracted. He was surprised to find how cold the girl was; not emotionally, but physically. Her flesh was chilling to touch, icy even, in places, and a coolness emanated from her. The skin he caressed was dry as paper, and the muscles in her arms and body seemed strangely, unpleasantly flaccid. He became more and more preoccupied by these peculiarities, and the girl must have noticed, because she urged him to finish what they had started.

He was glad, later, to be able to roll off her body because it had become, in spite of their activities, even colder. They lay together for a while on their backs, side by side and slightly apart, on the sand. When Nathan glanced at her, after they had both remained silent for some minutes, he noticed her skin glowed slightly green in the moonlight. He shut his eyes then and, as he had in so many similar post-coital situations in the past, began to wonder what he had let himself in for.

As if commenting on his thoughts, not very far away, someone laughed.

Nathan half sat up and looked around, feeling his own body freeze. The girl clasped him in her cold arms and pulled him back with a murmur.

He lay quite still in her embrace, and listened as something came towards them across the sand. He wanted to run, but the girl's arms held him down like ropes, and she clasped her hands across his chest to make her hold on him more secure.

Whatever was approaching was very close now, and Nathan squirmed free of the girl, finding it much easier to escape than he had anticipated, and stared into the dark towards the source of the sound.

A big grey dog was trotting towards them over the dunes. When it reached them it came to an abrupt halt, as though their nakedness had taken it by surprise, and its whole body became rigid. Its eyes were fixed on them and its nose, quivering slightly, was pointing straight towards them. Nathan re-cognised the creature as the one he'd seen being exercised by the couple on the promenade. Its master or mistress, who must have been responsible for the laughter he'd just heard, whistled from some way away. The dog twitched its ears, lingered as long as it dared, then bounded off towards its owners.

Nathan found he was shivering: from the chill of the girl's body, and from tension. He felt very wound up.

The night was warm and calm, but there was a scent in the air – of wood-smoke, and something else less pleasant – that made him deeply uneasy. Also, there was an angry red glow in the sky he had not noticed moments ago, that flickered almost like lightning. He reached for his clothes and started to dress. The girl made no attempt to detain him, but she said, 'Nathan, is something wrong? Do you have to go?'

'Christ, she knows my name,' he thought. 'How can she?'

He almost said, 'Who are you?' but realised he didn't really want to know. He looked down at her again. She was beautiful; there was no denying that, but now he needed to get away from her, and he hoped he would never see her again.

'Yes,' he said, 'I *do* have to go.'

As he strode away, he thought she said something about, 'The same time, at the same place,' but he didn't answer. He left her lying there on her side, gazing up at him. She was obviously in no hurry to get dressed, and seemed happy to stay where she was.

He went back along the promenade and down on to the beach. The tide had come in a long way, forcing him to stay close to the dunes. To his right, the smoky red glow had dwindled, but the smell remained. If anything, it was worse. Now, it was almost nauseating.

Someone shouted to him from in among the dunes: it sounded like a wordless taunt. He glanced across and saw two scrawny figures running along parallel with him, a dozen or so yards to his rear. Turning back, he discovered two more were on the beach behind him, and a lot closer. He had no doubt who they were.

He didn't look back again. He ran almost blind, unaware of the ground he covered, trusting to instinct to find his way back to the caravan. He was painfully aware of his injured foot, that he knew had opened up again, because he could feel blood in his trainer. The whole leg was throbbing and felt stiff. That slowed him down a bit, but he tried not to think about it, and reached the caravan sooner than he expected. He fumbled in his pocket for his key, aware that his pursuers were not far behind, jerked open the door, and literally fell inside. He forced himself to his feet again, and fastened the door shut, feeling almost triumphant.

He slumped on to his bed, reached up for the switch on the wall beside him, and turned on the light.

The woman in the denim jacket was sitting in one of the two easy-chairs the caravan contained. In front of her on a little table was the newspaper he'd taken to the dump with his other rubbish earlier. He knew it was the same one because it was stained with tea-bags and tomato soup he'd discarded. The woman had made some effort to flatten it out. She turned it round towards him, so he could read the front page, and tapped it with her finger.

Wearily, Nathan pulled the paper forward. The headline read:

FIVE LIVES LOST IN BEACH HOUSE HOLOCAUST

Four young people and a care worker died last night when their holiday home burned down. Firefighters were unable to approach the building because of its inaccessible situation among the dunes near Camber Beach. Police are treating the fire as 'suspicious'. A second care worker with the group, a young woman in her early twenties, is missing. A description of her has been issued, and police are appealing to her to contact them as soon as possible.

Nathan pushed the paper back towards the woman. 'So what?' he said.

She looked him straight in the eye, as though she wanted to hypnotise him. 'They were kids from the worst part of the city,' she said. 'The sort who'd been in trouble all their lives. They had various handicaps and they were dangerous, sometimes, to themselves and other people. We'd brought them for a holiday, Simone and I, partly at our own expense. We came here because we thought they couldn't do much mischief in a place like this. It's fairly remote. And there are no bad influences, or so we thought.'

'What has this got to do with me?' Nathan said. 'And how did you get in here?'

She ignored both questions. 'We'd worked with them for a year or two, and had really got to know them. They trusted us, we trusted them, so we thought we could put up with each other's company here for a week.

'But we were wrong about the lack of bad influences. Simone, the girl who was working with me, was the one who went astray, not any of the kids. She fell for a man who was staying in a hotel in town.'

Nathan stretched his leg and flinched at the pain in his foot, which felt about twice as big as it should have. 'I don't understand why you're telling me all this.'

The woman pointed to the lower part of the front page of the paper. 'Read that.'

He did, reluctantly. It was a detailed description of the missing girl. When he'd finished reading he said, 'But she's here: I saw her tonight.'

'I know,' the woman said. 'You screwed her.'

Nathan looked again into her immobile eyes, then hastily turned his attention back to the newspaper, though he didn't read anything written there. 'I don't get it,' he said. 'If *you* are here, *she* must have been the one who died in the fire.'

The woman shook her head. 'It was my night off. We gave each other two in the week. I went to the cinema; Simone should have remained here with the kids to see they were safe, and that they didn't get up to anything they shouldn't. She didn't stay though. When she thought the boys were asleep, she went out to meet this man. Someone she'd only met three days before, but she was already besotted with him! That's the way she was: there were some men, almost always good-looking philanderers, who she just couldn't resist.' Her down-twisted mouth writhed into a mirthless grin. 'I guess you know the type?'

She waited for some response. When none was forthcoming she said, 'It's hard to believe, but she found *you* irresistible.'

Nathan still didn't say anything. He was hardly aware what the woman was saying now because he was listening to something he could hear moving about outside the caravan.

'You told her to do it,' the woman continued, raising her voice, 'you made her lock the kids in the building and come to you. And she went: she met you on the promenade beyond the dunes.

'Sometime later one of the boys woke up and sneaked downstairs, to make some supper, I guess. When he went back to bed he must have left something burning on the gas. Most of the ground floor was on fire when I got back, just after midnight.

'I hadn't taken a key with me, as Simone was supposed to let me in. I broke a window but I couldn't get through the flames and smoke that came out at me. I screamed and shouted, but nobody heard me, and I panicked.

'My heart had been weak all my life, and it chose that moment to give up on me – just before the whole building, which was made mostly of wood, exploded into flame.'

'Look,' Nathan pleaded, 'I was never here before in my life: this is my first visit. I can't have had anything to do with all you've been telling me.'

'So you say, but are you sure?'

Nathan wanted to say 'Yes,' but didn't, couldn't. He wasn't any longer.

The woman shook her head. 'I don't think we can ever be *absolutely* sure of anything.'

'But I'd have remembered *something*,' Nathan protested, though he didn't sound convinced or convincing.

'I think you're beginning to. But, then, you see, we helped you to forget. It was easy enough to do. After all, there have been so many girls like Simone in your life that you've completely forgotten, haven't there? How many – fifty? – a hundred? And how many of them can you really remember, by name, even? Five? Ten? No, all we had to do was give your memory a nudge in the right direction, towards forgetfulness, to erase all recollection of Simone and what happened here last year from your mind. We had to do that, because we had to get you back. You'd not been happy here, had hated the place, and, without our intervention, you never would have returned. But we *needed* you, so we wrecked your life and *drove* you back, though no doubt you thought you were acting on your own volition. And it's all worked out very well, because *here you are*, just at the right time, one year after the event, on the anniversary of our deaths.'

'And the girl, Simone? What happened to her?' Nathan asked, after a long silence.

'She came back to the burning house shortly after I did, and realised at once what had happened. She found me before anyone else got there, and blamed herself for everything. Later, she walked out into the sea and drowned. Her body wasn't recovered for days. You never knew about *that*, however, because you didn't try to see her again: you left next morning.'

The woman rose out of her chair and stepped past him towards the door. Nathan tried to get up too, but his injured foot and the lower part of his leg were swollen and refused to bear his weight. Some infection must have got into the wound, and it hurt like hell. He fell down on one knee, then attempted to stand again.

He'd left the key to the caravan in the lock. He saw the woman turn it, push open the door, and throw the key far away into the dunes. She stepped back to let the others in, then went outside without looking back.

When he saw them close up, Nathan realised they weren't wearing masks, as he had supposed. Their faces, like their hands and legs and arms, were burnt black. Their clothes were scorched and smoke-stained. All four of them watched him with their blistered, glaucous eyes as he tried to crawl away towards the back of the caravan. He couldn't be sure, but he thought they were smiling. When he started to slide under the bed, one of them went down on all fours and bit his right ankle, attracted, perhaps, by the smell of blood and pus. He hauled Nathan back into the open with his jaws.

The other three moved in. They reached out for Nathan with the charred, charcoal-like stumps of their fingers, that they had used to write the graffiti messages on the outside of the caravan, and started to laugh. They sounded genuinely happy now, and were obviously eager to begin the anniversary celebration.

LEAVE ME ALONE GOD DAMN YOU

by

Joyce Carol Oates

In addition to being a respected novelist and story writer, playwright and essayist, Joyce Carol Oates is the Roger S. Berlind Distinguished Professor in the Humanities at Princeton University. She has won the National Book Award and is the 1994 recipient of the Bram Stoker Award for Life Achievement in Horror Fiction. She is the author, most recently, of *Zombie*, winner of the Bram Stoker Award for Superior Achievement in Novel, *What I Lived For*, nominated for the Pen/Faulkner Award, and *First Love: A Gothic Tale*. She has published three collections of her dark fiction: *Night-Side, Haunted: Tales of the Grotesque*, and *Demon and Other Tales*. Her short stories have appeared in *Omni, Playboy, The New Yorker, Harper's Magazine*, and *The Atlantic*, as well as in literary magazines and anthologies such as *Architecture of Fear, Dark Forces, Metahorror, Little Deaths, Ruby Slippers, Golden Tears, Off Limits: Tales of Alien Sex* and *Twists of the Tale: An Anthology of Cat Horror*, and has had stories reprinted in *Prize Stories: The O'Henry Awards* and *The Year's Best Fantasy and Horror*. She has recently edited the anthology *American Gothic Tales*.

Oates is prolific and fearless in her writing. She crosses genres with ease and is always receptive to a writing challenge. In this story she took my request for subtle and unusual motivation to heart – with this disturbing story the result.

LEAVE ME ALONE GOD DAMN YOU

_____

> We *must* repay both good
> and ill – but not necessarily
> to the one who did us the
> good or ill.
>
> Frederich Nietzsche

She was thirty-one. She was in control now. Her life was one of rules, prescriptions. The cardinal rule was *Take care, take time!* Patience, method, control. Waiting the necessary length of time (it might be less than a week, it might be as long as a month) required for the markings to heal.

Markings was the term she'd chosen, after some deliberation. She was a woman of principle, a woman of thought, a woman of shrewd premeditation. You don't earn a PhD from Yale in a difficult, competitive, state-of-the-art field by being an emotional child.

Markings, not *wounds*. For they were a special language, a sacred text.

'What a view! – beautiful.'

Like clockwork, that would be the first remark. A flattering exclamation.

Later would come the question, not overtly reproachful, not provocative exactly, yes but combative, sexually aggressive – 'Are you happy here, alone?'

The man would have entered her apartment that was an airy white space floating above pine boughs. He'd come, anonymous but for his name, whatever his name, Bob, Keith, Dwight, Frank, at her invitation of course, the two of them pleasantly drunk, or at least they'd had a few glasses of wine, and were feeling excited, aroused. The man would be smiling, or she would be smiling. That baring-of-teeth, that signal of hope. And more than hope. The man would have glanced about her sparsely furnished living room, he might be standing out on her eleventh-floor balcony, he might even have another glass of wine in hand, a cigarette, looking at her frankly now, his smile a little harder, with that air that was sometimes subtle and sometimes not so subtle, of masculine reproach. *Are you happy, here? Alone? A woman, alone?*

Sometimes she laughed. What could you do but laugh. *Leave me alone God damn you.* Though smiling, giving a perfectly sensible answer: 'Yes. Shouldn't I be?' Or, if she was feeling sexy, flirty: 'Sometimes yes. Sometimes no. Which is why I've invited you here.' So that her visitor would get the point without being exactly sure what the point was.

The primary sexual organ: the mouth.
The primary sexual stimuli: the mouth's utterances.

She was a linguist, a scientist of a kind. She looked upon the world as a place of species, specimens. The men whom she befriended, who came with her to her apartment, who were attracted to her, as she to them – what were they but specimens?

A man she would have met, for instance, in the museum café where she often went on free afternoons, a tall poised ashy-blonde woman in clothes of crisp neutral colours, sun-bleached, impeccably groomed, wearing dark glasses even in the building's interior. Or she would have met him in one of the new bookstores, or in the atrium foyer of her bank. The connection would have been made between them, an exchange unpredictable except in retrospect. And some hours later, or a day later, a week, there he would be stepping into her perfectly proportioned airy space overlooking Lake Bellaire and the oddly shaped water tower a mile or so distant and he would smile in that way that might turn suddenly uneasy, doubtful, combative. He'd have gone to stand by the sliding glass door of her dining room, unless it was the identical door of her bedroom, perhaps he'd pushed the door open and gone outside to stand on the balcony shading his eyes, peering at the city miles away, and she would come up behind him as if their roles were reversed and he was leading the way, she forced to follow. In that way of mild quizzical reproach she'd grown to anticipate, both to dread and to hope for. *Great place. Terrific view. But isolated, isn't it? Are you happy here, alone?*

Her *markings* were a kind of speech, of course. Sometimes a man warranted that kind of attention, most times not. She couldn't judge beforehand. To one of them, one of the first here in Houston, she'd said, lifting her eyes in a smile, voice low, throaty, girlish as in flirtation, 'Look, you can't hurt me! I don't love you yet.' And he'd stared at her, uncomprehending. After a moment he'd laughed, uncertainly, as if wanting to think she'd been joking; mocking the conversation between a man and a woman that might have otherwise have occurred.

A (sexual) specimen merely. Not one of those she'd confronted with her *markings*.

How dare you judge me. Judge my life. Who are you to judge me. Who are you to run your eyes over me like your fingers grasping, poking, kneading, prying.

Who are you to dare, who has given you ascendency over me. Who has raised you like God in His firmament His wild white beard and glaring eyes and enormous dangling penis aloft in the clouds to pass judgment on my life, to find me guilty, guilty of shame. To punish.

She was a linguist by training. It was therefore her privilege to penetrate meaning's surfaces, to expose secrets the way you crack a nut to expose its meaty interior. To decipher what lay within.

More difficult, more challenging was her own presentation of self. How to explain why she'd moved here, a Northerner from upstate Massachusetts, to this remote rural-suburban landscape of swampy bayous and high-rise condos, scrub pine and traffic-clogged interstate highways and 'corporate-industrial parks' south and west of Houston, Texas, not because she wanted to be alone – though of course she *was* alone – but because the job at the university here had seemed to her the most attractive, the most promising, the most challenging of the positions she'd been offered. And her apartment, on the eleventh floor of a sleek ivory-white stucco-and-glass building shaped like an upright iron, was the most attractive apartment building she'd seen that she could afford. In the distance the high-rise buildings and towers of Houston rose like dream-spires, now glaring in the white-hot sun, now fading in the humidity, dissolving in what sometimes appeared, at sunset, to be low-lying clouds, sweet-tasting orangy-toxic air. And close by was the lake that glittered like strips of glass, and spits of land where trees, shrubs, grasses grew in wild profusion. On the balcony you could not always distinguish, in raw gusts of wind, what was in fact toxic and what was purely natural – decaying vegetation, damp mucky earth, brackish water. *Are you happy here, alone!*

It required nearly an hour, sometimes longer, on the ex-pressway, to get to the sprawling, opulent campus of the state university at which, with her PhD in linguistics, she taught advanced seminars to graduate students and one immense, open-enrolment course in 'Arts of Communication' – too many miles for her colleagues to be invited to visit her. Too far for her to travel back to the university area, after she'd driven home for the day. How isolated she was, like a princess in a tower. There was a former classmate from graduate school, a woman, in Dallas, but that was many hours away; they spoke on the phone occasionally and made vague promises about getting together soon. No, she had no relatives in the area, no one else she knew in the entire state of Texas.

So the question was a natural question, perhaps. Her answer was the riddle.

Sexual intercourse: a solution to the problem of communica-tion.

She'd invented a wise European grandfather of peasant stock, yet educated too, somehow bookish, droll – he'd left a heritage of handy platitudes. *Take care, take time!* was one of his sayings. *Strike first, strike best!* was another. Or, *Strike first, strike last!* She believed he was a German grandfather. Yes, northern Germany. The region of Hamburg perhaps. A grand-father to whom she had no historical right. How shocked, how disbelieving, how hurt, furious her own family would have been if they'd known. It would have been hopeless to explain, and how could she explain? Better simply to outgrow them, their terrible dirt-dark memories. She would remain a kindly and dutiful daughter to them, at a distance.

Remember: patience. Even if she desired a man, even if she yearned to display her *markings* to him, she must wait until the exact, the perfect time. *Take care, take time!*

Since childhood she'd been highly sensitive to undercurrents of meaning in speech; since being trained as a linguist she'd made such subterranean meanings her speciality. She understood that meta-speech – the unconscious signals of facial expression, the body's movements, or arrested movements, subtle alterations of voice, tone – are as significant as words themselves. Yet, maddeningly, in the presence of others, she could not 'see' herself, and could not imagine herself. *As if I am blind and deaf, my powers taken from me.* Sometimes in the midst of a lecture at the university she heard her own voice, throaty, confident, authoritative, saw rows of strangrs, some faces uplifted, others downturned to notebooks, and felt an instant's panic *Who is this person? How have I become her?* yet the voice, the presence continued, unhesitating. Sometimes in the midst of a bright, chatty converstion with one of her male acquaintances, in those first heady, plunging minutes, she would hear herself speaking, not words but mere sounds, the melodic undercurrent *Love me? Love me? Love me? love me?*

In this year she'd moved to Houston, into the apartment floating above pine boughs at the edge of a glittering artificial lake, into an ivory-white stucco-and-glass building shaped like an upright iron, she'd brought several men home with her. If this was *home*, hadn't she the right?
For shame, her mother whispered. She'd long forgotten the particulars, perhaps shame has no particulars and is always and ever the same: *shame*.
   All of the men were strangers of course. Initially.
   One of her cardinal rules was: *Never a colleague. Never anyone who knows your name.*

She'd learned, in graduate school. How unwise to become involved with a man you must see routinely afterwards, no avoiding his eyes, his frowning stare, his too-glib greetings. No avoiding his avoiding of you, a yet more painful alternative. So in the Houston area where no one knew her, there were men, attractive men, seemingly available men, in any case eager, alert men, men to be sexually aroused, men faceless in memory encountered in bookstores, at films, in the art museum with its stark white walls and airy skylights and earthen-hued terracotta floors in which she felt rather at home, like a work of art herself – she made little attempt to retain names and faces if they began to fade.

Except: one of them was a man she'd begun to care for, seriously. At first, as if in disguise, he'd seemed like any of the others she'd known in Houston or in the north. Yet he'd returned, she'd wanted to see him again. He began to telephone often. Abruptly, it seemed he was *there*.

How emotions rose swift and unnerving in her, and in him as well it seemed, if she could trust him, the symptoms. She'd been alarmed yet elated, like a child hesitating at the top of a giant slide. *Should I? Dare I? Is there any turning back?*

She was reminded of the final conference she'd had with her dissertation advisor, at Yale. Smiling at the confounded man with her lashless eyes, cruel-plucked eyebrows, a pimply rash she'd provoked on her throat with unconscious digging nails.

With this lover, however, she would not lose control. There would be nothing unconscious, unmeditated.

And he'd come back to her apartment with her, at her invitation. Seeing the isolation of the area, the part-built condos, millions of dollars of abandoned property close beside jealously guarded private residential villages, the Bellaire Yacht Club, the artificial lake glittering like a mirror laid flat, rippleless, the ugly water tower and the distant shimmering spires of the city unreal as paper cutouts and the starkness of her apartment, and – he had not asked the question. And the next morning, he had not asked. Nor the next time he came to see her. She was waiting, shrewdly waiting for *Are you happy here, alone?* and had prepared her answer, yet he did not ask. He'd asked other questions, for of course he inquired into her life, warm and curious and not too inquisitive, and she inquired into his life, keeping her tone casual and spontaneous, not wanting him to guess how eager she was to learn of him anything that might be hopeful, promising. (Yes he was divorced, and yes a child – an eight-year-old son. A hole in his heart, then, she supposed. Such holes impossible to mend.)

There was a spell of his not calling, or possibly she hadn't answered his calls. And next time they met, on neutral ground, in a windswept plaza, he took her hand in a way he hadn't before, and said, not accusing so much as pleading, yet angry, too, she felt the trembling anger beneath, 'I don't understand you. It's as if there are two people inside you. The one I'm speaking with now, the one I know, or think I know – *you*. Then, when I leave you, the other seems to take control. She recalls our conversations wrongly. She distorts their meaning. She mishears words – if I've said, "I have to go home next weekend to visit my mother," she will remember, "I want to go home next weekend to visit my mother." She will remember my saying these words with a sneer, a look of defensiveness and reproach. She won't have seen *me*, at all.'

Hearing these remarkable words, this amazing speech from one who was inclined to quiet, understatement, she was astonished; and could not think at first how to reply.

Wanting to cry *No! No. There is no one in control but I.*

She was frightened, but fortunately she was wearing very dark glasses, and a silk scarf tied loosely about her neck, fluttering in the wind like agitated fingers. She leaned up to him, kissed him lightly on the lips, yet in such a way he would know he'd been kissed on the lips, and said, 'Well. We won't let *her* anywhere near, then, will we?'

For shame, shame. Touching yourself. Even in the bath, it's disgusting.

When does a child learn subterfuge? She'd asked the question, of course it was by now a much-rehearsed question, to her auditorium of undergraduates, many of them alert and attentive and smiling as they waved their hands or called out boldly – at the age of three? at the age of two? younger?

And what is the purpose of such subterfuge? she'd asked, quite enjoying her students' responses, as if they were wholly on

her side in this, children in league against prying, inquisitive
elders.

Except: one morning she'd awakened from a confusion of
dreams, dreams mixed with gale-force winds howling up from
the Gulf of Mexico, and saw to her dismay and chagrin that
she'd plucked out most of her eyelashes in the night, and so
scratched at her throat there was a raw, inflamed rash beneath
her jaw. And it was a Monday morning! Monday was her
longest, most complicated and usually invigorating, exciting
day at the university.

   She became brisk, practical. She took charge. As if another,
cruder person had wreaked damage that only she knew how to
remedy. She did in fact have a drawer of emergency items,
including false eyelashes, eyelashes not inordinately thick or
conspicuously 'glamorous' but simply substitute lashes exactly
the colour of her own. Of course, she owned attractive turt-
leneck sweaters. And a number of striking silk designer scarves,
to tie carelessly about her neck.

*Where? Well I don't know exactly, Eastern Europe I suppose,
I'm not the kind of person to dwell on the past, no family
trees, genealogical mazes for me thanks! I was born in 1965. In
the United States. The soil of Europe is soaked in blood
– that's not my continent, my continent is North America.
Why look back, why dwell upon the past – no thanks! What a
shame, dirty secrets. Actual dirt–filth, lice, rot. We were of a
people slaughtered periodically by people in the next valley
who spoke a different dialect, worshipped a different god. And
the Nazis, the young German soldiers grinning and panting
like dogs. There was a story told by the grandparents she
hadn't heard, she'd been shielded from by her parents so she
hadn't heard, it was simply not a story she knew. One of her
relatives who'd hidden fleeing Jews, possibly Jews who'd been
neighbours in Hungary near the Romanian border. And all of
them fed alive to the Nazis' starving dogs. But she hadn't
heard, and didn't know, and in any case such a story could not
be true.*

   *In any case the family name had been changed. Her name
had been changed. There was no connection, there was no*

history really. Her parents had shielded her from such know-
ledge and she hadn't heard and didn't know, no thanks!

In all places except one they were casual and spontaneous and
made it a point to laugh together. Glancing at them, you would
think they were lovers, attractive youngish people. Professional
people. But when they were alone together in her apartment
they were awkward, shy of speech. As if gravity had drawn them
to the apartment, to the very place where speech was difficult.
Their communication was touching, kissing. It was stroking,
caressing, playfully nudging. It was frequently lovemaking –
that solution, as she'd said wittily to her students upon more
than one occasion, to the problem of conversation. He was a
man who'd been a stranger initially and in many ways was a
stranger even now, though she'd told him x, y, z about herself,
carefully selected and rehearsed facts about herself, as she
assumed the facts he told her about himself were similarly
selected, rehearsed. She did not want to think that he might be
speaking more directly to her than she to him, that he spoke
from the heart, as the clumsy description had it. She did not
want to think that he loved her, still less did she want to think
she loved him unless in fact she understood that he did love her
and that the terms of his love for her were not negotiable but
absolute, fixed.

Yet she had the uneasy sense, which she'd never had before
with any man, that she'd already loved him, this stranger,
sometime in the past, and that her feeling for him now was a
kind of remembering. *It isn't possible, you know it. Is it
possible?*

There was the sense that she had no choice about it, her
feeling for him. That somehow it had been decided for her. And
he, too, knew. Yet could not speak of it, for the words were
lacking.

What frightened her: how their dreams meshed.

Confused like their limbs luxuriantly tangled together in the
aftermath of lovemaking. That torpor that becomes, by such
slow degrees you cannot discern one moment from the other, a
deep, physically embroiling sleep. And she was in terror that,
penetrating her dreams, he would penetrate certain secrets of

hers. He knew her name – the name her family had acquired, in
the United States. Yet perhaps he knew her true, her original
name, as well.

She trusted him with too much. She couldn't trust him!

Waking one morning after a few hours of fitful sleep, love
confused with dreams, disjointed windswept dreams, his physical weight, warmth, presence, pressure like a wall against
which she'd pressed, and abruptly she was alone – he'd slipped
out of bed, in stealth it seemed, for perhaps he, too, had been
feeling the terror of their closeness, and there he was standing
out on her balcony, the sliding glass open by several inches so a
chilly-misty wind eased through. It was not yet dawn: not six
a.m.: silent except for the wind. She followed the man out on to
the balcony, disguising her anxiety, smiling, brushing her hair
from her face, calling out in a pretence of boldness, intimacy,
'What on earth are you doing out here? – it's so early. It's *cold*.'
And he didn't turn to her, smiling, to embrace her, to shield her
from the cold. At another time he would have done so, without a
moment's hesitation, yet he did not, now. And the wind was out
of the east, bearing that sharp gassy odour she dreaded. And the
sky was mottled and grey as broken concrete. And the dream
city was obscured in mist, or fog, almost invisible. And this man
who'd shared her bed but was clearly a stranger, her lover of
several months but a stranger, stood leaning on the railing,
squinting towards the lake without at first acknowledging her
presence even as she stroked his shoulders and the tense
muscles of his back through the thin fabric of his T-shirt – he
wore undershorts, T-shirts to bed instead of pyjamas, when he
didn't sleep naked. And finally he turned to her, and asked, as if
it were a question he'd been pondering for a long time, 'Why are
you here, exactly?' and she was so startled she could not speak at
first, she'd begun to shiver yet felt the heat rise in her face as if
she'd been slapped, trying then awkwardly to make a joke,
'*Here?* – because you're here, I suppose.' He'd taken hold of her
hands as if to stop their nervous caressing of his body, and he
asked, 'I mean, why are you in Houston, why *here*?' and in that
instant she understood that he did not love her but perhaps
pitied her; she saw her apartment, the view from her
eleventh-floor balcony, through his critical, assessing eyes; she
saw herself through his eyes – an anxiously smiling woman of

thirty-one, an attractive woman whose youth was behind her, bare-legged, barefoot, making a pretence of gaiety in this gritty-grey air, dishevelled blonde-brown hair blown by the wind. There was a glare that seemed to emanate from the massed clouds and the steely, unreflective surface of the lake. The air tasted of metallic cold.

She turned from him, ran back into the bedroom and into the bathroom, shutting the door, locking it.

She'd known, of course. It was time.

For an hour then, perplexed, alarmed, he'd rapped on the door, pleaded with her. Spoke her name, and certain words – *honey, darling* – their intimate names for each other, rarely uttered aloud, and never before in such a tone. He asked what on earth was wrong? What had he said to upset her? Why wouldn't she unlock the door? Please would she unlock the door? He loved her, he was sorry, please would she unlock the door? But she held her ground, and did not weaken. She was crying softly to herself, inaudibly. Bitter salt tears she loved. How familiar to her the taste, and delicious. Until at last in the midst of the man's pleading, his veiled threat to call for help, to get someone to take the door off its hinges, she unlocked it, threw it open so he could see, staring in astonishment, her handiwork: the quick-feathery brightly bleeding slashes in her pearly skin, across her pear-sized hard breasts, even the nipples oozing blood, *you see I am serious, I don't stint on pain.* She'd employed several fresh razors, her slender fingers trembling yet skilled in the execution of such *markings*, such a beautiful mysterious language, this man had never seen before nor would ever see again. Her narrow ribcage, her breastbone, the smooth-healed soft skin of her abdomen and belly and thighs, a number of the scratches slick with blood, others scarcely more than hairline cracks in her flesh, almost invisible; tufts of her wheat-coloured kinky-damp pubic hair she'd torn out in derision, and the flesh there was starkly pale and beaded with blood like tiny jewels. The man had stepped back as if struck in the chest, he was murmuring what sounded like *My God! Oh no!* and may have said more, staring and incredulous as, triumphant, she advanced upon him, naked, shining, forcing him back, hands on her hips, jeering, as he could never have imagined her.

Crying, 'Leave me alone God damn you!'

Alone, alone – the syllables echoed faintly. Though in fact the apartment was empty, he'd gone away, fled like the others, and there was only the thin cold sound of the wind, the wind from the east, through the partly opened glass door.

BUTCHER'S LOGIC

by

Roberta Lannes

Roberta Lannes is a native southern Californian, who has been teaching junior high school English, art and related subjects for over twenty years. For twelve years she ran a commercial art business, and had gallery shows of her paintings and photography. In 1986 she began publishing science fiction and fantasy (after having published in literary reviews in college). Her short fiction has appeared in *Cutting Edge, Lord John Ten, Alien Sex, Off Limits, Dark Voices, The Mammoth Books of Werewolves and Frankenstein, Dark Terrors, Love in Vein 2, Darkside: Horror for the Next Millennium, Best New Horror*, and *The Year's Best Fantasy and Horror*, as well as various fantasy and horror magazines. Her one-act play, *Marionette*, was recently performed by the First Stage Alert Theater Group.

Behind the dull façade of American suburbs and 'normal' families in the 1950s, tamped-down passions and petty cruelties occasionally lurked. Lannes's story digs below the surface of one such family.

BUTCHER'S LOGIC

I grew up in the 1950s, in a sea of tract houses surrounded by orange groves. Shingled roofs on single-storey boxes, pruned hedges, snowy white sidewalks, clean streets and lots of space were things I took for granted. The neighbours were more alike than diverse, as they are now. In each home, for three square miles, were white, middle-class, upwardly mobile men with stay-at-home wives, their two or three generally well-behaved children, and a dog or cat. The eleven Rizzoli kids, and Mrs Coleman with her history of six miscarriages, were rarities.

But, from a child's point of view, the neighbourhood was full of drama and curiosity; from why Mrs Stedman dressed up each morning for the milkman to why Mr Wolfe was in a wheelchair and never came out except to chase kids from his lawn. And eerie Mr Melcher, the sneering butcher, and his meat locker. No one was allowed to see inside, not even his wife, and we kids were threatened with banishment into the great frozen void if we were trouble enough. Stories abounded of Mr Melcher cutting people up into steaks, grinding them until they were hamburger, and selling them to their own families. How he never let an ounce of blood touch his floor, so no one, ever, could find any evidence of a crime. Subject of great interest, yet feared by us all, we spoke of him only in hushed conversation.

My best friend was a boy, and because I was a pretty blonde girl this was a persistent source of upset to my jealous father. The fact that my friend was half Puerto Rican and half Afro-American turned my outwardly open-minded mother into a wary one. Jesse was tougher than my psycho younger brother, Kirk, a frustrating fact for Kirk, but a real blessing to me. My little sister, Trish, loved Jesse, as did I. He was an island of good will and true-heartedness in that ocean of bungalows, narrow minds, and mean spirits.

Jesse lived with his parents in the middle of an orange grove, just outside the perimeter of a new housing tract. His father, Monroe, was the grove caretaker; his mother, Cecilia, made and sold the most beautiful lace, crocheting everything from collars and doilies to tablecloths. They welcomed me into their home with honest smiles and sincere offerings, whether it be for water or an entire meal. Unlike my house where other children were allowed only during certain hours (when Daddy wasn't home), and then we had to play outside, regardless of the weather, the Simmonses only required their guests to be alive and well.

My mother feigned liberal ideals as I was growing up, such were the values our upwardly mobile neighbours professed. Along with some of the other local girls, I received a 'coloured' doll for Christmas (that was before I brought Jesse home). I named the doll Sophie. She disappeared a week after Jesse became part of my life. When I asked Mom where Sophie had gone, she told me she was filthy from my having dragged her everywhere, so she'd put her in the washing machine. At the age of eight, I was not ignorant regarding the physics of putting a doll with a porcelain head through the agitation of an ancient egg-beater of a washing machine.

I searched in vain through the garbage for pieces of Sophie. When I told Cecilia, she shook her pretty head, and clucked her tongue. 'I think your mother hid your Sophie from you 'cause she don' want nobody coloured in her house any more. Then she dump her with all that other give-away stuff at the thrift store.'

For weeks, I prayed it wasn't so. One day Jesse rode me over to the thrift shop on his bicycle. He'd told me we were riding to Lintner's, the five-and-dime next door. 'You gotta know one way or the other. "Wondering'll kill you," Momma says.'

Jesse pulled me inside. The musty smell of old clothes, yellowing pages of discarded books, and the oily scent of once well-cared-for furniture filled the air. The linoleum flooring curled up at its many seams, so we walked with caution.

'She's not here,' I protested, my eyes on the ground.

Jesse snorted. 'Over there. Look.' Gently, he lifted my chin. She was on the doll shelf, my sweet Sophie, her one eye shutting when her head slanted ever so little. I told Jesse I hated him and ran outside. I turned his bicycle over and hurried into Lintner's to lose myself in the racks of colouring books.

Eight is awfully young to lose faith in your mother.

After I forgave Jesse, I decided I would marry him when I was thirteen and have sixteen brown babies and be very poor, but extremely happy, all to show my mother and father how wrong they were about people and the world. If an eight-year-old girl could know true love, then I loved that nut-brown boy. For the next year and a half, he was my best friend.

When I was nine, my parents got us a dog. She was a boxer with the sweetest disposition, suffering us kids with immense grace. Jesse thought we should call her Sophie, after my doll, now long gone, but when I suggested it, Mom gave me 'the look'. Dad thought we should call her something we'd call a little sister. Kirk suggested 'Melon Head'. Trish liked the name Angel. No one objected, so Angel's what we called her.

Growing up without much physical affection, hugs and the like, we gave Angel all the tenderness we lacked. She responded by leaping at us and licking us with great abandon. My father, who about this time began his secondary career as an alcoholic, started kicking her when he got home, and Mom, incensed with us for not taking adequate responsibility for the dog's feeding and defecation, grew disapproving of our play. Jesse's folks told me they'd take Angel and make her a good home if my parents didn't want her. I had dreams of going to see Angel in the orange grove, knowing she'd thrive in the open space and the love the Simmonses could give.

One night, when Mom and Dad went out bowling, I was finally appointed babysitter. I'd reached the age (nine and a half) and stature of one mature enough to handle a brother whose sole joy in life was terrorising his sisters into locking themselves in the bathroom while he looted their secret caches of candy, and a sister so fragile emotionally that her consoling had become an art for me.

Angel served as an ideal buffer. We chased her, tossed her dog biscuits, hugged and wrestled with her until she grew reluctant, then downright unwilling. She chose to hide behind the sofa. I had the longest arms, so I reached back there, got a hold of her back leg and pulled. Hard.

She gave one quick, sharp cry, then let me yank her all the way out. We did our best to inspire her back into play, but she limped off, glancing back at me once. Later, I recalled that glance as being full of disappointment and pain, but back then I thought she was just dismissing us.

Jesse woke me the next morning by running a stick over my window screen. I hurried into pants, a shirt and sandals, eager to go outside. As I raced into the den, I saw Angel lying on her side, panting roughly, the entire carpet spattered with vomit, shit and blood. My heart stopped, my stomach clenched, and my mind wrapped around the thought that Angel was dying. I was afraid to touch her, scared I'd hurt her worse.

'Mom. Dad. Come quick. Something's wrong with Angel!'

Neither parent, at this point in our rearing, moved with any alacrity at our calls, long regarding any summons as 'crying wolf'. Eventually, my mother came out. Jesse, who was never allowed in the house, stood outside, listening.

'What the hell did you do to that dog!'

Angel's sharp cry and her backward glance came back to me with gut-punching force. Tears bled on to my face.

'Mommy, do something. Don't let her die,' I managed through my deep sobs.

By then, Kirk and Trish were up, standing in the doorway. Their eyes belied their fear, but they knew they hadn't been responsible. Even if they had been, they'd long ago figured out it was me, the eldest, whose job it was to be the scapegoat.

Mom turned to them. 'Do you know what happened to Angel?'

Trish ran to me, seeking protection and consolation. She was only five. She wouldn't need protection. Kirk, the sadist, chose the path of least resistance. He told the truth, a rare act for him – unless it meant I got in trouble.

I ached to go to Angel, tell her how sorry I was, and make it better. I moved towards her. I'd have walked through crap a foot deep, if my mother hadn't chosen that moment to bark, 'Don't you *dare* put a foot in that mess. You're going to be cleaning that carpet for a *week*.'

I looked back at Kirk, whose satisfied grin called up a mind-numbing rage in me. Mom grabbed my arm, pulling me to the linen cabinet to get towels for the floor. Once we stood before the cupboard, a few feet from where my father snored peacefully, Mom gritted her teeth and snarled under her breath.

'I can't believe we left you in charge for three hours and wake up to this. I don't want your father to see or hear any of it, understand? I'm taking Angel to the vet. And you're going to pay every cent it costs to get her fixed up out of your allowance. Meanwhile, you'll soak rags in soapy water and get every bit of that crap off the carpet before your father wakes up. If he finds one trace . . . '

I nodded, tears streaming. I just wanted Angel put back the way she was.

Jesse came inside after my mother left. He wanted to help me clean up and I knew there was no way to erase the scene alone. Kirk had taken off on his bike somewhere, and Trish went back to bed to cower.

We soaped rags until we were up to our shoulders in bubbles. Holding our breath, we scooped up faeces, clods of undigested dog biscuit and blood. Jesse never said a word, and all I did was sob quietly. When we had the major offending substances in the sink, then down the In-sink-o-rater, we took to our hands and knees to scrub away the stains. The only time Jesse spoke was to whisper that it was lucky we had tweed carpet.

Evidently Mom had left a note for Dad on the bathroom mirror, because when he walked into the den he was already steaming. Then he saw Jesse.

'What the hell are you two doing?' He grabbed the rag from Jesse and yanked him up to his feet. 'And what's *he* doing here?'

Jesse wrenched away and hurried to my side. I stood, rag dripping down my arms, nearly slipping on the wet broadloom.

'We had an accident this morning and I'm cleaning it up. Mommy said . . . '

'I want that boy out of here . . . now!' He glared at Jesse menacingly. He scared me, but Jesse was undaunted.

'Hey, Mr Sandler, don't take it out on her. I made her let me help.'

'Who do you think you are, talking to me like that?' Dad stepped on to the wet carpet in his leather slippers, reaching out to grab Jesse. Jesse pitched sideways to protect me, catching my father off-guard. Jesse never touched my father, there was a good three feet between them. When Dad's feet went out from under him and he landed on his butt, he shouted, 'That tar baby threw me on my ass!' The floor shook at his fall. 'Get the hell out of my house!' Trish peeked out from behind the door jamb, eyes wide.

Jesse looked at me, his expression a mixture of anger and hurt, shifting to resolve. I quaked in fear, unable to move.

'If he hurts you, I'll kill him.' That was the last thing Jesse said to me before he rushed past my prostrate father, awed sister, and astonished mother, just returning from the vet.

Instinctively, I knew better than to ask about Angel before showing concern for my father, but all my thoughts were for her. As my mother helped my father up and into his chair, she kept giving me 'the look'. Dad babbled on about suing the Simmons family, making sure that that nigger never set foot in his house ever again, and grounding me until I was seventeen.

As Mom tended to my father, I gathered up the rags and pail and went into the laundry room. The carpet was far from perfectly clean, my father probably crippled for life, I'd never be able to see my best friend again, and my beloved dog was probably unfixable. The year before, I lost my faith; now I was losing a piece of me. A sadness came to settle within my heart.

My mother found me standing at the sink a half-hour later, my elbows hooked inside to hold me up. I got my footing and turned to face her. She had a strange look, one I would now call spiteful, but back then it was intimidating, like all her 'looks'. She folded her arms and shook her head.

'Well, now you've really hit an all-time low. How stupid could you get? Bringing that boy in this house, after you've been told over and over. Doing such a sloppy job on the rug. God, what did you think you were doing there, painting? It's worse now than before. And your father . . . he's in such pain. What did that boy do to him?'

'I . . . I . . . ' Hopelessness robbed me of words.

'Well, serves you right, then. Just what you deserve. You killed that dog. Huh. She's *dead*.'

I felt nothing, yet everything was brighter-than-bright, distinct, and bottomless in the small space of the laundry room. My body was as cold as my big play magnet and just as hard. I closed my eyes, becoming stone inside and out. I heard my mother chuckle derisively, then pad carefully through the kitchen to the den.

That night, I dreamed I was in jail. Jesse drifted by the bars of my cell, whispering dirty words and telling me he would kill my father. I also dreamed Angel was alive and well, running across an ice field, catching hula-hoops in her teeth. When I woke up, I had to go to school and behave as if I was whole.

Jesse rushed to me the moment I set foot on the tarmac.

'Did he hurt you? You OK?'

I shook my head. 'Angel died. Mom told me I killed her.'

'Ach.' Jesse dismissed it. 'My momma'll tell you Angel didn't die 'cause of you. Your mother probably had her put to sleep. They have to shoot a horse if he breaks his leg, you know.'

'I broke her leg.' My lip quivered and tears filled my eyes.

'Then she had to be shot. It's better for her. She's out of pain, now.'

'I hope so.' I dragged myself towards the classroom, overwhelmed with sorrow. It would be many years later that I'd learn I'd merely dislocated her hip. That after the incident, she was too fragile to be around children. That my mother had told the vet to keep her, let someone with grown children have her. And finally, that Angel lived out her life not five miles from our house.

Jesse seemed to know there was more, and waited. When we sat in our chairs, I reached into my desk and found a tissue to blow my nose.

'Jesse, I can't see you any more.'

'Bullshit.' Whenever he cussed, I grinned. 'I'll see you at school. And you can sneak over through the orange grove when they send you to the store.'

I nodded sullenly.

At the time, doing what I wanted seemed a luxury I couldn't afford, and didn't deserve.

Two weeks later, I cut across the orchard on my way to the market. Cecilia opened her arms to me, kissing my face until it was wet. Monroe sat in his straight-back chair carving something ornate from a block of bass wood. He grinned at me, a mouth full of pearls.

'Jesse went to the market for me. He should be back any second. You wait?'

'I might get into trouble. I'm grounded. I should just go on ahead to the store. Maybe I'll see him on the way.'

Cecilia nodded, then reached over to her sewing box to take out a cloud of white lace.

'Here.' Cecilia handed me a lace collar she'd made. 'Wear it to church on that blue dress of yours.'

It was beautiful. But I was afraid to take it, certain that if my mother or father saw it, they'd know I'd been at the Simmons's and beat me silly.

Cecilia cocked her head, reading me. 'I think that maybe I oughta keep it here, jus' to keep it safe. For now, OK?'

'Yes, please.' I nodded. 'I'd better go.'

I hugged them again, and hurried back on to the path through the grove. Out of the corner of my eye, up ahead, I saw my father's shiny green Plymouth speeding up the road that ran along the length of the orchard. He had to have seen me. Damn. That was it. I was in for a beating.

I was shaking so badly by the time I reached the main road, I was sure I'd throw up. I searched for the Plymouth, keeping my head down, eyes jittering back and forth, hoping I wouldn't run into Jesse and get caught again. As I walked across the street to Pete's Market, I saw the front of my father's car peeking out from behind where the delivery truck dropped off meat for the butcher.

Pure fear drove me on to continue the errand. I wanted to turn and run, go bury myself in sweet loam under a tree in the park so that in time a new me would grow up through the grass. A whole me.

I stepped into the market, afraid every box and tin would betray my secret and tell my father where I'd been. I looked for him, but he was nowhere around. Behind the dirty strips of canvas that hung in the doorway to the storage area in the back, I could see Mr Melcher shutting the huge freezer door.

I set the list of things my mother wanted on the counter and Mrs Grant, a woman of few words, simply took it and handed it to her bagger, Chuck, who began gathering the items from around the store. I stood there, frozen, watching Mr Melcher wash his hands while Mrs Grant busied herself with straightening the gum in the candy rack. Mr Melcher kept looking at me, then back at his hands. His face was sweaty, though he'd just come from inside the freezer, as if he'd just cut up a lot of meat.

I jumped at the sound of the metal basket hitting the counter. Chuck had completed the list.

'That's . . .' Mrs Grant tapped at the adding machine keys, each computation making the sound of beans rattling in a tin can. 'Three dollars, seventy cents.'

I handed her a five and let her put the change in an envelope, as usual. She stared at me, as if sizing me up. When she handed me the envelope, she pinched her lips together, glanced back at Mr Melcher, then at me.

'You take that right home. No stopping.'

She lifted the bag of goods and settled it into my arms. I thought to suggest putting it in my father's car, which was right outside, but no one had mentioned him at all.

I went out of the front door, then hastily made my way around the back to see if the car was there. It was. I hurried behind a wall of thick hedge where I could see if he came out.

Mr Melcher came out after my father, grinning. I couldn't recall ever seeing Mr Melcher smile. While they exchanged words, my father rubbed his arms as if he was standing in snow. Then they shook hands, my father got into the Plymouth and drove off. Mr Melcher looked around the parking lot warily. He waited another minute then, satisfied, went back inside.

I hurried home, wishing the cold inside me gone. I knew I couldn't beat my father home, but I thought that, if I got there in time, I might see something pass between my mom and dad that would explain his behaviour. Perhaps I'd even hear their words. Understand. If I understood, maybe the awful feelings I had would go away.

The driveway and garage were empty except for my mother's two-tone Chevy Bel Air. Kirk was in the yard playing some war game with his awful demented friends. I went in the back door, face flushed, still cold inside, and terrified.

'I saw Dad out driving.' I was sorry the moment I blurted the words.

Mom set a clean pot under the counter, then took the groceries from me.

'It's Saturday. He was probably on his way to the office to finish up what he left last night.' She began pulling out the items one by one, ticking them off the list in her head.

'Chuck got everything. I just stood there. So if there's anything missing, you can blame him.'

'The envelope, young lady . . . ' She held out her hand, which I quickly filled. My mother shot me 'the look', then continued emptying the bag. 'Fine. It's all here. Now go to your room. No television.'

I shrugged. After nine years of being sent to my room, I felt as if it was my world. Once there, I spun waking dreams – I planned my wedding to Jesse, had us dancing on a beach in Hawaii, sang my heart out to the world, becoming famous, everyone loving and admiring me. I'd grow up to find part of the dreams – the sand between my toes as warm and real to me as it had been in the fantasies of my youth.

Monday at school, Jesse was absent. The teacher waited until we were all seated and quiet, then she sat down in a chair like ours, so she was looking into our eyes. It made everyone nervous. Miss Norman had never done that before.

'Class, I have something very important to tell you. One of your classmates, Jesse Simmons, is lost, or went with a stranger over the weekend, and his parents are worried sick. We don't want this to happen to any of you, so let's go over the rules about walking with a friend again.'

To me, her voice became a metallic rasp far down a long tunnel. I stared out of the window, imagining Cecilia and Monroe, holding each other, weeping, afraid their only child would never come home. Jesse's parents loved him, and their hearts were breaking. Wondering was going to kill them.

That night, at the dinner table, I couldn't eat. I was sick with sorrow, fear, and longing. I kept waiting for Mom or Dad to ask what was wrong, but no one bothered with me.

Finally, Trish asked me if she could have my peas. I nodded solemnly.

'Jesse's gone.' I sighed so heavily, I feared a sob would seep out.

Trish stopped spooning peas. 'Where'd he go?'

I looked at my father. His eyes remained riveted on his martini. My mother squinted at him a second, then reached for the mashed potatoes.

'Nobody knows. He got kidnapped, or something. The police are looking for him.'

'Maybe he robbed a bank,' Kirk offered, his future in crime suggested.

I managed a frown. 'Miss Norman lectured us about walking alone.' I stared at my mother. 'I guess you can't send me to the store without Kirk now.'

She looked at my father. Kirk whined, 'Aw, do I have to? She's older'n me.'

Dad pulled his eyes from his glass. They touched on me, then went far away. He grumbled to my mother, 'Solve this one. I'm going to finish my drink.' Then he got up and left the room.

Mom frowned at me. 'Eat or go to your room without supper.'

Kirk smirked. Trish shrank beside me. I shrugged, got up, and left. As I passed my father, he was slumped in his lounger, eyes shut. I imagined him in the electric chair, ready to fry, knowing one day I would make it happen.

But that night I sat on my bed, lights off, my face against the window screen. The cool night air stroked my cheek, and I breathed in the scents of night-blooming jasmine, hyacinth, and juniper. I wondered, for an instant, if Jesse's face was colder, if he smelled the carrion around him, then closed my eyes. There, in my mind, I saw Jesse on the beach in Hawaii, dancing beside Angel, waiting for me. Yes, I thought then, I'd find a way to be with them. Soon, but not before I told what I saw. My father rubbing his cold fat arms. Mrs Grant never looking me in the eyes. And Mr Melcher's lopsided grin.

A LIE FOR A LIE

by

Pat Cadigan

Pat Cadigan was born in Schenectady, New York, and now lives
in London, England, with her son. She made her first professional sale in 1980, and has subsequently come to be regarded as
one of the best science-fiction writers of her generation.
Cadigan is the author of three novels: *Mindplayers, Synners* and
Fools, the latter two of which won the Arthur C. Clarke Award
for Best Science Fiction Novel. She has recently published a
series of novellas about future Japan that will be incorporated
into her next novel and is working on a novel called *Parasites*.
Cadigan has also written non-fiction for *Omni* and *Mondo 2000*.
In addition to being one of the original 'cyberpunks' Cadigan has
written an amazing array of SF, fantasy, and horror stories
throughout her career, publishing in *The Magazine of Fantasy
and Science Fiction, Omni, Asimov's Science Fiction Magazine, Tropical Chills, Light Years and Dark, Little Deaths,
Alien Sex,* and *Blood is Not Enough*. She has had three
collections of her short work published: *Patterns, Home by the
Sea* and *Dirty Work*.

'A Lie for a Lie' is science fiction. It brings back Deadpan
Allie, a recurring Cadigan character last seen in dire straits in
'Dirty Work' and still top-notch at her job despite an extraordin-
ary handicap.

A LIE FOR A LIE

'Some things won't go away,' said the woman in the shiny black coat. It looked like leather sometimes and sometimes like vinyl, but it was actually a very glossy kind of cloth. Her yellow hair was equally glossy but her pale skin was dry and powdery; with the diamond eyes, she looked like a brittle doll. Very fashionable. My billing system said she was doing business as Faith Arsenault; she hadn't mentioned a name herself. 'Some things won't go away and some things won't come back. Do you know what I mean?'

Watching her diamond eyes glitter, I nodded. This seemed to sum up the human condition, actually – baggage you can't get rid of and grails you'll never find. Life considered as a helix of semi-hysterical frustrations.

'If there were any justice in the world, the two would cancel each other out, or at least balance. But they don't. Do they?' She added this last as if it had suddenly occurred to her that there might be some sort of justice in my world that wasn't in hers.

I only indicated that she should go on. I wasn't put here to provide that kind of answer. Two things I don't do: 1) affirm anyone's universe; 2) speak out loud. I suppose there's a third thing I don't do: lie. Not even by omission. So all those who come to me, including this woman, know I can't understand anything they say aloud, that it's actually coming to me via the aphasia translater in my left eye. Handy device for those who, for religious or philosophical or even aesthetic reasons, are opposed to surgery or nanotech. So why the hell not, anyway – the whole idea is, technology's supposed to give you a choice about what to do. And besides, aphasia can be tricky, even in this bright-and-shiny tech era. Sometimes you're safer settling for what's left than risking all for the sake of being able to speak or understand the noise that passes for communication.

And if the mind wanders some, that's all right – the translator stores and replays. Great feature. Maybe someday I'll admit I went for this not so much because I'm against surgery or nanotech but because I really like machines.

'No, they never balance each other,' the woman said decisively. 'This is why we have to balance things ourselves, however we can. Which is why I've come to you.' Since I don't speak myself, I tend to notice how people often talk about twice the amount they need to; with her, it was like she had to pile up lots of words as supports. She tossed a disk down on my desk and the holo popped on impact, rotating slowly in stop-action display. Good-looking man, young, but not too gaudy; nothing like a brittle doll with diamond eyes. I might have known.

'He's not as young as he looks,' she said archly. 'And I'm not as old as I look.'

In fact, she didn't look *old*. Her skin was firm, smooth, without flaw; no doubt the body under the coat was just as perfect. Nanotech's work is never done. It'll tone your biceps and triceps and quadriceps and all your other ceps while you sleep. If that's the sort of thing you can sleep through.

But it was all purely technical. It's the expression on the face that always gives the game away. I hear you can take classes in how to look *less* experienced, so as to give other people the impression that you're really as young as you're pretending to be. Personally, I think it would be hard to get through a class like that with – you should pardon the expression – a straight face. I couldn't, and there's no face straighter than mine.

'He stole my youth,' the woman said. 'That's why *he* looks so good and *I* look so tired and sad.'

She wanted her youth back? I popped Standard Disclaimer #4 up from the desktop: *There is no such thing as a time machine, only discrete memories and amnesia.*

'I'm not looking for my lost youth,' she said quickly. 'I want a piece of his soul'.

Oh. Was *that* all?

I wish I could describe how my translator communicated that one, but I can't get beyond phrases like *pictures of more than three syllables* or *words in mixed media*. Maybe someday I'll just throw all this over, become a conundrum artist, spend the rest of my life helping babies and mindsuck victims develop complicated brain paths.

In any case, regardless of how that particular request gets communicated, it's not as impossible as it sounds. In fact, it's not impossible at all. You can do plenty with a piece of someone's soul but most people choose to install it in a module and enjoy its company like you would a stationary pet or a mobile bonsai. Kulture Kritics call that social chewing gum, but what do they know? Frankly, I think they just won't admit they've ever been that lonely.

There are several ways to get a piece of someone's soul and most of them are legal. The easiest way is just to ask and see how much they want for it, except in the case of celebrities, where you have to go through the franchise agency. Of course, the agency will try to convince you that what you really want is to be enfranchised, so you just argue with them for an hour, or however long it takes, and then walk out with your module and your contract.

But regular people you can just ask. For a while, trading pieces with someone else was *mode de temps*, until the Devil's Market scandal hit. Then it became *très très mode* to claim that yours was among the pieces in the second-hand inventory the Brain Police confiscated. *Second-Hand Souls*, right. What a gold-mine for low-budget melodrama *that* was.

Then there was the rumoured traffic in unborn souls. Nobody proved that any such thing ever took place, though you still get this or that warpo claiming to have been victimised in the womb. But then, weren't we all.

If you don't know someone with the sort of soul you think you want a piece of, you can fish the personals. The advantage there is that everyone listed is willing, and most of them will give you a try-before-you-buy period, or a special temporary rental rate.

You can also go to a rental agency, though everything in it was acquired as pre-used to begin with. Proponents claim renting is less wasteful, but those who have tried it say there is something sad about a rented soul – something about feelings of rejection from too many renters and no permanent owners.

Then there are the semi-legal methods. You can rummage through their cast-offs, virtual and actual, and have a program put together a profile based on things like food and entertainment preferences, bill-paying patterns, education and job history and any other personal details you can scrape up. The result is supposed to be an approximation, and it's supposed to be sold that way, but there's a lot of fraud in the soul business.

There's even more fraud in the posthumous celebrity soul business, but all those snake-oil merchants manage to slip through the Celebrity Impostor loophole with stuff like *If You Were the King* and *The Next Best Thing To Being Her* and *E Equals MC^{You}*. And, of course, there are the stories that make the rounds every so often, that someone finally *did* get John Fitzgerald Whodoyoucallit's DNA to blossom and now there's a comatose clone in a vat dreaming a make-believe life while greedy soul-suckers cut pieces out and sell them. Maybe they're the same ones who handle the unborn stuff.

But assuming you can't find anything even marginally legal, or you have to have some particular person because you're hinky or kinky or in love or out for revenge – if there really is any substantial difference between one and another of those things – you can try breaking into some system that the object of your obsession is known to frequent and get a quick-and-dirty copy *sans* permission. Or you can hire someone like me to do it.

Some people believe you can stick pins in an effigy and make a person suffer; others think you can steal a copy of part of a person's essence and that person will be diminished. I've heard that there are still places in the world where the former works; the latter is usually treated as a case of copyright infringement, sometimes with punitive damages under certain circumstances, like the guy who stole his ex's rape fantasy and distributed copies to everyone in the New Jersey state directory. *New Jersey*. Now *that's* what I call *dirty*.

I didn't know if my fashionably brittle client had something like that in mind and I didn't want to know, though I made sure she was familiar with that case and some others. It only made her impatient. 'I told you, *I want a piece of his soul.*' The diamond eyes flashed; wincing, I wondered if the effect ever gave her a headache or an eye-ache. 'Sorry,' she said, 'It's a signal that my blood pressure is spiking. I need to tone it down.'

She sat for a minute with her head tilted back and her eyes closed. 'Better,' she said finally, opening her eyes and looking at me again. 'I *want* a piece of his soul. God knows, he's got more than a piece of mine.'

All lovers must say that at one time or another. Sometimes, it might even be true.

Raymond St Denis Nelblu sounded like someone you were supposed to *want*. I let the holo continue to twirl slowly on my desk while the online snoop pulled all of the guy's known details out of the usual sources. I kept watching his image while the refiner sifted out the mundane things – address, etc. – and put together a profile made up from his buying habits, spare time, and various miscellaneous stuff that seems irrelevant, out of character, or part of some larger, as yet unseen pattern. Or part of nothing, a mistake. Maybe someday I'll just admit to myself that I do this work because I'm pathologically nosy. I just love taking all that information about a total stranger and sticking it in my eye.

While I was sticking his stuff in my eye, I had the snoop pull data on Faith Arsenault. Yeah, I know what you're thinking: it's too good. The name even came through at first as icons for *church* and *guns*. Then *prayer* and *ammunition*. Sometimes, I think the aphasia translator has an independent sense of humour. But Arsenault is a very common French name, and there are as many people named Faith as anything else. And yes, she did a number of things under a number of other names, but Faith Arsenault was the name she had been born into, and the name under which she had loved Nelblu. Which was *not* the name *he'd* been born into.

Nelblu was a professional dreamer. Not a dreamfeeder, but a dreamer. There were those who would have said *con artist*, but I think of it the same way I think of performance art. No doubt there are people who dream more deeply, more vividly, and more coherently than average, and can provide, on command, an experience as satisfying and dynamic as anything you can get in a dreamland. I'm just not willing to believe that everyone who makes the claim is telling the truth.

I wouldn't have believed Nelblu was one of them except for the testimonials, or rather, the lack of them. Also the scarcity of his ads – the real ones don't have to advertise. Word-of-brain, you might say, gets around on its own.

Word-of-brain was still getting around on Nelblu in spite of the fact that he had settled on a short list of regulars and eliminated the waiting list. I didn't find Faith Arsenault on either list, under any of her names. I poked around in his recreation and leisure billing and not only didn't find Faith Arsenault, but didn't find any billing for that stuff, period. For the last decade, the bulk of his non-household expenses had been medical.

Munchausen was my first thought. It would figure; surgery as a metaphor for the creative process – getting cut open to put in new things, or cut out old things, or both. Creative types are all wild for metaphor; I figure it's the inexorable human drive to encode and decode. But the snoop didn't turn up any evidence that Nelblu was pretending maladies for attention and sympathy – the medical was all in-home stuff.

The rest of his life was uninteresting at first glance. Day-to-day chores like grocery shopping, laundry were all automated. Nothing unusual there, until you looked closer and saw that there wasn't any entertainment or travel or anything in the way of socialising, except for some media notices on a few highly publicised charity functions – Dream Maestro Joins Effort for Malaysian Memory Relief, Dreamer Adept Attends Benefit for Rebuilding the Library at Alexandria – where he had shown up via holo proxy. Not so terribly unusual, either; plenty of people do the same, sometimes for no real reason. But as far as I could tell, Raymond St Denis Nelblu hadn't been seen in public for fifteen years.

Well, that wasn't necessarily remarkable, either; lots of wealthy eccentrics disappear into their own self-contained worlds sooner or later. And as Nelblu's case showed, you didn't even have to be all that wealthy. Being a dreamer made him eccentric enough.

I had the snoop make another pass through the Dream Maestro's business history, just to make sure, but it came up the same – no transactions outside the small circle of regulars. Closed system? The arrangement looked funny no matter what symbols it was translated into. I decided to test it by sending for information on making an appointment to have a dream.

The answer was immediate: *St Denis has achieved Stasis and will not be seeing any new clients in the foreseeable future.*

Stasis? St Denis in Stasis. The image was arresting, dramatic, perfect. Ecological balance in a world designed by St Francis – no, wrong saint. St Francis had never been transfixed (in the soul business, you brush up on your hagiography or you could get lost fast).

Transfixed . . . the picture in my mind was of a man tied to a tree with arrows sticking out of his naked but otherwise perfect body. The expression on his face was not agony but a sort of hungry . . . *satedness.* I asked the translator for a retake, just to see if it could dredge anything further out of my own knowledge to convey meaning.

It gave me Elvis, onstage. For St Denis in Stasis? Obviously, some of the associations I was carrying around were too oblique even for me. I narrowed the context and asked for a new translation in terms of commerce.

I could feel the translator make the change, like someone sobering up on demand. The Dream Maestro had transformed his old dream-selling business into a private social club. You hear about this sort of thing happening from time to time – a group of people pool money and resources and have themselves declared a unit, which is a bit like a corporation without a product. If the money's invested wisely, it can last as long as most of the people in the arrangement.

The motivation for people doing something like that is always some kind of emotional fulfillment. It had to be something especially significant in this case because all of the members were, like St Denis himself, comatose.

It's a decadent society where you can be comatose by choice. Or aphasic, for that matter. As for people who choose to be comatose for the sake of someone like Nelblu – excuse me, St Denis – well, people will do for religious reasons things they would never consider for love or money.

Of course, if you were to add love or money to a religious motivation, you could end up with something akin to a force of nature, and about as unstoppable. St Denis's little circle had hardly formed around a fortune, and I doubted money was driving Faith Arsenault – the disk she had thrown down on my desk had contained a holo of the man himself, not a spreadsheet. Which made her more dangerous than someone looking for a big money prize. Moneygrubbers can be bought off.

According to my billing system, Faith Arsenault was more likely to buy someone off than be bought off herself; her wealth was a combination of elements which included currency but had more to do with leverage and position, what she knew and who knew her. Being excluded from the great man's little closed society must have wounded her like nothing else could. People like Faith Arsenault live on a crazy-angled plane, where they most want only what they can't buy, and keep trying to buy it anyway, even though they wouldn't want it any more if they could buy it. I'm not sure what they'd be more devastated by – the fact that everything *did* have a price after all, or that it didn't. I don't think even *they* know.

Even worse, though, was to have had it at one time and been helpless to prevent it from slipping away. Old billing records showed that Faith had once occupied a spot on the waiting list and later moved over – moved up? – to being a regular. At that time, no one but Nelblu had been comatose and he hadn't used the St Denis part of his name, or title, or whatever he called it.

It had taken just about three years for Faith Arsenault to move from the waiting list to the regulars and back to the waiting list before being cut off completely. She hadn't been the only person taken off the waiting list, and it was only a few months before the waiting list, too, was eliminated and the last of the chosen regulars taken into the group coma.

Coma was one of those things you had to have the temperament as well as the aptitude for. I could see why Faith Arsenault hadn't made the final cut; she just couldn't slow down enough. Well, some people don't, but it made me wonder what Nelblu had found attractive about her in the first place, not to mention vice versa.

Whatever it was had been enough to keep them connected for three years. I thought it was too bad that someone hadn't reminded old Faith that no matter how rough the ride is, any landing you can walk away from is a good one. But then, for some people, if it doesn't leave a scar, it hasn't happened.

On the other hand, the experience certainly had left its mark on her. Just how much of her soul did Nelblu have, as compared to how much she thought he had.

*

Nelblu might have had a good reason for locking Faith Arsenault out, and maybe I'd have done the same if it had been me. But that's not what I'm paid to think about. Nothing personal. If Nelblu had got to me first with a like request – get him a piece of Faith Arsenault's soul – I'd have just gone and done it. It would have been more difficult since she wasn't in the mindplay industry, but I'd have managed to scrape up something.

Of course, technically, St Denis wasn't in the mindplay business any more, either. I could have looked up some more of his ex-clientele but I had a feeling they'd all gone on to something else; otherwise, Faith Arsenault would have tried enlisting them in her crusade. She hadn't even mentioned anyone else.

It occurred to me that she hadn't even had the grace or sense to mention that he was comatose, alone or in a group. But she had to have known – had she thought it wouldn't matter? The comatose don't go around leaving traces and residue the way conscious people do, and dealing with a coma group is not the same as dealing with an individual. It seemed that things had a way of getting very complicated very quickly around Faith Arsenault. Which may have been why St Denis hadn't invited her to stasis. But that wasn't my concern, either. She was the one paying the bill and I was way too nosy to give her a refund and tell her to find another party to crash.

Sometimes it's good not to be able to talk to people directly, because you always end up chasing them down and baldly asking for things. If you can get them to come after you, they're so much more forthcoming. I sent the snoop out into the everywhere with a redesigned icon – St Elvis Sebastian, complete with arrows, but hanging from a cross of living wood, in the upside-down rapture of the Tarot's Hanged Man.

The responses weren't slow in coming. Most of them were requests for more details from people who wanted to meet the man pictured, but the last two were from St Denis insiders. One wanted to sell me self-help programs for achieving a stasis of my own. Figured; people who think they have all the answers are often only too happy to tell you what they are.

The other wanted to know how I knew Faith Arsenault.

*

Visiting the comatose below the consciousness barrier is – well, *odd*. The symbolism and the literalism are equally rampant and you can't always tell them apart. You don't always need to, but you won't necessarily know when you *do* need to. It was a situation I felt pretty comfortable with. The aphasia kept me from dreaming lucidly, which meant I handled my dreams pretty much the way I handled my waking life, and vice versa. Which is to say, everything was equally absurd to me, so I was right at home with the comfortably comatose.

Elective coma is something like hibernation and something like hypnotic trance and nothing like anything you've ever felt before. Trance-coma is something entirely different – you find nuns and monks in it for religious purposes, usually trying to get through all nine billion names of the godhead so as to bring on the end of the world and the promised paradise to follow. You'd find that goal much more understandable if you really believed that was the only way you were ever going to have any sex.

Elective coma is far less structured. Ordinarily. I've heard it described as a random walk through chaos. It's not as much like death as it is like the end of the world, single serving. Personally, I'm hard put to imagine how a personality wouldn't disintegrate altogether, but it doesn't. Chaos has its own structure and personality goes right to it – if it's the right kind of personality.

'*Exactly* right,' said the construct. 'In relation to all of the others in the mix, so that it can be in and of the phase space. Otherwise, the attractor cannot develop or be maintained.'

It was disconcerting to hear personality referred to as an *it*, especially by an it. The construct in contact with my left eye had made no effort even to suggest an artificially balanced androgyny. Sexless, raceless, faceless – an impossibly smooth, fluid, barely human outline. I wasn't sure what bothered me most – its lack of human characteristics, or the fact that I could understand its communication better than anyone else's, or that it didn't much feel like the same . . . what? person? entity? that had asked me how I knew Faith Arsenault. This thing wasn't given to curiosity. All its needs were taken care of. Maybe I was supposed to interpolate a soul from that.

Part of the advantage of being aphasic is never having to worry about expressing yourself coherently. I sent a sceptical pulse at the thing and waited to see how it would take that.

It paused; I could tell by the lingering aftertaste that I was on hold. While I waited, vision from my right eye began overlapping now and again, so that the sight of my office and the slowly twirling holo of Nelblu-the-man on my desktop melted in and out of the shadowy abstract I never bothered converting to a more standard environment. Lots of people will make an office or at least a room out of the join interface, but I don't bother. I don't stick a cable in my eye so I can be in a goddamn *room*.

Sometime later, the Hanged St Elvis Sebastian icon congealed out of the tints and shadows – first, the general outline of both cross and man, then the man. As I watched the image of the man become more distinct, he sprouted arrows in various parts of his body, but as if they were growing out of him rather than piercing him. He smiled, and the soft, sensual lips acquired a dimensionality they hadn't had before. This was no longer an icon.

Is this easier for you? he asked. *The entity registers your discomfort with the usual speaker. Also registered: absence of spoken language and presence of outside influence in this transaction.*

The translator assured me that the communication really was that stilted. It figured – communication by committee, of course. I've seen plenty of weird, bizarre and outré things, but I think the most grotesque is a group of people who have combined their personalities to eradicate the barriers between them. How unhappy did you have to be to do that? Or was *unhappy* too simple?

I sent him a picture that indicated I wasn't sure how many people I was meeting – him, several of them, or all of them.

There are no numbers here. Only the Blend and the Balance of the Marriage.

Marriage, my translator insisted, was the only word that fitted the concept, claiming my mind had assigned inaccurate or inadequate connotations to other terms. Maybe my translator really is capable of independent humour.

But then, I truly couldn't remember very much of what I had once associated with *marriage*, the icon or the concept. Maybe I could blame the aphasia for that. Or thank it –

There was a sensation of being *looked at*: perhaps *scanned* was more like it. Some unmeasured time after that, a blank wall encircled us and began to rotate, displaying pertinent scenes from the Holy Stasis of St Denis.

Like I said, what people won't do for love or money, they'll do for religious reasons. The desire for salvation is stronger in some people than the drive to reproduce. Of course, that does beg some questions: salvation *from* what, *to* what?

The scenes on the wall gave the story in overlapping fits and starts and jump-cuts, the Grand Apotheosis, from Nelblu the Dreamer to St Denis. In his dreams, yes, the very place. Dream charisma, that's what you have to have to persuade people to buy your dreams. Some have it, some are drawn to it, some are allergic to it. The sight of the holo twirling on my desk spilled over briefly and seemed to project itself among the images on the wall; then it was gone, though I could sense that the wall was echoing its movement.

The images that marked Faith Arsenault's tenure lasted barely as long as an eyeblink, but it *clunked*, somehow, like something big that had fallen down a steep hill. Or been thrown.

This was her *symbol*. The hanging man glowed brightly and I understood that he – they? – meant the emotion, not that actual image. Her *symbol*, her *desire*. *Not ours*.

I re-ran the brief *clunk* of Faith Arsenault's passage in the sacred story of St Denis. *You didn't exactly discourage her.*

She persisted. When someone persists, there isn't a question of allowing or discouraging. She persisted as she was: all of us persisted as we would become.

The symbols clicked along on the wall, as efficient and expressive as any words could have been. More so, actually; the translator gave me the full meanings, including the bits of truth that can be cut off when someone wants to shape a version of the truth. This gospel was no different from any other.

In every sacred story of salvation, there has to be at least one who *doesn't* get salvation. Because if everybody makes it, how do you tell the difference?

There's the *real* sacrifice, and it has a lot less to do with giving yourself up to some redeemer than it has with the unsuspecting offerings bedecked with jewels and flowers because they're going to be slaughtered.

Or, as in Faith Arsenault's case, burdened with everyone else's failings and cast out. Not that she understood what was going on at the time. She'd thought she was buying dreams, after all. Dreams from the very exclusive Dream Maestro Raymond St Denis Nelblu, who was only too glad to be rid of all the individual ambitions and frustrations suffered by himself and his following; things that kept them divided, or would have if Faith Arsenault hadn't come along to take them. And what great luck to find someone who could not only take them, but would pay for the privilege. Obviously a sign that their intentions would be blessed with success.

Old Faith had got it all completely wrong. She *did* have a piece of Nelblu's soul, the piece he hadn't wanted. And now he wasn't Nelblu any more, and he had nothing, absolutely nothing, of her, except the memory of her having been there. She was what they had given up to reach this blend and balance, to exist as the pattern of St Denis. The Marriage.

And the flesh was made word, and we dwelt among it.

Technically, that was none of my business, no matter how distasteful I might have found it. The Hanged Elvis Sebastian almost seemed amused, picking that feeling up from me. It let me know that even if I had loved the idea, there was no room for me. The Marriage had achieved its final form. Over time, it would become set enough that the extra bodies now maintained in coma could be disposed of, little by little, until there was only one to continue driving the configuration, from there to whenever entropy might set in. Assuming Faith Arsenault didn't hire someone to pull the plug first.

The hanging figure turned upright, plucked an arrow from its chest and held it out to me. It became a white rose. I didn't reach for it; the man left it hanging in the space between us, twirling slowly.

Then give her this and let her believe she has a piece of the Marriage.

Blood welled up between the petals and ran down the stem, dripping on the thorns.

I added an arrow, putting it through the rose's heart. *Isn't this more like it?*

The Marriage's response was a cross between an electric charge and the unrelenting grip of a vice, a stinging pressure that lasted for ever and was over in a flash. Somewhere in there, between the alpha and omega of the reaction, I saw the Marriage come apart.

It was less than a moment, but the members were all discrete. Then the spasm passed and it was the Marriage again, but in the aftermath, that moment-less-than-a-moment continued to exist. Not among them, but independently in the phase space they had built for their unity to exist in. It was a renegade spark, a comet on an unpredictable and irreversible path. Sooner or later, they would intersect with it again and there would be another shock, another separation. And then it would be gone, travelling away but bound to meet them again. Each impact would change things in that funny little reality until the time when it would hit them in just the right way and send them all careening away from each other for good. No more Marriage and, if they insisted on discarding the bodies, no more life to go back to.

I hadn't meant to do that; I didn't even understand how I had. And then the rose turned so I could see that the head of the arrow had become Faith Arsenault's head, features frozen in brittle triumph.

There was barely enough time to be shocked before the contract broke, and I found myself staring at the silent, rotating holo of Faith Arsenault's loss.

In my left eye, the cable disengaged, retracting the needle, several centimetres long but only a few Angstroms thick, that had penetrated the pupil to connect to my optic nerve and put me into the system. No more eyeballs-out-cable-in for me; the new systems are cleaner, safer, less wearing.

Cross my heart and hope to die; stick a needle in my eye. Funny, the things that come to you right after you break a mind-to-mind contact. Not to mention the things that endure and the things that don't. Pollution erosion did in Mt Rushmore, but kids' ritual rhymes go on, an oral tradition as old as – well, never mind. Oral traditions are not exactly my forte any more. But that's a funny thing, how history can get distorted, legends can blossom or wither, and auld acquaintance can be forgot until rudely brought to mind.

They had tried to hand me a lie to comfort her with – well, I suppose *lie* is an idea crueller than their intentions had been;

maybe *illusion* is more what they meant, but from Faith Arsenault's position all alone outside, there isn't a shade of difference between the two.

   . . . stick a needle in my . . .

I stuck the needle back in and let the system search, even though I knew it wouldn't come up with anything foreign. Faith Arsenault hadn't planted anything in my communications or my system; the arrow with her head had not come from her. I was just as pleased when I understood it had not come from me, either. The pierced rose was all from St Denis in Stasis, the Marriage; I could tell her to come and get it at her leisure. I could even tell her it was a piece of Nelblu's soul, sign here and here and here, and she would never be the wiser. It was a lie she would find easier to believe than the truth, that Nelblu and the rest had taken nothing of her.

But that wasn't quite true, either. You never get rid of anything completely, not out of the mind you don't. Associations stay, there *are* ghosts, and sooner or later something will activate them, a trigger word, a sensation, or, say, an image that brings to mind that auld acquaintance – or auld Faith – that should have been forgot.

Well, even if I said nothing at all, Faith would accept the icon of the pierced rose from me and treat it as if she had a piece of Nelblu's soul. Maybe that was ultimately what it was, after all; maybe the only real piece of Nelblu's soul was the image of the one thing that could destroy it.

I did consider attempting to tell Faith Arsenault the whole truth, I really did. What stopped me was knowing she wouldn't believe it, any more than the Marriage would believe it had contained enough of her to set its own destruction in motion. I guess that's because people tell each other too many lies, lies that they wish were the truth. Like Faith Arsenault and her dream of revenge. She wanted to believe she had hurt them, Nelblu and the others who had fitted in where she had been cast out. But she couldn't hurt them, because they were doing it for her. As she had been hurting herself for them.

But I don't lie, even by omission, and this would mean I had to. Only once, and for that, I wanted to hurt all of them. Which was another futile desire.

I settled for seeing it as a simple business exchange. A lie for a lie, and a truth for a truth, and maybe, in the end, that's all you can ever really get. I don't know, and I reserve the right to remain silent.

KEEPING ALICE

by

Simon Ings

Simon Ings lives in London, and sets much of his fiction there. He is the author of the novels *City of the Iron Fish*, *Hothead*, and *Hotwired*. His fourth novel, *Headlong*, will be published in the UK in 1997. Other recent projects have included a children's animation series, work with a German jazz band, and *Gloria*, a feature script currently in development with the British Film Institute and the BBC.

According to Ings, '"Keeping Alice" is completely autobiographical except for the plot, which is a damaged version of an Inuit folk-tale.' I pointed out to him that the sexual dynamics of this novelette are virtually the same as in his science-fiction story, 'Black Lotus'. We agree that we have no idea what this means regarding his psyche . . .

KEEPING ALICE

ONE

Unmistakably Alice, blinking the sun out of her eyes in the doorway of the Billy B. I leaned back on the bar. God, why did you have to give me what I want? But after what we'd been through, she and I, I told myself to wait, to watch. See how she moved and if she smiled. See if there was anything beyond her lips and hips I recognised.

She was nothing like my dreams: heels; an ankle-length beige sheath dress; black hair cropped short; eyes bedroom-bruised by blue shadow. It unnerved me, that I should have recognised her so easily, who did not look at all like her I'd known.

It made no sense, her wanting to come in here. I wondered, dressed like that, what was her proper place? I did not know. A dismal irony, this: to think young enough to build a place like Billy B's, and so lose the scent and spoor of your own generation.

Like me, she was too old for this place. A man of our age strays in, he feels for the coat-hook under the bar trim, the space-cadet decor confuses him, and he thinks for a moment it's the mid- to late 80s again. The women are smarter and, seeing a flash of Umbro or Adidas, depart: 'No atmosphere!'

Alice came over to the bar, heels on parquet clicking counterpoint to *Wow War Tonight*, and perched uneasily on a bar stool. Turning her back on me she studied the place: the soft orange walls, the Billy B logo stencilled across them in gun-metal blue. Reed-like lights tall as street lamps leaned over the stairwell to the basement bar: cylindrical shades on green stalks.

'Can I get you something?'

She glanced at me; looked again, seeing who I was.

'Vodka? We freeze it.'

She smiled. 'Sure.'

'Which?' I pointed at the blackboard – frozen flavoured vodkas were our speciality. While she read I watched her, tried to figure out what she was feeling.

'*Aero*?'

'We're out. There's chocolate orange –'

'Christ.'

'White Toblerone?'

'How do you do that?'

'You leave bits of the chocolate in the bottle. Or there's lemon –'

'Lemon, then.'

'Jackie? A *Citron*, and a Caramac.'

'How can you drink that stuff?' she said.

'Try some?'

She sipped, grimaced. 'I might have known you'd pick something like that.'

She asked me if I worked here. I told her how the place was mine and how I sat here every day, like a dusty and only occasionally wise owl, navigating styles and trends.

'Very Bohemian,' she said, meaning a compliment.

The real Bohemians hang on the other side of Bateman Street, sprawling across the burst second-hand sofas of the Living Room to a soundtrack by Transglobal Underground. They leaf through *Dazed and Confused* for Rankin's white-room portraits, Ellis's postfeminist crotch-shots: 'Diamanté handcuffs! Beyond me . . . '

I knew I was talking too much. For six years I had heard nothing from her. I couldn't bear the idea that she would sound as different as she looked. I forced myself to shut up.

She looked around the bar again. 'The girls,' she said. 'They all look like Elina Lowensohn.'

'So do you.'

'No I don't.'

'You're so thin.'

'I'm too tall.'

She had an hour to kill, she said, between a screening and a dinner date.

'A film?'

She nodded, volunteering nothing more.

I drained my glass. 'Another?'

She peered into her lemon vodka as though trying to see what was wrong with it. 'A beer maybe.'

'So Alice – what do you do?'

'I'm an actress. didn't I say? Broke, of course.'

'In an Issey Miyake dress?'

She plucked at the skinny-rib material complacently. 'Appearances.'

'Christ, you've changed,' I said. I tried to make it a joke but my voice wouldn't co-operate.

It turned out she wasn't an actress at all; she was a dancer. The film she'd been to see was an experimental short made for TV. They transmitted it recently. She's naked in a water-tank: she's beautiful.

'I danced with DV8,' she said, 'and VTOL, for a bit.' But the names meant nothing to me. She fell silent. I realised then it wasn't her strangeness was making our talk so hard; it was me: my own fear and desire. So I tried over again, but by then it was late and she had to go.

I walked her to the door. Opposite, outside the Carlisle Arms, girls in plain jean jackets drank from sleeves of Foster's in the sun. (Downstairs in Billy B's, that would be some sort of statement; a new front in the denim-Lycra wars.) We said goodbye. We didn't kiss. We made no stupid promises to call. I let her go.

Six years of dreaming, wishing it would all come right for us at last. Now, for reasons I understood but could not face, I let her turn the corner, out of sight.

TWO

North of Bristol city centre, in a bowl where three streets meet, Montpelier, year by painful year, bootstraps itself into some New Age version of gentility. The Farm Shop's not the mouldy muddle I remember, the juggling store has moved, and in its place the Pacifica offers 'Little strips of Sesame Spiced Chicken and Green Capsicum served with Warm Mango Sauce'.

The rest changes hardly at all. In the Old England the jukebox still plays Pink Floyd. The faces there are different, but the crowd hasn't changed: white boys in dreadlocks or shaven-headed with limp Jesus beards; girls in cotton shifts and unlaced army boots.

Walk up to Richmond Road, and up again, past Greenpeace-stickered windows and plastic stained-glass whales: you'll find a path beside the Malting House. There's a view of the suburban rail-line here: it's far below you, obscured by brambles and hawthorn, overgrown with knap-weed and broomrape. The footpath meantime slides off to the right and steeply down, following a muddy path between sunflowers and tomato canes, peas and potato plants to St Werburgh's. I was born here, in the dark: a house surrounded by allotments on the unlit gravel track that leads to St Werburgh's City Farm.

A child's idea of a house: plaster-grey walls, square windows either side of the front door, the upper storey blank; a steeply pitched slate roof and, at its centre, four ornate clay chimney pots from a single stack.

I remember foxes and old French roses: Céleste with its grey-green leaves, its few but wicked barbs and soft pink blooms. Broom and yellow buddleia; pipistrelle bats, dropping like scraps of shadow from the bows of the birch trees. Grass snakes. A plum tree gone bad.

One night, suddenly, everything was different. The wall which had hidden the house from the lane was missing. In its place there was a swing, a sand-pit, fencing, bedding plants. Once dark with ivy, rambler roses, wisteria, overtowered by matted clouds of raspberry and bramble, now the house shone out from the mottled charcoal of the hill like a splash of dirty paint. A security light blinked on above the porch, dazzling me. Inside, childish voices raved; bedtime versus *Blade Runner*.

As my eyes adjusted, I saw that the new owners had laid a patio around the house; around that lay an earthen scar, graphic and precise, broken by clumps of wilted Busy Lizzies. Trays of bedding plants stood by the door. Behind them, in a tangled heap, the children's mountain bikes.

I stared and stared, hating what they'd done and at the same time understanding it. They had children; they had to take care. In hot summers, laburnum trees make poisonous seed-cases. They'd cut them down, and planted floribunda.

It used to be a mess. A complete mess. Riotous, impending. Blown. I couldn't criticise. I remember one night when I was drunk I too had taken a hammer to it all: *'I'm going to tidy this up!'*

I first met Alice in my mother's shop. An index card in the window said we stocked the widest range of Personal Development Cards in Bristol; Alice wanted some.

'But you want to start with something gentle,' her boyfriend warned her, in a thin Swansea accent. His hair was in dreadlocks; clotted in some places and eaten through in others, they resembled small dead mammals hung from his head on a string. From out his heavy metal T-shirt, his arms were hairless, grey and thin as driftwood on Porthmadog beach.

She was after tarot cards; Aleister Crowley's pack. I got them off the shelf.

'Not them,' he advised her warily. 'No, you want something simple, like Aquarius.'

I put them back and showed her the Aquarius deck instead.

She leafed desultorily through the cards. 'But they're all airbrushed.' Rat's-tails of unwashed chestnut hair were entangled in her ornate Tibetan earrings. Her Bali batik bodysuit was old and stretched; she had gathered it around her waist with a leather money-belt.

'You don't want anything with attitude,' he said.

'Yeah,' I said, parroting received wisdom, 'the Crowley deck can really do you in.'

'But the Fool's only a head-shot,' she complained, pointing at a card. 'I thought he was supposed to be stepping off a cliff?'

'Not necessarily,' he said. 'Besides, you want something made for Now, made for Today.'

'Anyway,' I said, making a guess at who would pay, 'the Aquarius is only fifteen quid.'

'But –'

'You want something easy on the eye, to start,' he said.

I put the cards back in the pack and sold it to him. He gave it to her. She gave him a thin smile.

'Jubiaba' was my mother's name for it; I called it 'Crystal Balls'. The board outside boasted incense, posters, semi-precious stones, pendulums, tarot cards, runes and wands. In the

window we had Jubiaba Wondermix Smoking Mixture, pipes for
toking bad dope from St Pauls, a Gandalf-shaped hookah and
Mayan Music Balls: steel, with a bell inside, there came with a
note which read, 'Because they are hand-made, no two balls ring
alike.' Some didn't ring at all.

Inside the shop, scented candles gathered dust beside a
hardboard shelf of well-thumbed books; Papus and Gareth
Knight and Unwin's reprint of Mouni Sadhu. Laminated posters
of dolphins regularly fell off the walls and some of the braver
customers said, 'It's not as much fun as Chachi's,' which, with
its candles, scarves, postcards and knick-knacks, a little way
down Perry Road, made colourful a trade my mother plied with
such numbing sincerity.

I saw Alice again at a party held by some regulars at the Old
England. They were squatting a five-bedroom country house in
Compton Dando and the eviction order had just come through.
They were giving the place a farewell trash.

I drove there in my mother's van, the Old England's barmaids
in the back, squealing. 'I know what I'm doing!' I snapped. But I
shaved a few corners anyway, adding to their adventure, and felt
old for no reason.

The back lawn of the old house had once been screened by tall
trees, but the recent storms had all but destroyed them; you
could see straight through to the garden. Firelight reflected
muddily off the green tin walls of Commer vans. Tents and
teepees made strange, angular shadows under the trees. About a
hundred people were crowded round a bonfire of floorboards and
old furniture. Someone was lugging round trays of Stella Artois,
a quid a can, and there was this argument raging about them
costing 95p in the shops and where did the other 5p go? Like it
mattered.

The latest Skinny Puppy album blared and ground away
inside a large shed. The treble frequencies vanished into the
pine, leaving only a back-beat; a bass line sampled from a
wrecking yard, it thudded away like some monstrous heart.

I went over to the bonfire and sat down on a felled tree trunk
next to three old men. The one nearest me was saying to the
others, 'Do you believe?'

I looked around for someone I knew.

'Do you believe in the afterlife?' He smelled of stale whisky and sweat and something chemical – Vim, I think. 'I believe that when we are parted on the last day, we won't ever see each other again.'

'Look, we went to Amsterdam, and what did we do? Fuck all.' I turned to the argument breaking over my head. A youth with dope-puffed eyes was trying to reply, but he was so stoned he couldn't get the dreadlocks out of the way of his mouth; belatedly I recognised Swansea Accent. He had a different T-shirt on: Hawkwind, the Black Sword tour. He was trying to speak, he was moving his mouth, his brow was furrowed with concentration; no words came.

'I lived with you six months, and what did I do all that time?' The girl was her I'd seen before; wild and filthy hair and silver earrings. Tonight she was wearing cut-off jeans and a Bali-print vest; silver fish dangled from her ears. 'Cooked. Kept house for you. Cleaned after you. And you spent the whole time in Abi's lorry.'

Welsh managed a murmur.

'What? Oh. Yeah. *Trailer*. Sorry. Abi's fucking *trailer*.' She walked off to the house alone; I followed her.

The place was a mess of bottles, plates, half-eaten food; plastic washbowls full of pungent punch, thick and blood-like under weak fluorescent light. She was standing by the open fridge snapping open a can of lager. She looked at me and nodded a greeting and swept her bangles free of her wrists.

'How's the tarot deck?' I asked her.

'It's shit.'

I found a half-full bottle of Wray & Nephew, slugged from it, wiped the neck and handed it her.

'I don't need that.'

'Yes you do.'

The rum slid down her throat as smooth as milk. 'Alice,' she said.

'Charlie.'

We went through to the hall.

'Who's Welsh?' I asked her.

'I spent winter with him.'

'Amsterdam; good choice.'

'You were listening!'

'Did you go to Icebreaker?'

'Where? No.' She thought about it. 'We went to Bulldog's.'

'Bad news.'

'And we went to the Heineken brewery, but it was closed.'

'Did you eat at Egg Cream?'

'No.'

'We should go,' I said, enthusiasm getting the better of me as usual.

'Yeah,' she said, 'sure.' Like I was taking the piss or something.

Just then the front door glass blew in. A bloody hand reached through and fiddled with the lock. Alice stepped back and took my arm. The door opened and a drunk boy slouched in, trailing a guitar.

'Sorry!'

He wandered into the living room and struck up the refrain of 'I Wish I Was Back Home In Derry'.

Alice, shivering in the gust from the open door, looked around at the paint-spattered carpet, the inept graffiti on the walls, the shattered light-shade over the door and the fragments of coloured glass. 'They've ruined it.'

'It's how they like it.'

'That's not the point.' Her look was helpless, melancholic.

I went down the hall and swung the door shut. Coloured glass crunched beneath my feet. I pulled a blue square free of its twisted leading and gave it to her.

She didn't know what to do with it. I took it back off her. 'Close your eyes.'

'What?'

'Close them.'

I stood beside her, raised the jagged colour to her face: 'OK.'

She stared round the blue-tinted room, wide-eyed like a child.

I said, 'We could go to Amsterdam.'

The Fool's number is Nought. The Fool's clothes are ragged and he is being attacked by a dog as he marches along. He carries a bag slung over his shoulder on the end of a stick. The Fool ignores the cliff's edge beneath his feet because he no longer thinks about his earthly body: the pure light of the spirit shines down on him and white roses grow at his heels.

*

Later, we went back to the garden. A flare of light from behind the bonfire caught Alice's attention. In the gap between parked wagons two women, breathing fire, laughed and staggered, swinging brands. Bottles of kerosene stood at their feet.

One was thin, the other fat. The thin one was new to it: afraid.

'Harder! Blow harder!'

'The fat one, look!' sighed Alice.

Her flare was huge: white hot in its centre, with a broiling yellow tongue. When her breath failed her the flame shot back into her mouth. She dropped the brand and took a step back, rubbing vigorously at her lips.

Alice laughed. 'I want a go!'

'Go ask her, then.'

'You know her?'

'She's my mother,' I replied.

Alice took the dole and earned pin-money playing flute outside The Knot, her mouth pinched, eyes slightly crossed with concentration, as though she were trying to spit with accuracy into the plate at her feet. Yachts lay at anchor in the dock behind her. Across the water, in the Arnolfini arts centre, the Cholmondeleys ran a masterclass, gallery staff unwrapped Anne Whiteread's plaster-casts, and in the bookshop upstairs Zone's *Fragments for a History of the Human Body* were on sale for £30 a volume.

'What's the use of it?' said Alice, unconvinced, as I leafed through Volume One.

'Just keeping up to date,' I said, glancing through a chapter entitled 'Indian Speculations about the Sex of the Sacrifice.'

'You read stuff like that for the shop?' she asked, as we took our seats by the window in the bar downstairs. Outside, beyond the Lloyds Bank car park, rose the narrow but expensive terraces and overtowering trees of Brandon Hill.

I shook my head. 'It's hardly "Crystal Balls" material.'

Alice didn't like it when I did or read or listened to something for its own sake; she always wanted there to be a good reason for everything. In love, I took no notice; blaming, if I had to, Swansea Accent. I figured six months in his camper van in Merthyr Tydfil was enough to blunt anyone's enthusiasm for the world.

'You can borrow it if you want,' I said, pushing the book towards her.

'No, thanks.'

The prince kisses Sleeping Beauty; she wakes confused, so weak she cannot stand, with pasty skin, and a bad taste in her mouth. The prince puts his arm round her, makes simple meals to soothe her shrunken stomach, massages her back: so I with Alice; I enjoyed the world for both of us, held coloured glass before her eyes, and tried at every turn to make her smile.

Sometimes I tried too hard.

'Leave her alone,' my mother said.

'Please.'

'I don't smoke, Charlie,' Alice insisted.

'They're Beedies! They're from India!'

'Shut up, get us a drink.' When my back was turned, 'He does go on,' my mother said, and Alice laughed.

Behind the bar of the Arnolfini, screening off the kitchen, sheets of frosted glass bore shelves of unfamiliar drinks. Krupnik, Starka, Topiaka, Jarzebiak. Carefully I climbed the metal stair back to the tables.

Alice stared. 'What's that?'

I sipped my brownish slurry, wincing as the citrus hit the back of my jaw: 'Frobisher's Red Orange.'

'Christ, Charles, I asked for something *normal*,' Mother bitched, fighting with the cantilevered plug that sealed her bottle.

'Mum, it's Grolsch. It *is* normal.'

Alice picked up hers and read, 'Banana beer?'

'Shit, Charlie.'

'Mother –'

Alice took a swig. 'No, wait, it's great.'

I drowned whole seconds in her smile.

'I need a piss.'

'Mum, mind the step.'

'Suck eggs, son,' she snarled, swinging her mighty hams over the form bench.

'Your Mum's so *cool*,' Alice enthused.

On the opposite side of the dock the wooden wharves were a muted red.

'I wish I had a mum like that,' she said.

A sleek little yacht with 'Laser' written on its side bobbed before them.

'What did your schoolfriends think?' she asked.

I began sketching the yacht with my fingernail in the soft varnish of the table.

'I suppose she must be more like a big sister than a mum.'

'Yeah,' I said, 'that about sums it up.'

Alice frowned at me, like my irony was hard to read or something.

I shrugged. 'What?'

'What are you doing?'

'Drawing boats. Look.'

'Charlie?'

'What?'

'Well – talk to me!'

I sighed, said I was sorry, and picked the varnish from my nails.

'What's with the boats?'

I didn't want to talk about it; not with Mum around. With a mother like mine you keep your wishes to yourself. I pointed out of the window. 'Since I was a kid,' I said, 'I've dreamed of owning one.'

'A boat?'

'A speedboat.'

'Why?'

So I might leave the dock, turn right, sliding past the bright blues and Mediterranean pinks of the Cumberland Road terraces, slip under the Avon Bridge, past Nightingale Valley and Observatory Hill, into the Severn and the sea –

'Ow! Shit!' Mother had scraped her shin again on the metal step. 'Why can't we drink in a real pub?'

She meant The Farm on Hopetown Road, a minute from our home. It was bounded to the south by the city farm; its café and community rooms shadowed the pub lawn, all soft lines and tree-branch window frames like overgrown garden ornaments, or a Yes album cover brought horribly to life. The pub was as eccentric in its way: a regular-looking house on a regular-looking street; sitting outside, you couldn't help but feel you were invading someone's private lawn.

Mother drank Ruddles County here each night at sunset, greeting people with the smallest of unsmiling nods. All here knew her, many loved her; loved me too, who had been brought up on this lawn as much as anywhere. The Farm crowd were our family, familiars, an inner court. Here Mum belonged, cross-legged on the slope up to the little sheds, once piggeries, where new, unwary drinkers, getting up after their Founders or their Best, cracked their heads on the low beams. Mum enjoyed playing with the children, most of whom she'd known since birth. The game was simple; she would sit, taking no notice, and the kids did what they would around her, chasing, dancing, sometimes singing in a ring, sensing in her gravity and bulk something resembling a natural principle. Titania to her dungareed and Baby Gap-clad court, Mum, with a blink or a gesture, somehow engaged their respect. No tantrums broke out around her, no hair-pulling or mean faces. Here, if nowhere else, Mum broadcast gentleness.

'She's amazing,' Alice said.

'This place is home for her.'

Alice looked at me like I was trying to explain something away.

'What?' I said.

'Nothing.'

'Look,' I said, losing patience, 'she's my mother. You don't have to sell her to me.'

'I'm not!'

'I know who she is.'

A child's idea of a house. Step under bramble, cross the lawn, crush speedwell underfoot, and find Alice prone, blushed by the sun, against a ground of lavender and wild strawberries.

Smell the sunlight on her skin as she undresses you: sweat heavy with the scents of phlox and rosemary; on her neck, Turkish delight of mingled rose; under her breasts, the soft tang of pineapple sage.

'Oh Charlie, I was asleep.'

Her thighs surround you; she tastes of forest loam, mushrooms, game.

'Stay there. Stay there always, Charlie. Live there. Get inside.'

Rose-heads blow and fall. Scatter the petals on her breasts, see how they stain the light, glowing beneath their curve of shade. Stroke her moisture out into your hand and see it spark in the sun from your fingers like static, while she hunts you for tastes of her own.

'Break me. Do it.'

Give with a cry into her hands, her mouth, the damp between her legs. Her nails are black with dirt, her knees are stained, her breasts are scratched and sore from rubbing in the grass. She rides you into the earth. Her hands cover your face. The smell of crushed grass drowns you.

'Cold now.'

Dress each other, kissing for hours as the light declines. The flowers give their last, valedictory burst:

'Such beautiful scent!'

The flowers here are old; irreplaceable perhaps. Moss roses: Little Gem with tiny crimson flowers; the purple lavender of William Lobb. 'That one's Henri Martin –'

Alice laughed.

'What is it?'

'You don't have to do that.'

'What?'

'You're always trying to impress!'

She hadn't understood me at all. 'I'm not trying to impress anyone. I'm just interested, that's all.'

'Leave some space for me, then, Charlie, if that's what it is.'

'What?'

'Let me be eager, too.'

Hurt, I pulled free of her embrace. 'I do!'

That summer was relentless. It never rained. Around us, the crane's-bill melted into brown crusts over the cracked earth; the old cherry tree died; the lawn was crisp and sharp against our backs. We kissed thirstily, sucking at each other, parched.

Late afternoon, we would dress and follow the path between garden plots to The Farm, where mother would be waiting.

'Hello, Tina!' Alice had taken to kissing my mother on the cheek.

'Hullo, love.'

After an hour of this the three of us would walk back to the house to eat. Mum made a great show of hunting out special herbs from the chaotic borders by the back door; Alice was fascinated.

While they picked and sniffed among the shrubs, I'd do what I could with the garden. Watering the cherry had done no good, and now the plum tree was dying. It was late August: I remembered bright red plums, sometimes flushed yellow. This year the leaves had come out silvered and crinkly, and what fruit there was was deformed and attracted all the pests. I'd tried pruning the tree the year before and some of the branches had split. Flat purple fungus appeared on the dead wood. Wasps had burrowed into a cracked bough.

Mother picked a sprig of rare sage. 'Smell. Go on.'

Alice lent her face into my mother's open palm. 'It's just like pineapple!'

I went inside and took down mother's *Good Housekeeping* gardening manual.

Plum Sawfly larvae, I read.

Brown rot. Honey fungus.

'Mum, I *want* to drive,' I said.

'Get in the back with Alice; don't mind me.'

'Mum –'

'Come on, it'll rain!'

Alice and I climbed in the back of the van. The previous winter I had knocked up a rough plywood bench over each wheel arch. We sat opposite each other, clinging to the sharp edges of the Escort's frame as mother bullied us on to the M32. 'Bloody taxis!'

It was August bank holiday; that morning, a refreshing dampness in the air had signalled summer was about to end.

'Where do you want to go?' I'd asked Alice the week before. Our appetites were dulled by all the summer afternoons we'd spent in Mum's garden. We were still promising each other that we'd go to Amsterdam, but it never seemed to happen.

'I want to see the sea,' she said.

'OK.'

But though I warned her several times, that evening Alice told my mum what we had planned and Mum, being who she was, wanted to join in. 'I can drive!'

There was surf in Cornwall; I'd wanted to drive out and hire a board.

'But that will take all day!' my mother said.

'So what?'

'Besides, Alice doesn't swim.'

It was news to me: 'Alice?'

Alice shrugged.

Mum tutted. 'How could you not know?'

'How about Pembroke?' I said, a sinking feeling in my gut.

'What, drive all that way?'

'*I* would,' I said.

A pregnant pause contained all else I'd say, were Mum and I alone.

'I just want to see the sea,' Alice said.

The A370 joins the coast at Weston-super-Mare; it is separated from Marine Parade by walled lawns, the grass shorn and brown like parcel paper.

The bus station stood here once; now only Baker's Coaches works straight off the road, offering day-trips to local sights and shops: 'The Zummerset Cider & Cheese Shop for that "Tasty Gift".'

A small tractor decked out in plywood steam-engine livery pulled toy railway coaches with rubber wheels the length of the Parade. Signs pasted up by the shelters advertised the town's attractions: 'An evening of nonsense with Jethro' ('Slightly Naughty', it confessed in small type, underneath); 'Jimmy's Bursting with Laughter Show'. A trip on the *Taurus* or the *Silver Spray* might have shown us Brean Down from the sea: 'the historical fortress and wartime defences'.

Walking south down the Parade, Brean Down rose before us out of the shallows like an island with steep banks, connected to the land by a spit of sand. Indeed, that's how it used to be but, since the Bleadon Levels were drained for farmland, that spit, though you can't see so from here, fans out around the far side of Brean Down: acres of mudflats; sodden pasture; parks for static caravans.

'Must we go all that way?' my mum complained.

I set my teeth. 'Yes,' I replied.

There were no sea defences here, just a knee-high wall, its top

eaten away leaving varicose patterns in the stone. The sea was
so far out it looked as though you might walk straight to Brean's
rugged slopes over the sands. Every year some tourist tries it in
his Daihatsu and goes home wet and broke, by bus.

We passed the Tropicana, its sandstone frontage mutilated by
purple and lime window-frames. 'Let's go in!' Mum said.

The heated pool was full of kids. There was a fountain, and a
flume. 'We should have brought costumes,' I fretted, but Mum
and Alice hadn't waited for me; they were already past the sign
about the cafe's 'huge large bursting breakfasts' and were half
way to the bar.

'What do you want?' Mum shouted back at me.

I shook my head.

'Alice, love?'

'Half a cider, please.'

We took our seats.

You couldn't see the sea from here. Disconsolate, I stared out
at Marine Parade: parked cars, low walls and guest-house roofs.

'Jesus, I'm tired already,' Mum said.

'It's really not that far,' I promised her.

'It's nice in here.'

An hour, then another hour dripped away, Mum with her
gas-pumped beer, Alice with her cider; the smell of old
breakfasts.

'Oh, cheer up,' my mother said, then got up and went to feed
her change into the Andy Capp game in the corner.

'What's the matter, Charles?' Alice asked me. 'Can't you just
relax?'

'OK,' I sighed, folding my arms, 'OK.'

Later, on the Parade, we passed an ice-cream stall. 'Alice? Do
you want one?'

Mum wouldn't allow me even that. 'I'll get them! Let me get
them!'

'Mother –'

'Oh, come on,' she said, with false lightness, 'let me do it:
she's family now!'

Walking to the foot of Brean Down we passed a café whose back
garden, bounded by a high concrete wall, was given over to a
tropical bird garden. A gravel drive led past the wall to the foot of

the outcrop, where concrete steps zigzagged steeply up. Caged
birds' song played counterpoint to Mother's moans all the way
to the top. Once or twice I reached out for Alice, thinking to
draw her away from Mum's baleful bitching, but the cider had
made Alice morose and clumsy and she wouldn't take my hand.

A grassy path cropped short like a golfing green led along the
tops, bounded by banks russet with dead ferns. Mum and Alice
stood, lost and weary, surveying it all with dull expressions.

'The fort's this way, come on!'

Mother waved me away. 'You go on, Charlie. We'll follow.
We're tired.' Then, as I turned, 'Be careful!' she said, the way she
used to when I was little.

'I'll leave you my balls for safe-keeping, shall I?' I retorted.

But Mother's whale-like fat absorbed my barbs without a
wound: 'What was that?'

'Don't let the wind blow you away,' I said.

Alice shot me a look. I shrugged and walked away.

Bringing them here – making of a dull day something a bit
different – had been a mistake. Knowing that, a calmness
overtook me. The mistake made, I might as well enjoy what I
could. Hawthorns, shaped and shrunken by the wind, hid
stonechats and rock pipits. Chalkhill blue butterflies played
around my feet as I walked. Watching them, I glimpsed a white
rock rose. I knelt and ran my fingers across the five simple
petals, as perfect in their way as lotus blossom. I remembered
the Fool, roses round his ankles as he steps blithely into space:
'Alice. Here! Come see!'

She was a long way back now, dawdling with my mum. The
sea breeze snatched my words away from her. 'What?' she
demanded, cross.

'A rose. It's rare!'

'What?'

Something snapped in me. I stood up, strode on, giving up
even on her. 'Charlie, what?' She sounded hurt. Well, so was I; I
did not turn round.

Near the end of the outcrop there is a trig-point and from here,
because of the convexity of the slope ahead, it seems you can see
all the way to the end of the headland to the sea; you feel
cheated. 'Where's the bloody fort?' Mum shouted. Alice
laughed.

'It's further on.'

'Under the sea!'

'It's not far now.'

'It's a fucking submarine pen!'

'Mum –'

'Are you sure you've got the right hill?'

'Charlie,' said Alice, 'come back now. I'm tired.'

'That bird place was licensed!'

I went on, ignoring them both.

The slope, steepening at every step, filled me with the giddy sense of slowly and unstoppably falling into the sea. Then the ground fell away, revealing suddenly a level scarp. Cattle grazed before the fort; I stopped to take it in. Built in the 1860s to receive Napoleon III's assault, it had been refortified for both World Wars. Behind me, to each side – hidden only seconds before by the slope – were pillboxes, gun emplacements and tracks for heavy artillery.

I slipped and slid down to the moat, its bottom paved with concrete slabs. A modern concrete bridge led into the fort. Beyond the original barracks, gun emplacements from more recent wars abutted older armouries: drab temples open to the sea, big rusted I-beams poking up from concrete floors.

A gun-rail followed a weathered finger out to sea, stopping suddenly where it plunged to Howe Rock. Here a final shelter looked out to the channel, and the fortified island of Steep Holm. As I watched, a speedboat rounded the battlemented rock. I squinted at it, trying to work out what it was: a Martinique, maybe; but as it turned the faring looked all wrong; perhaps a Camargue 46. From here, the man steering the boat looked no older than me.

I sank on to my haunches, picked a pebble up and threw it at the sea. It clattered on the rocks, fifty feet short.

The speedboat vanished into the sun.

Behind my eyes I pictured it: Alice, bare beneath her cotton wrap, sprawling on the prow; Nightingale Valley; Observatory Hill; the Severn; and the sea –

Cursing, I stood up and turned back the way I had come. I'd never have a speedboat, living like I was, a helper in my mother's shop, an ironist selling personal development and health stones to London burn-outs, indulgently semi-retired in the comfortable terraces of Brandon Hill and Clifton.

For years I'd stood still gazing at the world, afraid to touch, eating my mother's food. I'd lost myself in Bristol, all its places, all its people, sucked up every taste till, drowsy, I slept replete in mother's house. And after all, I'd earned nothing. No speedboat. No family that I wanted, and no life.

I knew then that I'd have to leave; and out of pride as much as love, I would take Alice with me.

A gentler path leads from the fort and back over Brean Down. It's metalled for the most part, hedged by early-fruiting brambles, gorse and fern. Past the gun emplacements of Sprat Beach, the hawthorn closes in, hiding a view of Weston-super-Mare beneath the slopes of Worlebury Camp. The track turns and rises up the hill and here I found Alice and Mum at last, giggling together, heads bent in conspiracy, on a broken concrete platform from which you saw, laid out like a model, the garden of caged birds.

'What's up?' I asked.

One of the parrots had learned to wolf-whistle.

I followed Mum and Alice down to where a low sea wall divided pasture-land from the sedge-banks covering the mud of the estuary. Signs by every gate across the embankment warned of sinking mud. Ahead, flat-topped Compton Hill rose out of the levels like a gigantic burial mound and to the right, the skyline was saw-toothed with the silhouettes of caravans. The stone dressing of the sea wall petered out as the embankment turned left towards the ferry. Steps cut into the mud led to a line of rotted planks and a primitive landing-stage. My shoelace came undone and I slipped on the bank. 'Oh do your shoes up!' Mother laughed.

'Fuck off,' I said, beyond caring; Mum told Alice about the time she took me to London and I fell into the Thames by Cleopatra's Needle.

The little rowboat could only take two passengers. Alice and my mother climbed in, laughing. The boat wallowed under Mother's weight. Alice sat facing me, but she wouldn't catch my eye. She was trying to laugh and chew at the same time. Mother must have bought her a Mars bar or something. She looked so young there, in the prow: a little girl, chocolate all round her mouth.

THREE

'Ipanema' (literally, The Place of Dangerous Water) is a raw, sensuous solo using movement, texts and shamanic outpourings to explore conventions of feminity. On a stage lit by dreamy, piercingly blue television screens a naked woman, silenced behind a bird's beak, methodically unpicks a wedding dress. Evoking fairy-tales and mythic labours, 'Ipanema' is permeated by an atmosphere of mute sacrifice and emotional endurance. Theatre-maker Kim Uckridge has worked with some of the greats of American experimental theatre including Jack Smith and Charles Ludlam before joining dancer/performance artist Alice Young. As the Stitched Sisters, they have generated 'performance/environments' in unexpected sites, from a garden shed to a 12th-century Leper Chapel. 'Ipanema' is a development of 'The Girl from Ipanema', a Chisenhale Dance Space commission.

Charlie?'
  'Yeah?'
  'It's Alice.'
  'Hi.'
  'I got your number from Billy B's.'
  'Yeah?'
  'Was that all right?'
  'Sure.'
  'It just felt strange, the other day. Walking out like that.'
I bit my lip.
  'I wondered if you'd like to meet.'
  'OK.'
  'Or if you don't –'
  'I do.'
  'Charlie?'
  'I do. A lot.'
  'That's great.'
  'Yeah.'
  'Where?'
I did not know where she belonged. 'You pick a place.'
  'I'm performing all this week,' she said.
  'Can you make lunch?'

'I thought maybe you could meet me after I was done.'
'OK.'
'I'm at The Place. It's on Duke's Road, near Euston station.'
'I'll find it.'
'I'm staying out of town, I can't stay late.'
'OK.'
'Just a drink, OK?'
'OK.'
'Tomorrow?'.
'Sure.'
'I'm not ringing too late, am I?'
'What? No.'
'Good,' she said. 'Tomorrow?'
'Tomorrow. What time?'
'I'm through about ten.'
'Ok.'
'Charlie?'
'Yeah?'
'Don't see the show.'
'No?'
'It's kind of strange. I'd feel embarrassed. Charlie?'
'Goodnight, Alice.'
'Well, goodnight,' she said.

It was 10.40 when she finally emerged, wrapped up in a blue nylon parka that extended past her skirt. She wore opaque black tights and Caterpillar boots. Her eyes were heavy with kohl; big silver hoop earrings emphasised the bob-cut of her hair.

'Tonight's our last night here,' she said, excusing her lateness. 'There was packing to do.'

'Did the show go well?'

'I guess.' There was a sticking plaster on her cheek. 'I bumped into something. It's nothing. In the wings; I tripped.'

'An exhausting show?'

'I guess.'

The café at The Place was itself a rehearsal room: a mirrored wall, black rubber flooring, exercise bars around the walls, an old piano.

'Do you take the show elsewhere now?'

'We're off to Belgium in a fortnight, for a festival.'

'Sounds good.'

She would not look at me.

'I'm glad you called,' I said.

Silence.

Then, 'You must meet Kim,' she said. 'I'll go get her.' She got up and crossed the room, losing herself momentarily in the parti-coloured crowd at the bar.

I looked for the defining ingredients of the people here, recognising in the bright red lipstick of the girls, their shaven hair and self-conscious gestures a family likeness to the crowd at Billy B's. But there was something fractious here, some undercurrent of anxiety stronger than that at Billy's and at the same time more in-turned.

'Kim, this is Charlie.'

Kim nodded, unsmiling, and settled her bulk uncomfortably into the seat opposite mine.

She wore a nose-ring. Her black T-shirt concealed the true extent of her huge breasts. The pale brown hair over her eyes was long enough to make a cow-lick, but the rest was shaved. Her eyebrows and eyelids were even paler than her hair: she wore no make-up and her grey eyes, lacking definition, seemed to swim about their sockets as she looked from side to side, avoiding me.

'Alice told me not to see the show,' I said, 'it's such a pity.'

Kim shrugged.

'We go to Belgium soon,' Alice repeated.

'Have you a good venue there?' I asked.

Kim wrinkled her nose. 'Yeah,' she said.

'Did it take long to make the piece?'

'Ages,' Alice said.

Kim's eyes bobbed round to face her. 'Not ages.'

Alice backed down quickly: 'No, not *ages*; several months.'

Kim leaned on the table. It rocked. I grabbed my bottle of Beck's to stop it falling. Kim got up.

'It's good to meet you,' I said.

Kim mumbled something in reply and turned her back on me.

Alice watched her go. 'We work a lot together,' she said, as though this were an explanation.

I said, 'Are you sure you won't have a beer?'

Alice looked at her watch. 'I really haven't time.'

'When have you got to go?'

'Kim and I have a train to catch at quarter past eleven.'

I stared at the table. The emptiness of what we'd said so far combined suddenly with the sterile whiteness of the walls and the bare fluorescent lights over the temporary bar. 'Christ, Alice.'

'What?'

'Nothing. Nothing.'

'Have you anyone now?'

I stared at her.

'Anyone special?'

'No.' I was taken aback by her. Why – and why so suddenly – should she have asked me that? I thought her question might be leading somewhere, and I didn't know whether to be pleased or afraid. The cold blue silence of our absurdly brief 'evening' was somehow comforting; an ice-pack on a bruise. I wasn't sure I wanted anything else.

'Oh, Charlie –'

'What?'

She looked around. 'God, but I hate this place.'

'Let's go,' I said.

It was nearly time for her train, so I walked her down Dukes Road, past Wellcome's green glass monolith and through the ill-lit scrap of park separating the station from the road.

'We've still got ten,' I said. 'Come on, I want to show you something.'

'What?'

'Come on!'

'Charlie, I haven't time!'

'There are later trains, surely.'

'I have to go back with Kim.'

'Why?'

'I have to.'

'Tell her you'll be late.'

She let go of my hand. 'Stop it,' she said, too loud.

'What?'

'Stop bullying me!'

'I'm not!'

'You are! You haven't changed. Look here! Eat that! Do this! *Shut up*, Charlie.'

I stared at her.

She held my gaze a long while then turned away, back towards Euston station. She looked at her watch. 'Christ, I'm late.'

I followed her. 'I don't know what to say!'

'I know.'

We got there with minutes to spare. 'Goodbye, then,' she said, fussing at the Band-Aid on her cheek. It was paining her suddenly; the gluey bit was over the cut.

I helped her pick it free. 'I don't know what you want from me,' I said.

She said, 'Sorry I got so cross. I thought it would be different.'

'"It" meaning me.'

'Perhaps.'

'I'm not a bully, Alice. I just like sharing things.'

'Whatever.'

'*Alice.*'

The cut started to bleed again. 'Let go,' she said. 'Oh God.' A drop of blood fell on her parka.

I handed her my handkerchief. 'It's clean.'

She pressed it to her face and looked up at the board to find her platform.

'Number ten,' I said.

'Right. Thanks.'

'Alice.'

She looked at me.

'She asks for you sometimes, I said. 'Why don't you go and see her? She's still where she was.'

She laughed at me. 'Charlie, you're amazing.'

'What?'

'You know I won't. You know I can't. That's why you offered, isn't it?'

I had no idea what she meant. 'It's up to you,' I said.

FOUR

Three months or so after our day trip to Brean Down, Alice and I moved to south-east London. I'd rented a top-floor conversion on Adelaide Avenue, not far from Ladywell station. Looking east to the worn terraces of Lewisham, I was filled with excitement. People work hard in places like this, thinking one day to escape. I'd been too long without that urgency, that will to win, that fear of anonymity which drives the world to work. Here at last there would be no distractions: no more friends-of-friends' neighbours, no six-hour-long 'quick cups of tea' all ending in a joint, no Old England crowd, no parties. I would work.

We arrived at night to find the electric didn't work. 'He said it would be on,' I apologised.

Alice tripped up on an edge of carpet and slid down the couple of stairs between the bedroom and the living room.

'Bloody hell, Charlie,' she complained, picking herself up, 'what is this place?'

Each room was on a different level to the others: at the time I'd thought it gave the place character. But the conversion was shoddy and superficial; there were badly laid oatmeal carpets in every room, and the smell of fresh paint lingered where they'd painted matt white over everything, including the handles of the doors.

We left our belongings locked up in the van for the night, bought fish and chips from a Chinese round the corner and ate them in the dark on the floor of the living room. Outside, sodium-orange rain plashed the bare black branches of the trees round Hilly Fields.

Alice sobbed. 'I don't know why we're here!'

Looking at things was all I knew, so I tried my hand at photography.

Cranes built fifty years ago for the war were still in use in Surrey Docks; re-jigged by jerry-builders for heavier and heavier loads, they resembled gigantic dustbins with pipe cleaners sticking out of them. I spent weeks with a second-hand Pentax ME Super, cataloguing condemned buildings and defunct machinery. Lengths of pipe. Rusted diesel pumps. Signs so eaten away I could only guess at what they once said. I spent a whole day on a fluorescent blue rope that lay fused to a quayside road; it had been rolled over by so many vehicles, it had melted into the concrete. It looked like strange seaweed, stranded by the tide.

What I was doing had all been done to death before, of course; I had been covering old ground. But someone found my naiveté fresh enough to set me up an interview at Goldsmiths School of Art.

I spent the first half of that year scraping up money for school. I didn't know who to approach. Ignorance made me pushy. I even pestered Saatchi & Saatchi's personnel department. 'I'll do anything,' I told them. I wore them down until finally they put me in touch with a motorcycle despatch firm, hoping perhaps I might top myself. I bought a clapped-out Honda Super Sport; I worked hard; I earned money; I learned London.

An agency found Alice a clerical job in a life assurance company on Gray's Inn Road. Strangers from regional offices would yell at her for things she didn't do. On Fridays the men would all walk in with new ties and ask the women to pick a winner, but they never asked Alice.

Term began. I bought a Fuji GX680 and lugged it round in a bright orange Peli Protector case, an industrial-sized tripod under my arm. I buttonholed passers-by and snapped them against a wall in Farringdon. 'Take off an item of clothing, anything you like, and hold it up.' I didn't know what I was doing.

There were classes in business, in marketing, in design. I read the style magazines, listened to the music, bought the clothes: Alice didn't like them, they reminded her of the office.

'They're nothing like office clothes,' I complained, working the buttons shut on a Cordings shirt.

But Alice had no eye for these things. She spent all her money on day-trips to Bristol and came back wearing some old jumper of mine my mum had dug out of a closet for her.

We didn't look right together any more: Alice shopped in Camden Market; I bought khakis from The Gap. On the street, we made no sense.

'It doesn't matter,' Alice said. 'It doesn't fucking matter. Christ.'

With Alice in Bristol most weekends, I spent the time in Tottenham Court Road Tube snapping commuters as they blurred past Paolozzi's murals. I used Ilford XPS: developed on colour stock, it came out green, or sepia, and after further

games with Goldsmiths' chemicals, it soon lost all similarity to
the world I knew, becoming a different land entirely.

*His oddly mediated photographic style suits their obliquity,
their lack of cohesion, their effervescent – one might almost say
contingent – appearance; as though they were lit by polarised
light from another sphere.*

'Charlie, I *can't* go back. They told me I had to wear a shorter
skirt!'
　'So what? They're your legs: use them.'
　'Not like that.'
　'Why the hell not?'
　'It's degrading.'
　'It's a game.'
　'I won't.'
　'OK! There's other jobs.'
　'I'm going back to Bristol.'
　'Back to what? Busking in the Broadmead? Pulling cider?'
　'I was happy.'
　'You were nowhere. You were in Merthyr fucking Tydfil.'

*Print weaves through the interstices of his more recent, sepia-
tinted photographs, images of almost sinful opulence superim-
posed heavily one upon the other, so that to decipher them is to
act out a cerebral moment from some 1930s serial.*

'Tina's place, hello?'
　'Is Mum – Alice?'
　'I'll just get her.'
　'Alice!'
　'Hiya, kiddo.'
　'Mum?'
　'What's up?'
　'Just saying hi – was that Alice picked up the phone?'
　'Yeah.'
　'Well bring her back, damn it; she can't have known it was
me.'
　'She's gone to bed.'
　'Bed where?'

'Bed here.'
'Since when?'
'Where else should she kip?'
'But she's got friends.'
'Well what am I?'
'So, can I speak to her?'
'I said, she's gone to bed.'

I came away from this extraordinary installation feeling I had been initiated into some diplomatic overclass; as though his images of people, his assemblages of haute couture and designer goods had uniquely qualified me for vodka martinis in the lobby of a Vietnamese restaurant in Melbourne, and later, perhaps, for complaining about the temperature of the wine to a servile railway representative on the first-class sleeper to Bangkok.

Alice wrote to me every week. Mum was paying her to work mornings at Crystal Balls; 'She gave me my own Crowley deck as a present – cool!'

They'd been to lots of parties together. 'Tina and me were fire-eating at this benefit in Wyke. It was great.'

If she needed a bit of extra money she bartended at the Tube Club on Frogmore Street. 'John Otway was playing at The Fleece last Saturday. The PA was shit, but it was OK.'

I really should have seen it coming. All the clues were there.

'You should know,' she wrote. 'I'm seeing Tina seriously now.'

From The Farm, the house where I was born is only a few minutes' walk. At the top of the road, an unmetalled lane leads off left to the fields of St Werburgh's City Farm. Some of the plots are deserted, overgrown; others a confusion of netting and bamboo, tilled earth, artichokes and gooseberries and young fruit trees. Empty plastic lemonade bottles, their bottoms cut off, are planted neck first in the soil, root-feeders for huge squashes. Other plots are laid fallow under old cardboard and rolls of carpet; rotting, they enrich the soil.

The track ends, and a metalled path goes up the rise to Ashley Hill and Bishopston. Field scabious and bird's-foot trefoil thrive on the limestone ballasts of the rail embankment. Chicken wire fences the path, a frame for dog-rose and early-fruiting bramble.

The house is on your right. You can't miss it, even at night: it's the only one around.

I arrived in Bristol about six in the evening. I went to The Farm but Mother had already left. I drank steadily until closing time, then made my way home. I wasn't expected. I let myself in quietly. 'Hounds of Love' was playing on the stereo in the living room. Mother was kneeling topless in front of the sofa, her face hidden between Alice's spread legs.

When I was a child I used to hide in the gap between the lavender bushes and the back wall of the garden: I fled to the back door. The narrow passage was full of gardening things; I stumbled over buckets; I trod on a rake and the handle swung into my face. I staggered bloody-nosed and stubbed my toes on a toolbox. 'This place is such a fucking mess!'

Mother was hysterical. I listened to them getting dressed.

'Nothing's ever in its proper place round here. I'm sick of it!' I picked up the toolbox and threw it against the back door. The glass shattered. Something crushed my foot. I reached down, picked it up, swung it against the door. It opened.

'I'm sick of all of this,' I said, swinging at the brambles and the roses. I saw I had hold of a hammer.

'Charlie, put it down.'

'You never kept the place straight, ever.'

'Charlie!'

I started hacking at the plum tree. Brittle branches snapped and tore. 'She was mine, you selfish bitch.'

'Charlie,' said Alice, 'come inside.'

'I'll pay you back,' I said.

Afterwards we told anyone who asked it was an accident. Perhaps it was. I don't remember.

Just the hammer in my hand.

Mother, trying to stop me.

'All overgrown,' I said, 'all gone to seed, you stupid cow!'

She looked at the hammer. 'Charlie?' she said.

'Charlie,' said Alice, from the open door.

I looked at Alice. 'Go inside.'

'*Charlie –*'
I turned to my mother.
'I'm going to tidy this up.'

FIVE

'You didn't tell me she was blind,' said Alice.

I bent down and picked up a pebble with a hole in it. 'She had a stroke last year.' I slipped it into my pocket.

Bone chips from Mum's ruined nose had penetrated her meninges. The doctors mapped them on a scan, but could not operate. Year by year a sliver had been edging slowly and inexorably towards a blood vessel. When at last it tore, it put her in the dark.

'She seems strong,' Alice said. 'Lucid.'

I volunteered nothing, still not clear why I was here, why Alice should have invited me. She lived in Kent now, sharing a house with Kim in Tenterden. The Stitched Sisters: inseparable.

Alice had said stay the weekend, but in my unease I still hadn't taken my bag from the car. Kim was in the studio working and it was bright out; Alice suggested we go to the beach. Camber Sands: we drove through a uniform landscape of dikes, winding roads through tall grass, isolated houses and reclaimed pasture, bounded only by the old coastal hills of Rye, miles inland and – straight ahead – the heat-hazed blocks of Dungeness. We parked, and clambered up into the dunes. Pillboxes from the last war lay at crazy angles in the sand, as though they had been carelessly dropped from the air.

The beach was endless, clean and bright. Children were playing in the surf. Through my Ray-Bans the scene had that limpid, undersea quality you find sometimes in the paintings of the Hampstead set.

'She rallied well, except her eyes,' I explained. Then: 'I'm glad you visited her.'

Since the accident I've been paying for Mum to stay in a nursing home in Bath. I visit every year or so and smuggle in some beer. 'They've got this widget thing now,' I told her, 'it tastes fresh out the keg!' She recognised me eventually.

There was a dark line on the horizon: a bank of low blue cloud, heading for land. We threw pebbles into the waves as we walked. 'Kim and I are leaving for New York next week,' she said.

'How long will you be gone?'

'A year.'

I was afraid to ask if I'd see her again.

She must have been about twenty-eight; there were creases round her soft, bruised-looking eyes which only made her gaze more mesmerising as she stared past me out to sea. 'There'll be a storm tonight,' she said. The skin around her jaw was impossibly delicate, paper over bone: beauty so fine it is its own *memento mori*.

I picked up a stone and skimmed it. It bounced twice and vanished. 'I wish we'd done this sooner,' I said. I'm not sure what I meant.

The dunes fall abruptly away here, replaced by shingle banks. The Kit Kat Café sells inflatable rafts and ice creams and, according to a sign in the window, Pukka Pies. I wondered what they were but when I went inside to buy ice creams the assistant didn't know. The place was barn-like and empty so we sat outside, shielding our eyes against the Persil-white garden furniture, and shivered as the first storm-cold reached land.

An elderly couple sat nearby, watching fatalistically as a fat eight-year-old girl wobbled back towards them, dripping ice cream down her suit.

'Mind the shingle!'

There were trampolines not far away. The girl bit fiercely into her cone, her teeth impervious to cold; once it was gorged inside her she went over to have a go. 'I need a leg-up!'

'No you don't.'

'I do, I'll hurt myself!'

I said, 'Maybe if I'd kept my temper on Brean Down, things would have worked out.'

Alice stared at me.

I stared back. 'What?'

'What on earth made you say that?'

I thought of pillboxes, of reclaimed pasture and endless shallows. It was strange how Alice, living at the other end of the country, should bring me somewhere so redolent of Weston-super-Mare.

Alice and Kim lived in a renovated oast-house. I followed Alice up waxed stairs and dumped my bag in a circular white-painted room, converted from the place where hops were dried. It had a conical wood roof that creaked in the wind, a futon on a hardwood base and, by the stairs, a Japanese flower-arrangement. 'This OK?'

'It's wonderful,' I said, staggered.

She showed me over the rest of the house: Kim's studio, awash with books, scattered CDs, half-complete models and constructions. The dining-room floor was flagstoned; African textiles hung from the walls. There was a bathroom on the ground floor with a sunken marble Jacuzzi. A transparent resin loo seat contained plastic shells and gold starfish. 'Kim made that!' Kim herself, her bulk accentuated by stiff dungarees, was busy in the terracotta-tiled kitchen, tending Le Creuset pans on a designer hob.

We went into the living room. A Japanese wide-screen TV was tuned to a shopping channel. Opposite, a French window stood open on to the newly planted garden. 'Come and see the trees!'

From the patio a lawn swept down to a barbed-wire fence. The grass was dug up everywhere; damp gusts bent the new trees easily.

'What are they?'

'Cherries. Plums. It's going to be a riot.'

I sat down heavily in front of the TV while Alice went to help Kim with the food.

There was one advertisement which seemed to go on for ever. 'If you use plastic bags, then you need the Super-sealer!' the voice-over enthused; but having established that the Super-sealer sealed plastic bags, he didn't know how to stop.

'The Super-sealer, an extraordinary sealing device for plastic bags!' he exclaimed. I went back to the window and breathed in the scent of lavender and phlox and sage. *A riot*. My head swelled with pernicious memories. I came back into the room and he was saying, 'any plastic bag can be sealed with the Super-sealer!' I looked round for the remote. In a final desperate bid for attention, he offered me two Super-sealers for the price of one, 'one for the car and one for the home!' The advert didn't seem to end; it just tailed off into some rambling monologue about garden centres. I couldn't work out whether it was an

advertisement or not. I went down to the kitchen to see if there
was something I could do.

Kim was feeding Alice something from her hand. I watched as
Alice lent her face into Kim's open palm. 'It tastes just right!'

Dizzy, I leaned against the lintel.

'Charlie?'

I stared at Kim: the familiar unsmiling, uncompromising
bulk of her. 'It's not over.'

'Is he all right?'

Her resemblance to my mother was uncanny. 'You've carried
on,' I said.

'Open the door, love. Charlie, take my arm. Come on outside.'

'I didn't stop it after all!'

Storm clouds raced towards us. They were so close, you could
have touched them.

'Charlie, what's the matter?'

I clutched my sides against horrible laughter.

'Charlie? Is it your heart, Charlie?'

Great blue clouds, so low it was as if you could reach up and
swirl them with your fingers. A faint, erratic light swamped us.
My pulse thundered. I said, 'I've got to go.'

Half way out of the drive I remembered I'd left my overnight
bag in the house. I didn't go back. I turned up the heat, slid a John
Lydon CD into the slot and turned the headlights up against the
crashing rain.

I never did get that speedboat I wanted. But I drive a Hennessy
Viper Venom 550. It can hit sixty in under four seconds, it's got
an eight litre V10 with a custom-ground camshaft and hardened
push-rods, and now and again – topping 200 with the hardtop on,
or tramlining on a bend – it feels as though the land has turned to
sea.

A PUNCH IN THE DOUGHNUT

by

David J. Schow

David J. Schow lives in southern California with his wife, Christa Faust. He is known primarily for his powerful, award-winning short fiction, and for editing the anthology *Silver Scream*. He has had two novels published, *The Kill Riff* and *The Shaft*. In 1989 he branched out into films and television, scripting 'the unsavoury activities of such social lions as Leatherface and Freddy Kreuger'. He also is credited with writing the script of *The Crow*. His short fiction has been collected in *Seeing ·Red*, *Lost Angels*, and *Black Leather Required*.

And what the author thinks of revenge:

'Feel like your world is spinning out of control? That friends of some vintage are abruptly going all loopy on you, doing insane things, reproducing, or becoming actively toxic? Emotional hydraulics kicking into overdrive and golden time? Is the amplifying theistic hysteria accompanying our final approach to the year 2000 making you want to call a friendly phone psychic *right now*?

'You're feeling the press of the Millennium on your brain pan. It's all part of what the venerable Adam Alexander has duly christened the Great Despair (for which he has my thanks, here in print) . . . and you, the reader, are urged to keep this in mind when the cranked-up ambient craziness in the air, all around you, right this minute, threatens to tip you over.

'Then again, you could just go kill whoever fucked around with you. They should have known better.'

A PUNCH IN THE
DOUGHNUT

———

It is said to be a dish best served cold, and that the best way to achieve it is by living well. These are civilised sentiments, cunning and barbed in their decent way, and their principal drawback is that they cannot satisfy the hotter and more immediate needs, such as the desire to make a meat cleaver part of your enemy's profile, on the spot.

Durkins' opponent tonight was the sort of rubicund bigmouth he had always fancied his polar opposite. A typical braggart with a bullying mien, Calloway had always been loud, swaggering, self-inflated. They had become friends precisely because they were so different.

It is said that the first impulse is to share good news; the second, to bludgeon someone with it. That was how it had started, really, between Durkins and Calloway; one of those dick-measuring bouts they had both enjoyed in their youth. Durkins liked competition, but now petty contests seemed hyperbolic and pointless. He billed his moody funk to the Great Despair.

Supposedly a signifier of the onrushing millennium, the Great Despair was proof that the whole world's accustomed way of life would expire not with a bang, but with endless whimpering. Passing comments would be quoted so those who ventured the comments could be sued. Misunderstandings would flourish and paranoia reign. Once everybody took offence at everything said by everyone else, regardless of intent, then there would come true freedom of speech – because all would be talking, and none listening. It was either the Great Despair, or everyone around Durkins was flushing their sanity at the same time.

Calloway was a tourbook of failed addictions; ex-alcoholic,

former coke sniffer and basehead, veteran of AA and NA and support groups aplenty, multiple divorcee and expert liar. He had winnowed his remaining compulsions to what he considered to be the least debilitating group. He was still what his twelve-step pals would call a sex addict, but who cared? He chainsmoked, but that was better than drinking or basing, right? Most of the considerable energy he had previously devoted to chemical recreation and ducking the police was now focused on . . . gossip.

Calloway was a man who could not keep his mouth shut at gunpoint, and only stopped talking when he was asleep. He was one of those members of the human species who feels an unregenerate drive not to *share* whatever facts he collected, so much as to amplify and disburse them. He was a lousy chess player.

Durkins was a man who, in the middle of his life, had just discovered that people often chose their 'ages' early and stuck by them no matter what the calendar said. Calloway, for example, had turned seventeen and stayed there for over twenty years. He was still there, tending seventeen. Durkins, though the same age as Calloway, felt much older, less brash, hardly impulsive at all any more. In comparison to Calloway's glandular, loud-speaker approach, Durkins had lived long enough to learn that keeping his mouth shut was, frequently, better strategy in the war-zone of human relationships. To him, that meant keeping things to oneself rather than automatically spraying half-facts and innuendo in every direction like shrapnel. It meant not comporting oneself like an adolescent. Like Calloway.

Especially when the rumours concerned things that were personal and private; particularly when there could come consequences; most emphatically when the say-so was targeted right on Durkins' reputation.

Calloway, conversely, wore his personal and private 'tragedies' like badges of honour: 'Don't tell me; I'm a three-time winner on the Wheel of Divorce!' Do not pass GO; proceed directly to detailed and entertaining anecdote. That sort of thing. Usually the omitted aria in what was inevitably an opera was the one pointing out that none of these 'tragedies' had impacted Calloway in any real way – he was too emotionally shallow and infantile for any grown-up difficulty to bother him for longer than it took to aver blame. But he was fun to listen to.

Durkins had in large measure straightened out his life by evacuating straights from his life. His chess game had improved. Now happier than he could remember being in the past decade, and despite all the glad-handing of assorted media (this season, at least) toward his preference, he nonetheless found himself the object of ridicule and attack, thoughtless, abject and utterly unexpected.

The reason? Mario, Durkins' current lover, who had replaced Jeanette, his ex-wife.

In a fist fight on Durkins' front lawn one memorable day near last Thanksgiving, Mario had calmly bested the thrashing, flailing, and clearly unhinged Jeanette, who was now busy seeking her inner child within the safe confines of a minimum-security therapeutic facility. Charges and counter-charges had been disposed of in one day, and all of a sudden Durkins felt as though he had got a reprieve on his entire life. *The Tragickal Comedy of Lady Jeanette* had been his biggest excursion so far into ritualised abuse.

This dramatic conflict had sent all their mutual acquaintances scurrying to one corner of the ring or the other. At the time, Durkins smugly observed that only his already handicapped 'friendships' had bailed on him (not counting Calloway, who was yet to betray); he did not miss them. The blowouts were always losers anyway; best to plane them free and refinish the life in a richer tone. That was cold but practical, as Durkins tended to be whenever he sensed his own flesh getting flayed.

Durkins informed Calloway, in the course of casual conversation, that Jeanette was history and Mario would be staying with him for a while. The situation was basically a healing one.

Calloway had turned and bitten.

That simple update was all the impetus Calloway had needed to start braying, going all cross-eyed and slack-jawed whenever he deployed the word 'faggot'. He made it well-known that Jeanette had enjoyed his heroic phallus on more than one occasion while she was vampirising Durkins' bank account and soul. That Durkins was a textbook exemplar of the term pussywhipped. Had been, always would be, nyahh, nyahh, it figures the guy's a queer.

Mario offered to break a few of Calloway's bone groups.

Durkins kept his opinions to himself, holding back, waiting. Inside his gut, however, he ached. Why couldn't the son of a bitch just shut his face? That was easy, wasn't it? Just stop talking.

The answer, the *true* one, could only sting him as well: Calloway, righteous gender bigot, had real honour the way Mongol rapists had scruples.

It came back to Durkins, through mutual ears, that Calloway's next salvo had gone something like this: 'Well, he can't say anything, y'know, because basically he's got a little dick and he can't fuck, at least not women, that's what *I* heard, 'cos he's major fag-o-rama, likes taking it up the Hershey Highway, I mean, I ain't got nothing against those people except AIDS, but gee, what am I gonna say to a fuckin *homo*? And he's like *shaking my hand* and shit, probably thinking about putting his tongue up my butt. I thought this guy was my friend, and now it turns out he's a doughnut puncher?'

Durkins considered Calloway's insultable attributes, from the brain-dead surfer 'do ('spike the top, buzz the sides and leave the back long') to the classic bay window (one of those pendant bellies pop science currently blamed on surplus testosterone); from the hours logged on his Bowflex, which had popped his jaw muscles like golf balls and thickened him like a steroid junkie, to the hours logged beneath the sun in pursuit of a terminal cancer tan. *He looks exactly like a beer commercial,* Durkins realised, *pure tough-dood manqué.* He kept it to himself. To respond, to say or do anything, would mean escalation, which made Durkins a victim of terrorism.

Mario piped in with an offer to 'punch Calloway's doughnut, permanently'. Durkins told him never mind.

It came back next that Calloway had asserted Durkins' professional 'success' in commercial photography was entirely beholden to a daisy chain of gay old boys snaking back to the beginning of Durkins' career as a guy who shot pictures of refrigerators for ad layouts. Every photograph clearly told the tale that the guy was a big pansy! Those shots just oozed fagitude! Where Calloway's patented, hyberbolic rants once had been amusing by their sheer volume – exaggeration being a cornerstone of good comedy *and* manliness – his style retained significantly less entertainment value when

Durkins was the exclusive bullseye.

Durkins concluded that Calloway was so overpoweringly macho, turned up so high for so long, that this was the *only* response of which his ex-friend was capable, given the Nazi limits on his horizon for human interaction. Calloway literally could not help himself, nor stop his big flapping mouth from dropping open, full bore, to spew fresh bile whenever the opportunity arose to slander Durkins – the former friend who had become a sex traitor.

To be sure, Calloway's entire identity hung between his legs. Which explained the smell, thought Durkins . . . but he kept it to himself because it was cheap and vindictive. No one wins a turd fight because, in the end, everyone is covered in shit.

But he and Calloway frequently encountered the same people, and since no input at all was coming from Durkins, Calloway persisted in recycling old invective, cranking it up higher with each unanswered barrage. The truth would never deter Calloway from eventually fabricating an entire alternate life for Durkins, if Durkins never hit back and never provided anything new to ridicule. Therefore, whenever Durkins crossed paths with the tiny subset of friends still common to both of them, most of the dish would focus on the latest 'Durkins story' from Calloway – all of it quite innocent of the fact that the two had not even spoken for over a year. It happened just often enough to annoy and irritate Durkins, a recurrent itch that could be scratched and exacerbated, or ignored at the risk of becoming malignant.

Calloway had become dandruff on Durkins' soul.

Durkins knew it was all a goad, of course; he was supposed to get hot, and react rashly. That was the whole point. Durkins resented any attempt at manipulation. He hated being forced to do anything.

Mario reminded Durkins that he knew 'a guy' who had done time for rape and arson. The guy owed him a favour.

Calloway did what Calloway did, on and on, never lacking wind or grist. Didn't this man ever acquire *new* enemies?

Then it occurred to Durkins that Calloway was the sort of man who kept friends in reserve, to sacrifice as needed in order to avoid any culpability for his own life. By claiming Durkins' head had swelled as a penalty of his perceived 'success', Calloway handily processed his own guilt over his go-nowhere avocation – a minor skill at handicrafts that had expressed itself in the manufacture of smoking paraphernalia (a train wreck of interests, when Calloway's life had hit the freebase speedbump) and little Tolkienesque figurines of bisque. By berating Durkins' sexuality, Calloway fortified against his own insecurities. And by telling tales out of school, no matter how outrageous, Calloway remained very much the gregarious social lion, thereby guaranteeing himself a constant supply of bodies to throw in the lawnmower path of responsibility.

Durkins realised this is what most people thought friends were 'for'.

Mario offered to have Calloway murdered by a couple of gentlemen who guaranteed the body would never be found and were willing to 'do a job' – for a friend – for 500 dollars. Durkins said he'd think about it.

Calloway kept on keeping on.

It was no surprise, then, when Calloway accepted Durkins' unexpected invitation to coffee, so things between two estranged friends could be worked out without any more hassle. They chose neutral ground, a coffee shop neither had entered before. This was no longer the bygone era of Beard-O's java emporium, where they'd once maintained a favourite table from which they over-caffeinated and attacked any and all topics as a team.

Calloway saw Durkins waiting in the booth, but pit-stopped at the restroom before sitting down. Durkins knew Calloway had a bladder the size of a grape.

'This is a shock,' Calloway said, sliding in behind still-steaming coffee. 'Man, I thought you and me were on the outs for good.'

An understatement, thought Durkins. 'I don't think the sort of damage that got done is fixed with a Band-Aid.'

'We both said stuff and did stuff we shouldn't have said and did.' Already, Calloway was segueing into his shuck-and-jive routine, the extravagant gestures, the serpent bobbing of head and shoulders. 'I mean, I've seen you ice out your friends, man, and when you freeze them out they're frozen out for keeps, but I thought that if you were in, you were in for good, you know, for better or for worse? I mean, I'm willing, I guess – otherwise I wouldn't be seen in public with . . . you know.'

Durkins let that one pass; a free throw. He knew that in some furrow of his brain Calloway was keeping score on who ranked whom, how well, and how many times. 'You were saying you knew how I felt,' he said, 'about friends who have stabbed me in the back.' The part Durkins kept to himself was the codicil specifying that he had no *friends* who had stabbed him in the back.

'Now, wait a minute. You have a lot of stuff to answer for, too.' His coffee habit was to let his cup cool to warm, then drain it all at once. He tried to force the steam from his cup to wane by gazing abstractedly into it. Durkins realised Calloway was not ready to meet his eyes. 'I mean, I was upset. I even talked about it with my sponsor, and I told him how you –'

'Don't start that,' said Durkins, overriding him.

'Start what?'

'That useless game where one of us throws up a sin to counterbalance every sin done by the other. The slap-jack of human guilt. Let's just bypass that one entirely.'

'Bypass it? Then I guess you don't really want to talk about any of this stuff.'

'I don't want to uselessly talk about it.'

'Oh, wow, then I guess you get to decide what's relevant or not.'

'Not really.' Durkins was not about to fall for the psychiatrist's trick again. Calloway had learned it from a therapist. When one feels threatened or attacked and two-way conversation will only aggravate the conflict, fall back on merely repeating the last few words of what your opponent says and add a question mark. '*I have issues with my mother.*' You say, '*Oh? You have issues with your mother?*' They say, '*Yes*'; do not pass GO; proceed to anecdote. Use as needed.

Refills came and went. Calloway hit the restroom again. Did he have crib notes in there or something?

Durkins decided on a move of equal diversionary value, which was to bend the conversation away from the scab Calloway was so eager to pick. To steer it back towards the sort of side-road that had made their talks more entertaining, back in the days before they had to be grown-ups. Durkins stared fixedly at Calloway's coffee cup while waiting for his chatter to trail off.

'What?' Calloway stared at the cup in his hands, thrice refilled already.

'There's lipstick on your cup.'

Calloway reversed the cup and saw the sneaky smear of crimson. 'Aw, shit.' He flagged down a waitress and solicited a fresh refill in a fresh container; it was bad enough he was just as good as kissing somebody he hadn't even met, somebody who might not even be a *girl* . . .

'Oops, sorry,' he said to Durkins, shifting his crosshairs away from the waitress, who had laughed at his joke.

'Let's just say I was very upset,' Durkins said, as a link. 'I could have done all sorts of nasty shit; the sort of stuff we used to talk about doing to Beard-O.'

'Aw, Jesus, Beard-O,' laughed Calloway, unloading a pound or so of dispenser sugar into his new cup. 'I wonder what's up with that guy?'

Beard-O was Bernard Carney, a fat guy with oft-voiced aspirations of being a science-fiction writer instead of manager of an espresso bar. He was forever labouring over some never-glimpsed novel or screenplay, droning into any trapped or willing ear about artistic integrity. He had used up decades this way and, as far as Durkins knew, was still manning his post, frothing mochaccinos for yuppie losers and eyeing, these days, younger and younger women. The coffee bar had been one of those places Durkins and Calloway had hung out in for almost a year, then abandoned. Since so much of Durkins' perception of Beard-O had been through the Calloway filter of ridicule – Calloway had naturally, unobtrusively got Beard-O's backstory before anyone – Durkins now wondered if the real Beard-O might be more interesting . . . once subtracted from Calloway's histrionic 'take', of course.

These side-roads efficiently wasted another hour. It became clear to Durkins that Calloway would prefer to avoid the whole fag thing, at least in Durkins' presence.

'I don't think that Mario guy is ever gonna like me, no matter what,' was the closest Calloway would swerve to the topic.

He doesn't like you because you insulted him – and me – about a million times, and never to our faces, Durkins thought.

What he said was, 'No, he just wanted to kill you about two dozen different ways, everything from blow guns to wire-guided missiles.'

Calloway made a face. 'It figures. *Blow* guns.' He made a fist and punched upwards into the air. 'Missiles.' He shrugged, as if to shrug off change that might threaten his lock-stepped prejudices. 'Guess I better check my coffee for poison, huh?'

'No. I didn't poison your coffee,' said Durkins. *Look at him. He's dying to ask how I could ever find a man's hairy rump 'appealing'. Instead, he'll dance around it all night.* It was time to steer the talk again. 'Do I look like one of the Borgias to you?'

'Shit, man, you can poison someone with household cleaner. Windex and shit under your sink. Drain-O.'

'Yes, but all of those are easily detectable. And there's the danger of emesis – vomiting, to you.'

'Speaking of which, I'm going to the bathroom again, to hurl.' By now both of them had been up and down to the john several times; coffee was a great leveller. Durkins already knew that Calloway had ducked into the restroom before sitting down the first time to assure himself that his appearance was suitable not only for possible combat, but also to magnetise whatever stray bimbos happened to be running loose tonight.

'More strychnine,' he commanded of the waitress. 'You know all about my coffee habits. You could hide something in all the sugar I pour in.'

'No, I thought of that,' Durkins went on. 'Too obvious. The best way for a poisoner to work in this century is to combine poison with a skin absorption compound. Or give them diamonds.'

'Diamonds aren't poisonous,' said Calloway. 'Are they?'

'No. But what is a diamond? Remember what they always said about diamonds?'

'That they were for ever.' Calloway's entry-level schooling flooded back. It didn't take long. 'That they were the world's hardest substance.'

'It was reading that diamond dust is the world's hardest abrasive, because it doesn't degrade. It actually was a rather popular method of assassination during the Renaissance.'

'It was big in the Renaissance, huh?'

'Yes, because if one ingests a quantity of diamond dust, the little pieces are embedded in the alimentary canal by the peristaltic motion of the digestive tract.'

'Don't you just pass it?'

'No. You can't. The millions of tiny little splinters just keep working their way deeper and deeper into your tissues. You'd have to locate each individual mote of dust with a microscope and extract them through surgery, which is impossible. And since the chips never wear away, they just keep sanding away your insides until you die.'

'Ouch.'

'Yeah, the pain is supposed to be astonishing. The other thing is that it can take up to six months to completely kill you – which is the big drawback. It's hideously efficient, surefire, but it takes too long to kill. Most poisoners want their victims to die fast.'

'Gah. That's too nasty even to think about.' Calloway made a face and cleared his throat. 'Where do you get diamond dust, anyway?'

'No idea.'

The silence hung like a humid drape between them. Calloway fiddled. He smelled like he was on the verge of bolting, so Durkins got on with it.

'Basically, the thing I wanted to tell you, before we get sidetracked again –' he permitted Calloway to share a quick smile at that '– is that I know things have changed. They won't be the same for you and me. They might get better, but it'll never be what it was. One of the reasons I wanted you to come here tonight was so I could look you right in the eye and say, whatever was said, whatever was done, starting now, I forgive you.'

Calloway nodded in cadence with Durkins' speech, weighing the words in his mind. Normally, Calloway's most unerring skill (after imposing his flaws on others and berating them for same) was in skating from emotional destruction without ever picking up the karma check. Not his fault, not ever. His ego was a bottomless reservoir of extenuating circumstances.

'Wow,' he said.

Durkins observed with amusement the elaborate way Calloway glanced at his watch. It took him fifteen minutes and two more cups of coffee to work his way up to some lame excuse about having to cut it short and be somewhere – almost as if *he* had slipped diethylene glycol into Durkins' drink and was fighting a ticking escape clock.

Durkins had read about diethylene glycol. Too obvious.

Calloway glanced at the check for the coffee but did not touch it. Durkins nodded to indicate it was on him, and, with this last danger of responsibility erased, Calloway fled as gracefully as possible, absolution shoplifted and in his pocket, more coerced than earned. By Calloway's own compass, he was now free to pillage anew.

One of the precepts Durkins had brought to this meeting, tonight, was *tell no lies*. He had not been asked the hardest potential questions, but he had come through the ordeal of seeing Calloway one last time and suffered no major scars on his brain. He had not lied, not once.

It was true, for example, that Durkins had no idea where diamond dust could be obtained. In fact, the whole suggestion had been Mario's.

He had not put poison in Calloway's coffee.

And, in a perfect invocation of the Great Despair, Calloway had listened to Durkins' words, but not heard a thing because he was so anxious to be heard himself.

So they had enacted one of their old-style talks, bringing the past up for one last gasp by digressing on to the topic of poisoners and poison. A recreation of the way they once related, as opposed to how they saw each other now.

On his way home, Durkins felt unburdened enough to whistle. The red lipstick he had used to mark Calloway's cup was disposed of in the first trashcan he came to.

UNFORGOTTEN

by

Christopher Fowler

Christopher Fowler lives in London and runs a film promotional company and a movie development company. He has published six novels including *Rune, Red Bride, Darkest Day, Spanky* and *Psychoville*. He is also the author of four story collections, *City Jitters, City Jitters 2, The Bureau of Lost Souls* and *Flesh Wounds*.

Fowler is adept at bringing London alive, first in the novel *Roofworld*, an imaginary place high above the city streets, then in his short-story collections. He continues to depict London in all her manifestations . . .

UNFORGOTTEN

―――――

It cannot think, of course; fanciful to imagine it could, for how would so many millions of lives make themselves heard, distilled into a single voice? But if – just if – there was such a thing as a collective intelligence, what would it be saying now, the voice of London?

During the trial of Captain Clarke at the Old Bailey in 1750, the court became so hot that the windows had to be opened, and the foul germ-laden stench from nearby Newgate Prison that blew in killed everyone sitting on the window-side of the court – all forty-four people.

'How much do they want for the sale?'

'Three hundred and seventy grand. That's what they figure it's worth at today's prices.'

'I'm in this business to make a living, not to be bent over a table and fucked stupid.'

'I'm sorry, that's what their man told me to tell you.'

'Well, you can tell them –' The door opened behind Marrick and his exhausted secretary stuck her head into the room. Marrick nearly fell off his chair trying to see who it was.

'For fuck's sake, Doris,' he exploded, 'will you stop creeping around like Marley's fucking ghost?'

'I'm sorry, Mr Marrick, I'm about to vanish for the night, and your wife is here.' Doris tossed the information into the room like a lit firecracker and beat a hasty retreat.

Marrick banged his chair upright. 'Harrods must have declined her credit cards again. This is all I fucking need. Excuse me, gentlemen. Jonathan, see if you can talk some fucking sense into the sales agent. Try to make him see that I'm not a completely heartless bastard. You know – lie.' The door slammed and he was gone in a cloud of acrid cigar smoke.

Jonathan Laine didn't much like his boss; the man had no respect for anything or anyone. Adrian Marrick trampled a path through life in a cheap suit, shouting and shoving all the way. The technique worked, up to a point, but Jonathan could not see the company expanding beyond this dingy Holborn office. There were barriers of class in the city, invisible lines that could not be crossed by a marauding loudmouthed oik from south London.

Jonathan was not complaining; at the age of fifty-seven he was at least still employed and making a subsistence wage. His boss was just past his twenty-fourth birthday, and although it sometimes seemed strange to be working for such a young man, Marrick possessed a cunning far beyond his years. He could even be fun in an appalling way – chain-smoking, swearing, drinking and dealing through the property market – and he was a good teacher so long as you remembered to isolate the immoral and illegal elements of his advice. His observations about his fellow man could be jaw-droppingly crass, and yet there was often a horrible accuracy to them. He was part of a new generation whose tastes were decided by price. 'You owe us, old sport,' he would say in one of his magnanimous after-dinner moods. 'We're burying the past, chucking away the old rules. Giving commerce a chance to breathe.'

Jonathan considered himself to be a reasonably moral man. He had never meant to end up working in a place like this. The pleasures of his life stemmed from peaceful pursuits, his interests inclined to classical studies. He had always held an unformulated plan in his head to succeed as some kind of architectural historian. Instead he had married young, looked after his parents, raised a child, suffered a nervous breakdown. He had been sidetracked by his need to make money, distracted by the fuss of living, misrouted from his original goal. And now, here he was in the centre of one of the most historically important cities in the world, and the only work he had found since the death of Connie was in property speculation, helping to asset-strip and destroy the very thing he cared about most dearly. A typical Gemini trait, he thought, to be both destroyer and creator. Well, one day he would find a way to repay the debt, redress the balance. Until then . . .

He turned back to a desk smothered in unprocessed documents. Darren, the office junior, was laboriously clipping surveyors' reports together and arranging them in files. Today's problem had been growing for a while now. The building in question was a run-down Victorian house presently occupied by an electrical appliance contractor. The freehold was owned by the Japanese property congolmerate Dasako, and the lease had been granted on a short-term basis that was now reaching an end. Jonathan's case notes ran to dozens of pages. Marrick was desperate to purchase the building outright because it stood between two other properties he owned under different company titles. Individually neither was worth much above land value, but collectively they represented a highly attractive proposition. Jonathan assumed that ownership of the third building would increase across to the other two, but Marrick had never explained why he wanted to own such a large chunk of property. He never explained anything. He was guided by an unerring instinct for making money.

Jonathan was sure that Dasako had no knowledge of Marrick's involvement in the surrounding offices; the names on the company records would mean nothing to them. Even so, their asking price for the soon-to-be-vacant property was way too high. The area would not support such a valuation. There had to be a reason for pricing themselves out of the market, but what could it be?

'Tell you what   said Marrick in the pub later that evening, 'I've got an idea   and he threw Jonathan a crooked grin which normally meant something dishonest was coming. He made a meaty fist around the handle of his pint, his rings glittering like gold knuckle-dusters. 'Get me the plans for the city block, would you?'

'The whole block?'

'Yeah. There's something I remember seeing the last time I went over the place. I've got a feeling we can stitch up these tossers without moving a fucking muscle.' He drained his glass and banged it down, then felt his jacket for his cigars. 'Three hundred and seventy K for an almost derelict building, bollocks! I know their fucking game.'

'You think they're going to find a new tenant?'

'Nope,' said Marrick, lighting up an absurdly large cigar. 'Of course not. Crafty bastards have other plans. They're gonna get it listed and restore all the original features.' He sucked noisily at the stogie.

'How can you be so sure?' asked Jonathan, shifting beyond his boss's smoke-ring range.

'Ah, well you see, while you're still snuggled up in bed in your pyjamas dreaming about retirement, I'm up with the fucking larks collecting information, and I hear that Dasako are currently employing the services of a design company that specialises in restaurants. Fucking great big Conran-style eateries that seat 700 diners at a time. If they get a restaurant in that space and it's a success, we'll never fucking get them out.'

'So what do you propose to do?' asked Jonathan. He ran a hand through his straggling grey hair and waited while his employer picked flakes of tobacco from his lip.

'I'm gonna buy 'em out, pull the whole lot down and resell. It's worth fuck-all as it is. The upper floors are falling apart. Just get me the plans of the block.'

The teeming humanity that passes through London as the centuries rise and fall! The sheer weight of life borne by such a small area of land! The city transforms itself from a Roman capital with an amphitheatre, forum and basilica, its Temples of Mithras and Diana giving way to the spired cathedrals of Christianity. Walls, gates and defences rise, parish churches are built over Saxon villages, medieval commerce packs the streets with wood-beamed houses, and the kaleidoscope of history spins wildly on through coronations, insurrections and disharmonies, mutiny and jubilation eliding past, present and future. And through these pullulating voices one word is heard most clearly; Charles I, stepping up to his execution before jeering crowds in Whitehall, turns to his bishop-confessor and cries, 'Remember!'

When old London Bridge was widened in the 1760s, it was realised that the new footpath would have to cut through the hundred-year-old tower of St Magnus the Martyr on the eastern side of the bridge. Incredibly, Sir Christopher Wren had built the church in anticipation that this problem would occur a century

later, and had already provided the tower's arches with removable sections to create such a passageway.

London's building plans are a mess. The Second World War saw to that. In some parts of the capital virtually every other building was destroyed in the firestorm of the Blitz, and the once-elegant streets gaped like the rotten teeth of a corpse. Between six p.m. and nine-thirty p.m. on Sunday, 29 December 1940, the second great fire of London occurred when the German Luftwaffe dropped 127 tons of high explosive and more than 10,000 incendiary bombs on the city. A famous photograph of that night shows St Paul's rising unharmed through a raging sea of flame.

Jonathan looked up at the squat brown building standing between two fifties' office blocks and tried to imagine how it had been that terrible night; the din of tumbling masonry, the blasts of the firefighters' hoses. He had been two years old and living far away, in north Yorkshire. 'London Can Take It' – some motto. But the city had managed it in the past, so many times, surviving the plagues and the fires only to be brought to its knees at the end of the twentieth century by traffic and developers. A city as old as Christianity itself was fighting for its life. Jonathan pulled the camera from his jacket and snapped a few shots: the grimy storefront with the yellow plastic sign reading AIKO ELECTRICS, the four floors of crumbling Victorian redbrick (third and fourth clearly on the verge of collapse), the ill-fitting modern roof; what an invisible, unimpressive – and unlisted – building it was. Perhaps it deserved to be pulled down. It wasn't always a good idea to cling to the past. Marrick would have no qualms about demolishing the Albert Hall if it suited his plans.

But then he looked up at the building again and tried to imagine it restored and filled with people. That was when he noticed the details; the dusty turquoise glazing bars on the tops of the third-floor windows, the swagged ornamentation on the broken rainwater head at the top of the drainpipe, the rusticated keystone above the archway leading to the building's side-alley, and he realised then that a magnificent building was hiding behind its wounds and beneath a caul of dirt; that it could all be restored, because it had been a restaurant once before, long ago, and Dasako had spotted it even if Marrick hadn't. On the pavement was another tell-tale sign; a shattered section of black and white mosaic in which the name of the establishment would have been set in curlicues of brass. And most miraculous of all, there on the wall beside the door, a battered cone of blackened metal, a snuffer! These rarely spotted pieces of street furniture were used to extinguish the tar-covered brands of the link-boys who escorted the restaurant's visitors through the unlit streets. Dasako's architects had seen all this. The Japanese respected the traditions of the past. With patience and planning, they would allow this building to spring to full-blooded life once more, filled with gaiety and beauty. Its restaurant would stand as a magnificent testament to the pleasures of the past, and the possibilities of the future.

But there was something else here as well, something that could only be seen away from the light, something less wholesome and only just hidden from view. Jonathan could feel the strange sensation creeping across him like a stormcloud obscuring the sun. There was something here that hid within the bricks. The weight of history was giddying, and he felt suddenly sick. He ceased pacing in order to catch his breath, then walked on past the central building, turning the corner at the end of the block. Three buildings constituted its longest side; the other three sides were shorter, comprising two buildings each. The one in the centre of the long side, the building owned by Dasako, grew narrower towards the rear and was truncated to allow a central courtyard within the block, although according to Marrick little evidence of this could be seen from its windows, the courtyard having been largely built over.

Jonathan looked up at the rapidly darkening sky and felt a speck of rain. At his back, traffic thrummed endlessly around a one-way system towards Hackney Town Hall. He realised with a start that he was standing near the spot where he and Connie were married. The little church had been demolished in the seventies to make way for wider traffic lanes. In his mind's eye he saw Connie turning on the steps and crying delightedly, confetti drifting from her shoulders as a passing car sounded its horn in celebration. Harder to see her now, of course; harder each day to capture each retreating memory.

He pocketed the camera and turned his collar up, preparing for his next stop – the building registry office just behind Lombard Street. Why did Marrick want plans for the entire block? What was going through his mind? Sometimes his cunning displayed the most surprising lateral thinking. As he headed for the Old Street Tube station, the only certainty Jonathan had was that money would once more change hands in deceitful circumstances.

London is an old, old woman, heartsick and tired. Her aches have now grown into a solid constant pain, nagging and unrelieved. To have survived the poverty, the misery, the riots, the ravages of sickness and disaster; to have outlived the numbing terrors of the bombs – and for what? To see the city's heart torn out and cast aside, to see her body desecrated and her soul destroyed. She has always fought back, but now her fighting days are at an end, and the battle is all but lost.

There is little that is truly Christian about London. Hawksmoor's churches have long been noted for the strange profanity of their design. The building of Bush House will never be completed. If you walk through the western colonnade which connects the Strand to the Aldwych, you'll see that one of the building's columns has an incomplete capital in order to comply to an old adage: 'Perfection is an attribute of Allah; Impiety to achieve perfection.'

Jonathan had to support the drawer of the plans chest on his bent knee in order to remove the architectural layouts without damaging them. They appeared to have been drawn in the 1930s and poorly updated in the late fifties. Presumably there were earlier versions stored somewhere, but nobody seemed to know where. The paper was fine and brittle, carelessly stored beside a radiator for too many years. He gently laid the plan to one side for photocopying, and noticed the scrap of map wedged beneath it. It was old, certainly early nineteenth century. His finger traced a path across botanical gardens in faded emerald ink, through the fields of Kensington, over meadows and market gardens to the straggling canalways and riverbanks of north London. He loved maps. To be perched dizzyingly high in the

clouds from the cartographer's viewpoint, peering down across a
metropolis that is trapped for ever in a single moment . . .

'Are you going to be much longer with that?' A listless
secretary clumped past. There was a vague, unfocused hatred in
her eyes, a suspicion of age, of gender, of everyone and
everything. Jonathan so often saw it in the eyes of the young. He
reluctantly closed the drawer and rose. He could spend all day
here, sifting through the blueprints of the past, but Marrick
would have a heart attack. As soon as his copies were ready he
folded them into his case and stepped back into the penetrating
rain.

He found the drawing at his local library, in a book on
Edwardian London. An attentuated young lady in a peach-
coloured gown with a fur collar was alighting from a carriage
on the arm of her evening-suited beau. In his free hand, the
man held a top hat and a pair of white gloves. Rain glossed
the street. The restaurant before them was a shimmering wall
of light. Great chandeliers sparkled above the elegant dining
lounge. The maitre d' stood beneath a silvered canopy awaiting the new arrivals. A copperplate sign was illuminated by
rows of dazzling bulbs: La Belle Epoque. Of course. The place
was world-renowned. Jonathan pored over every detail. You
could even see the snuffer beside the entrance. It all looked so
– what was the word? *Swanky.* An Americanism, but quite
old and entirely appropriate. He savoured the picture, longed
to tear it out and hide it inside his overcoat. Instead he rose
and returned to his cold flat above the fishmongers in the
high street, to pass the evening in his books and his
dreams.

'Piece of piss,' said Marrick, wiping a chunk of bread around his
plate and popping it in his mouth. 'Between the end of Aiko's
lease and Dasako's application for listed building status, I
bunged an offer in to them. Two hundred and sixty K.'

They were having lunch several weeks later in a vast and
deafening Wardour Street restaurant. Marrick hated the food
but ate here because it was fashionable. The hard wooden seats
were designed to discourage lingerers, and Jonathan had to shift

awkwardly about to stop his legs from going numb. 'I don't understand,' he said as the appalling truth sank in. 'Why would they have accepted such a bid?'

'Because they can't build a restaurant there any more. No fucking planning permission. Modern laws require safety exits, and they ain't got any.'

'I'm sure I saw an alleyway at the side of the building. Couldn't they have applied to make use of that?'

'Could have done if it was theirs, old fruit, but it's not. It belongs to the building next door, my little auction-purchase. Their bloke contacted me and tried to get the right-of-way signed over.'

'And what happened?' asked Jonathan, dreading the answer.

'I told him to fuck off, obviously.'

'But surely they can appeal?'

Marrick looked at him suspiciously and seemed about to speak, then changed his mind. 'No,' he said finally, raising his glass and draining it. 'They can't appeal. How can they build exits when the only other properties bordering theirs are mine? Anyway, the deal's already going through. Their hands are tied good and proper. They'll find some other dump to tart up. I'll have all three buildings down within a month, crash, bang, bosh, clear the space and flog it off as office units. I feel like celebrating. Let's get another bottle of this, if we can find a fucking waiter.'

It made perfect sense, of course. He'd seen it on the map, but had chosen to ignore an obvious truth; the three properties were worth more knocked flat and sold in newly arranged packages of landspace. The packages could be tailored to suit modern business requirements. London's existing old buildings found it difficult to incorporate the conduits that were required to carry computer cables. In Jonathan's mind the golden windows of La Belle Epoque dimmed, the glittering crystalline structure dismantled itself and disappeared into the night, leaving behind a deep, dirty pool of shadow. He could not bring himself to hate Marrick; he was merely disappointed that the past had been cheated out of a chance to return.

The spirit of London sinks from a powerful roar of flame to a single glowing ember, and soon that too will be extinguished.

*For cities, like people, must eventually grow old and die. Even a
city as ancient at this . . .*

**Scotland Yard, named after the palace where the kings of
Scotland lodged when visiting London, is founded on the site of
an unsolved murder. Multilated portions of a woman's body
were secreted on the building site in the 1880s, and the officers
of the C.I.D. were never able to discover the identity of the
murderer or his victim.**

Jonathan turned on the desk light and tilted back the green glass
shade, then unfolded the photostat across the cleared surface of
his desk. Marrick was planning to inspect the vacated premises
with him tomorrow. After that it was simply a matter of sorting
out the paperwork and waiting for the demolition order to be
cleared. He withdrew a magnifying glass and checked each of
the rooms and staircases in turn. Something about the map
bothered him. Or rather, something about the way it matched
the experience of actually visiting the property. He checked the
specifications of each of the buildings against the photographs
he had taken, but the anomaly eluded him. Why couldn't he see
it? Something was wrong, something at the heart of the land
itself. He removed his reading glasses and massaged the bridge
of his nose. Perhaps the answer would come to him tomorrow.
He refolded the map, switched off the desk-lamp and wearily
headed for bed.

'I don't know why they had to turn the fucking lights off,'
moaned Marrick as he and Jonathan passed beneath the cracked
AIKO sign and entered the ground floor of the building. 'Look at
it out there, ten in the morning and you'd think it was fucking
midnight. Did you bring a torch?'
   'Yes. The main staircase is to the rear of this room.' Jonathan
clicked on the flashlight and raised its beam. The showroom had
been stripped to a few piles of mildewed carpet tiles and some
battered old shelf units. It smelled bad – damp and sickly. From
far above them came the drone of heavy rain and the warble of
sheltering pigeons. They reached the foot of the stairs and
started up.

'I wanna make sure they cleared everything out. Barney couldn't get here this morning, his wife's sick or something.' Barney was an ex-bouncer and former prison warden whose aggressive temperament perfectly qualified him for his position as Marrick's site manager. Unpleasant things happened in Marrick's company that Jonathan did not know about, that he could not allow himself to discover. Not if he wanted to keep his job and his sanity.

Although Marrick was young, he was considerably over-weight; the stairs were already defeating him. He reached the second-floor landing and looked up through the centre of the well, catching his breath. 'You can check out the top two floors, Jon, make sure we ain't got any squatters. Fucking hell, it stinks in here.'

Jonathan stopped on the staircase and stared out of the rain-streaked window into the centre of the block, where the backs of the buildings met.

Rooms. Something odd about the rooms. He studied the brick walls of the courtyard formed by the other properties. He felt as if he had a cold coming on. Getting his jacket so wet hadn't helped matters. He should have bought himself a new umbrella. He sneezed hard, wiped his nose on a tissue. Spots of dark blood, a crimson constellation. He looked from the window again. The bricks. That's what it was. The bricks to the right of the window. They were in the wrong place. There should have been an empty space there. It was marked on the map, but not there from the window.

There was one room too many.

'Adrian, come and look at this a minute.' He beckoned Marrick down and pointed from the glass. 'There shouldn't be another room in the centre-well. The old wall to the right, do you see?'

'Yeah, so?'

'It's not on the plans.'

'Why would that be?'

The brickwork was ancient, and the spaces between the blackened bricks were filled with bedraggled weeds. Near the top of the wall was a tiny window less than a foot long. There was no glass in it, just a single iron bar running across the gap. Jonathan frowned, trying to understand. 'The 1933 plans were

drawn over much older ones, but when they traced the new
buildings in, they didn't add the existing layout.'

'So what was there before?'

'I don't know. The original drawings have been lost, misfiled
somewhere.'

Marrick looked at him as if he was going senile. 'I'm not
following you, Jon.'

'There was another building already here at the centre of the
site, or at least part of one. A very old one. Look at the bricks.
There must be an entrance to it.'

'Wait, before you go off on a fucking treasure hunt, how
about we finish what we came here to do?'

'This building has been cleared.' Jonathan scrubbed his fist
across the filthy pane. 'We have to find a way into that room.'

'Why?' It was useless to assume that Marrick had a natural
sense of curiosity, so Jonathan appealed to his greed. 'It could
have been sealed off for years. There might be something of
value in there.'

'If there was, it was probably nicked years ago. Someone's
bound to have been in there already.'

'I think that's unlikely. There's no immediate access, and it
looks like it belongs to part of another building. It's hard to
even see.'

'Hmm. You have a point there.' They both started looking
for a doorway. There was nothing on any of the landings, or on
the second floor. At the bottom of the stairs they found a door
leading to a basement, but it was locked and there was no key.
Marrick picked up a chunk of discarded pipe and smashed at
the lock until the damp wood around it splintered and fell
away.

'Fucking hell! What died?' Marrick waved a hand in front of
his nose. 'Shine your torch down there. These steps look
rotten.' The beam rippled back at them. The whole of the
basement was under an inch of filthy water. On the far side
was an arched passage. Jonathan instinctively knew that this
way the way to the room at the centre of the building. He'd
seen this type of layout in old architectural books. 'We have to
go over there.' He pointed at the arch.

'You're joking. These shoes cost a fucking fortune. I'm not
going down there.'

Jonathan's torch caught a stack of planks piled under the stairs. It was a simple matter to lay them like duckboards across the basement. The ceiling was low, and Marrick swore spectacularly as he banged his head. They arrived at the far side of the room, and Jonathan reached out to touch the heavy oak door set before them. He could hear running water. The torch illuminated the source through a crack in the wood; a brick channel filled with sluggishly moving liquid, cut through an arched tunnel that led off to an iron gate in the wall. 'The Fleet,' said Jonathan excitedly, 'it's a tributary of the Fleet.'

'What the fuck is that, a river?'

'Certainly a river. It was used as a rubbish dump for centuries. Runs from Hampstead down to Holborn and right across London.'

'What do you mean "runs"? It's still there?'

'It was finally channelled underground at the end of the eighteenth century, but the main part is still used as a sewer. There's a whole network of tributaries attached to it, and this looks like one of them. A lot of basements used to have access to the city's sewer system.' Marrick had lost interest. He pulled at the edge of the door, and it shifted inwards.

'Doesn't look like it's being used any more,' said Jonathan. 'The water's clean.' He shone his torch further along the channel and found another, much smaller door. This one was painted black and studded with iron bolts. 'That has to be the way to the centre-well.'

They carefully stepped across the open water-pipe and examined the door. It was set two feet from the ground, presumably to keep the area behind it dry and avoid the danger of flooding.

'It's locked. I wonder who has the key.'

Marrick dug about in his pocket and produced a handful of loose Yales. 'Take your pick, there's these and dozens more of the bastards back in the office.' But all of them proved too small to fit the lock.

'The mechanism will probably need oiling, anyway,' said Jonathan. 'We wouldn't be able to shift it by ourselves, not if it's been shut for years.' They resolved to come back down on Monday morning.

*

London was once settled much lower in the ground. Layers
were added: strata of gravel and stone and tarmacadam; layers
of bones, the residue of corpses stricken by pestilence and
firestorm, three decades of cholera victims, the sickly paupers
from debtors' jails and workhouses, the silent majority of the
city. Denied a voice in life, how they longed to speak and be
heard.

The first tunnel under the Thames was a private enterprise built
by Marc Brunel and opened, after considerable loss of life, in
1843. Within fifteen weeks, a million pedestrians had paid a
penny each to walk through it, but the novelty wore off fast, and
for the next decade the gloomy arched passageways underneath
the river became the favoured haunt of thieves and prostitutes.

Jonathan was unable to find a key which would fit, so Marrick
asked his site manager Barney to take the door off its hinges.
Barney did so that Monday morning, following Marrick's
instructions not to go inside. Marrick, who fancied himself as a
bit of an Indiana Jones, was determined to retain that privilege
for himself. Later on in the afternoon, as the biggest storm of the
autumn broke over their heads, Jonathan accompanied his
employer back to the cellar, and they crossed the sewage
channel to the door in the wall.

Barney had set the square iron panel to one side. Marrick
assumed proprietorial charge of the flashlight and, now wield-
ing a crowbar in his other fist, shore his beam ahead into a
rubble-filled corridor. Jonathan followed him through, pausing
beside a crumpled sheet of newspaper, *The Daily Sketch*, 18
May 1949. He rose, disappointed, hoping to find something
older. At least it was dry in here. They had to be under the
centre-well of the buildings now. The room he had seen would
be above them at the end of the passage and to the right.

'I don't know why I'm fucking wasting my time down here. I
should never have let you talk me into this.' Marrick picked his
way across the littered floor, leaving Jonathan to fend for
himself in the dark. From far above them came the distant
rumble of thunder, like masonry being emptied into a skip.
Jonathan listened to his boss's muttered complaints, knowing
that the merest sliver of hope would drive him forward. 'You

never know what we might find,' he said. 'There, at the end, where you just pointed the torch. What is that?'

Twisted curlicues of iron hung from the ceiling. A number of sections had rusted through, and lay on the floor like giant fruit-rinds. Marrick cast the beam upwards. 'Looks like part of a staircase,' said Jonathan.

'Not like any fucking staircase I've ever seen. You reckon this room of yours is above here?'

'There's nowhere else it could be.' He raised his eyes to the stained plaster ceiling and saw the slightly protuberant square of plaster in the corner of the passage. It was half the size of the first door, but large enough for a man to climb through. 'There's your door,' he said excitedly. 'There should be an iron ring set flat in the front section, buried under the plaster.'

'How could you know that?' Marrick stopped and stared back at him through the glare of the torch beam. 'You haven't been down here before.'

'I've read about these things. It's a relic room. Lots of wealthy old houses used to have them. You built a special room, just a small one, and sealed a treasured possession inside, and built the rest of the house around it.'

'Then what?'

'Then nothing. You sealed the room up from the outside and forgot all about it, and the building would have good luck all its life. It was a pagan thing. By giving up something precious you appeased the household gods. The old Roman habits died hard. Not all Londoners were Christians, you know.'

Marrick's eyes glittered in the gloom. 'So you reckon there's something really valuable in there?'

'There could be, I don't know. They tucked away all sorts of belongings. Gold candlesticks, silver and pewter plate, chalices, they were all popular sacrifices.'

'Reading all them books of yours finally paid off, eh?' Marrick thumped the ceiling square with the end of his crowbar. The plaster coating that covered it sounded thin. A few more thumps rained wafer-fine pieces on to his shoulders. It only took a few minutes to reveal the edges of the door. When he shone the torch back up, they could both see it; a dirty iron ring, recessed into the square.

'Give me a hand here,' said Marrick, thrusting the torch at

him. 'Hold that steady.' His fingers followed the outline of the ring and dug around it, pulling it down towards him. As he brought his weight to bear on it, the door grudgingly opened downwards in a shower of plaster fragments.

'Christ, this thing must be on a fucking spring,' Marrick cried. 'I can barely hold it.'

'Do you want me to help?'

'You'd give yourself a hernia. Just grab the bottom corners as soon as you can reach them.' He was right. Jonathan could feel the power of the door as it tried to close itself. Marrick moved the torch to the inside of the hole. Pinpoints of reflected light glittered back. 'There's definitely something in there all right. Keep a hold on the door.'

Marrick braced his feet against the walls and raised his arms into the open hole, pulling himself up. 'Used to – ugh – do this sort of thing in the gym,' he gasped through gritted teeth. As his torso, his legs and finally his expensive Italian shoes disappeared into the hole, Jonathan shoved against the door with all his might to keep the heavy spring from slamming it shut.

'What can you see?' he called.

'Hang on a minute, let me get my breath –' Marrick shone the torch around the room, which was less than five feet square. The air was thick and old, but breathable. His head brushed against the brick ceiling. Beside him at head-height was the tiny window he had seen from outside.

'Plate,' he called down finally. 'Silver plate by the look of it.' He shifted his feet either side of the trapdoor hole. A great mound of the stuff was stacked in a corner. Each piece was twice the size of the average dinner plate. It looked like the municipal tableware they used for mayoral banquets. He bent down and pulled the largest one free in a cloud of straw-dust. It was badly tarnished, but he could still make out the leaping stags, the coat of arms, the portrait of some ugly bird in a pointy headdress. His heart was beating faster. Even an idiot could see that this lot was worth a fucking fortune. He turned it over, and there on the reverse was an inscription, hard to read because the 'S's were substituted with 'F's, but the date was clear: 1503. Dear God in Heaven, he was rich.

'Here, cop hold of this.' He passed the plate down to Jonathan, who was propped against the trapdoor and had trouble accepting the heavy metal dish. Marrick switched the torch into the opposite corner, no more than two feet behind him. His mouth fell open.

Jonathan's arms were tiring. He was not sure how much longer he could manage to keep the door down. Beyond in the darkness he could hear the steadily augmenting sound of rushing water. The deluge above them was filtering through the pipes of the building and swelling the sewer channel. 'Hurry up,' he called anxiously. 'The storm's bringing a lot of water down.'

Marrick did not hear. He was staring back at a dead body. It was centuries-dead and dried out, so that it appeared as little more than a skeleton with yellow skin vacuum-formed across its bones. It was small, just over four feet high, its head tilted back and its jaw wide open so that it appeared to be laughing, or screaming. There were iron rings around its wrists, manacling it to the wall. They seemed unnecessarily heavy on such a small frame. A chill crept over Marrick as it occurred to him that the poor creature had been chained up alive and left to die here, and that it was probably a child.

'Oh, Christ –'

'What's the matter?'

'They walled up something precious to bring themselves luck –'

Several things happened at once just then. An enormous roll of thunder made itself heard all the way to the basement, there was a sudden renewed rush of water through the sewer duct, and Jonathan started in surprise, moving his shoulder from the trapdoor. The spring tightened, the lid swung unstoppably up and slammed shut with a deafening bang. For a moment both men were shocked into silence. Then Marrick began shouting and thumping about in his tiny cell, but the sound of his rage was not enough to carry clearly through the heavy sealed door.

Marrick stood up sharply and cracked his head on the ceiling. His heart was pounding in the darkness. The walls pressed forward. He was unable to catch his breath. Claustrophobia hemmed him in. The dead air in his throat stifled him. He gasped and bellowed at Jonathan, every filthy insult he could conjure, and threw himself to the floor in an attempt to dislodge the trapdoor. But it was somehow arranged so that it could only be opened with the iron ring outside – and only he had had the strength to pull it down. Jonathan would never be able to manage it alone. He forced himself to calm down for a moment. Barney. Jonathan would have to go and get Barney. He might still be at the office. He wished he had not left his mobile phone in his briefcase on the ground floor. 'Jon,' he shouted at the floor, 'call Barney. Get him!' He held his breath and listened, but all he could hear was the rain outside and the distant rushing water below. 'Jon, for fuck's sake, what are you doing?' His voice rose in fright as the beam from the torch grew yellow and died. He dropped to his knees and scrabbled at the seams of the unmoving door until he could no longer feel his fingers.

Jonathan made his way back along the passageway in total darkness. He soaked his legs crossing the sewer duct, which was now overflowing the sides of the brick channel. A faint light showed from the distant cellar entrance. When he reached the top of the stairs, he collected Marrick's briefcase. Then he went back to the rumbling river.

Positioning himself by the water that boiled and rushed through the iron grating, he emptied the contents of the case, Marrick's pens, his mobile phone, his cocaine, his lunch receipts, and all the contracts he had drawn up for the purchase and eventual demolition of the building. Jonathan watched as they passed through the wide iron mesh on their underground journey to the city's dark heart.

'There are no kind gods,' he said aloud. 'The price of true belief will always be terrible.'

Back on the ground floor he studied the huge plate Marrick had passed to him, the lauded ceremonial plate commemorating the death of Elizabeth of York, daughter of Edward IV, sister to the murdered princes in the Tower, beloved mother of Henry VIII. On the back was engraved an elegy, written for her by Sir Thomas More. He was holding a cornerstone of history, long thought lost, finally restored to safe hands. He would never know what else the *oubliette* contained – apart from the large useless article that would now serve the birth of a new urban deity.

Several days later, Jonathan returned to the stairwell window and looked out into the centre of the building. It was a still, sunny day, and a sparrow perched on one of the sturdy weed-stems that sprouted from the wall of the hidden room. Jonathan stared at the tiny window with the thick iron bar across it, and occasionally – as if it could sense that someone was watching – a pale face, despairing and nightmarish, passed before the gap like the moon fleetingly glimpsed through clouds. It was a sight that he would never forget, an eternal penance. His skin prickling, he hastily returned to the warm city streets and the choking traffic beyond.

There is a brief respite in the sobbing, crying maelstrom. The city's agonies are temporarily assuaged. A sacrifice accepted; a building restored. For the most fleeting of moments, the tough old woman raises her crumpled face to the sun and smiles.

A century and a half ago, within the thick Wren walls of the Theatre Royal, Drury Lane, a body was discovered with a dagger in its ribs. Somebody was murdered in the theatre and quietly bricked in. Nobody knows why, or whether the victim was still alive when the last brick was cemented into place.

O, RARE AND MOST EXQUISITE

by

Douglas Clegg

Douglas Clegg was born in Virginia but has lived in Los Angeles for eleven years. He has published the novels *Goat Dance, Breeder, Neverland, The Dark of the Eye* and *The Children's Hour*. His short stories have been published in the magazines *Cemetery Dance, Deathrealm,* and *The Scream Factory* and in the anthologies, *Love in Vein, Little Deaths, Twists of the Tale: An Anthology of Cat Horror* and in *Best New Horror* and *The Year's Best Fantasy and Horror*.

When he was nineteen, Clegg relates, he worked in a nursing facility. He badly wanted to know elderly people, having no grandparents himself past the age of five or six. So after his shift, he'd go and sit in someone's room and listen to their stories. What he heard was not always wonderful. Men and women would talk about their lives, and they'd complain bitterly about those who never loved them enough. What he sometimes heard through their stories was something they themselves did not know they were revealing – that these people speaking were the ones who had thrown away love, and trampled on it; had loved the ones who did not return their affection, and had abandoned the ones who *did* for shallow reasons. Clegg wanted to find a metaphor for that love, for the kind of young man who chases and cultivates love. And he has, in this gardener who adores flowers.

O, RARE AND MOST EXQUISITE

'What is human love?' I have heard my mother ask, when she was sick, or when she was weary from the rotted-wood dams of marriage and children. It's a question that haunts my every waking hour. I, myself, never experienced love, not the kind between a man and a woman. I once learned about it second-hand. When I was seventeen, I worked in a retirement home, in the cafeteria, and on my afternoons off I went up to the third floor. This was the nursing facility, and I suppose I went there to feel needed; all the elderly patients needed attention, often someone to just sit with them, hold their hands, watch the sun as it stretched down across the far-off trees heavy with summer green. I don't know why I was so taken with the older people, but I often felt more comfortable around them than I did around my peers. One day, an old man was shouting from his bed, 'O, rare and most exquisite! O, God, O God, O, rare and most exquisite creation! Why hast thou forsaken me?' His voice was strong and echoed down the slick corridor; his neighbours, in adjacent beds, cried out for relief from his moans and groans. Since the orderlies ignored all this, routinely, I went to his room in order to find out what the trouble was about.

He was a ruffian. Bastards always live the longest, it was a rule of thumb on the nursing floor, and this man was a prince amongst bastards. Something about the lizard leather of his skin, and the grease of his hair, and the way his forehead dug into his eyebrows as if he were trying to close his translucent blue eyes by forcing the thick skin down over them. He had no kindness in him; but I sat down on the edge of his bed, patted his hand, which shook, and asked him what the matter was.

'Love,' he said. 'All my life, I pursued nothing but love. And look where it's gotten me.' He was a rasping old crow, the kind my brother used to shoot at in trees.

'Did you have lunch yet?' I asked, because I knew that the patients would become irritable if they hadn't eaten.

'I will not eat this raw sewage you call food.'

'You can have roast beef, if you want. And pie.'

'I will not eat.' He closed his eyes, and I thought he was about to go to sleep, so I began to get up off the bed. He whispered, coughing a bit, 'Bring me the box under the bed.'

I did as he asked. It was a cheap strong-box, the kind that could be bought in a dimestore. When I set it beside him, he reached under the blankets and brought out a small key. 'Open it for me,' he said. I put the tiny key in the hole, turned, and brought the lid up. The box was filled with what appeared to be sand. 'Reach in it,' he said, and I stuck my hands in, and felt what seemed to be a stick, or perhaps it was a quill. I took it out.

It was a dried flower, with only a few petals remaining.

'Do you know about love?' he asked me.

I grinned. 'Sure.'

'You're too young,' he said, shaking his head. He took the dried flower from my hand, and brought it up to his nose. Dust from the petals fell across his upper lip. 'You think love is about kindness and dedication and caring. But it is not. It is about tearing flesh with hot pincers.'

I smiled, because I didn't know what else to do. I wondered if he were sane; many of the patients were not.

He said, 'This is the most rare flower that has ever existed. It is more than seventy years old. It is the most valuable thing I own. I am going to die soon, boy. Smell it. Smell it.' He pressed the withered blossom into the palm of my hand, and cupped his shaking fingers under mine. 'Smell it.'

I lifted it up to my nose. For just a second, I thought I smelled a distant sea, and island breezes of blossoming fruit trees and perfumes. Then, nothing but the rubbing alcohol and urine of the nursing floor.

'I will give this to you,' he said, 'to keep, if you promise to take care of it.'

Without thinking, I said, 'It's dead.'

He shook his head, a rage flaring behind his eyes, a life in him I wouldn't have expected. 'You don't know about love,' he grabbed my arm, and his grip was hard as stone, 'and you'll live just like I did, boy, unless you listen good, and life will give you its own whipping so that one day you'll end up in this bed smelling like this and crying out to the god of death just for escape from this idiot skin so that the pain of memory will stop.'

To calm him, because now I knew he was crazy, I said, 'OK. Tell me.'

'Love,' he said, 'is the darkest gift. It takes all that you are, and it destroys you.'

And he told me about the flower of his youth.

His name was Gus, and he was a gardener at a house that overlooked the Hudson River. The year was 1925, and his employer was an invalid in his fifties, with a young wife. The wife's name was Jo, and she was from a poor family, but she had made a good marriage, for the house and grounds occupied a hundred acres. As head gardener, Gus had a staff of six beneath him. Jo would come out in the mornings, bringing coffee to the workers. She was from a family of labourers, so she understood their needs, and she encouraged their familiarity. Her husband barely noticed her, and if he did, he wouldn't approve of her mixing with the staff.

One morning, she came down to Gus where he stood in the maze of roses, with the dew barely settled upon them, and she kissed him lightly on the cheek. He wasn't sure how to take this; she was wearing her robe, as she always did when she brought the coffee out to the men, although it revealed nothing of her figure. She was the most beautiful woman he had ever seen, with thick dark hair, worn long and out of fashion, a throwback to the long Victorian tresses of his mother's genera-tion. She had almond-shaped eyes, and skin like olives soaked in brandy – he had never seen a woman this exotic in Wappingers Falls, which was his home town. She smelled of oil and rosewater, and she did not greet him, ever, without something sweet on her lips, so that her breath was a pleasure to feel against his skin. She drew back from him, and with her heavy accent, said, 'Gus, my handsome boy of flowers, what will you find for me today?'

When she kissed him on the cheek, he waited a minute, and then grabbed her in his arms, for he could no longer contain himself, and they made love there, in the morning, before the sun was far up in the sky.

Gus had girls before, since he was fourteen, but they had been lust pursuits, for none of the girls of the Falls, or of Poughkeepsie, or even the college girl he had touched in Connecticut, stirred in him what he felt with Jo. He called her, to his men, 'My Jo', for he felt that, if things were different, she would not be with this wealthy man with his palsied body, but with him. Gus and Jo, he wrote it on the oak tree down near the river, he carved it into a stone which he had placed in the centre of the rose garden.

He knew that she loved him, so he went that day to find her the most beautiful flower that could be had. It was a passion of hers, to have the most beautiful things, for she had lived most of her life with only the ugly and the dull. He wished he were wealthy so that he might fly to China, or to the South of France, or to the stars, to bring back the rarest of blooms. But, having four bits on him, he took the train into New York City, and eventually came to a neighbourhood which sold nothing but flowers, stall upon stall. But it was mid-summer, and all the flowers available were the same that he could grow along the river. As he was about to leave, not knowing how he could return to his Jo without something very special, a woman, near one of the stalls said, 'You don't like these, do you?'

Gus turned, and there was a woman of about twenty-two, he guessed. Very plain, although pretty in the way that he thought all women basically pretty. She was small and pale, and she wore no make-up, but her eyes were large and lovely. 'I've been watching you,' she said.

'You have?'

'Yes. Do you think that's rude? To watch someone?'

'It depends.'

'I think it's rude. But then,' she said, smiling like a mischievous child, 'I've never been ashamed of my own behaviour, only the behaviour of others. I'm ashamed of yours. Here I've watched you for fifteen minutes, and you barely took your eyes off the flowers. How rude do you think that is? Very. You like flowers, don't you?'

'I'm a gardener. I take care of them.'

'Lovely,' she said wistfully, 'imagine a life of caring for beautiful things. Imagine when you're very old, and look back on it. What lovely memories you'll have.' Although she seemed forthright, the way he knew city people were, there was something fitful in the way she spoke, almost hesitant somewhere in the flow of words, as if all this snappy talk was a cover for extreme shyness. And yet, he knew, city women were rarely shy.

He had not come all the way to the city to flirt with shop-girls. 'I'm looking for something out of the ordinary.'

She gave a curious smile, tilting her head back. She was a shade beautiful in the thin shaft of daylight that pressed between the stalls. She was no Jo, but she would make some young man fall in love with her, he knew that. Some city boy who worked in the local grocer's, or ran a bakery. Or, perhaps, even a junior bondsman. She would eventually live in one of the boxcar apartments in Brooklyn, and be the most wonderful and ordinary bride. She would have four children, and grow old without fear. Not like Jo, who was destined for romance and passion and tragedy and great redemption, not Italian Jo of olive skin and rosewater. The woman said, 'I know a place where you can find very unusual flowers.'

'I want a beauty,' he said.

'For a lady?'

Because Gus knew how women could be, and because he detected that he might get further along with this girl if he feigned interest in her, he lied. 'No. Just for me. I appreciate beautiful flowers.' He felt bad, then, a little, because now he knew that he was leading her on, but she seemed to know where the interesting flowers were, and all he could think of was Jo and how she loved flowers. Gus was considered handsome in his day, and women often showed him special attention, so he was used to handling them, charming them. 'I need a beauty,' he repeated.

'I'm not saying beautiful,' she cautioned him, and began walking between the stalls, through an alley, leading him, 'but unusual. Sometimes unusual is better than beautiful.' She wore a kind of apron, he noticed, the long kind that covered her dress, and he wondered if she were the local butcher's daughter, or if she were a cook. The alley was steamy; there was some sort of kitchen down one end of it, a Chinese laundry, too, for he smelled the soap and the meat and heard someone shouting in a foreign language, but nothing European, for Gus knew how those languages sounded, and this must've been Oriental. The woman came to an open pit, with a thin metal staircase leading down to a room, and she hiked her apron up a bit, and held her hand out for him to steady her as she descended. 'My balance isn't too good,' she told him, 'I have a heart problem – nothing serious – but it makes me light-headed sometimes on stairs.'

'There're flowers down there?' he asked, as he went down the steps slowly.

'It's one of my father's storage rooms. He has a flower shop on Seventh Avenue, but there's an ice house above us, and we get shavings for free. They stay colder down here,' she said, and turned a light up just as he had reached the last step. 'There's another room three doors down, beneath the laundry. We keep some there, too.'

The room was all of redbrick, and it was chilly, like winter. 'We're right underneath the storage part of the ice house.' As the feeble light grew strong, he saw that they were surrounded by flowers, some of them brilliant vermilion sprays, others deep purples and blacks, still more of pile upon pile of dappled yellows on reds on greens. 'These are all fresh cut,' she said, 'you can have any you want. My father grows them underneath the laundry, and when he cuts them, we keep them on ice until we ship them. Here,' she said, reaching into a bowl that seemed to be carved out of ice. She brought up tiny red and blue blossoms, like snowballs, but in miniature. She brought them up to his face, and the aroma was incredible, it reminded him of Jo's skin when he pressed his face against her breasts and tasted the brightness of morning.

The woman kissed him, and he responded, but it was not like his kiss with Jo. This woman seemed colder, and he knew he was kissing her just because he wanted the blossoms. He remembered the cold kiss all the way to the big house, as he carried his gift to his beloved.

Jo was shocked by the tiny, perfect flowers. He had left them for her in a crystal bowl of water on the dining-room table so that she would see them first when she came to have breakfast. He heard her cry out, sweetly, and then she came to the kitchen window to search the back garden for him. She tried to open it;

but it had rained the night before and all that morning, so it was stuck. She rushed around to the back door, ran barefoot into the garden and grabbed his hand. 'Sweetest – precious – blessed,' she gasped, 'where did you find them? Their smell – so lovely.'

He had saved one small blossom in his hand. He crushed it against her neck, softly. He kissed her as if he owned her and he told her how much he loved her.

She drew back from him then, and he saw something change in her eyes.

'No,' she said.

When the flowers had died, he ventured back into the city, down the alley, but the entrance to the pit was closed. He rapped on the metal doors several times, but there was no response. He went around to the entrance to the ice house, and asked the manager there about the flowers, but he seemed not to know much about it other than the fact that the storage room was closed for the day. Gus was desperate, and had brought his month's pay in order to buy armloads of the flowers, but instead, ended up in an Irish bar on Horace Street drinking away most of it. Jo didn't love him, he knew that now. How could he be such a fool, anyway? Jo could never leave her husband, never in a thousand years. Oh, but for another moment in her arms, another moment of that sweet mystery of her breath against his neck!

He stayed in the city overnight, sleeping in a flop house, and was up early, and this time went to the Chinese laundry. The man who ran it took him to the back room, where the steam thickened. Gus heard the sounds of machines being pushed and pressed and clanked and rapped, as a dozen or more people worked in the hot fog of the shop. The owner took him further back, until they came to a stairway.

'Down,' the man nodded, and then disappeared into the fog.

Gus went down the stairs, never sure when he would touch bottom, for the steam was still heavy. When he finally got to the floor, it dissipated a bit, and there was a sickly yellow light a ways off. He went towards it, brushing against what he assumed were flowers, growing in their pots.

Then, someone touched his arm.

'Gus.' It was the woman from the week before. 'It's me. Moira.'

'I didn't know your name,' he told her.

'How long did the flower last?'

'Six days.'

'How sad,' she said, and leaned against him. He kissed her, but the way he would kiss his sister, because he didn't really want to lead her on.

The mist from the laundry enveloped the outline of her face, causing her skin to shine a yellow-white like candles in luminaria, revealing years that he had not anticipated – he had thought she might be a girl in her early twenties, but in this steam, she appeared older, ashes shining under her skin.

'I loved the flowers.'

'What else do you love, Gus?'

He didn't answer. He pulled away from her, and felt the edges of thick-lipped petals.

She said, 'We keep the exotics here. There's an orchid from the Fiji Islands – it's not properly an orchid, but it has the look of one. It's tiny, but very rare. In its natural state, it's a parasite on fruit trees, but here, it's the most beautiful thing in the world.'

'I never paid you for the last flower.'

'Gus,' she said, and reached up to cup the side of his face in the palm of her hand, 'whatever is mine, is yours.'

She retreated into the mist and, in a few moments, laid in the palm of his hand a flower so small that he could barely see it. She set another of its kind into a jewellery box, and said, 'This is more precious than any jewel I know of. But if I give it to you, I want you to tell me one thing.'

He waited to hear her request.

'I want you to tell me – no, promise me – you will take care of this better than those last ones. This should live, if cared for, for over a month. You do love flowers, don't you?'

'Yes,' he said, and, because he wanted this tiny flower so much for his Jo, he brought Moira close to him and pressed his lips against hers, and kissed around her glowing face, tasting the steam from the laundry. He wanted it so badly, he knew this flower would somehow win his Jo. Somehow, she would manage to leave her husband, and they would run away together, maybe even to the Fiji Islands to live off mango and to braid beautiful Jo's hair with the island parasite flowers.

Yet, there was something about Moira that he liked, too. She wasn't Jo, but she was different from any woman he knew. When he drew his face back from hers, her face was radiant and shining, and she was not the middle-aged woman he had thought just a minute ago. She was a young girl, after all, barely out of her teens, with all the enthusiasm of fresh, new life. He wondered what his life would be like with a girl like this, what living in the city with her would feel like, what it would be like to live surrounded by the frozen and burning flowers.

There were tears in Moira's eyes when she left him, and he sensed that she knew why he wanted the beautiful flowers.

And still, she gave him the rare and exquisite ruby blossom.

The tiny flower died in fourteen days. Gus could not return to the city for over six weeks, because a drought had come down the valley, and he had to take special pains to make sure that the gardens didn't die. Jo did not come and see him, and he knew that it was for the best. She was married, he was merely the gardener, and no matter how many gorgeous flowers he brought to her, she would never be his. He thought of Moira, and her sweetness and mystery; her generosity was something he had never experienced before in a woman, for the ones he had known were often selfish and arrogant in their beauty. He also knew that the old man must suspect his over-familiarity with Jo, and so his days would be numbered in the Hudson River house.

One afternoon, he took off again for the city, but it took several hours, as there was an automobile stuck on the tracks just before coming into Grand Central Station. He got there in the evening, and went to the Chinese laundry, but both it and the ice house were closed for the day. He remembered that Moira had mentioned her father's shop, and so he went into the flower district and scoured each one, asking after her. Finally, he came to the shop of Seventh Avenue, and there she was, sitting behind a counter arranging iris into a spray-like arrangement. She turned to see him, and in the light of early evening, she was the simple girl he had seen the first day they had met. How the mist and the ice could change her features, but in the daylight world, she was who she was!

'Gus,' she said, 'I thought you weren't coming back. Ever.'

'I had to,' he said, not able to help his grin, or the sweat of fear that evaporated along his forehead, fear that he would not find her. It was like in the moving pictures, when the lover and his beloved were reunited at the end. He ran around the counter and grabbed her up in his arms, 'Oh, Moira, Moira,' he buried his face in her neck, and she was laughing freely, happily.

She closed the shop, and pulled down the shade. 'Gus, I want you to know, I love you. I know you might not love me, but I love you.'

Gus sighed, and looked at her. Here he was, a gardener, and she, a flower-shop girl, how could a more perfect pair be created, one for the other?'

'There's something I want to give you,' she said.

'You've given me –' he began, but she didn't let him finish.

'Something I want to give you.' She began unbuttoning the top of her blouse.

When she was completely naked, he saw what was different about her. 'I told you I had a heart problem. I could never give my heart freely, knowing that I was like this. Different.'

He stepped back, away from her.

'Who did this to you?' he asked, his voice trembling.

She looked at him with those wide, perfect eyes, and said, 'I was born this way.'

The threads.

There, in the whiteness of her thighs.

He was horrified, and fascinated, for he had never seen this before.

Her genitals had been sewn together, you see, with some thread that was strong, yet silken and impossibly slender, like a spider's web. She brought his hand there, to the centre of her being, and she asked him to be careful with her. 'As careful as you are with the flowers.'

'It's monstrous,' he said, trying to hide the revulsion in his voice, trying to draw back his fingers.

'Break the threads,' she said, 'and I will show you the most beautiful flower that has ever been created in the universe.'

'I can't.' He shivered.

Tears welled in her eyes. 'I love you with all my being,' she said, 'and I want to give you this ... this ... even if it means ...' Her voice trailed off.

He found himself plucking at the threads, and then pulling at them, until finally he got down on his hands and knees and placed his mouth there, and bit into the threads to open her.

There must have been some pain, but she only cried out once, and then was silent.

Her labia parted, curling back, blossoming, and there was a smell, no, a scent, like a spice wind across a tropical shore, and the labia were petals, until her pelvis opened, prolapsed like a flower blooming suddenly, in one night, and her skin folded backwards on itself, with streaks of red and yellow and white bursting forth from the wound, from the pollen that spread golden, and the wonderful colours that radiated from between her thighs, until there was nothing but flower.

He cupped his hands around it. It was the most exotic flower he had ever seen, in his hands, it was the beauty that had been inside her, and she had allowed him to open her, to hold this rare flower in his hands.

Gus wondered if he had gone insane, or if this indeed was the most precious of all flowers, this gift of love, this sacrifice that she had made for him.

He concealed the bloom in a hat-box, and carried it back to the estate with him. In the morning, he entered the great house without knocking, and his heart pounded as loud as his footsteps as he crossed the grand foyer. He called boldly to the mistress of the house, 'Jo!' he shouted, 'Jo! Look what I have brought you!' He didn't care if the old man heard him, he didn't care if he would be without a job, none of it mattered, for he had found the greatest gift for his Jo, the woman who would not now deny him. He knew he loved her now, his Jo, he knew what love was now, what the sacrifice of love meant.

She was already dressed, for riding, and she blushed when she saw him. 'You shouldn't come in like this. You have no right.'

He opened the hat-box, and retrieved the flower.

'This is for you,' he said, and she ran to him, taking it up in her hands, smelling it, wiping its petals across her lips.

'It's beautiful,' she said, smiling, clasping his hand, and just as quickly letting go. 'Darling,' she called out, turning to the staircase, 'darling, look at the lovely flower our Gus has brought us, look,' and, like a young girl in love, she ran up the stairs, with the flower, to the bedroom where the old man coughed and wheezed.

Gus stood there, in the hall, feeling as if his heart had stopped.

'It was three days later,' he told me, as I sat on the edge of the nursing room bed, 'that the flower died, and Jo put it out with the garbage. But I retrieved it, what was left of it, so that I would always remember that love. What love was. What terror it is.'

The old man finally let go of my arm, and I stood. He was crying, like a baby, as if there were not enough tears in a human body to let go of, and he was squeezing his eyes to make more.

'It's all right,' I said, 'it's just a bad dream. Just like a bad dream.'

'But it happened, boy,' he said, and he passed me the flower. 'I want you to keep this. I'm going to die some day soon. Maybe within a month, who knows?'

'I couldn't,' I said, shaking my head. 'It's yours.'

'No,' he said, grinning madly, 'it never was mine. Have you ever been with a woman, boy?'

I shook my head. 'Not yet.'

'How old are you?'

'Seventeen. Just last month.'

'Ah, seventeen. A special time. What do you think human love is, boy?'

I shrugged. 'Caring. Between people. I guess.'

'Oh, no,' his smile blossomed across his face, 'it's not caring, boy, it's not caring. What it is, is opening your skin up to someone else, and opening theirs, too. Everything I told you is true, boy. I want you to take this dried flower –'

I held it in my hand. For a moment, I believed his story, and I found myself feeling sad, too. I thought of her, of Moira, giving herself up like that. 'She loved you.'

'Her? She never loved me,' he said. 'Never.'

'How can you say that? You just told me –'

His voice deepened, and he sounded as evil as I have ever heard a man sound. 'Jo never loved me.'

I looked again at the dried flower. He plucked it from my fingers, and held the last of its petals in his open palm.

He said, 'You thought that was Moira? Oh, no, boy, I buried her beneath the garden. This is Jo. She finally left her husband for me. And then, when I had her . . . O, Lord, when I had her, boy, I tore her apart, I made her bloom, and I left her to dry in sand the way she had dried my heart.' He laughed, clinging more tightly to my arm so that I could not get away. 'Her flower was not as pretty as Moira's. Moira. Lovely Moira.' He sniffed the air, as if he could still smell the fragrance of the opening flower. 'I made Jo bloom, boy, and then I stepped on her flower, and I kept it in darkness and dust. Now, boy, *that's* what love is.' He laughed even while he crushed the dried blossom with his free hand.

'O, rare and most exquisite!' he shouted after me as I pulled away from him, and backed out of that madman's room.

'O, why,' he laughed, 'why hast thou forsaken me?'

MARTYR AND PESTY

by

Jonathan Lethem

Jonathan Lethem is the author of the Crawford Award-winning novels *Gun, With Occasional Music, Amnesia Moon,* and *As She Climbed Across the Table.* His collection of short fiction, *The Wall of the Sky, The Wall of the Eye,* was recently published by Harcourt, Brace. He lives in New York, He also has a regular online interview show on *Hotwired.*

Certain professions seem to breed a more active rivalry between long-time partners than others. Comedy, for example. For the husband and wife team George Burns and Gracie Allen, their collaboration worked until she died. After all, Burns would quip, all *he* had to do was stand there, *she* did all the work. Jerry Lewis and Dean Martin's act, on the other hand was not as long-lived. So think about them as you read the next story.

MARTYR AND PESTY

He was on a talk show, live, plugging his new TV series. My old partner, the fuck.

'What happened to the two of you?' asked the host. Sycophantically, that's the word for it.

The fuck took a deep breath. The set was bare. The host leaned in and furrowed his brow. I understood suddenly that this was no flashy Letterman appearance, five minutes, ten quips, and off. They were going to get serious, talk for an hour.

The fuck was going to reach deep.

'Andrew, when I left –' he sighed '– when I left Richie, that was the hardest thing I'd ever done. Not just in my career. The hardest thing in my *life*. Richie and I had come up together. He'd been everything to me. The hard knocks – we took it all side by side. Side by side, Andrew.'

'I thought he left the act,' said the host, Andrew Whatever.

'No,' said the fuck, full of pretentious sorrow. 'No, I forced him to. I knew it was over, I knew my artistic challenges were elsewhere. It's a hard feeling. I denied it in myself. But I made things impossible. I made him go, at that level.'

'And so much good came your way, in the following years,' said the host, his reverence infinite. 'It must have been hard on you two.'

'*Terribly* hard,' said the fuck. 'For years we couldn't talk. You know that, it's old news. We *cared* for each other, Andrew, we still felt the *love*, but we never spoke.'

'But you're saying the connection was there. Most people felt you probably didn't like each other –'

'No. No.' He shook is head gravely, with gravity. 'No. People can say the cruellest things. No. We loved each other. Even if we didn't talk for thirty years. Didn't matter. He knew. I knew.' He was playing the victim for both of us, speaking with that angry, persecuted edge. 'He was the funny one, Andrew, did you know that?'

'Really?'

'I got all the laughs, but it was him, his timing, his impeccable instincts. That's why my humour had to go in a new direction after we split. Because our act, it was all him, Andrew. Him, him, him. He was the funny one. I was just *basking* in it.'

'Then why – why did he stumble so badly afterwards? The drugs?'

'Don't say it. That's a slur, Andrew. That's beneath you. He, he –' He winced, put his finger to his brow. 'Richie didn't know how to turn it on and off like a tap. He was all instinct. I was the brains, I was the deliberate one. My act, crazy as it looked, was *craft*. With Richie, you couldn't put a finger on what he did that was so brilliant. He was flying by the seat of his pants.'

'How is he now? Is he OK?'

'He's good, Andrew. You won't believe this, but we talked just last week. He's taking care of himself. He's straightened out his money troubles, some friends pitched in –' here the fuck winks '– and he's laying off the blow. He's looking great. Andrew, you would not believe how *good* he looks.'

'So the bitterness is gone?'

'What Richie and I have goes back all the way. The bitterness, as you call it, was always exaggerated. Even when we were out of touch, *I knew he loved me*. How could it be any different?'

Enough. Enough. I reach for the phone.

My agent hasn't heard from me in four years. He leaves messages, I don't return the calls. But I know where he is at this moment, because I know him. He's watching the fuck.

'Dennis.'

'Richie, my God.'

'He's saying we're in touch.'

'Calm down.'

'He's saying I was the funny one, Dennis. He's saying he lends me money. He's saying he broke up the act.'

'This is news for you, Richie, that he's a liar? Forget him. Tell me how you are.'

'Sanctimonious bastard. I broke up the act. He never lent me a dime.'

'Richie –'

'I want to go down there. Tell me where it is.'

'You can't –'

'Tell me.'

On screen they're switching to a clip from his new show. The fuck leans back smugly in his chair, hands templed together. The clip starts: he plays a Latin American dictator.

'Somewhere on 54th – Richie, you don't want –'

'Screw you. I'll ask the cabbie.'

I loaded up and went.

I burst in only ten minutes before the end of the hour. I had to wheedle and threaten to get inside, but I never had to whip it out. The set was just cameramen and technicians, no studio audience. I lurched in front of the main camera, towards the host's table.

'Hey, Brains!' I said. 'Reunion time!'

'Richie,' said the fuck, stunned.

'This is remarkable,' said host Andrew for his invisible audience.

'We're back!' I said with a big mugging wink into the nearest camera.

'Richie, sit down,' said the fuck. 'We'll talk. Andrew was just asking about you.'

'No, Eddie. You stand. You get up. We're doing the act. Announce us, Andrew.'

'Uh, ladies and gentlemen . . .' said Andrew, faltering.

'Come on,' I said. 'Proud to present –'

'Yes, indeed,' said Andrew. 'Really proud and astonished to present, together again for the first time in –'

'Thirty-four years,' the fuck supplied edgily, keeping his eyes on me.

'– thirty-four years, the two and only, Martyr and Pesty!'

The fuck got out of his seat.

As he came towards me across the stage I caught sight of myself in the monitor.

The fuck was never a handsome man. But he aged well. He's made of money. He holds himself stiffly, and his hair is fake, but his skin is good and he looks like money.

I look like shit. I scare myself.

Andrew and the fuck must have thought a monster arrived on

the set. I'm patchily bald and I have a thin scraggly beard. My nose is red and pitted like a cartoon drunk's. I'm so hunched my arthritic shoulders are practically higher than my head.

Oh well. Here comes the fuck. Time to be funny.

'Well, Pesty, long time no see.'

'Let's sit down, Richie.' He didn't want to do the act. He tried to take my arm.

'Don't call me Richie,' I said, pulling away. 'Call me Martyr. Let's give the folks a good time.' I gestured at the camera.

He didn't know what to do, whether to play along. How to make me go away. I heard him pitch his voice a little higher, going into character. 'Well, Martyr. Quite a little surprise your coming down to the studio like this.'

'I thought you might need my help. Andrew seemed to be giving you a hard time.'

'I – uh –' His voice was still doing Pesty, but he couldn't bring himself to take the characteristic jabs at me. He couldn't do it.

'What's the matter?' I said. 'You don't look so good.' The perfect set-up. Take it and run, you fuck.

'I guess I don't have the heart for this, Richie.' His voice dropped. 'Can't we just sit and talk?'

'Gosh, Pesty. I guess so. First tell the folks how it was me that left the act first.'

'Richie.'

'I'll take that as confirmation. Now what's this about lending me money?'

The fuck began to see, began to understand. He looked cornered, like a rat in a box. 'I never lent you money, Richie. OK?'

'Fair enough. Now tell them how you think I was the funny one.'

'*What?*'

'Tell them I was the funny one.'

'I said that, Richie, were you listening? I *said* that. Tell him, Andrew.'

'It's true,' said Andrew weakly.

'I said you were the funny one, that it all came from you. That you had that instinct, that it was nothing without you. I said you were the funny one.' In his hysterical insistence I heard his voice rise, involuntarily, to that Pesty squeak.

I took out my gun. He gasped and stepped backwards. 'That's a lie,' I said.

'You're funny,' he said, holding out his hands.

I shot him through the heart.

'You're such a fucking liar,' I said to his corpse. 'I never was funny, never a day in my life. I was the straight man.'

FOREIGN BODIES

by

Michael Marshall Smith

Michael Marshall Smith was born in Knutsford, Cheshire and grew up in the United States, South Africa and Australia. He now lives in north London with his girlfriend Paula, two cats, and 'enough computer equipment to launch a space shuttle'. His short fiction has been published in *Omni*, *Peeping Tom*, *Chills*, *Dark Voices*, *Shadows Over Innsmouth*, *The Anthology of Fantasy and the Supernatural*, both *Darkland* anthologies, *Twists of the Tale: An Anthology of Cat Horror*, *Best New Horror* and *The Year's Best Fantasy and Horror*. He has won the British Fantasy Award for short fiction twice and the August Derleth Award for his critically aclaimed first novel *Only Forward*. His second novel *Spares* was published in the UK by HarperCollins. He is currently scriptwriting the mini-series adaptation of Clive Barker's *Weaveworld*, and is working on other projects as a partner in the Smith & Jones production company.

Smith invites the reader into the everyday world of his characters and, just when you're getting comfortable, something weird and disruptive is unleashed.

FOREIGN BODIES

'Well?' I said.

'Well what?'

'You know very well. What happened last night?' There was a pause, and John laughed. I groaned loudly, enjoying every minute. 'You did it again, didn't you.'

'Yes.'

'She stayed round yours.'

'Yes.'

'You berk. You utter spanner.'

'It wasn't my fault.'

'Yeah, and try telling her that. Another scratched fixture, was it?'

'Nope. Reached the finishing post.'

'You idiot.'

'Twice.'

I sighed theatrically, and John laughed again, slightly embarrassed. He knew what I was going to say, not least because he agreed with me.

'You've been a *very silly boy*, haven't you.'

'I know, I know,' he said happily.

'What *happened*? We spoke, what, three hours before? I thought you'd told her it was just going to be a meal.'

'I did.'

'So what happened?'

'Well we were there, mid-evening, in this restaurant I wanted to try. That Bolivian place.'

'How was it?'

'Fucking terrible.'

'What, worse than that Korean?'

'No, not that bad, obviously. But still bad.'

'Anyway.'

'There we were, it was all going fine, and then suddenly she looked at me and said, "You know what I suggested last time?", and I said, "Yes . . ."'

'What, about why don't the two of you just do it anyway?'

'Exactly. And so she said, "Well, how about it?"'

'And you said, yes.'

'Well what *could* I say?'

The answer, of course, was nothing. I knew this, to my cost, but I continued giving him a hard time for a while, and then we signed off the phone and got on with our jobs. John didn't mind the jokes too much: I think it was the equivalent of doing a penance. Talking to me after an ill-advised Sexual Encounter was the nearest thing he was going to get to saying twenty Hail Marys.

There are some men who will go out, see a woman they fancy, and chat her up. I know it happens because I've heard about it, seen it, marvelled at it. I've never done it myself. In all the time I've been meandering around the planet, I can honestly say I have *never* had the courage, confidence or whatever it is that it takes to be as proactive as that.

But, on the other hand, if you're a reasonable-looking bloke, keeping half an eye open but never really trying very hard, there's a certain kind of situation you're going to find yourself in. While not especially charming, I can string sentences together. While not handsome, I don't inspire outright terror when I hove into view. More importantly, I can listen. Boy, am I good at listening. And therein lies the problem, because there is a certain type of woman out there for whom I, and men like me, appear to be the answer. These women are intelligent and attractive, interesting and sophisticated. They are all, unfortunately, also as mad as snakes.

In the two years I was a single variable, I spent time with four women of this type. They were either people I worked with or met through friends, and I didn't approach a single one of them. They started it. I'm not boasting or gloating here, completely the opposite. Think about it. With the way society is at the moment, women don't approach men. They don't need to. Your average woman spends enough time fending off members of the opposite sex without starting trouble for herself. So what does that say about the women who do such a thing? It says they come with problems. It's different in some other countries, America for example, where perfectly sane women will sometimes make the running. In England it doesn't work like that. Or it doesn't for me, anyway. I was approached by four women, of widely differing ages, appearances and personalities, and I ended up spending time with them purely because I didn't realise that's what I was doing until it was too late.

And the simple fact was, each of these women was mad.

That sounds sexist, or misogynist. It's not. Not deliberately, anyway. There are a vast number of disastrous men out there, too. I'm probably one of them. I'm not characterising the female sex as in any way unstable. If anything, I'm taking the blame back, because I can't understand how some women get the way they are unless it's through a long-term, recurrent, almost *concerted* campaign of subtle mistreatment by men.

My point is, I'm the guy they latch on to when someone else has brought them to that state. These other men sow the seeds through years of desertion, mixed messages and callous indifference, and then they trade up to a younger model and abandon these women to the world. The women regroup, do their jobs, live their lives and carry on, all the time keeping an eye out for someone who looks nice. Someone who looks like they're not going to hurt them, who looks as though they'll listen.

In other words, looking for someone like me. And the sad punchline is that, despite appearances, I'm just as bad as everyone else, and I'm the last thing that they need. I'm just another one of the guys they've met before, but with a slightly kinder smile and an even colder heart.

Or was, anyway. After two years of sexual hit-and-run accidents, each of which left me feeling more damaged and damaging than before, I simply gave up. I gave up right at the start of another one, finally having the experience and bloody-mindedness to spot it for what it could become. I backed out, pulled down the shutters, and resolved to sit tight for a while. If I wanted company I had my memories, and if I wanted sex I'd hot-wire my imagination or rent a bloody video. Sounds pathetic, but it's not. There are advantages to virtual relationships. They don't leave you with someone you don't know to talk to in the morning, someone's calls you have to take when you've got nothing to say. They don't present you with someone's faith to destroy when you never promised them anything.

And then, out of the blue, I met Jenny. I made the effort for once, and she reciprocated sanely and slowly, and suddenly everything was different.

John was still in the position I'd been in a year before, and although I'd never met her, this girl Tamsin fitted the mould perfectly. She was supposed to have temporarily split up from someone else, someone who was bigger than John, had a flashier job, but who happened to be out of the country. John had met her through the usual splatter of coincidence that in retrospect looks too dark and foreboding to be the result of pure chance. He had, to give him credit, pegged her as an 'interesting person' from the very first date.

At first fairly subtly, and then with surprising persistence, Tamsin had suggested a period of casual acquaintance, to include excursions into the sexual arena. This period would end with no strings, it was proposed, when her boyfriend returned from abroad. She would go back with him, John could get back to his life, and everything would be neatly tidied away.

Though this was the sort of suggestion which is supposed to get male hormones ricocheting round their glands in a frenzy of joy, it had struck John as rather odd, In my capacity as a scarred general of former such ill-fated campaigns, he chewed it over with me. My advice had been this.

Don't even fucking *think* about it.

Why?

Because.

Because it wouldn't work that way. Because the sex wouldn't be as good as he hoped, and wouldn't make him any happier. And because when you've slept with someone once, there's no good reason for it not to happen again – and once it's happened twice you're in a relationship, never mind what it says in your contract.

I could picture, almost as though it was happening in front of me, what would take place the evening before Tamsin's boyfriend returned. She'd meet John for a drink, in some pub that meant something to both of them. The stage would be carefully set. John would be nervous, but relieved that the strange interlude was over. Men know better than anyone that you don't get anything for free, and few things make you more nervous than an apparent gift from the gods. John would buy a couple of drinks and sit down, ready to be hearty and make the usual promises of friendship, and then Tamsin would speak.

'Well,' she'd say, and pause, and smile brightly, 'what are we going to do?'

John would cough, and stare, and ask what she meant, and then it would all come out.

She'd changed her mind. After all, there was something between them, wasn't there? Something *important*. She was going to tell her boyfriend she'd fallen in love with someone else. He'd be angry, of course, and she'd have to move out of his flat, and she'd have nowhere to stay . . . but between her and John, and the love that they shared, she was sure they'd be able to work it out.

When someone says something like that to you, you're not allowed to just run yelping out of the bar, although that's much the best thing you could do. There are rules of human engagement. And so John would swallow, try not to pass out, and settle down to having one of the worst evenings of his life. There would be tears, brave smiles, and a horrendous scene in a public place. Possibly screaming. I've seen it happen. After four hours he'd think he'd got away with it, and would limp sweating back to his flat.

Then the next day the calls would start, and the letters, and the visits. John would spend a month looking like a hunted animal, and would eventually emerge bewildered, frightened, and feeling absolutely terrible about something he'd never done.

And if he was anything like me, in four months he'd end up doing exactly the same thing again.

I knew John well enough to be able to plot all this with absolute confidence, and so I told him to stay well clear. He was my friend, so he listened, and thought about it, and realised I was speaking not with forked tongue.

And then, being a man, he'd gone ahead and done it anyway.

Two days later I was sitting at my desk again. I spend a lot of time sitting there. Working at it, rather less.

I was staring out of the window, watching with interest the

antics of a cat in the garden across the road, and I was smoking. I am a keen, dedicated, probably almost *professional* smoker, and recognise a period of time I call 'a cigarette's worth'. It's about five minutes, the length of time it takes to smoke a fag, but the actual duration isn't really the point.

Thus, when I'm supposed to be working, I'll take a break to do a cigarette's worth of reading, a cigarette's worth of leafing pointlessly through magazines, or a cigarette's worth of staring into space. This is different from the usual reading, leafing through magazines and staring into space which I do when I'm supposed to be working – though I'll almost certainly be smoking when I do those too – in that it's a conscious decision, a marked-off period of time during which I am deliberately, instead of merely effectively, not working.

When the cat finally rolled and tumbled out of my field of vision I sighed, and instead turned my intellect to the task of staring at the computer and randomly spiralling the cursor round the screen. This, I find, can keep me occupied for hours. Sometimes, as that afternoon, I dally with a variant of the technique, which involves clicking the mouse at intervals while I'm spiralling. This is both pointless and silly, as sometimes it accidentally moves some of my folders around on the computer desktop. But that's all right, because I can then do a cigarette's worth of moving them all back so they're neat and tidy again.

When I finally started to resurface from my reverie, I noticed that I was whirling the cursor over the folder which holds my letters. I could tell that at a glance because I'd once spent most of an afternoon making its icon look like a little letter coming out of an envelope.

I work for a number of people in a variety of capacities, but I can't honestly say I represent value for money to any of them.

I double-clicked on the folder to open it, and stared vaguely at the sub-folders inside, each labelled with the name of the person to whom the contents had been sent. The names on some of them were enough to make we wince, without even exploring the terrible stuff inside. Like I said, I advised John on the basis of my own experience. Ginny's folder was there, as was Jackie's. Yvonne's and Mel's, amongst less frightening ones holding letters to various other exes, friends and the tax office. There was also, I noticed, a folder which didn't appear to have a name. I was about to investigate when the phone rang.

It was John, and he'd done it again.

I should stress here that, despite appearances, John and I are not a couple of typical lads who can't wait to swap tales of sexual derring do. Over a long and arduous period we've earned our Politically Correct badges, and are in any event both fairly private people. I would never discuss Jenny with him even if he asked, which he simply wouldn't. Reports on random sex are different, though – it's more like a sports news update. And don't try telling me that women don't do it too.

The last time we'd spoken John had sworn curiosity had now been satisfied, and that he wasn't going to end up in bed with Tamsin again. I'd been sceptical. If someone wants to do it again, how are you going to avoid it? Turning down a man is one thing: women have a right not to sleep with someone if they don't want to, and many men will respect that, intellectually if not in practice. Being denied sex is one of the key features of being a male earthling, and it's only the grace with which you accept it that determines how you're perceived.

Turning down a woman is something completely different. Turning down a woman, when she has taken that step and made that offer, comes across as such a wholesale rejection, such a spine-chillingly loud slap in the face, that it's almost impossible to do, however much you want to.

John had gone out to dinner with Tamsin, armed no doubt with the best of intentions, and it had happened again.

Sighing heavily, I got down to the task of telling John yet again that he was making a mistake. I see it as my role in life, discouraging other people from having fun. We knocked it back and forth for a while, and then there was a pause.

'There's something else,' he said eventually.

'Oh yes?' I said. 'What? She doesn't believe you've got someone else?' John had told Tamsin that he too was loosely attached to someone abroad, and that she was coming back soon. I'd liked the way he was thinking, but hadn't held out much hope that it would make a difference.

'No. She told me that she'd taken something. She took something last time as well, apparently.' I assumed that he was talking about drugs, and was about to wax indifferent when he continued. 'Last time it was photos.'

'What do you mean?'

'Last time she stayed round mine, when I was in the shower, she took some photos from the flat.'

'She did *what*?'

'She had prints done, large prints, and then gave the originals back to me this morning.'

'Photos of what?'

'Of me.'

I didn't say anything for a moment. I was reeling slightly. Though I enjoy being proved right as much as the next man, I didn't like the sound of this.

'Where were they? I mean, were they just lying around, in a drawer, or what?'

'They were in an album. It was on my desk.'

'Did you show them to her?'

'No.'

'She just opened it, without permission, and took the photos.'

'Yes.'

'That's not ideal, is it?'

'No.'

'And now she's taken something else?'

'Yes.'

'What?'

'I don't know. She wouldn't tell me.'

At the weekend John called me again. Jenny and I were splatted in front of the television, stupefied with pizza. When the phone rang Jenny advised me to ignore it, but I always find that very difficult to do if I haven't spoken to my parents that day, which I hadn't.

So I answered it, and on finding it was John settled back to banter with half my mind, while trying to keep track of whatever it was we were watching. A documentary on cane toads, I suspect. Jenny had just walked out to make some coffee when John stopped abruptly, and said he wanted to ask me a favour. Something in the tone of his voice made me sit up and tune out the toads, despite the fact that they were cutely rolling on to their backs to have their stomachs rubbed, just like my cat used to do.

John wondered whether Jenny and I could be talked into going out the following night. The fact that he was asking in those terms made it obvious what he was really saying. I asked, and he admitted that a double date was what he had in mind.

I breathed out heavily for comedy value, pretending that what he was asking was a bit of a tall order. Normally he would have got the joke. He didn't. He rapidly said that he wouldn't have asked, except he didn't know what else to do. Tamsin had phoned him at least three times each day since they last saw each other. He was calling from his office rather than home, late on a Sunday afternoon, because pretending he had work to do was the only way he'd been able to avoid spending the day with her. Nothing else he'd been able to come up with, from the fact that he was tired to claiming that he needed to paint the ceiling, had dissuaded her.

Because, after all, she could come and help paint the ceiling. And if he was tired, well, they didn't have to *do* anything, did they? She could just come round, bring some food, and they could curl up together . . .

When he got to that point, I stopped pretending and rapidly agreed, making it clear what I was doing and waggling my eyebrows at Jenny for her approval. She rolled her eyes but then nodded with a smile. '*Men*', she was clearly thinking, and who can blame her. I made arrangements with John to meet him at a cinema in town the following evening.

When we'd finished I put the phone down and sipped my coffee. Jenny nudged me a few minutes later to bring me out of my reverie, but it stayed on my mind. John was a calm, level-headed person. He'd known what he was getting into – I'd warned him often enough.

I could understand him being rattled. But he'd almost sounded afraid.

I had to spend the afternoon at a client's on Monday afternoon, which I didn't mind too much. It meant I could drink their coffee and waste their time, instead of merely my own. I hung around till half six and then went round the corner to meet Jenny in a pub.

When we left an hour and a half later, we were both in high spirits. Neither of us had bothered to eat any lunch, and after three drinks in quick succession we peered rather owlishly at each other when we re-emerged into the fading light outside. Hand in hand we walked down the street towards Oxford Circus, and when we looked across at each other and smiled I sent up a silent thankful prayer To Whom It May Concern.

There'd been times when I thought I would never have this again, when I thought I would spend the remaining evenings of my life nodding in polite fury at the utterances of someone I didn't really know, never mind like, much less love. It wouldn't have been their fault, nor even really mine. It's simply the way things are when people come together out of hurt rather than happiness. When you try to use people as Band-Aids you merely re-infect the wound, and every moment you spend with them is like a speck of glass working itself deeper into your flesh. If it gets in far enough then the wound closes up, sealing the alien matter inside you. Women are used to having their lives and bodies invaded: men aren't, and so I think they struggle against it more. On the outside everything looks good enough, and only you can feel the fresh little cuts that tear every waking moment. The only way to get it out is to rip yourself apart, and so instead you sit and nod, and pretend that nothing matters.

The difference between that state and the one I felt with Jenny was the biggest difference in the world, and as we careered slowly down the pavement towards Piccadilly I gripped her hand very, very tightly.

We were a few minutes early at the cinema, and while Jenny went off to the toilet I sourced a large amount of soft drinks from the counter in the centre of the foyer. I considered buying a tray of tacos, cheese and jalapeños, and then patiently talked myself out of it. There are things one likes that one simply should not have, and in my case thin slivers of green plutonium are among them. As I counted out my change I thought I saw some familiar colours pass by on one side of me, but when I looked up Jenny hadn't yet returned, and there was no sign of John.

I took the drinks, stood next to one of the free-standing ashtrays, and set about mainlining as much nicotine as I could before the show started. It's impossible to find a cinema you can smoke in these days, though I see that talking, clearing one's throat repetitively and loudly explaining the plot to your neighbours are still very much allowed. Jenny still wasn't back, but that didn't surprise me. I know what happens in women's toilets. They step through a portal to another dimension, where they assume their true form and gambol through dream-lit forests, tarrying a while on their home planet to bask in the last moonglow of autumn, before returning to the cursed twilight of this dread prison world. At least, I assume it has to be something like that. I can't see any other conceivable explanation.

I was about half way through my first cigarette when I spotted John on the other side of the room. He was wearing his leather jacket, hands thrust deep in pockets, and craning his neck as he looked round the foyer. People kept coming between us and so I had a minute to observe him, and to see that a woman of average build was standing fairly close to him. She had her back to me, but there was something familiar about her, and suddenly I knew what Tamsin had taken the last time she'd stayed at John's. She was wearing one of his sweaters, a sweater that Jenny and I had given him at Christmas.

I faltered, stopped waving, and withdrew my hand, needing a moment to assimilate this.

OK, so it wasn't any big deal. A jury of her peers would be unlikely to give her the death penalty. But it was wrong. It was wrong in some way that seemed to strike at me personally.

When Jenny and I had chosen the sweater we hadn't been going out with each other for very long, and she had only met John on one rather stilted occasion. John and I never exchanged more than perfunctory gifts, and so I'd been surprised at her suggestion that we look for a sweater for him. He'd commented on his wardrobe when they met, apparently, bemoaning the fact that he never got round to buying anything presentable. I understood that Jenny's desire was due partly to the fact that she was simply very nice, but also out of a wish to start forging a bond between her and my best friend, so we'd had a merry time trawling round a variety of men's clothes shops before finding one we both thought he would appreciate.

He'd liked it, and wore it often. And now this woman had taken it without his permission, and was wearing it as proof of a relationship which John didn't want to have. OK, it was his fault for not being strong enough to keep away. But this was something else, something more than a misjudgment on her part, more than demanding too much too soon. This was invasive.

John eventually saw me, and I smiled and started towards them. At the same moment Jenny emerged from the women's toilets, and we reached them at about the same time. Doubtless reading John's face, Tamsin turned to face us.

When I saw her my heart stopped, and I felt as if I had fallen suddenly into a dream of freezing water. The brief, liquid spell came and went in a moment, and I dragged my eyes off her to listen to what John was saying. I heard the words, but couldn't make any sense of them. My mind was elsewhere.

I'd met Tamsin before, and her name was not Tamsin.

When the film finished at half past ten, I wanted to go. I'd spent most of the film taking covert tooks to my left, where 'Tamsin' had been sitting, and while the initial spasm of complete panic had passed, I still felt extremely bad. I wanted to say goodnight and go home, but the look in John's eyes told me that my job wasn't yet finished.

So, after a pointless few moments of dithering, we went round the corner to a pub John and I occasionally drank in. Tamsin took John's hand and led him to a table. I asked everyone what they wanted to drink, avoiding Tamsin's eye, and went towards the bar. On an afterthought I diverted my course towards the Gents. What I wanted most of all was a chance to think without anyone being able to see my face.

When I was there I splashed cold water over my hands and rubbed them over my cheeks and forehead. Then I just leant on the basin and stared at nothing at all.

I'd seen Tamsin before. More than that. I knew her.

Sometimes when you catch a half-glimpse of someone across the street you mistake them for someone else, most likely a person you're missing, or whom you've just loved and lost. This was not like that. This was not a chance similarity. This was the actual person herself.

The problem was, I didn't know who the fuck that person was.

When we'd stood in that little foursome in the foyer, John making the introductions in an endearingly embarrassed way, I'd felt my mind running at screaming pitch, trying to resolve the question of who she was. But I knew that there was no solution, that however fast my mind ran the wheels were being held off the ground. I had no recollection of this person whatsoever, except for the fact that I knew her.

My memory's fine, in case you're wondering. I may not always pay my Visa bill on the nail, but I don't forget names and faces. As far as I could remember – no, fuck that: it's for sure, and definite. I'd never met this person. But I knew her. I'd never known her name, but I knew it wasn't Tamsin.

Jenny had noticed the sweater immediately, and preoccupied as I was I'd felt the ambient temperature drop by about ten degrees. She knew about the photos, and about the second 'borrowing.'

'That's a nice sweater,' she'd said, with a smile that was bright enough to blind. The girl had nodded self-deprecatingly, and took a step closer to John, who was sending me signals I couldn't interpret.

'It looks just like one of John's,' I said woodenly, staring at him. 'You know, the one Amanda gave you.'

Amanda was John's fictitious girlfriend, an imaginary medical student allegedly out of the country doing an elective in Canada. I know it sounds vile to have ploughed straight in like that, but I was all over the place. It was a wonder I could say anything at all, and not surprising that I fell immediately into my programmed role. I had a job to do, and I was going to do it, not least because now I'd seen Tamsin, or whatever her name was, she was sending shivers up my scalp. There was something very wrong with this picture, and the worst thing was that I didn't know what it was.

'It's the same sweater,' Tamsin said, smiling winningly. 'John lent it to me.' The look in John's eyes as she said this confirmed what I already knew. No he fucking hadn't.

But she'd turned up this evening wearing it, and he could hardly have demanded she take it off. Why? Because she doubtless had nothing else with her, and nothing on underneath. But that wasn't the real reason. The real reason was that you simply can't do that kind of thing.

After all, she'd only borrowed a sweater. It wasn't a crime, was it? And she'd only done it so she could have something of his with her, so she could smell him while they were apart. That was sweet, loving, a sign of how much she was beginning to care: surely not a reason to be shouted at?

With each moment I spent in this woman's company I was feeling worse and worse. And the next thing that we did, after John had stocked up on soft drinks, was to go and sit together for nearly two hours. Tamsin ended up between me and John, and I had Jenny on my other side. We sat, in the darkness, and the film went on, and I have not a clue what it was about. Sitting next to Tamsin felt about as comfortable as sitting next to a corpse, and all I had in my head was one thought.

Why did I think I knew her?

Eventually I left the pub toilet, and bought the drinks. When I returned to the table I was expecting to see Jenny sitting with her arms folded, looking stern and ill at ease. Instead I was perturbed to see her chatting affably with Tamsin. John looked up, took his drink – and Tamsin's – and then carried on listening to what the girls were saying. He didn't try to catch my eye, and neither did Jenny when I sat down. In fact, as far as I could tell, normality had broken out all around me. The undercurrents and strangeness had disappeared, except in one place. My head.

We stayed in the pub until it shut. I probably said about thirty words while everybody else chattered away, having what appeared to be a good time. I tried to start a subsidiary conversation with John but it petered out almost immediately, partly out of my frustration at his apparent refusal to receive the messages I was sending. He was sitting close to Tamsin, his arms behind her on the bench, and every now and then she'd let her hand fall on his knee. I felt like a jealous lover watching them together, but I simply couldn't understand what was going on. At one point her eyes fell on mine and I looked away quickly, almost as if they'd burnt me.

When we were standing outside, the foursome dividing into two pairs again, I threw one last rope in John's direction and asked if he wanted to share a cab. He said no, he was fine. Tamsin put her hand in his, looked at me, and they walked off up the road.

As soon as Jenny and I were in a taxi I started talking fast, and didn't stop for several minutes.

What, I enquired, the *fuck* did John think he was doing? If he wanted this thing to stop before it got any further, why was he playing up to it? Why was he sitting in a pub next to a woman he didn't know – and who kept rifling through his possessions – and looking like he was enjoying himself?

'What was he *supposed* to do?' Jenny demanded eventually, when she could get a word in. 'Sit there looking miserable?'

'Yes,' I shouted, 'yes, that's *exactly* what he should have done. Otherwise it'll be taken as a sign. Otherwise, what was this evening about?' Jenny tried to interrupt, but I overrode her. 'As far as she's concerned, this evening will now have been about John introducing her to two of his best friends. It's just going to make things worse. Now, for the first time, she's going to have something solid to clobber him with when the time comes.' Without knowing I was going to do it, I savagely mimicked Tamsin's rather hard-edged voice. 'There *must* be something between us, John, because you went to all the trouble to introduce me to your friends.' I paused, and furiously lit a cigarette. 'He's digging his own fucking *grave*.'

'Put that out, would you, mate,' the taxi driver said firmly.

'Jesus fucking Christ,' I muttered, and ground the cigarette out in the ashtray.

Taking her time, speaking calmly and rationally, Jenny told me I was over-reacting. She pointed out that they'd seemed to enjoy each other's company, and suggested that maybe John was changing his mind. She enquired as to what it was exactly that I had against Tamsin, and went so far as to offer the opinion that imputing such cold-hearted deviousness to a woman qualified as misogynism.

At this I turned and stared at Jenny, feeling the blood drain from my face. We teetered for a moment on the brink of a vicious argument, and then I calmly but firmly stood down.

Like everyone else, I only know one side of the sex war story, but that doesn't stop me being right every now and then. I wasn't saying Tamsin was a mad woman. I was simply saying she was mad. Mad men would doubtless behave in ways that I would find equally abhorrent. I'd just never had the misfortune of getting emotionally entangled with one.

The whole discussion was nonsense anyway, because it was the furthest thing from my mind. I was trying to focus on it purely as a way of forcing out the other thoughts that were shouting for my attention. Because after an hour sitting in the pub looking at her, I still knew both that I'd never seen Tamsin before, and that I knew her very, very well.

'What about the whole sweater issue, then?' I said finally. 'What about that?' Jenny smiled and rolled her eyes. I remembered briefly that the last time I'd seen her do that was when John had asked me if we'd come out tonight, to dilute the presence of a woman he didn't want to be with. I didn't bother to mention it.

'John lent it to her. What more do you want?'

I sighed and stared out of the window, willing myself to calm down. Ultimately, it wasn't my problem. It wasn't my fucking problem.

'What's so strange, anyway?' Jenny said suddenly. 'She's well-spoken, obviously intelligent, and she's certainly pretty.' She paused, and the cab seemed to go very quiet, with just the sound of wheels on wet pavements outside. '*You* looked at her often enough.'

I resisted the urge to whimper as the last sentence curled lazily in front of me, like a live electricity cable on wet grass. Then I clamped my mouth over Jenny's. After a few moments the cab driver coughed aggressively enough to stop us and so we sat in companionable silence instead: Jenny humming quietly to herself, me wishing fervently that I belonged to a species that reproduced by binary fission.

Next morning I was at my desk at nine o'clock sharp. There was no one there to see it, but it made me feel diligent and worthy, and there was moreover a reason for it. The portable handset of the phone was sitting in front of me, and for once I'd remembered to replace it on the charger unit before going to bed, so the batteries were good and full.

John got into work at nine-fifteen, and boy was he going to have a phone call waiting for him.

While I waited for the time to roll round I booted the computer into life and gazed upon the outside world with reasonable good-will, sipping a cup of coffee. In the cold light of morning the state I'd got myself into the night before seemed unnecessary, even ludicrous. I'd mistaken Tamsin for someone else, that was all, and if John was now intent on seeing her, then that was no one's business but his. I was feeling good, looking good, and juggling three oranges in one hand.

None of that is true, unfortunately.

I was staring out of the window, rather than gazing, and my jaw was set. I hadn't slept well, and there were shadows under my eyes. The morning light was not cold, merely bright, and it was failing to do what it was supposed to. It was failing to make me feel any better.

I wanted to call John, but I felt nervous about doing so. I wanted to believe that last night had just been some weird mental belch on my part, but I didn't. I'm not a complete idiot. If I feel something, really feel it, it's not suddenly going to go away. It's not a whim. It's real.

When we'd got home the previous night, Jenny had gone straight through to get ready for bed. As she wears not only make-up but contact lenses she generally starts about half an hour before me, so as only to have about another half hour's worth to do by the time I come through. I padded around in the kitchen, preparing to make tea and corralling up the ashtrays, and then I wandered into the living room.

It didn't matter where I was. I was in the same place wherever I was standing, and I finally knew what was wrong.

Three years ago, before the mad women period, I had a girlfriend called Karen. She was the last real person I dated. Karen was fun, warm and a very good friend, but she had some problems. We talked them back and forth over the years, tried different ways to work round them, and in the end she went to a psychiatrist. He started her off on hypnotherapy, and during the second session the bombshell landed.

There were things in her life, events, which she had completely blanked. I'm not saying what they were, because it's her life, but they're the kind of things you really don't want happening to you. These events had taken place mainly when she was very young but a few when she was older, and then had simply disappeared from her mind as if they'd never happened.

Except they hadn't, of course. They were still there: she just didn't know about them.

They'd been blanked.

It's not like forgetting. When you forget you can remember, given the right cues. When you blank something, it's like someone throwing a coin into a pool of opaque water when you aren't looking. However hard you stare at the surface, you're not going to know that the coin is there. You may experience ripples every now and then, and you may realise that *something* is buried inside you, but unless you're taken back in time to see the coin sink, the event simply never happened for you.

I was at home when Karen came back from the breakthrough session, and I can still remember the look of horrified astonishment in her eyes. The rug had been pulled out from beneath her in a way that normally only happens in dreams, and she didn't know what to trust any more. What else might she have forgotten? What else had happened that she hadn't been a party to? It was a bit like living a completely normal human life for thirty years and then overhearing someone say it was about time they whipped your motherboard out and upgraded the CPU.

'What?' you think, feeling very cold inside. '*WHAT*?'

As I stood in the living room waiting for the kettle to boil, that was how I felt, and as I sat at my desk the next morning, I felt exactly the same.

At that moment the phone rang, scaring me half to death. It was John, bizarrely. He thanked me and Jenny for coming along the night before, and said he hoped we'd had a reasonable time. As he talked about the film I listened to him carefully, wondering if he was an impostor. Finally, I said something.

'So. You had a good time last night, did you?'

'Yeah, great.'

'And afterwards?'

John laughed, and I nodded to myself and grabbed the computer mouse, nervously making the cursor move around. Careful not to prejudge the issue, I asked if he'd found out what Tamsin had taken.

'Oh yeah. It was just that sweater.'

'But you lent that to her, apparently.'

There was a brief pause, and then John laughed again. I couldn't tell whether he thought I was being weird, or if he was covering up some confusion of his own.

'Yeah, well I probably did. I was quite drunk that night. No big deal, anyway.'

'No. So. Has she taken something this time?'

'Yes, I expect so.'

'And you don't know what.'

'No.'

'She's a one, isn't she,' I said, and we laughed again.

I dropped the subject. I wanted very much to tell John how the sight of Tamsin had affected me, but I couldn't. Believe me, no one hates tension more than I do, the feeling that 'nobody knows but me'. If there had been any point in mentioning it to John, I would have done. I couldn't. It would have felt like I was prying, which was a big change from the last time we'd spoken about it.

I'd been on the brink of telling Jenny the night before as we lay in bed, but again I hadn't. With Jenny in particular it would have led to a conversation that would not have been helpful. I could still picture the live cable in my head, and I wasn't going anywhere near it.

So John and I chewed the rag a little longer, arranging in our roundabout way to play pool at some unspecified venue on an undetermined date in the future. I was only listening with half an ear, watching the cursor whirl round the screen.

Then suddenly the cursor was over my letters folder, and I wasn't listening at all. I opened the folder, grunting distractedly in response to John's ongoing banter, and saw again the folder without a name. Yesterday it had merely made me curious. Today, for some reason, my reaction was far more extreme. I stared at it, mouse still, my heart feeling as if it was in an elevator that was slowly going down and down, way past the ground floor and further still with no end in sight.

I signed off the call and sat and stared at the folder. It looked no different to the ones called Ginny or Mel, except that it didn't have a name. Or it did, as I discovered through a little technical messing around, but it was a special one. It was simply a space.

I hesitated for a long moment, with the cursor hovering over the folder. Then I double-clicked, and the folder opened. Inside was a list of files, eight in total. They didn't have names either.

It was possible that the folder could have been named accidentally, that I'd carelessly deleted everything but a space character. It was inconceivable that I would have done that with the eight files within it. I must have done it deliberately. Needless to say, I had no recollection of having done so.

Wincing slightly, I opened one of the files at random. The computer whirred into life, loading up my word-processing software. A few seconds later I knew what the file was.

It was a letter of a type I've written several times, examples of which were currently residing in the 'Jackie' and 'Yvonne' folders, as well as in 'Ginny' and 'Mel'. A letter which said that while we'd had some fun, I didn't really feel that things could continue in the way they had. That I didn't feel that I was up to the rigours of a full-blown relationship, and didn't want to let them down. A letter that struggled valiantly not to say 'Christ, *I didn't ask for any of this*. All I wanted was a friend: *you* were the one who pushed things in this direction', a letter which tried to pull the blame on to me instead, in the hope of an easy getaway.

Reading the letter made me cringe way deep down in my soul. It was one of mine all right. I recognised the studious reasonableness, the calm hatred, the cultivated air of distant melancholy. Between the lines it said that I *was* to blame, that I should have had the sense not to get involved when I knew I couldn't deal with it. That I was just another bloke, as shallow as the rest, who'd taken what was on offer against his better judgment, because he didn't have the character to turn it down. It was the letter of a confused child, denying responsibility for his actions by using all the tricks of an articulate adult.

The only problem was, I didn't know whom it was to.

There were references in the letter to events, to times and places. None of them rang a bell. A few lines didn't make any sense at all, unless they were in-jokes I'd shared with the person I'd been writing to. One read: 'I'm ready for the airlift to Bourbon Street.' I knew Bourbon Street was in New Orleans, but apart from that it was meaningless as far as I was concerned. It didn't make me smile sadly, as similar parts of the letters to Ginny or Jackie would have. It was simply baffling.

I read the letter three times before sitting back with a cigarette, distractedly rubbing my temples and swigging from the cup of luke-warm coffee. The letter made perfect sense. To me, anyway. But then it would. I'd obviously written it.

But to *whom*, for fuck's sake? To whom, and when?

Without closing it, I opened another letter from the folder. This one was lighter in tone, but just as impenetrable. The fact that I sounded more relaxed probably meant it had been written earlier than the first one. Probably, but not necessarily. With Yvonne, for example, there had been two waves, a second period of light-heartedness after we'd explicitly agreed that it was all just in fun, that we weren't playing for keepsies. Then, of course, the agreement had fallen apart, soon after she had put her apartment on the market.

'Why did you do that?' I'd asked, dear old stupid me. 'So I can come and live with you,' she'd said, smiling as if she'd finally given in to what I'd always wanted. Yvonne had been bright, funny and a successful businesswoman. She had also tried reasonably hard to slash my face with a breadknife.

I spent the next hour reading the rest of the letters, trying to get them into some sort of order. It should have been easy. They should have triggered an unwelcome series of memories which would have helped to put them in context. They didn't. They didn't trigger anything at all. They just read like a distillation of the letters from the other four folders, as if someone had fed them into a computer and the machine had spat out an averaging of them all.

In the end I just sat, staring out of the window. I couldn't see what was beyond the glass, and if the phone had rung I probably wouldn't even have heard it.

I was remembering Jackie, who'd once jumped so massively during a horror film that she'd sprayed an entire carton of popcorn over me and the surrounding rows. She had been nice, in retrospect, simply a little wary and uptight. I was too fucked up by the time I met her to be able to tell the difference. I was remembering Mel, who kept insisting on taking me to little out-of-the-way upmarket cafés, each full of older versions of herself. Each was presented like a prize, and each held some glorious memory for her that she would recount at stupefying length while I twisted with boredom in my seat. I was remembering Ginny, whom I'd really liked, lying her head upon my chest in bed and telling me she'd slept with her ex-boyfriend that afternoon.

I was remembering Yvonne, who had a habit of pointing at me whenever she said something, head cocked one side. At first I'd found this endearing: by the end it symbolised everything I hated most about her. When I thought of the others I could remember the line of their jaws, the curve of their hair, at least something personal about them and the way they looked. With Yvonne, only coldness and fear and that pointing finger.

I was remembering the fact that she'd rung me up two days after my cat had died and asked me out to dinner. We'd stopped seeing each other three weeks previously, at my insistence, but we had a quiet and friendly meal. She was very supportive about my cat, because she'd known how much he meant to me.

During the meal she gave me a shirt that she'd bought. She'd seen it in a shop, she enthused, and simply *had* to buy it for me. The best manipulators are always those who've been manipulated to death themselves. Afterwards she drove me home, and asked if she could stay. After all, she'd helped me – surely I could do the same for her? I said no, and eventually left the car, clutching the little bag with my shirt in it. I felt awful, but what else could I have done? I couldn't just leave it there, and even she probably knew in her heart of hearts that she'd only bought it to make me feel I owed her.

I stood in my apartment and watched as she sat crying outside for half an hour, and then she left. She returned at three in the morning, and rang the doorbell until the house shook and I had to let her in. She then very loudly regressed to the age of five on my living-room floor, and appeared to think I was her father. She grabbed a couple of knives from the kitchen, offered to cut herself up for me, and when I demurred, tried to cut me up instead.

It was, without exception, the worst night of my life.

It was only much later that I realised that she'd already sounded concerned when she'd rung up to ask me for dinner, as if she knew something would be wrong. Before she could have known I would be grieving for my pet, before she should have been aware that Spangle had died, apparently run over in the street by a car whose driver didn't stop.

I sat there and remembered all these things, watching them process in front of me like ghosts down a spiral staircase. Pieces of glass, still left inside, waiting to be recalled so they could shift and cut again.

But I couldn't remember a single thing about the folder of un-named letters, or whom I'd written them to. And all the time I sat remembering a name kept hammering in my head, a name I didn't even believe in.

Tamsin.

I worked for most of the afternoon on autopilot, bashing together some stuff for one of my major clients. It wouldn't matter that it was a bit below standard: they hardly ever noticed what I did so long as it was done on time.

Jenny got back from work at about seven, and we sat and chatted for a while before she got on with cooking dinner. It would make more sense for me to cook, given that I'm kicking around the house all day. But she's better at it and enjoys it, whereas I don't. It's one of the many things I'm completely talentless at.

She had the radio on in the kitchen while she was cooking, and when the phone rang shouted for me to get it. I picked it up and walked towards the window in the living room, away from the arrhythmic shouting that passes for popular music these days.

When I'd switched the phone on I said hello. There was no answer, and I was in the middle of shrugging and putting it back when a voice spoke.

'Hello, David,' it said.

'Hi. Who's that?' I asked cheerily, assuming it was one of Jenny's mates, all of whom are much better at remembering my name than I am at recalling theirs.

'It's Tamsin,' the voice said.

There was a very long pause, and I unconsciously moved a little further away from the kitchen door.

'Oh. Hello,' I said warily. She laughed, a sound which had about as much humour in it to me as a recording of someone long dead.

'Hello. Are we going to go on like this all night?'

I didn't know what else to say. In the end all I could come up with was an enquiry as to how she was.

'I'm fine,' she said, as if sharing a private joke. 'Excellent, thank you. How are you?'

'I'm – look . . .' At that moment Jenny called to me, asking who it was. Without thinking, I said it was a client, and Tamsin's laugh carried to me from the phone. 'Look,' I said, feeling guilty and implicated, 'what can I do for you?'

'I don't know. What do you suggest?'

'Well . . .'

'I was just calling to say hello. After all, we know each other.'

'Yes,' I said, a little stonily.

'I got the impression last night that maybe you don't approve of me.'

'What John does is up to him.'

'I'm not talking about that. You acted as if you didn't like me.'

'I . . . look, I hardly know you.'

'No?'

'No,' I said firmly. 'After all, we only met last night.'

'That's right. Well, it was nice to talk to you, David.' At her second use of my name I felt something clench inside me. I'd noticed yesterday evening that she was a little familiar with it, and it's something I don't like. It's too personal, somehow. When someone uses my name like that, it feels like they're claiming squatter's rights on my soul.

'And you, Tamsin,' I said. She laughed yet again.

'We'll meet again,' she said. Then the line went dead.

I felt like a bastard as Jenny commiserated with me over clients who think they can call you up at all hours, but I wasn't going to tell her who it was. I was quiet over dinner, and ate little. For the rest of the evening Jenny retreated to the sofa with a book, looking puzzled as I blanked my mind with work.

As soon as she'd gone to bed I called John. He sounded a little tired, but I ploughed on regardless. Tamsin could only have got our number from John's address book, and I'd come up with a pretext to get him to look for it. After a little preliminary chat I went for it.

He said he'd do it in the morning. I was about to press him, and then realised why he was sounding strange. There was someone with him, and she would have already returned his book. I apologised for disturbing him, put the phone down and went to bed.

Nothing untoward happened the next day. That's the only way I can put it. I got up, did my work, spent the evening watching a film with Jenny, went to bed. That was it.

Or nearly it. Each time the phone rang I expected it to be someone I didn't want to talk to, and after a while I just put the answering machine on and turned the volume down. I even considered taking half an hour mid-afternoon to go through the box file of letters and mementoes I kept in the bedroom cupboard, looking for something, anything. But I didn't. I could remember what was there.

In the evening John called, and we arranged to play pool the following evening. I did some more work, and Jenny finished her book, and then we went to bed. At some time in the night the phone must have rung, because when I got up the next morning the light on the answering machine was flashing.

Whoever it was didn't leave a message.

John got to the pub before me, and was sitting at the bar making short work of a Budweiser when I turned up. We got another round and headed downstairs to the cold and deserted pool room. There was only one table, but as no one else seemed to realise it was there, we rarely had much competition.

We didn't say much for a while, as was our wont. Eventually John said I looked tired, and I agreed that I was. I went on to say that he was looking decidedly spruce for someone who was involved in as much nocturnal activity. He smiled, and straightened up. He looked at me for a moment, paused, and then spoke.

'Well, you would know.'

'About what?'

John laughed, and then appeared to make a decision of some kind.

'She told me,' he said. 'I don't mind.'

'About what?' I repeated.

'About you and her. You could have said, but it's not a problem.'

'John, what are you talking about?'

'About Tamsin,' he said, and for a moment he looked annoyed. It took me a moment to realise, because I'd never seen him look like that. Not at me, anyway.

I was completely confused. OK, so he knew she'd called me. Surely it wasn't that big a deal.

'John, she just called me. To say hello, allegedly.'

'When?' he said. 'When was this?'

'The night before last.'

'I didn't know about that.' I stared at him.

'Well then, what the fuck *are* you talking about? She called me. That's why I wanted you to look for your address book. She must have taken it last time she was at your place.' John just looked at me. 'John, if there's anything else, you're going to have to spell it out for me, because I've no idea what you mean.'

John laughed angrily, and slammed his glass down on the table. I jumped, visibly.

'I'm talking,' he said, slowly and clearly, 'about the fact that you and Tamsin used to know each other. That you had an affair. That you fucked each other. Is that clear enough?'

For a brief, absurd moment, I was four years old again.

When I was four, my parents had a vine in the back garden on which chilli peppers grew. Time and again I was told not to eat them, and so I didn't. I was relatively well-behaved in those days. Then one afternoon I touched one of the fascinatingly plump and glowing chillies, and a little while later was in agony, my lips burning as if they were pressed against an oven door. My parents, of course, assumed I'd eaten one of the peppers. But I hadn't. All I'd done was accidentally rub one of my fingers against my lip, and that had been enough. As they applied ice to my lip and ice cream to my mind, my parents good-naturedly said they'd told me so, told me not to eat the peppers. When I protested that I hadn't eaten one they just smiled. The fact that they weren't shouting or angry made it worse. I hadn't eaten one. I hadn't eaten a pepper.

And so with John. I denied it. I said I'd never met her before, and it was true, but I felt like a liar. John didn't believe me. I tried to tell him about the way it had felt when I'd first seen her, when we'd all met in the cinema, but he took it the wrong way. As far as he was concerned, what she'd told him was the truth. He was on the other side of the wall, and I couldn't reach him, no matter what I said. What's more, he now thought that I was trying to reactivate the affair behind his back.

I got angry myself, furious that he would rather believe someone he'd only met a couple of weeks ago. Again and again I said I didn't know her, that I didn't know her at all.

'Then how come,' he shouted eventually, 'how come she knows *everything* about you?' He slugged back the last mouthful of his beer, and then he stormed out of the pub.

I just sat still for a moment, shocked. My mind couldn't process what had just happened, not on top of everything else. Then I grabbed my coat and ran out.

I jogged down the road in the direction John would have taken, but there was no sign of him. I walked quickly back up to the pub, struck by the thought that he might be sitting fuming at one of the tables round the other side, but he wasn't. He'd gone.

I did a cigarette's worth of leaning against a nearby wall and smoking, in the hope that he'd reappear, but he didn't. In the end I walked to the nearest phone box, and left a message on his machine saying that I had to talk to him. I didn't have to load fake sincerity into my voice: the real stuff was there in spades. I hoped he'd be able to tell that, even if these days he was choosing to believe Tamsin rather than me.

Then I walked home. I could have taken the subway, but the thought of going underground and standing fretfully on the platform for ten minutes didn't appeal. I didn't think I could stand still for ten seconds, never mind longer. I turned in the direction of home, and walked stiff-legged up the road.

It was just turning dark by then, and the streets were deserted. I guess it was soap-opera time, or dinner time, or some other period where everyone else just happened to be otherwise occupied. I felt completely and utterly adrift, examined and found wanting. I couldn't explain why I'd felt the way I had on meeting Tamsin. I couldn't explain the letters either, but it wasn't as if they were to her. The letters I'd written to Yvonne were called 'Yvonne 1' to 'Yvonne 14'. I'm organised like that. The letters in the folder with no name had no names, so they couldn't be to Tamsin: otherwise they'd be called Tamsin 1 to 8. They were to someone with no name.

To no one at all.

It didn't take more than half an hour to get home. I was striding quickly, wanting to be inside, anxious to be somewhere where I could be surrounded by things I recognised and understood. I found I was muttering and swearing to myself, on the verge of tears. I hadn't felt like that since the excruciating night three years before when I'd broken up with Karen. I was frightened to discover that side of me was still intact, that beneath the carefully cultivated exterior a lonely and hurt little boy was still jabbering and screaming to itself.

By the time I got to our street I was almost running. I ran up the stairs to the flat, and was fumbling with the keys when the door opened and Jenny was standing there, looking sane and wonderful and whole. She was surprised to see me, but as I started upon the drawn-out process of feeling my way towards an explanation, I realised that there was something a little strange about her. Not strange, exactly, but 'public'. She wasn't being quite herself. I asked her if she was OK, and she nodded vigorously.

'Oh yes,' she chirped as she headed up the couple of steps which led to the kitchen. 'We've got a visitor.'

John had come to our flat. He'd thought better of his outburst, realised I was telling the truth, and had come to talk it out.

It wouldn't be ideal with Jenny around, but I felt so anxious that frankly any resolution seemed welcome, even if it meant a tense hour or so with her. It felt as if the last few days were drawing to a point, a moment when, finally, the world was going to start making sense again.

That's what I thought as I strode across the kitchen towards the living room, feeling nervous but glad of something concrete to say and do. That's what I was expecting as I walked into the living room and looked across at the sofa, ready to be hearty and businesslike and to talk to John like we always used to.

I wasn't expecting to see Tamsin.

I stopped moving a yard or so into the room and just stood, mouth open. I'd been so convinced it would be John that I'd almost been able to see him sitting tensely on the edge of the sofa, feeling a bit of an idiot. But it wasn't him. It was her.

This can't be happening, I thought. This is fucking *Fatal Attraction* and it isn't happening to me.

'Hello, David,' she said, looking up bright-eyed over the cup she was sipping from. She was holding it a bit strangely, but I was too stunned to work out in what way.

'Tamsin was nearby and stopped in to say hello,' Jenny said, unnecessarily. I stared at her while she was saying this, but there appeared to be no subtext to the announcement. 'Isn't John with you?'

'No,' I said. 'No. He went home.'

'Oh,' Jenny said, puzzled. 'Why?'

As I struggled to come up with an answer, I glanced at Tamsin. She was smiling, a little cat smile that curled up at the corners into a mind whose strange angles I was still struggling to comprehend. 'Ask her,' I wanted to say. Why don't you ask *her* what happened this evening, and why?

In the end I just shrugged, and said that the pool hadn't been happening, and that John was tired and called it a day. I sat down on the sofa next to Jenny, making it as clear as I could without recourse to speech that I felt there was one person too many in the flat. No one appeared to be listening on the body language wavelength.

'We were just talking about holidays,' Jenny said, and for nearly the first time I felt a twist of irritation with her. I can't do that kind of conversation, as she fully well knows, can't sit and swap sentences on subjects which are of no interest to me. What is the fucking point? I don't give a shit what other people are going to do for their holidays. Why should I? It's just white noise, information which has no impact on me. Sitting and listening to it very rapidly drives me into a state of cold and furious boredom. I don't ask for in-depth discussions of weighty issues – I hate those too, as it happens – but I can't sit and listen to people reading out the ingredient list of their lives.

'Oh yes?' I said, hoping to kill the conversation stone dead.

'Tamsin's hoping to go to New Orleans,' Jenny continued with, as far as I was concerned, a surreal level of enthusiasm.

'Why?' I said. I knew I was behaving badly.

'Oh, just everything,' Tamsin said, and Jenny nodded at me, as if this explained something. 'French toast, the old town, jazz. I've always wanted to go. It sounds wonderful.'

'Holidays are always wonderful,' Jenny chipped in tellingly. 'They take you out of yourself, don't they?'

'That's it,' Tamsin agreed. 'That's exactly it. Sometimes when I'm sitting at my desk, doing something boring, I wish it could happen right there and then. I wish I could just be airlifted straight to Bourbon Street and sit on the pavement drinking cold beer and listening to "Dixieland". Don't you feel like that sometimes, David?'

As I stared horrified into her eyes, I had a tiny flicker. A half-image passed through the back of my mind, a picture combined with a fragment of sound, a wisp of scent, a beat of atmosphere. A glimpse of the side of someone's face, the sound of a tenth of a word being spoken. The noise of a pub, the smell of beer on a warm evening. Like a memory it was there, a half second of the past, and then it was gone, unrecoverable.

From that moment I knew that I couldn't try to explain away what was happening. It must have been me who was there, in that pub. That moment was part of me. Something was forgotten, and I had to find out what it was. I must have been there, doing that, at that time, with someone. Someone, but I didn't know who.

'David doesn't dream about things like that,' Jenny said suddenly, covering what must have been a very pregnant pause. 'He's happy.'

'Is he?' Tamsin asked. 'He doesn't sometimes want to call up his clients in the wee small hours and shout abuse?' I shivered, but Jenny didn't notice. I hadn't said anything like that since we'd known each other. But I used to. I used to all the time. 'Or put razor blades in the parcels he carefully sends to them?'

'Stop talking about me as if I'm not here,' I said, mainly to convince myself that I was. 'No, I don't wish any of those things. I'm happy now. I've got Jenny, for a start.' I hadn't said this for political reasons, but it went down well with her, and she looped her arm around my back.

Tamsin just looked at the two of us and smiled, that little cat smile that made we want to take a hot iron to her face. Somehow this woman was holding everything I had in her hand, and she was waiting to clench her fist. I didn't know why, or what she was waiting for, or how much longer she'd hold off.

Suddenly I knew what I had to do, what I should have done half an hour before. Thinking rapidly, I groaned and went through a great show of irritation at my forgetfulness, tutting and virtually slapping my forehead in order to get the message across. Tamsin and Jenny stared at me with bright smiles.

'What an idiot,' I said, shaking my head. 'Got to go.' I stood up, and reached for the car keys.

'Where?' Jenny asked.

'To see John,' I said. 'Completely forgot something.'

'Can't you call him?'

'No,' I said. 'Got to get something from him.' It was weak, and I knew that Jenny wasn't convinced, but by that time I was backing towards the door. Unless one of them was prepared to call my bluff, they couldn't stop me going. 'Won't be long.'

I turned on my heel and walked rapidly through the kitchen, willing them not to say anything, hoping against hope that Jenny wouldn't come up with the bright idea of suggesting that I give Tamsin a lift somewhere. I heard her call out just before I got to the door, but I ignored it, shut the door quietly after me and ran downstairs.

I went through two red lights on the way to John's, using all the rat-runs I knew to get me there as quickly as possible. Tamsin – or whatever her real name was – was building a trap around me. I didn't know what kind, or why, but she was. The only way to stop the circle from closing was to jam something in the way: to ensure that John knew what was going on. I had to speak to him. I had to convince him that he was dealing with someone whose word could not be trusted. Not even on something as basic as her name. How I could do that without knowing what her real name was remained to be seen. But I had to do it.

When I pulled up outside the house that held John's flat I was relieved to see that his light was on. I'd spent the last five minutes of the drive convinced that he might have gone to my place, or even that something might have happened to him. There was no reason for the latter suspicion, none at all, but once it had entered my head there seemed no way of dislodging it. But he was obviously home, and would have heard the message I'd left on the answer machine. That was good.

I strode up to the door and pressed the entry-phone buzzer briefly. It was one of our running gags, seeing how short a buzz we could generate. Partly a joke, partly a subversive dig at all those in the world who leant on buzzers until the whole building shook. It was a good buzz, short and probably barely audible. I knew he'd be impressed.

There was no answer. Puzzled, I pressed again, less briefly this time. After a pause a burst of feedback leapt out of the speaker.

'John,' I said. 'It's David.'

'Hello, David,' said Tamsin's voice. 'Why don't you come up?'

I stared at the speaker, feeling sick, and then I took a quick step backwards. As a blurred afterthought I moved so that I remained close to the front of the building, so that someone looking out of John's window wouldn't be able to see me.

Heart pounding, I gazed unseeingly out across the road.

There was no way.

No way she could have got here more quickly than me.

No way.

'What are you doing here?'

At the sound of his voice I refocused suddenly to see John walking down the pavement towards me. He was still wearing his coat, and looked cold. Moving quickly and silently, as if in a dream, I raised my hand to my lips and ran towards him. He stared at me as I grabbed his arm and pulled him towards the car.

'Dave . . .'

'John, get in the car,' I hissed. 'Just get in the fucking car. Please.'

He got in.

It took an hour, but in the end I did it.

I didn't say anything as I drove. I glanced across once to see him sitting looking affably out the front, and decided against breaking the silence. I hate talking about important things when I know I'm about to be interrupted by trivia such as getting out of cars and buying drinks.

I drove to another pub that we sometimes went to and bought a couple of beers. When we were comfortably seated, when John had been for a piss and I'd lit a cigarette, I began.

I told John again that I'd never met Tamsin before. He started to twist slightly in his seat, but I ran over him. I told him that I'd just got home to find Tamsin in my flat, talking to my girlfriend, and that she'd made a reference to something that had spooked me. I told him that there was no way she could have beaten me to his flat. He nodded at that one: he's been driven by me, and knows the routes I take. I realised suddenly that he had only my word for the fact that she'd been there when he turned up, but he didn't question it.

He believed me, finally. At least, he believed that I'd never gone out with Tamsin. I firmly drummed into John the precise number of times I'd seen or spoken to Tamsin, and what the circumstances had been. He seemed willing to disregard anything Tamsin said which contradicted my version, and that was enough to be going on with. In my relief I was willing to back off the weirder stuff. It seemed the right thing to do. I think John was inclined to see it as slightly hysterical exaggeration on my part, done for comic effect. I wasn't prepared to sound any stranger than necessary, so I let it go. The sentences concerning it washed down through the conversation and disappeared, leaving us with something more explicable. A mad woman.

In the end I drove him home, and felt a weight lift from my shoulders as our familiar banter started up. As he got out of the car he laughed and shook his head.

'I should have known it was bollocks,' he said. 'In all the time I've known you I've not seen you even *look* at a blonde, never mind go out with one.

I laughed, and waved, and drove away and because I was so relieved that I'd sorted things out with John it was only when I'd got about half way home that I absorbed what he'd said. When I did I steered the car over to the side of the road and just sat for a while, engine idling, staring at the condensation on the window.

Tamsin's hair was brown. A rich, dark brown. Exactly the kind I liked.

When I got home I smoothed over my abrupt departure. Tamsin had stayed another five minutes after I'd left, apparently, and then gone to take the Tube. I nodded distantly. It didn't make any difference. If she'd left a second after I had she still couldn't have beaten me. I tuned out while Jenny free-associated on the subject of holidays, and worked on a way of asking a question so that it wouldn't cause trouble.

'Tamsin's hair,' I said, eventually, with the air of someone who thought it looked terrible. 'Is it natural, do you think?'

'Oh yes,' Jenny said seriously, giving the subject the full weight of her attention. 'You can't fake a blonde like that.' I nodded, dismissing the subject, but Jenny held on to it. 'Do you like it?'

'Babe, you know I prefer brunettes,' I said, in a just passable Bogart voice, and Jenny laughed. She knew.

So did Tamsin. Perhaps that's why I was seeing someone different. They saw blonde Tamsin. I saw someone with dark hair who didn't have a name. I thought it was more likely that I was the one seeing the truth.

She had power of some kind. That was clear. What was less apparent was what the fuck she wanted.

The subject changed and we watched some television and went to bed and I lay all night staring at the ceiling, feeling as if the sky had gone and I lay cold and exposed beneath the dark well of space.

And the next morning it started in earnest, and the ending when it came was inconclusive and added up to nothing.

I was sitting at my desk, as ever. I felt hollow, too blank to be tired. It was grey outside, and the leaves of the trees which lined the other side of the road were stirring constantly and silently behind the glass of my window. Jenny had gone quietly to work at half past eight, and since then it felt as if I hadn't heard a sound.

Until the phone went, and I dropped my cigarette. The ring isn't that loud, but it was much closer than I was expecting. I realised that the phone was lying to one side of the desk. I'd forgotten to put it on the charger overnight. Again.

It rang twice more, and then I picked it up.

'Hello,' I said.

'Hello, David,' said a voice, and in a way it was almost a relief.

'Tamsin,' I said.

'No,' she said. 'You know it's not. You know that's not my name.'

'Yes,' I said.

'So what is it?'

'I have no idea.'

'Bullshit. You know. You just don't fucking remember.' I was startled by the tone of her voice. For the first time it had lost its gloating pseudo-politeness and was on the verge of anger. The sound of it raised hairs on the back of my neck, and I didn't want to hear it get any worse. But I didn't know. I simply didn't know.

'What do you want from me?'

'What do I want?' she shouted, and I could feel myself shrinking with a familiar fear. 'What do I *want*? You're such a shit, David, such an utter, fucking *shit*. You fuck me up, throw me away, and you want to know what I *want* from you?'

'Tamsin, I . . .'

'DON'T CALL ME THAT!'

'I don't know what else to call you . . .'

I stopped not because I'd run out of things to say, or because I was interrupted, but because I heard the all too familiar tones the handset makes when the battery has run out. The line went dead, and I was just trying to decide whether to run to get the other line in the bedroom, or just to be thankful that the conversation was finished, when I heard Tamsin's voice again, coming from the phone.

'Yes you do,' it said. 'Yes you *do*. And you'd better remember, because I need to know.'

'Can't you just leave me alone?' I stuttered, not knowing if she'd hear me. The battery indicator light had gone out. The phone should have been dead.

'Why should I? How can I? If you don't even have the decency to remember my fucking *name*?'

'Please,' I said, 'please, just go away.'

'I can't,' she said, abruptly no longer sounding angry.

Then there was no more sound. I looked at the handset. The battery indicator was still out. Our last couple of sentences couldn't have happened. I put the phone back on the desk. I didn't want it recharged.

Her name wasn't Tamsin. She'd admitted it now. I had to find out what it was, or remember it. Until that happened, it would go on, and from the tone of her last sentence I wondered if it was more than that. Maybe it wasn't just me who was being persecuted. Maybe I was involved. Perhaps she *couldn't* go until I remembered who she was.

Maybe she really didn't know.

I spent the rest of the morning ignoring my work, just thinking until my brain hurt. I couldn't get anything to come. I couldn't think of anyone who I'd shared dreams of New Orleans with. I couldn't remember who the letters were to. In the end I called John, from the phone in the bedroom. The first minute or so of conversation was a little stilted, and I wondered how long it would be before our shouting match had completely left both our minds. But it relaxed soon enough, and after a while I asked him.

'John, got a weird question for you.'

'The answer's no, Dave. I like and respect you, but I simply can't do that other thing. I'm just not attracted to you in that way.'

'Very funny. Since Karen, how many girls have I been out with?'

'Is this a rhetorical question?'

'No.' There was a pause, and all of the light-heartedness went out of John's voice.

'Are you OK, David?'

'Not really. How many?'

'Well, there was Ginny, then that one I never met . . .'

'Jackie.'

'Yeah, her, that skinny one – Mel, was it? Oh, Christ, and that complete nutter. Yvonne. Whatever happened to her?'

That was something I'd often wondered, exactly what had happened to Yvonne, why she'd backed off in the end.

'She went away. Eventually.'

'Right. So, four.'

'That's what I thought.'

Back in the living room, I stood and looked out of the window at the drizzle. Outside on the pavement the cat ran past, as if fleeing from something. But they always look like that: probably it was only the rain.

Time felt like it was shortening, speeding up, as if something I didn't understand was getting closer. Confirmation from John that there couldn't have been anyone else should have made me feel better. It didn't. Instead it opened up a portion of my mind which hadn't really been paying attention. It melted suddenly, as if I was relaxing a muscle which I hadn't realised had been clenched for months, maybe years.

There had only been four. There was no one else.

Tamsin had to be one of them.

I turned and walked back into the bedroom. I opened the cupboard and sat down in front of it. Reaching beyond the hanging tails of coats and shirts I found my box file. For a moment I just let my hands rest on it, sensing that I could simply leave it there, that its contents could remain half-buried.

But half-buried is not enough. You can put rubbish as deep in the bin as you like, and cover it with whatever you can find, but it will still be there. Even when the truck has come to take it away you'll know, know that somewhere the evidence remains. It may be hidden so deep that no one will ever find it, and it may be destroyed, but you'll still know it's there, or that it existed once.

Once a coin has been thrown in the water, it's always going to be lying at the bottom of some pool or other.

I pulled the box out and opened it on my lap. Unlike the files for my 'proper' ex-girlfriends, the contents were a jumble: letters, cinema ticket stubs, wine corks and dried-out flowers mixed together so thoroughly that they could have related to just one person. I pulled out a couple of letters and glanced at the writing on them.

Letter from Ginny. Card from Mel. Unwisely, I glanced inside. There, in an untidy Biro sprawl, was a message saying that she thought she loved me. Carefully phrased, so as not to go too far out on a limb, but there in black and white all the same. Cringing to the depth of my soul with shame, I put it back in the envelope. I hadn't loved Mel, or any of them. It wasn't that I had taken advantage. I simply hadn't felt anything at all.

Two consecutive postcards from Jackie. The first a tirade. The second a numb acceptance. A CD single of the theme song from a long-forgotten film which I went to see with Mel, a song which would have been 'our tune', if we'd stayed together long enough to have one. If I hadn't left, walked out dead into the night, leaving her tearless and bewildered.

Rain spattered against the window suddenly, and I looked up. I caught a glance of a photo of Jenny and me which hung on Jenny's side of the bed. Her face looked down at me, brown from the holiday she'd been on before we met. It was a pretty face, but it took me a moment to recognise it. Even longer to recognise myself.

I pulled another handful of letters from the box, mostly from Ginny. It was odd I couldn't find anything from Yvonne. I must have thrown them away. I was still leafing through cards and letters, feeling more and more horrified at myself, when my heart nearly stopped at the sound of the doorbell. Scattering the contents of the box I leapt awkwardly to my feet.

In the hall I paused. We don't have an intercom system, and so I had to go downstairs to answer. I didn't know whether I wanted to. After a pause the bell rang again, and I opened the door to the flat and walked slowly down.

No shape bulked through the glass of the front door, and when I opened it, there was nobody there. On the mat lay a small bundle wrapped in brown paper, and I picked it up and closed the door.

In the bedroom I took the paper off. Inside, damp from the rain, were seven letters. They all bore the same address, written in my handwriting, and none of them had a name. Sitting suddenly down on the bed as my legs went from under me, I took the letter out of the first one. It was neatly laser printed, and I recognised the typeface. I recognised the contents too. It was the first letter from the nameless folder. No name at the top, but my initial at the bottom, and a kiss. A kiss.

Another splatter of rain hit the window but I barely heard it as a crowbar made of pieces of folded paper forced the doors of memory wide. Fragments came at first, and then whole scenes, pushing through the cracks like eyeless animals from the ground. In slow motion, my vision blurred, I reached down and pushed my hand through the articles scattered around the box file on the floor, the remains of what should have been friendships, the debris of shattered people. The person I had thought was me watched as someone else searched for what he knew was there to be found.

A small bottle, and a key.

I found them.

The key fitted a door which I now remembered. The bottle held formaldehyde, and something else. The last joint of a finger, a finger which always used to point. Something which belonged to a woman whose face I could suddenly recall.

The rain was so furious that I had to lean forward and peer through the windscreen, and I skidded at one junction and nearly totalled a cyclist.

On the passenger seat lay the letters, though I didn't need the address any more. The bottle was in my pocket.

The road was in the tangle of dead streets between Finsbury Park and Archway, an area I'd unconsciously avoided for two years. As I drew closer I noticed how many windows were still boarded up, the remnants of some developer's dream which had never come to fruition, waiting out the fallow years in a little patch of temporary ghost town. Most of the houses had already been abandoned when I'd last been there, when I'd last visited Tamsin Road.

The closer I got the slower I drove. It wasn't reluctance. I knew I had to go. It was caution, because of the wetness of the roads, and it was because I didn't trust myself to drive with so much still flooding into my head. It was like discovering a new room in a house which has always seemed too small, except that I knew this room from before.

Turning into Tamsin Road was like finding a drawing you did as a child. It's a short street that curves, and on both sides the eyes and mouths of the buildings were boarded over and nailed shut. Dirty fragments of litter scuttled down the gutters, but not as much as you'd expect. No one was coming here to top the level up, and I suspected that if you caught one of the fleeing fragments of newspaper with your foot the date would be from some years ago. From 1993 itself, perhaps, the year I'd last been here.

I pulled up outside number twelve and killed the engine. After gathering up the letters I got out of the car, locked it and walked up towards the door. It was two years older and grubbier, paint peeling a little more, but I recognised it. For a brief moment I thought of the people I knew, of John and Jenny, and realised that they were somewhere in the city now, doing their jobs and – who knows – maybe thinking of me. But I wasn't there any more.

I was here again.

I felt in my pocket for the keys and slipped it into the lock. She gave me the key herself, obtained by some means from the company she helped to run. I don't think they were the people who were planning to redevelop the area, but I can't remember. I hadn't blanked that fact, like all the others, but simply hadn't listened when I was told. I listened to her a lot at first, because she was funny, and clever in a brittle way. But after a while I didn't listen to her at all, like I didn't really listen to Mel or Jackie, or even to Ginny, whom I'd liked.

The lock turned with a little effort, and I let myself in and closed the door. The hallway was dark, but I saw the letter lying on the mat and picked it up. It was the last one, covered in dust and beginning to discolour, with the address in my writing but no name at the top. I added it to the others and walked quietly to the stairs. After turning for no reason to look at the dirty yellow light which seeped through the boards across the door's thin and filthy window, I went upstairs.

The door was shut. I'd always closed it after me, as if that would make some difference, as if throwing something away and piling rubbish on top would really hide what was at the bottom of the pile. Realising I was crying, I rubbed the back of my hands across my eyes and turned the handle of the door.

The room was exactly as I now remembered it, though deeper in dust. It was brighter than the rest of the house, more light coming through the windows, which had been papered rather than boarded over. The corkscrew we'd opened our wine with lay by the wall, and the mattress where we'd fucked was still beneath the window, now heavily stained with damp.

I walked to the middle of the room and looked down, and was not surprised to see that the ragged patch of carpet looked as though it had recently been disturbed. Slowly I sat down cross-legged next to it, and took the bottle out of my pocket.

We hadn't needed to come here. I had a flat, and so did she. We'd just done it occasionally to be different, to be sleazy in the way that middle-class yuppies sometimes think is exciting. We came on autumn afternoons, each letting ourselves in, then shared a bottle of wine and had sex on the mattress and carpet and floorboards; her eyes flat with lust and hurt, mine with lack of feeling. Rubbed into the walls of the dead room I could almost smell the only two emotions I ever experienced in it: jittery, perfunctory desire, and bored, selfish remorse. The first time I'd said I didn't think our relationship was going anywhere was in this room, but of course we'd come back several times after that. It was if I deliberately ended up sleeping with women after saying we shouldn't, as if I wanted to hurt them as much as possible. I didn't. I just followed the line of least resistance, lived out my programming like an abandoned automaton.

I smoked a cigarette, ground it out on the floorboards, and then reached out and pulled up the carpet. The boards looked loose, as indeed they were. Not knowing how she'd look, or caring, I pulled the middle one up, and then the two on either side.

She lay there, caved in and empty, body curved a little because she had been too tall to fit in the space. A last faint remnant of the smell I'd buried drifted up, but not much. Not as bas as it had been when I'd come here before, on the seven occasions I'd come and sat with her, watching the body decay, seeing the parts I'd kissed or sucked decomposing into sludge.

It wasn't just that she'd killed my cat. It was what she'd done to me before that, or helped me do to myself. Every time I tried to break loose from her she appeared in front of me, and diverted me to the side. She needed me to say I loved her, and manoeuvred me until I did, standing in her kitchen, at her office, and blurting it out in the hope that she'd stop crying. That was the only time I've ever lied in a sentence with that word in it, and it was the beginning of the end for me, the last time I could tell the difference between loving and not caring. That was when my feelings finally died, where I lost the battle to keep myself alive.

She was mad, but she was also a little girl who deserved and needed someone better than me. She killed my cat to try to keep me, and when I realised what she'd done I killed her back. I rang her up at work and hinted that I wouldn't mind an afternoon behind papered windows, and she'd purred and said she'd be there as soon as she could. I knew she would. Being fucked in the afternoon by someone she knew didn't care about her was exactly the kind of self-inflicted wound she was incapable of rejecting.

I was standing behind the door when she walked in, and brought a brick down on her head as hard as I could. It took a couple more blows to finish the job, but I got there in the end. I cut off part of her pointing finger to prove to myself that I was free, put it in my pocket and then just sat next to the hole I'd made in the floor.

I wrote the first of the letters in my head as I stayed with her that afternoon, a letter that I needed to write. In these years since Karen I've had someone in my mind, someone I will be able to care about, someone I will come back to life for. Yvonne hadn't been that woman, and neither were Mel or Jackie or Ginny. That woman had no name, no address. She was the best of all of them, the opposite of their worst, all of that and more. She was me, I suppose, transposed and set apart, an idea to comfort me across cold evenings and grey years. Sometimes I'd thought I could almost picture her, almost smell her skin.

But she was everyone, and no one, and I never found her.

In my head I wrote a letter to that woman, pretending she really existed. Maybe, for a while, I even believed she did. I went home and typed it, and then posted it to Tamsin Road. I didn't know where else to send it.

A few days later I came back, picked up the letter in the hallway and read it out to what was under the floorboards. As a punishment, I suppose. To show her what I would have written if she had been the one, if she hadn't got a name.

I wrote seven more letters, but on the last occasion I didn't come to read. By then it didn't seem so important, because I'd given up. The letters had started to follow their own course, to replicate the only kind I was capable of writing. I could make up dreams like going to Bourbon Street, but I couldn't carry them through. Without the nameless woman to hold me, I couldn't keep them alive. Soon afterwards I must have blanked it altogether.

I didn't kill Mel or Ginny or Jackie, in case you're wondering. They didn't kill my cat. I'm not a violent man. I was just trying to find someone who was never really there.

After I'd looked at the remains for long enough, I opened the bottle and tipped the finger joint out on to the floorboards. I picked it up and placed it as close as I could to what was left of her right hand. Then I took a pen from my pocket, wrote her name at the top of the letters and on the envelopes, and placed those in there with her. The letters had never been to Yvonne, or to anyone who'd really existed. But they had confused what was left of her, and until she knew her name, she wouldn't be able to go.

I kissed the tip of my finger and touched it to where her lips used to be, remembering for a moment how much fun she'd been in the beginning, how often she'd made me laugh. Then I replaced the floorboards one by one and moved the carpet back over them. I ground the bottle to fragments under my foot, took a last look round, and then left. The key I dropped down a gutter as I got into the car.

I spent two hours driving, but have no idea where I went. Round and round the backstreets, not paying attention, just trying to find my way back to the present. When I'd come far enough I pulled over at a public phonebox and called John.

Tamsin had already called him. Her boyfriend had returned, and she'd decided to stay with him. She felt it was for the best that they never see each other again. John sounded both relieved and mildly put out by the news. I said I'd call him soon.

I went home, changed my clothes, and then sat at my desk watching the clouds. After a while Jenny came home, and I stood up to give her a hug. I could see in her face when we parted that it hadn't been tight enough, but it was the best that I could do.

People always have names. Yvonne, or Jenny, in the end it doesn't make much difference.

Not tight enough is the best that I can do.

SHIPS

by

Michael Swanwick and Jack Dann

Jack Dann is author or editor of over thirty-five books. His short
fiction has appeared in *Asimov's Science Fiction Magazine*, *The
Magazine of Fantasy and Science Fiction*, *Omni*, *Playboy*, and
other venues. His latest novel is *The Memory Cathedral: A
Secret History of Leonardo da Vinci*. Forthcoming is an
omnibus collection of the novels *Starhiker*, *Junction* and *The
Man Who Melted*; a short-story collection entitled *Jubilee and
Other Stories*, and *Counting Coup*, a contemporary road novel.
Dann is also working on a novel about the American Civil War
entitled *The Silent*. Based in Melbourne, Australia, he 'com-
mutes' to New York.

Michael Swanwick's *Stations of the Tide* was honoured with
the Nebula Award in 1992. His works, alone and in collaboration, have been nominated for the Nebula Award nine times,
the Hugo Award four times, the Arthur C. Clarke Award and the
World Fantasy Award twice, and have won the Theodore
Sturgeon Award. His novels include *In the Drift*, *Vacuum
Flowers*, *Stations of the Tide* and *The Iron Dragon's Daughter*.
He has recently finished *Jack Faust*. His short fiction has been
collected in *Gravity's Angels*. He lives in Philadelphia, Pennsy-
lvania with his wife Marianne Porter and their son Sean.

This science fantasy is one of the stranger and least traditional
stories in this volume. It has a colourful and brutal cast of
characters sailing a most unusual ship. Think of it as a depraved,
surrealistic homage to Milton's *Paradise Lost*.

SHIPS

I was dead.

That before all: I was dead and buried. Time passed and I took no notice of it. My body rotted. The vermin of the earth came and feasted upon my flesh.

It was then that my third eye opened. An area in the centre of my wallet-brown skull seemed to melt, and my questioning vision stared upwards, seeing through the coffin, through the soil, through the roots of the grass above, seeing as clearly as ever I had when I was alive.

I knew my mind's eye was blue, though I could not say how I knew. Perhaps it was some sort of sympathetic magic, for I was staring at a clear blue sky that curved above me, flawless as the finest example of the ceramist's art. And though I well knew where I lay, I felt that I was at long last home.

I could remember my funeral, the incense, the last screams of . . . Anastasia? A woman, definitely. I could feel the wood and silk of the bier beneath me, mountains pressing upon me, even as the darkness swirled like wind, like smoke. I lay detached and emotionless, my thoughts slowly dissolving with death and my senses numbing into a synaesthesia of colour and sadness and memory and sound and

Then here. Blue eye. Open.

As the ships came towards me, skimming over sand, blowing slight tails in the dunes.

A kind of lightness seized me, lifting me up into the blue mirror of my eye. It was as if God had hooked a finger under my chin and held me dangling over the shimmering, the oceanic surface of my old life.

I waited.

The nearest of the ships, a three-decked frigate of a hundred guns, hove to, kicking up a light spray of golden sand. I thought I

felt a grain or two strike my face. The creatures aboard the ship
– demons? angels? – crowded the rails and hung from the
shrouds. A thin, almost skeletal figure stood on the raised
quarter-deck, looking-glass tucked under his arm.

With a pang of what emotion I now cannot say, I recognised
him.

It was me. What I was seeing was either a doppelganger, a
ghost . . . or else the real Auberon Chang.

For an instant, I felt a vertiginous turning, so that I became the
other Auberon Chang, standing aboard the frigate, and I thought
his thoughts, scanned the dunes with his baleful eyes, saw *me*.
Our shared imagination quailed at the sight. He saw an open
grave, violated brown bones, maggots caught as if in the webs of a
hundred spiders. But the webbing was rotting musculature, and
my skull was eyeless, for eyes were to the small workmen of the
soil a delicacy beyond even flesh. Thoughts turned to darkness,
emptiness, and when I awakened (as myself, as the Captain of
this impossible ship) I found myself on the forward deck, looking
out into the starry darkness.

The sands were far behind us. Incredibly, we were sailing in
the ebony blackness of space. The stars were so sharp and
bright, so hot and cold in their redness and demon-fire blues
that it hurt the eye to look into them. And below, far below,
the earth rotated like a blue dream, or a last thought.

'Sir! Permission to approach.'

I turned, middle fingers linked behind my back, and nodded
to the crewman waiting by the mainmast. He came to me,
hauling by the scruff of its neck a wretched thing, pallid and
afraid, but undeniably human. *The cabin-boy*, whispered a
voice in my head.

'This'n here was caught stealing food, sir.'

The cabin-boy twisted his head around suddenly, snorted as
if to clear his throat, and spat at me. It was a shocking gesture,
wild and suicidal. Wiping my face in disgust, I could not but
admire him for it.

'Take him aft,' I said (and all the while thinking how
pathetic a being this less-than-mannikin was, what a horrid
existence he must lead, how deserving he was of compassion).
'Have him hanged.'

*

The hanging was held as a formal discipline, with a colour guard and three drummers. The crew was assembled to watch as four demon sailors pulled the creature kicking and struggling into the air. They hauled on a rope that ran through a block-and-tackle hung from the fore yardarm and with each smooth motion the cabin-boy was jerked another yard higher. His hands had been tied behind his back. His face darkened from red to blue, a knot of agony. It was a gruesome sight.

'Enjoying yourself, Captain?'

I turned into the grinning, many-toothed face of the first mate. *Starbuck*, my interior voice whispered, *a most dangerous subordinate*. 'State your business, sir,' I said coldly.

His smirk retreated from his face, but lingered beneath the skin, like a hyena waiting just beyond the lion's reach. 'We've passed the beacon star, sir. It's time you opened our orders.'

'I'll be the judge of that, Mr Starbuck.'

'Yes, sir.'

'Have you so little to occupy your time, Mr Starbuck, that you must involve yourself in second-guessing your superior? Do the men find your supervision wholly superfluous?'

An involuntary snarl distorted Starbuck's narrow face before he could hide it with a bow. Chastened, he made his respects and backed away.

The cabin-boy's struggles were more desperate now. He had turned black, and blood poured from his nostrils – it made him seem a minor goblin. He could not die, of course – not here, not now – and so it was possible to extend his punishment as long as desired. For ever, if necessary.

'Cut him down,' I said at last. 'You know where to send him.'

When I returned to my quarters, three bells later, the cabin-boy was awaiting me. His eyes were red with hate, but he made no protest as I turned him around and pulled his ragged trousers from his smooth young flanks. He allowed me to bend him over the cot submissively enough, and made only a single gurgling noise – a whimper, almost – when I entered him and took my pleasure.

After I had slaked my lust, I poured water in a basin and laved my privates. Then I adjusted my clothing. The cabin-boy pulled up his rags and watched sullen and unblinking as I opened the ship's safe and removed the packet of instructions under which we sailed. It had been sealed in red wax with the Sigil of Baphomet. I tapped the parchment bundle thoughtfully against my lips.

'Brandy!' I snapped. 'And then get out!'

Alone, I sprawled in the captain's chair – mine was the only berth in the ship afforded this dignity – and drank deep from a cut-crystal tumbler. The liquor was as brown as amber and as delicious as old sins recalled in tranquillity.

I broke the seal.

The orders were brief and to the point. Nevertheless I studied them for a long time. Though I had long been expecting something of the sort, and had indeed argued for it in clandestine councils, still it was a shock to come upon the moment itself.

'Here it is, then,' I murmured.

With sudden resolution I strode up on deck. 'Starbuck!' I shouted. 'Assemble the crew!'

He materialised at my elbow. 'Twice in one watch? It's not good discipline, sir.' Eyes glittering with an avaricious hunger for me to show weakness or indecision. But I had a trick up my sleeve worth two of his.

'Bugger discipline! Line 'em up and serve out three tots of rum-and-sulfur for every man-jack of them.'

'Three!' Starbuck cried in involuntary amazement.

'Do it now, sir,' I said quietly.

In minutes the crew was assembled in crude, undisciplined ranks before the mainmast. Their grog was served out, and this effectively divided their attention between curiosity and anxiety for the devilish liquor they knew better than to drink before my command to do so. At my direction, Midshipman Coffin stood by the mast. The cabin-boy deposited a small chest at my feet.

'Mister Coffin!' I barked. 'Strike the colours.'

Demon mouths fell open in amazement, revealing arched rows of pointed teeth, fangs, tusks the hue of old ivory. Tattooed faces turned upwards, aghast. A Babel of hoarse whispers arose from all sides. Out of the corner of my eye I saw Starbuck's hand surreptitiously close around the hidden dagger he thought I didn't know about. The silk flag of the Old Order floated gracefully down, as white and delicate as a hanky dropped from an old lady's hand. From the chest I'd had removed from my cabin I drew forth new colours. Up they went.

The crew stared up at the banner under whose aegis we now sailed. It was as black and featureless as the black flag of anarchy. But the black of *our* flag held an infinitely more fearsome meaning.

A horror-struck silence descended upon the ship. Before it could break, I held out my hand. The cabin-boy placed in it a leather cup identical to those the crew themselves held. I raised it in a formal toast.

'Blood and damnation! Fuck the grail.'

I drained the thing in one gulp.

It took an effort to maintain my countenance, for the drink came from Hell's own cellars and was fit only for the degraded palates of such as sailed before the mast. But somehow I managed to keep a granite face. And the crew, nothing loath for a drink upon any occasion, knocked their own back.

While they were gasping and wheezing and laughing, I raised an eyebrow at Starbuck. He nodded to Coffin, who jumped atop the taffrail and whipped off his hat. 'Hip-hip –' he cried.

'*Huzzah!*' the crew roared.

'Hip-hip –'

'*Huzzah!*'

'Hip-hip –'

'*Huzzah!*'

I allowed myself a tight little smile of satisfaction. The moment when the men might have turned against me was past. They were mongrel curs to their very bones, with a cur's mentality: to attack upon show of weakness and to fawn and grovel before the hand that wielded the whip. I had acted with the high-handed assurance of a master of beasts. There would be no mutiny. My command was safe.

And we were rebels now.

Fuck the grail.

So began the great enterprise: with three cheers and a command to the steersman to abandon our prior course for a sharp veer into the starry wastes. Inevitably the first excitement of rebellion was swallowed up by the inescapable routines of duty, unchanged by our new status. Decks still needed swabbing, and sails trimming. Days, weeks, months, and years passed in the regular monotony of shipboard life, broken into dogwatches and the clocking tolling of bells and shrill of whistles. I grew to know and hate my officers and crew as intimately as they did me.

The strange transformation of the cabin-boy escaped my attention for so immoderately long a time that when I at last had my revelation, it was already undeniable in its nature.

It happened at the end of the third watch. I had seized the cabin-boy by the shoulders preparatory to entering him, and one hand slid forward and down to his chest, which I on occasion grasped and fondled during the act. Sliding under his loose tunic, it encountered what was unmistakably a woman's breast!

I drew back from him. He waited motionless, incurious.

'Strip,' I commanded.

I watched avidly as he obeyed. In the gloom, he might have been mistaken for a slender woman. His hips had widened. He now had, as I have said, slight breasts. There had been a general shifting of fatty deposits. In other, less obvious ways he was no longer entirely male.

Wonderingly, I lit a lantern and scrutinised his body with care. There was an unforced femininity to his form and features. His neck was long and smooth. The gentle swell of his belly brought back ancient, longing memories. His penis, for which I had no use, had shrivelled to the size of an infant's. He was all but hermaphroditic.

'How has this happened?' I demanded.

He shrugged. 'It's what you wanted.'

'Explain yourself!'

He gave me a look sharp as a fox's. 'Yer the Captain and I'm just the cabin-boy. You want something – what'm I s'posed to do? Might not want to obey. Ain't got no choice.'

I questioned him further, but he was a creature of little intellect. I was the Captain and that meant I got my way. In his simple philosophy, that explained all. Still . . .

Was it possible? Had my desires – my *needs* – been slowly altering the creature in the course of the endless series of sodomies I visited on his body? It seemed inevitable. Those same lusts that overmastered me, it would appear, were capable of overwhelming their object as well.

I laid him down on the cot upon his back for the first time and studied his form with a cold and unsympathetic eye. Then I entered him from between his legs, as I would have a woman.

'Let's get to work,' I growled. 'You have a long way to go.'

Within the year, the creature was no longer male. Its hair had, at my insistence, been left uncut and hung half way down its back. Its breasts, pale as alabaster and pink-tinged at the tips, were full as ripe pears, the skin fine to the point of translucency. Its vagina was a detailed work of art, identical in every respect to that of one particular woman from my long ago and otherwise forgotten past.

On the day when it was at last clear that no trace of its penis, of its maleness, remained, I asked a question I had never directed at it before. 'Do you have a name?'

It shook its head, not meeting my eyes. I took its chin between thumb and forefinger and lifted its gaze to meet mine. The coals of rebellion glowed therein, as hotly banked as ever. That I had very carefully left unchanged.

'I will call you Anastasia.'

She flushed, but said nothing.

'The body's done,' I told her then. 'Let's start working on the face.'

Already I could see the ghost of a different set of features lying just beneath the skin, like the face of a drowned woman glimpsed through murky water.

From that night on, Anastasia lived in my cabin; and like an artist who, knowing that a madonna resides within the stone he's working, chips away blindly until he 'finds' the form residing there, so did I mould her features, sometimes with fornications and sometimes with curses and beatings. I knew not what I wanted until the features manifested themselves in a series of tiny miracles of the flesh: pale blue eyes flecked with silver, hair as black as obsidian, a swarthy complexion. A narrow, aquiline nose and high cheekbones combined with a full mouth and a heart-shaped face to give her the appearance of a feral saint, the obscene sweetness of an angel blessed – or cursed – with free will.

She lay beside me when I slept, and upon awakening I would examine her to see what had changed, what had become defined, what had become more perfect, for her journey was to nothing less than perfection. Long before she was done, she was so beautiful that it hurt me to look upon her.

I talked with her for hours, teaching her to respond as Anastasia herself would. I gave her warmth and intelligence and a certain calculating curiosity. I gave her a smile so bewitching it made me want to wrap my hands lovingly about her throat and choke her senseless. I formed her mind as carefully as I did her body.

When she accompanied me topside, the crew would stare at her with the flat, cannibalistic gaze of a hungry rat considering its own children. She held herself stiffly then, chin high, trying in vain to hide her fear from me. She was never – never! – more deliciously desirable to me than she was then. Back in my cabin, I would take her while the terror still flowed from her body in great waves of pheromones.

I was living in a fool's paradise.

The watches passed, the men rotating like the dark hands of a clock that was the frigate itself, measuring out the futile parsecs of eternity. We sailed beyond the final dim stars of existence and into the void beyond. And there came at last a day when a thin line of light appeared in the distance, almost impossible to see, bisecting the universe.

The cliffs of Heaven.

The cliffs grew, incandescent white and brighter than any sun, for month upon month. By imperceptible degrees they towered so high over the ships that their tops could not be seen without looking up. Sunglasses were doled out to all the crew, and even so the cliffs could not be looked at directly for long without the eyes watering.

The mere sight of that ancient stronghold of the great Enemy sent the crew into frenzies of loathing. In their emotional state they committed even more atrocities than usual. Disciplines, floggings, tortures, became a daily entertainment. Yet, 'We're detecting no more than one crime in ten,' Starbuck reported.

'Then punish 'em ten times over for those you do.'

Black specks against the more-than-Arctic dazzle, the gathering fleets were at first no more significant than a swarm of midges set upon attacking a continent.

But as more and more ships joined the gathering, by the dozens at first, and then the hundreds, congregating into the thousands and millions, the brightness diminished. We grew into the billions, and became a great cloud, a storm, and still we grew. Our numbers surpassed comprehension. The wave of hatred that preceded us was like a great fist smashing into Heaven's face. The cliffs cracked and shattered, crumbling, into the void even before we reached them.

By the time we passed the coastline our armada seemed not just a threat but Fate itself.

Midshipman Coffin had good reason to believe that he would not prosper were Starbuck first-in-command. So it was he I chose to operate the capstan that lowered me in a rope-and-basket contraption alongside Sophonisba, the frigate's painted figurehead. She was an enormous carving, three times my own height, and I felt ridiculously diminished dangling before her, one hand clapped to my hat lest it blow away and the other clutching a little iron hatchet.

Imperiously, I rapped with the blunt end of the hatchet on the nearer of the figurehead's matronly breasts.

With a groan of pain her lips moved. 'Why did you awaken me?' she asked. 'When will you let me die?' I swung slightly in the stellar breezes and quickly wrapped my hatchet-arm around one of the basket's guy wires. Her eyes remained dull and wooden.

'Prophesy for me.'

'Death,' she said. 'Damnation. Eternity. Futility. All this you knew long ago and without my intervention. If you will not let me die, then at least let me sleep.'

Outraged, I slammed her cheek. The hatchet bounced off, leaving behind a gash in the wood. 'Awaken! The fleets are gathering. This is not the universe as it once was. Stretch your thoughts, look out across the plains of destiny. Give me tidings dire enough to glut my hunger for them. Tell me of horrors too fearsome to hear.'

Now, as if a disguising mist had blown away from her, a knowing light kindled in Sophonisba's eyes and her wooden substance was transported briefly to flesh. Blood trickled down from the hatchet-scratch but she paid it no mind. A wondering expression came over her. Where her gaze went, mine could not follow.

'Speak!'

She said nothing at first, and then: 'I see angels dying. I see your ship destroyed and its crew as well. All that is good will be defiled; all that is evil will come to naught; I see destruction without purpose and desolation without end.'

I could not help but gloat. This was better than I had dared hope for. 'More!' I demanded. 'Tell me more – and worse. Make me despair.'

Sophonisba nodded, all but invisibly, and her lips moved.

'Why did you agree to this?' she said. It was Starbuck's voice, sullen and suspicious. 'If Captain Chang were to discover us – and in his own berth!'

A trill of laughter such as could have come from but one throat. 'What does it matter to you, little man? You'd spit in the Captain's soup if you had the chance. Are you afraid to fuck his whore?'

I screamed.

'You lie, you lie, you lie!' Sophonisba's face was lifeless again, and I was slamming it repeatedly with the hatchet. In my fury I smashed off her nose entirely and splintered both eyes blind, rendering her permanently useless to the ship. Then I was roaring to Coffin to crank up the basket, crank up the basket, the damnable basket, damn you sir, up!

Sophonisba did not lie.

Starbuck lay, hairy-bellied and naked, upon the formerly crisp linen of my own sheets while Anastasia crouched over him, sucking his soul out through the conduit of his filthy little spigot.

My thoughts were like rabbits fleeing from dogs, scattering across empty fields in futile quest of a safe cranny. A single lamp glowed, flickering with every movement of the ship, which was considerable, for our inverse tau was enormous now as we continually closed upon the limiting speed of light. Even as I

stood, hatchet raised, before Starbuck and Anastasia, overwhelmed with blood lust and horribly, unspeakably, *enjoying*
it, stars were being born before the bow and dying in our wake.

With a shriek Anastasia leaped from the bed, yanking the
sheet after her. It hid one breast, one thigh, a parody of modesty.
Leaving her lover uncovered and vulnerable to my eye. And
helpless before my hatchet.

I chopped off his hands.

I hacked out his liver and his heart. I sliced through the
tendons on the backs of his calves so that he must henceforward
not walk as a man but crawl as does a serpent. His cock and balls
I flung out of the porthole into the great vacuum mouth of the
universe.

Finally I gouged out both of Starbuck's eyes and cast them
after his privates. Let him stare for ever into infinitude and
glory. Let him suffer.

Leaving his mewling remains behind, I seized Anastasia by
the wrist. I could smell Starbuck's musky sweat all over her,
like rot in salt-pork.

I hauled her, naked and squealing, to the forward hold. The
only light came from a single green-glass bull's eye lantern.
Demon sailors started to their feet at my entry, rolling down
from hammocks, rising from dice games and rat-baitings. 'You
dog-fucking bastard!' Anastasia raged. 'I'll make you crawl for
this. Oh, sweet suffering, the things I'll make you do!'

I flung her down before the crew.

Some things are too vile to describe. I stood watching until
there was not the least remnant of humanity left in the thing
that had for a brief span been Anastasia.

Then I left.

Time passed. The watches accumulated like pearls deposited by
divers.

One night I was wrenched awake from the cold dreamlessness
of sleep by a great pain in my temples. I pressed my hands
against them, as if the pressure could keep my head from
bursting open. In the shaving mirror upon the wall I saw that my
forehead was purple and bruised and my face swollen, as if from
a hundred agonising blows. I could hear my teeth cracking and
feel my jaw begin to break as the side of my face tore open.

Something inside my skull was struggling to get out, striving to be born.

In a frenzy, I threw open my medical kit and seized a vial of heroin. I cooked the solution and prepared a syringe with a long, curved needle designed for this express purpose. Then, peeling back an eyelid, I slid the needle between eye and socket and shot its load directly into my brain.

It took three slugs to lay the pain to rest.

I was sitting on my berth considering what to do next when the air was split by the shrilling and brazen clangour of every whistle and bell in the fleet being sounded at once. The thunder of cannons and demon drums swelled and merged into a roar the like of which had not been heard since that Word was spoken which began existence by shattering the primal mono-block. I leaped up, heart pounding, exultant.

The battle had at last begun.

We were in the vanguard of the fleet, right on the front line, but even so there was time to prepare. I had the ship's carpenter fasten an iron band about my forehead so that whatever lay within could not escape, and then turned my attention to the conversion of my ship. The internal bulkheads were taken down and the gunnery crew ran out the cannons. Weapons were served out to our marines and the fire-buckets filled with sand.

With a mighty creaking and groaning, the ship began to absorb the masts and extrude wings. Chitinous plates accreted over the hull and antennae sprouted above the mandibles at the prow. All around us ships were growing simple and compound eyes, proboscises, gaiters, stings, and ovipositors, legs and tibia and spiracles, each according to its nature and genus. Steam issued from the cannon barrels and filthy holds still damp from piss and sweat. One by one the chittering voices of our unholy vessels rose up, merging into a single howl of despairing wrath.

My ship was the first to land on the icy desert plain.

Our multitudes rained down, frigates and cruisers and schooners and galleys and bomb vessels: ships of the line, swift chargers and cumbersome gunboats, all become locusts, hornets, wasps, mantises . . . Folding their wings and striding forward to ravage the fields of eternity. Marines crawled like ants down their ropes by the millions to defile the golden sands with shit and sacrilege. Briefly, we were unopposed.

Then the lookout screamed in rage and fear as a storm of angels kited up from the distant mountains. These were the lowliest of the adversarial forces: its cherubim, those spirits so beautiful they were physically nauseating to look upon; gleaming towers of muscle and steel, wheels of whirling blades, hallowed and perfect; wings that billowed like sails, of such delicate construction that a soap bubble would be considered gross by comparison. Serene and pitiless eyes.

'Mister Coffin!' I cried. 'Ready a salvo. On my word.'

The closest of our enemies raised their lances. Needles of ruby light pierced carapace and armour plating. The boatswain's mate fell screaming to the deck, black bile gushing from his chest and back. Midshipman Coffin raised his hands to his mouth to form a megaphone. I glared them down. 'Steady!' I barked. 'Not yet.'

The sacred *pneuma* rose up from our assailants in an invisible, lilac-scented cloud, driving the lesser demons mad and causing others to retch blood. 'Not yet,' I repeated. We could not fight them with bullets and shot, for we were *materia*, the real, the tangible, and that would be relinquishing one's essence, one's flesh and inner self to our opponents. But hermetic science (and swords and fists) would suffice to rid us of their oppression for ever.

'Fire!'

The cannons blasted billows of black smoke into the attacking ranks. I had had them loaded with ancient injustices – the tears of the innocent, the screams of children, the prayers of the betrayed – and they wrought massive destruction upon the cherubim, who fell, broken, down the welling light to a land that blackened under them, each blasted angel staining and despoiling great swathes of the infinite plains.

So went the battle, bloody and disastrous for both sides. We were so perfectly matched that our struggle could only end in mutual and universal annihilation. But the advantage was ours, for it was the black flag of Annihilation under which we sailed, and the final end to suffering and punishment we sought. Our ships, driven by the strength of resentments older than the universe itself, cut through the Enemy in phalanxes, crushing with thoraxes wet with blood, spearing with claw and comb. An immense wasp exploded by our starboard bow and its crew were picked off before they hit the sands, eviscerated, mutilated, and eaten by the vengeful Defenders. A broadside caught an archangel square in the eye and he went down in explosions and gouts of blue flame.

I was the rattle and the sabre. The fleets radiated out from my perfect fury like iron filings caught in a magnetic field. I was the very centre, the focus, the eye of the hurricane. The children of wrath flocked to me like moths, and like moths they died in untellable numbers and unspeakable agony.

We fought for aeons.

Until finally, having exhausted all the ship's powder and its crew as well, Midshipman Coffin and I stood shoulder-to-shoulder on the blood-slick deck, faced with one final invading angel – a seraph. It was possible that he was the last of his kind.

The angel's strength was prodigious. With one blow of his fist he crushed Coffin and swept his body over the rail. With a second, he smashed my cutlass to flinders.

Dropping the hilt, I threw myself at the seraph; we locked arms about each other. My rib splintered and cracked. Machine oil dribbled from his jaw and puffs of steam leaked from his joints. He forced that beautiful and pitiless face so close to mine I could see nothing else and murmured, 'Look into my eyes.'

Startled, I did. In all that inhuman visage of titanium and steel, only the eyes were organic. They were set into gimbals, held in place by pronged needles, and manipulated by gears and servomechanisms. Even so, I recognised them.

They were Starbuck's.

Those eldritch eyes blazed with amusement at my shocked recognition. Fleetingly I felt that what I fought was no more than an automaton, a marionette, the cat's-paw for forces beyond my comprehension. That all this, my glory and all-destroying triumph, were no more than a cruel and pointless shadow-play. Then I overbalanced and fell, pulling the seraph with me to the deck. For an instant my arm was free.

I seized the broken hilt of my cutlass and ran its twelve inches of jagged blade into the angel's abdomen. Hot ichor steamed over my clenched fist. For a long moment we lay thus, locked in homicidal embrace, and it was good, oh very good indeed, this moment was, far better than ever sex had been.

But even as I savoured my victory, the Starbuck-eyed seraph rose up beneath me one last time. His blow was like lightning! I ducked its full force, but still his fist glancingly struck my forehead – and the iron band shattered!

Underneath me, laughing, the angel crumbled to nothing.

My pain was beyond expressing.

I rose to my knees, clutching my head in agony. I screamed as flesh extruded from flesh, essence from essence, physical being from the stuff of my own body. Weeping bloody tears, I could barely look at the separate thing that arose from me, even as it tore the umbilicus of flesh connecting us. Liquids gushed away, weakening me, strengthening *her*.

Anastasia.

She rose up before me, shaping herself even as I watched. Wet and slick as a newborn infant, but proud, fearless – a warrior queen. She was infinitely stronger than I; she had clarified. Her body, nude, was less flesh than light; radiance itself, a steady candle. I groped for a weapon, any weapon, even as the ship, creaking and groaning, shifted underfoot.

Asastasia kicked me in the side. Ribs splintered.

I screamed.

She seized me by the pigtail and hauled me, struggling, to my feet. 'Where is my body?'

'I –'

She struck me in the face. Blood and spittle flew. 'Don't talk – go!'

Half-blind with pain, I led Anastasia down into my dreadful vessel's hollow innards. The hold was lit only by the feeble phosphorescence of its dying flesh. In the trembling dark, a-reek with gore and maggots, I sought out the mutilated remains of what had once been Anastasia and before her the cabin-boy.

It had been kept in an airless closet with a single bucket used to bring its slops and remove its leavings. When I unlocked the door, I was hit with the stench of gangrene. It had lost both legs and arms; the stumps were tied up with leather thongs. Its dugs were empty sacks, its face a noseless horror black with necrosis.

That blind and fish-mouthed face gaping up at me, idiotic in its misery, was all but unrecognisable.

Anastasia drew in her breath with a short, sharp hiss. But she only said, 'Carry her.'

I picked the body up and discovered that it was almost liquescent. It sloshed like an overripe pear. Anastasia walked us to the sailmaker's cupboard and from it took needles, canvas and leather. Swiftly, she fashioned a kind of saddle for her one-time body and a harness for me.

'Strip,' she commanded.

I obeyed.

Her body stirred slightly. A sort of coughing noise hacked and rattled in its chest and for a horrified instant I thought it was laughing at me. But then in a tiny, mewling voice, it said, 'I want . . . I want . . .'

'Hush.' Anastasia's voice and face were like stone. 'I know what you want.' She called upon her powers and was abruptly clothed again, in the good wool of my second-best dress uniform. She hung a gilt-framed mirror in the air and fluffed the jabot so that the lace stood up crisp and white. Her hair she briskly brushed and pulled back into a pony-tail. She dashed on a touch of scent and made certain that the bow was perfectly straight.

Smiling her wrath, she turned upon me.

What at last she was done amusing herself, I was strapped and saddled like a mule. Her body was placed on my back.

Anastasia slapped me on the rump. 'Move!'

We made our way up on deck. The corpses of my crew were strewn about. I looked upon them and felt nothing. Beyond, the immense insect-ships were breaking up and burning on the sands. Brown as lacquered wood, they kicked and struggled like dying cockroaches, their substance shifting in the golden light, disintegrating, degrading, rotting. The stench was terrible, the stink of elimination pits and extermination camps. So far as I could see, only we two had survived the holocaust.

We passed through the silent battle-grounds.

Gagged, harnessed, and bent over by the weight of Anastasia's mutilated body, I made my painful way across the sterile plains of Heaven.

*

How long did we travel? Hours? Days? Centuries? We did not
sleep and there were no events to divide the eternal emptiness of
the desert sands. I began the trek rabid with humiliation and
inwardly raving for revenge. But the unvarying drudgery of
passage leached away my passions a breath at a time, until all
my past took on the unreality of a story told one time too many
and I began to forget even my own name.

Finally, my senses numbed and emotions at zero, we came to
a place where the unvarying sands stretched to infinity to all
points of the compass. A place where all directions were one.

Anastasia's body was finally and undeniably dead. She unsad-
dled it and lowered it to the ground. Then she created a shovel
and thrust it in my hands.

'Dig!' she commanded.

I delved the hole true and to the square: eight feet long, four
feet wide, and six feet deep, with straight edges and crisp
corners. Even Anastasia could find no fault with my work.

Her corpse lay alongside the grave. When I was done, she
edged a foot underneath and unceremoniously rolled it in. It fell
face upward.

Dead blue eyes stared up at me.

In that dizzying, vertiginous instant I remembered everything. All this had happened before, not once but innumerable
times. Always to the same weary conclusion.

Exhausted and drained of emotion as I was, I would have made
my peace with Anastasia if I could. But after all I had done to her,
what overtures of mine would she accept? What words were
sweet enough, grovelling enough, *true* enough? None that
human tongue had yet spoken.

Still – the alternative was unthinkable. I had to try.

But as I turned to speak, I saw Anastasia fade away, like
smoke, like wind, like darkness.

And when I looked back, there were ships coming across the
sands. I saw and, seeing, understood and, understanding, des-
paired.

The ships skimmed lightly over the golden sands, blowing
slight tails in the dunes. A fresh and untouched flotilla,
amnesiac, flagged by a schooner whose rails and shrouds were
thronged with grotesques who were all aspects of a single
woman. One among them, I knew, would love me despite

herself – and pay dearly for doing so. The captain stood on the raised quarter-deck, looking-glass tucked under her arm, harshly beautiful, eyes stern beyond all reason. It was Anastasia's turn again.

This time the ships were hers.

This time we would sail to Hell.

AFTERWORD

According to Jack Dann, 'Ships' came to life as a literary game on the Genie Information services. 'Michael Swanwick dropped into my topic some time in 1994 and typed in the first four lines of what was to become our story. Then he challenged me to best what he had written. This was a case of write or be humiliated online. Old-world macho in cyberspace. I couldn't resist, and we wrote several more parapraphs back and forth on Genie. I thought that was the end of it . . . until I received the first nine pages in the mail. Michael had done an initial conforming draft of the opening . . . which I took back to Australia. The rest of the story was written – and brainstormed – on e-mail.'

THE DREADFUL DAY OF JUDGEMENT

by

Ruth Rendall

Ruth Rendell is a major writer of psychological suspense novels. She has won three Edgar Awards from the Mystery Writers of America and four Golden Daggers from England's Crime Writers' Association, and is the author of over thirty novels, including *Going Wrong*, *Live Flesh*, *The Crocodile Bird*, *Simisola* and *The Keys to the Street*, and as Barbara Vine, *A Dark Adapted Eye*, *A Fatal Inversion*, *Gallowglass*, *Anna's Book* and *No Night is Too Long*. In addition, she has published six collections of short stories.

'The Dreadful Day of Judgement' takes place in a setting most readers would prefer to avoid – a cemetery. The story was originally published in Rendell's collection *The Fever Tree*.

THE DREADFUL DAY OF
JUDGEMENT

There were four of them working in the cemetery. They were employed by the city corporation – to do what? Even the foreman was vague about their duties which had not been very precisely specified. Not to clear the central part, certainly, for that would have been a task not for four but for four hundred. And a wild life sanctuary, for which purpose it was designated, must be wild. To tidy it, then, to remove the worst signs of vandalism, to carry away such gravestones as had fallen, to denude certain of the many winding paths of the intrusive bramble and ivy and nettle. When they asked the foreman whether this should be done or that, he would say to use their own judgement, he couldn't be sure, he would find out. But he never did. Sometimes an official from the corporation came and viewed the work and nodded and disappeared into the hut with the foreman to drink tea. As the winter came on the official appeared less often, and the foreman said it was a hopeless task, they needed more men, but the corporation could no longer afford to spend the money, they must just do the best they could.

The hut was just inside the main gates. The foreman had a plan of the cemetery pinned to the wall next to Gilly's calendar of the girl in the transparent nightdress. He had a kettle and a spirit stove, but the cups and the teapot had been brought by Marlon who got them from his mother. The hut was always hot and smelly and smoky. The foreman chain-smoked and so did Marlon, although he was so young, and everywhere in the hut were saucers full of ash and cigarette stubs. One day Gilly, who didn't smoke, brought into the hut a tin can he had found in an open vault. The foreman and Marlon seemed pleased to have a new, clean ashtray, for they never considered emptying he others but let them fill up and spill about the floor.

'Marlon'd be scared stiff if he knew where that came from,' said John. 'He'd die of fright.'

But Gilly only laughed. He found everything about the cemetery funny, even the soldiers' graves, the only well-tended ones, that the Imperial War Graves Commission still looked after. In the beginning he had amused himself by jumping out on Marlon from behind a monument or a pillared tomb, but the foreman, lethargic as he was, had stopped that because Marlon was not quite as they were, being backward and not able to read or write much.

The main gates hung between what the foreman called stone posts but which John alone knew were Corinthian columns. A high wall surrounded the cemetery, which was of many acres, and the periphery of it, a wide space just inside the wall, had been cleared long before and turfed and planted with trees that were still tiny. This was to be a public park for the townsfolk. It was the centre, the deep heart of the place, once the necropolis for this mercantile city, that was to be left for the birds and such small animals who would venture in and stay.

Many species of bird already nested in the ilexes and the laurels, the elms and the thin, silver-trunked birch trees. Crows with wings like black fans, woodpeckers whose tap-tap-tapping could be heard from the almost impenetrable depths, little birds which even John couldn't name and which crept rather than hopped over the lichen on the fallen stones. It was silent in there but for the rare rustle of wings or the soft crack of a decayed twig dropping. The city lay below, all round, but in winter it was often masked by fog, and it was hard to believe that thousands lived down there and worked and scurried in glare and noise. Their forbears' tombs stood in rows or gathered in clusters or jostled each other haphazardly: domed follies, marble slabs, granite crosses, broken columns, draped urns, simple stones, all overgrown and shrouded and half-obscured. Not a famous name among them, not a memorable title, only the obscure dead, forgotten, abandoned, capable now of nothing more than to decree a hush.

The silence was violated by Gilly's talk. He had one topic of conversation, but that one was inexhaustible and everything recalled him to it. A name on a tomb, a scrap of verse on a gravestone, a pair of sparrows, the decorously robed statue of an angel. 'Bit of all right, that one,' he would say, stroking the stone flesh of a weeping muse, his hands so coarse and calloused that John wondered how any real woman could bear them to touch her. Or, lifting the ivy from a grave where lay a matron who had married three times, 'Couldn't get enough of it, could she?' And these reflections led him into endless reminiscences of the women he had had, those he now possessed, and anticipations of those awaiting him in the future.

Nothing stayed him. Not the engraved sorrow of parents mourning a daughter dead at seventeen, not the stone evocations of the sufferings of those dead in childbirth. Some of the vaults had been despoiled and left open, and he would penetrate them, descending subterranean stairs, shouting up to John and Marlon from the depths that here was a good place to bring a girl. 'Be OK in the summer. There's shelves here, make a good bed, they would. Proper little boudoir.'

John often regretted the thing he had done which made Gilly admire him. It had been on his first day there. He knew, even before he had done it, that this was to show them he was different from them, to make it clear from the start that he was a labourer only because there was no other work obtainable for such as he. He wanted them to know he had been to a university and was a qualified teacher. The shame and humiliation of being forced to take this unskilled work ate into his soul. They must understand his education had fitted him for something higher. But it had been a foolish vanity.

There had been nothing in the deep cavity any more but stones and dead leaves. But he had jumped in and held up a big pitted stone and cried ringingly: 'That skull had a tongue in it and could sing once. How the knave jowls it to the ground, as if 'twere Cain's jawbone that did the first murder!'

Gilly stared. 'You make that up yourself?'

'Shakespeare,' he said. 'Hamlet,' and the awe on Gilly's unformed pug-nosed face made him go on, excited with success, a braggart in a squalid pit. 'Prithee, Horatio, tell me one thing. Dost thou think Alexander looked o' this fashion i' the earth? And smelt so? pah!'

Marlon had gone white, his face peaked between the falls of thin yellow hair. He wore a heavy blue garment, a kind of anorak, but it gave him a medieval look standing there against

the chapel wall, an El Greco sky flowing above its tower, purple
and black and rushing in scuds above this northern Toledo. But
Gilly was laughing, begging John to go on, and John went on,
playing to the groundlings, holding the stone aloft. 'Alas, poor
Yorick . . .' until at last he flung it from him with the ham
actor's flourish, and up on the path again was being clapped on
the back by Gilly and told what a brain he'd got. And Gilly was
showing what he was and what all that had meant to him by
demanding to have that bit again, the bit about the lips that I
have kissed I know not how oft.

Marlon hadn't laughed or congratulated him. Bewildered,
frightened by the daring of it and the incomprehensibility, he
fumbled to light a fresh cigarette, another of the sixty he would
smoke that day. Cigarettes were all he had, a tenuous hold on
that real world in which his mother, sixteen years before, had
named him after a famous actor. The smoke flowed from his
loose lips. In a way, but for that cigarette, he might have been an
actor in a miracle play perhaps or in a chorus of madmen. On
that day as on all the others that followed, he walked behind
them as they made their way back through the shaded aisles,
under the leather-leaved ilexes, between the little houses of the
dead.

In the hut there was tea to be drunk, and then home, the
foreman off to his semidetached and his comfortable wife,
Marlon to his mother and stuffy rooms and television commer-
cials, John to his bedsit, Gilly (as John, the favoured, was not
privileged to be told) to the arms of a casino owner's wife whose
husband lacked a gravedigger's virility.

The chapel was built of yellowish-grey stones. It had an
octagonal nave, and on its floor thin, hair-like grass grew up
between the flags. To one of its sides was attached a square
tower, surmounted at each angle by a thin ornamented spire.
The four spires, weather-worn, corroded, stained, were like four
needles encrusted with rust. The workmen used the chapel as a
repository for pieces of broken stone and iron rails. Even Gilly's
bullying could not make Marlon go inside. He was afraid of
Gilly and the foreman, but not so afraid as he was of the echoing
chapel and of the dust beneath his feet.

Gilly said, 'What'd you do, Marl, if you turned round now and
it wasn't me here but a skeleton in a shroud, Marl?'

'Leave him alone,' said John, and when they were alone in the nave, 'You know he's a bit retarded.'

'Big words you use, John. I call him cracked. D'you know what he said to me yesterday? All of them graves are going to open up and the dead bodies come out. On some special day that's going to be. What day's that then? I said. But he only wobbled his head.'

'The dreadful Day of Judgement,' said John, 'When the secrets of all hearts shall be revealed.'

'Wouldn't suit me, that. Some of them old skulls'd blush a bit if I told them what I'd been getting up to last night. The secrets of all hearts? Open some of them up and I'd have a good many blokes on my track, not to mention that old git, you-know-who. Break his bloody roulette wheel, he would.'

'Over your head, no doubt,' said John.

'A short life and a randy one, that's what I say.' They came out into the cold, pale sunlight. 'Here, have a shufty at this. Angelina Clara Bowyer, 1816 to 1839. Same age as what you are, mate, and she'd had five kids! Must have worn her old man out.'

'It wore her out,' said John and he seemed to see her with her piled plaited hair and her long straight dress and the consumption in her face. He saw the young husband mourning among those five bread-and-butter-fed children, the crêpe on his hat, the black coat. Under a sky like this, the sun a white puddle in layered cloud, he came with the clergyman and the mourners and the coffin-bearers to lay her in the earth. The flowers withered in the biting wind – or did they bring flowers to funerals then? He didn't know, and not knowing broke the vision and brought him back to the clink of spade against granite, the smell of Marlon's cigarette, Gilly talking, talking, as boringly as an old woman of her aches and pains only he was talking of sex.

They always stopped work at four now the dusk came early. 'Nights are drawing in,' said the foreman, brewing tea, filling up with dog ends the can Gilly had found in the grave.

'When'll we get it over with?' Marlon faltered, coming close to the stove, coughing a little.

Depends on what we've got to get over,' said the foreman. 'Digging a bit here, clearing a bit there. My guess is that council fellow'll come round one of these days and say, That's it, lads, now you can leave it to the squirrels.'

Gilly was looking at his calendar, turning over the November nightdress girl to the December Santa Claus girl. 'If I had my way they'd level it all over, the centre bit, and put grass down, make the whole place a park. That's healthy, that is. Somewhere a young kid could take his girl. Lover's Lane Park, that'd be a good name. I'd like to see real birds there, not them bloody crows.'

'You can't do that,' said Marlon. 'There's the dead people in there.'

'So what? There was dead people round the edges, but they took them up. They done something – what they call it, John?'

'They deconsecrated the ground.'

'Hear what John says? He's educated, he knows.'

Marlon got up, the cigarette clinging to his lip. 'You mean they dug them up? There was others and they dug them up?'

''Course they did. You didn't think they was under there, did you?'

'Then where'll they be when the Day comes? How'll they lift up the stones and come out?'

'Here, for Christ's sake,' said the foreman, 'that's enough of that, young Marlon. I don't reckon your mum'd better take you to church no more if that's what you come out with.'

'They must come out, they must come and judge,' Marlon cried, and then the foreman told him sharply to shut up, for even he could be shaken by this sort of thing, with the darkness crowding in on the hut, and the heart of the cemetery a black mound horned by the spires of the chapel.

John wondered what church Marlon went to, that of some strange sect perhaps. Or was it only his incomplete brain that distorted the accepted meaning of the Day of Judgement into this version of his own? The resentful dead, the judging dead, lying censorious in the earth.

For his part, he had at first seen the cemetery as no more than a wooded knoll and the stones no more than granite outcroppings. It was not so now. The names in inscriptions, studied by him quietly or derisively read out by Gilly, evoked images of their bearers. James Calhoun Stokes, 1798–1862, Merchant of this City; 'Upright in all his dealings, he stood firm to meet his

Maker'. Gilly had an obscene rendering of that, of course. Thomas Charles Macpherson, 1802–79, Master Builder; 'Blest are the Pure in Heart'. Lucy Matilda Osborne, 1823–96; 'Her submissive duty to her husband and devotion to her sons was exceeded only by her pious adoration of her God'. John saw them in cutaway coats, in bombazine gowns, or night-capped on their deathbeds.

But Marlon saw them as a magisterial procession. Listening, watching, waiting perhaps for the ultimate outrage.

'What a load of old cobblers! You'll be down there yourself soon, all the fags you get through in a day.' Gilly sat on a toppled stone, laughing. He had been telling John more about the casino man's wife, trying to find among the statues they had piled up one whose figure might be comparable to hers. Britannias, muses, embodiments of virtues or arts, they lay prostrate, their blank grey or bronze faces all staring upwards at the clouded sky.

'What are we going to do with them?' Marlon said in the voice that was as desperate when he asked about trivialities as when he gave his prophet-like cries.

'Ask the foreman,' said John.

'He won't bloody know.' And Gilly lifted on to his lap the bronze that was nearly nude, just veiled over her loins with metal drapery. 'Randy old devil, he must have been, that Sidney George Whatsit, having her sitting on top of him when he was dead.'

'He was a historian, the plaque says,' said John. 'She's supposed to be Clio, the Muse of History. That's why she's got a scroll in her hand.' And then, because he was bored with Gilly and afraid for Marlon, 'Let's stick them all in the chapel till the council guy comes.'

But Gilly refused to abandon the huge joke of caressing the bronze. Every reachable inch of her anatomy was examined until, suddenly, he jumped up, leaving her to roll into one of the muddy ruts the truck had made, and ran up to the pillared monument from whose dome she had toppled. He stood inside, a satyr, John thought, in a temple defiled by northern rains. He threw up his arms.

'I said you was a randy old goat, Sidney, and so you was! I had a bird called Clio once myself, real hot stuff.' His shouts

punctured the thick greyness, the silence, the fog-textured air.
He leapt down the steps, kicking a gravestone here, a marble urn
there, and perched on a broken column. 'Come out, all the lot of
you, if you want, only you can't because you're bloody dead!'

And then Marlon made a horrible sound, the moan a man
makes in sleep, in a nightmare, when he thinks he is screaming.
He got into the cab of the truck and hunched there.

'You stupid bastard.' John picked up Marlon's fallen cigarette
packet, brushed the grit off it. 'D'you have to act like a kid of
ten?'

'Got to get some sort of kick out of this dump,' Gilly said
sulkily. 'Dead-end hole.'

'Well, that's what it is, isn't it? What d'you expect? A bar?
Booze? Bring on the dancing girls?'

Gilly started to laugh again, picked up his muse again. 'I
wouldn't mind this dancing girl. Don't reckon they'd miss her,
do you? She'd look OK in my place. I could stand her on the
table.'

'What for?'

'People have statues, don't they? They've got them in the
town hall. It'd give my place a bit of class.'

'Come on,' said John, 'let's stick the lot of them in the chapel.
The foreman'll do his nut if he sees you going off with that. She's
too big to go under your jacket.'

So they piled the statues and the urns into the chapel, and
Gilly amused himself by shouting insults and obscenities
which the lofty walls echoed back at him, black pigeons, white
doves flapping from the crannies in fear.

'What d'you do in that room of yours, John? Must be a real
drag all on your own night after night. Fancy coming over to my
bird's place? She's got a real dishy friend. We could have
ourselves a ball, and I don't mean wining and dining.'

No, thanks, John said, and softened his refusal by saying he
had to study which impressed Gilly. It wasn't that he was a
prude so much as that the idea of association with Gilly's
friends offended some snobbish delicacy in his nature, some
fastidiousness. Better the speechless company of James
Calhoun Stokes and Angelina Bowyer and the historian, better,
in the evenings, the dreams of them and the wonderings about
their lost lives. Though, in refusing, he thought it likely that

brash insensitive Gilly might not take his no for an answer but
turn up one night with his girl and that other girl to rout him
out. He feared it a little, but not with Marlon's obsessional dread
of threats from another world.

When at last Gilly did come, it was on a cold moonlit night,
and he came alone.

'I'm going to split,' said Gilly, 'I'm getting the hell out. All
good things come to an end. You can tell the foreman in the
morning, OK? I'm going south. I've got a girl in London,
worships the ground I tread on, poor cow. She'll take me in. But
that's between you and I, right?'

'But why?'

'He's found out, her old man, and I reckon he'll have his
heavies out gunning for me. He's beat her up – bunch of bloody
gangsters that lot are. I'll miss her.' The tears stood in his eyes,
and John stared, amazed, confounded. 'Poor cow,' said Gilly, the
epithet an endearment, a caress.

'D'you want me to come to the station with you?'

'No need for that. I only come in to tell you to tell the
foreman. Anyway, I got something to do first, get that statue,
that Clio. The train don't go till eleven, and I want her.' He
turned half away. 'For a souvenir like, she's the dead spitting
image.'

'You'd go into the cemetery tonight, for *that*?'

'Like I said, I want her.' His eyes, glazed, held a pathetic
hunger. Of love, in those bare words, he had expressed all he
knew how to. On lechery only he was articulate. 'It's
moonlight,' he said. 'I've got a torch. I'll climb the wall.'

'Goodbye, Gilly,' said John. 'Good luck.'

In the morning the sky was copper, grey above, reddish on the
horizon where the sun hung. The Winter Solstice had come.

'It's like the end of the world,' said Marlon.

The foreman came in, rubbing his hands. 'Going to have
snow before the day's over. Gilly's late.' John told him Gilly
wasn't coming in. He didn't tell him why not, and he expected
an outburst. But the foreman only stuck out his lip and put
the kettle on and helped himself to one of Marlon's cigarettes.

'No loss, that,' he said. 'We shan't miss him. And if I'm not
much mistaken we'll all be laid off by tonight when this dump's

snowed up. You'll be able to get yourselves dug in nice for Christmas, lads.'

Marlon showed no inclination to leave the stuffy warmth of the hut, where the foreman now had a brazier of coke, for the raw air and yellowed dimness of the cemetery. But the foreman wanted to be rid of them, to be on his own, to be idle and warm in peace. He took down Gilly's calendar and pushed it among the glowing coke, and the last John saw of it was the glossy tanned body of a naked girl gyrating in the fire. They moved out into the chill of the shortest day, the foreman hurrying them along by cleaning frost off the truck's windscreen himself.

John expected trouble from the boy, so forbidding was the cemetery in the gloom and under that strange sky. But Marlon, when John had repeated several times that Gilly was not coming, when this had at last sunk in, became more cheerful and more like a normal person than John had ever seen him. He even laughed. He pushed John about in the cab, and when this made the truck swerve, he hooted with laughter.

But when they had come to the centre and were working on clearing the main aisle, he fell silent, though he seemed tranquil enough. All those months John had longed for peace, for a respite from Gilly's ceaseless bragging and innuendo, but now he had it he felt only uneasy. Being alone up here with Marlon had something to do with it. He despised himself for being afraid of a poor retarded boy, yet he was afraid. The thickening atmosphere was part of it, and the windless cold, and the increasing darkness like an eclipse, and the way Marlon would stand for whole minutes on end, staring vacantly, swinging his spade. But what made him long for the snow to begin and drive them back to the hut was Marlon's new habit, now Gilly was not here to deride him, of touching the gravestones and seeming to whisper to them. That he did this reverently and cautiously did nothing to ease John's mind. It was as if he were placating the dead, assuring them that now all would be well. And John had an awareness, growing in intensity as the time slowly passed, that the cemetery had somehow undergone a change. For him it had been just a place to work in, later an abode of sadness and the lost past, never till now macabre. Perhaps much of this feeing was due to the strangeness of the day itself, the permanent twilight, the knowledge that in these hours the earth had turned to its ultimate distance away from the sun.

Yet it was more than that. That might account for the distortions he seemed to see, so that the tombs appeared more closely crowded and the chapel tower taller and darker, but not for his sensation that there had taken place in the cemetery since he had last seen it, some upheaval and some outrage. It was when these fancies grew so strong as to make him imagine some actual physical change, the positions of the slabs and stones altered, that he looked at his watch and told Marlon they could stop now for their midday meal.

The foreman said to bring down one truck-load of rubble from the chapel, and then they could knock off. The sky had lightened a little, becoming uniformly livid, but still they needed the headlights on. The pale misty shafts of light probed the undergrowth and died into blackness. They parked beside the tower.

'Can you make an effort and come in?' said John, 'or do I have to do it on my own?'

Marlon managed a sheepish, crafty smile. 'You go first.'

The rubble was heaped against the furthest side of the octagon. He saw Gilly before he got there. Gilly was lying on his back among the muses and the virgins, his head, his face, a mass of black clotted blood to which fragments and crumbs of stone adhered. Clio, memento of love, had rolled from his grasp. His eyes still stared, as if they still saw those meters-out of vengeance.

'Gilly, Gilly!' John cried, and the eight walls called back, 'Gilly, Gilly!' – calling them to Marlon as he came through the tower and into the nave.

Marlon did not speak Gilly's name. He gave a great cry.

'The dead people came out! The dead people judged him! The day has come, the end of the world . . . the Day, the Day, the Day!'

From the eaves, out of the broken roof, the birds came, circling, cawing, a great rush of wings. And the echo roared like a knell. John stumbled out after Marlon, after the flying figure that cried like a prophet in the wilderness, into a whiteness that cleaned the world.

In great shaggy flakes, the snow had begun to fall.

A FLOCK OF LAWN
FLAMINGOS

by

Pat Murphy

Pat Murphy has published four novels, *The Shadow Hunter*, *The Falling Woman*, *The City*, *Not Long After* and, most recently, a historical feminist werewolf novel, titled *Nadja: The Wolf Chronicles*. A portion of this novel ('An American Childhood', published by *Asimov's Science Fiction Magazine* as a novelette) was a finalist on the Hugo ballot. She has also written numerous stories, some of which have been collected in *Points of Departure*.

Her second novel, *The Falling Woman*, won the Nebula for best novel published in 1987 and in the same year, her novelette 'Rachel in Love' won a Nebula, *The Isaac Asimov's* Reader's Poll, and the Theodore Sturgeon Memorial Award. More recently, *Points of Departure* won the 1990 Philip K. Dick Award for best paperback original and her novella *Bones* won the 1991 World Fantasy Award.

When not writing science fiction she writes for the Exploratorium, San Francisco's museum of science, art, and human perception.

I heard Murphy read this story at a science-fiction convention. Before I sat down I asked if she thought it was something I could use for *Omni* or for any anthology I was working on – because I make it a rule not to attend readings of stories I may want to consider; hearing a writer read her story colours for ever the way the editor *reads* that story. She said 'Nah' so I sat and listened. And afterwards, told her I wanted it for my revenge anthology. She looked at me doubtfully for a few minutes and then said, 'Oh yeah, I can see that,' or something to that effect.

It certainly makes for a nice change of pace.

A FLOCK OF LAWN FLAMINGOS

Live Oak Estates was a pleasant little townhouse development in a pleasant little California town. I lived there peacefully enough, until Joan Egypt moved in and everything changed.

I met Joan Egypt on a sunny autumn day. I had just pulled into my car port when I saw a moving van pulling away from the townhouse next door. It was late in the afternoon, and I was coming home from work – I'm the librarian at the local elementary school. I had spent the day preparing for the first day of school.

Cardboard boxes were stacked on the front lawn of the townhouse. From the sidewalk in front of my house, I could see through the open front door into the living room. The room was crowded with more cardboard boxes. From where I stood, I could read the black scrawls that identified the boxes' contents. 'Dance masks – Tibet & Mongolia', read one. 'Zuni fetishes', read another. 'Shrunken heads', read a third, 'Handle with care'.

I was hesitating on the sidewalk, wondering if I should welcome the newcomer to the neighbourhood, when Joan Egypt stepped out the door, heading for one of the stacks of boxes on the lawn. She was a tall woman with a tangle of curly white hair. She wore khaki pants with button-flap pockets and a flame red shirt. She grinned when she saw me on the sidewalk. 'Hello, neighbour,' she called.

'Hello.'

'It really isn't all shrunken heads,' she said, waving a hand at one of the boxes. 'A few shrunken heads, a few blow guns and darts, and some other artefacts from the Jivaro culture that I picked up on my last trip to Ecuador. And a few pickled heads from New Zealand. But I thought the movers might handle it with more care if they thought it was all shrunken heads.'

I managed to nod in agreement, while wondering how and why anyone would pickle a head. 'I suppose you're right,' I said slowly. 'Movers can be so careless.'

She held out her hand, still grinning. 'I'm Joan Egypt. Just call me Joan.'

I shook her hand. Her grip was solid and confident and I could feel callouses on her palm. She was not, I thought, the usual sort of person to move into Live Oak Estates. 'I'm Nancy Dell, your next-door neighbour.'

'Glad to meet you, Nancy,' she said. 'It's nice to be back in the States.' She told me that she had just returned to the USA after spending the last decade abroad. 'Field work in a variety of places,' she said. 'Indonesia, South America, Nepal, Tibet, Siberia.' She was an anthropologist, it seemed, and she'd come to our town to teach at the community college. 'I thought I'd settle down for a time,' she said. 'Just for the hell of it. This seems like a nice, quiet place to live.'

'It's very quiet,' I agreed, wondering how she would adapt to the quiet life. The townhouse complex was a very orderly place. Several acres of identical houses, painted in earth tones, each with its own tiny front yard. Once, a young couple had painted their door bright red, but Mr Hoffer, the head of the Live Oak Estates Home Owners' Association, had spoken to them about it. They repainted it brown and moved soon after.

'I need a little peace and quiet,' she said, gazing into the distance. 'I had to leave my last post rather quickly. There was an incident . . .' She stopped in mid-sentence and waved a hand dismissively. 'Let's just say it was time to leave.'

I was trying to think of how I might tactfully find out why it had been time to leave when I heard Mr Hoffer's footsteps on the sidewalk. 'Hello, ladies,' he called.

Mr Hoffer was a retired minister. Every afternoon, he strolled through the development, alert to breaches of the regulations established by the Home Owners' Association and to any other changes that might adversely affect his property values. He wore, as always, brown polyester sansabelt slacks and an immaculate polo shirt. He had a bad knee so he carried a burnished wooden cane, with which he gestured when he wanted to make a point. He was a stern, uncompromising man who showed too many teeth when he smiled.

'I'm Pete Hoffer,' he said, holding his hand out to Joan. 'You must be the proud new owner of this lovely corner house.'

'Yes, I suppose I am,' Joan agreed as he pumped her hand.

'Welcome to the community,' he continued. 'As you probably know, I'm president of the Live Oak Estates Home Owners' Association.'

'Why no, I hadn't realised.'

'I certainly am, and I wanted to make sure that you'd been properly apprised of the regulations by your realtor.'

'The regulations?' Joan looked faintly bemused. 'I suppose they might have been in the papers that I signed when I bought the place.'

'It's really quite simple,' Mr Hoffer exlained. His voice had the soothing tone of a man who had offered sympathy and counsel in a professional capacity. 'You've agreed – just as we all have – that you will not alter the external appearance of your home. The regulations list some of the troubles we've had in the past. You'd be surprised at the sort of things people will do. There was one family, for example, who left a packing crate on their front lawn for three full days! I finally had to ask them to remove it.' He was staring at the boxes on the lawn as he spoke, and he thumped his cane on the sidewalk for emphasis.

'I can't imagine what they were thinking,' Joan murmured.

'Of course not. Well, if you notice any irregularities in the neighbourhood, please be sure to call on me.' Mr Hoffer shook her hand again and walked briskly away.

'Interesting,' Joan said, watching him turn the corner at the end of the block. 'Is that true about the regulations?'

'It certainly is.'

Joan glanced at my house. 'What about those flamingos on your lawn?' she asked, pointing to the pink plastic lawn flamingos on the grass by my front door.

'Oh, you can have a few lawn ornaments,' I said. 'Lots of people do.'

'I see,' she said, nodding thoughtfully. 'But you can't change the external appearance of your house.' As she spoke, she began strolling down the sidewalk, examining the houses one by one. I followed, puzzled by her seeming fascination with this minor regulation.

We passed the Arveys' house, where a stone duck followed by

seven stone ducklings waddled across the lawn. A few doors down, on the Winfreys' lawn, a stone garden gnome stood by the flower bed.

Nothing unusual – just bird baths, flamingos, and the like – until we reached Mr Hoffer's house at the end of the block. In the alcove beside his front door, a life-sized, marble statue of the Virgin Mary stood, her hands spread in benediction. A pedestal elevated the statue by more than a foot, so that she smiled sweetly down on passers-by.

'That's Mr Hoffer's place,' I said. 'The statue was a gift from his parish when he retired.'

Joan nodded and turned back in the direction from which we had come. 'I see that there's room for some individual expression in lawn decoration at least,' she said.

'Of course,' I agreed. 'Of course there is.'

The next day, I stepped out of my house and discovered a flock of flamingos on Joan's lawn.

I hadn't realised how very pink lawn flamingos were until I saw fifty of them, standing in a cluster on the square of neatly mowed grass. Twenty-five flamingos stood tall, raising their heads high. The other twenty-five were in the other traditional lawn flamingo pose, necks lowered close to the ground.

Joan was putting the last flamingo in place as I stepped out of the door. She waved cheerfully when she saw me. 'Good morning,' she called. 'It really brightens the place up, don't you think?'

'Oh, yes,' I said politely. 'It's very bright.' From up close, the flamingos seemed even brighter, an expanse of pink punctuated only by the white spots that marked their eyes. I got in my car and headed to work, the flamingos a blur of pink in the rear-view mirror.

That afternoon, when I came home from work, I saw Joan and Mr Hoffer standing on the sidewalk. They were deep in discussion. I parked my car and strolled over to join them.

'It's quite clearly against the regulations,' Mr Hoffer was saying.

'I don't think it's quite so clear-cut,' Joan disagreed calmly. 'The regulations expressly permit traditional lawn decoration, and I don't think there's any lawn decoration much more traditional than a flamingo. Why, Nancy told me that she's had hers for years.' She turned an innocent gaze in my direction.

'That's true,' I said slowly. 'And no one has ever suggested that my flamingos might be a problem.'

Mr Hoffer glared at me. 'Your flamingos are not a problem.' His voice was rising. 'You have the normal number of flamingos. But this is not normal.'

'Now, Mr Hoffer,' Joan began, 'you'll find that standards of normalcy vary from culture to culture. Take, for example . . .'

'In this culture, it's not normal to have more than two flamingos,' Mr Hoffer interrupted. 'And if you can't interpret the regulations correctly, I suppose we'll just have to make them more specific.'

'Now, Mr Hoffer,' Joan began again, but he was already hurrying away down the sidewalk, planning, no doubt, an emergency meeting to amend the regulations. 'I seem to have upset him,' Joan murmured. 'I just thought they would look festive.'

There was, of course, a meeting of the Home Owners' Association. It was attended by Joan, myself, Mr Hoffer, and the five other members of the board. We sat in metal folding chairs in the Live Oaks Community Centre, a small inhospitable building beside the swimming pool. The Community Centre had been intended, I believe, to serve as a site for parties, community lectures, and other gatherings. But Mr Hoffer kept the key, and as far as I knew, no one ever borrowed it.

Mr Hoffer explained the purpose of the meeting very briefly. 'There are entirely too many flamingos on Ms Egypt's lawn,' he said. 'I recommend that we set a limit on how many ornaments a lawn can sustain.'

Before the others could speak, Joan raised her hand. When Mr Hoffer called on her, she delivered a short, and I thought very interesting, lecture on flamingos and their habits. 'I think we need to consider the natural history of the flamingo,' she began quite seriously. 'These birds are extremely gregarious. In their natural habitat, you would never see a single flamingo; you would never see a pair of flamingos. Never. It just doesn't happen. In Madagascar, they gather in flocks of hundreds. As far as the eye can see, the shoreline is crowded with flamingos.' She

waved a hand, gesturing at the white plaster walls that surrounded us as if, just beyond them, we could see flamingos in
their flock.

'They squabble and nest along the shoreline. At night you can
hear them honking like geese. When the flock takes flight, the
flapping of their wings is like thunder. They wheel overhead, as
pink as a cloud touched by the setting sun.'

She lowered her hand. 'Yet we keep our flamingos in lonely
pairs. Our children will grow up thinking that this is a natural
situation: two flamingos, all alone. I think it's rather sad.' She
studied the faces of the board. 'On my front lawn, I have, as
much as is possible with the materials at hand, recreated a
natural situation for these plastic flamingos. Perhaps you can
think of it as an educational display.'

When she sat down, the board remained silent for a moment.
Then Mr Hoffer spoke briefly on how this extreme sort of
behaviour could cause all of our property values to plummet.

The discussion of precisely how the regulations should be
amended was lengthy. The existing regulation read: 'Homeowners may, at their discretion, install lawn ornaments depicting traditional subjects.' Mr Johnson, a young, upwardly mobile
bank manager, sugggested putting the words 'a few' in front of
'lawn ornaments'. Mrs Michaels, a retired accountant who had
been calmly knitting through all the talk, looked up from her
work to complain that the wording Mr Johnson had suggested
would necessitate removing some of the seven stone ducklings
from Mrs Arvey's lawn. Seven was, after all, more than a few –
but no one had ever complained about Mrs Arvey's ducks. In the
end, they agreed to insert the words 'a traditional number of', so
that the regulation read: 'Homeowners may, at their discretion,
install a traditional number of lawn ornaments depicting
traditional subjects.'

As Joan and I walked home from the meeting, I offered my
sympathies. I had, after all, gone to the meeting to support her.
No one ever attended meetings of the Home Owners' Association. 'It's really too bad,' I told her. 'I liked looking out my front
window and seeing all that pink.'

'Yes, I think they're quite festive. And biologically accurate,
as well.' Her tone was thoughtful, and I wondered if she was
thinking of trying to ignore the board's dictates.

'I'll help you take them down, if you like,' I said quickly.

'I suppose I do have to take them down,' she said.

I nodded. 'I think so. Over the years, I've found that it's easier to live within the regulations.'

She nodded and continued walking, frowning a little. We were walking past Mr Hoffer's house, with its neatly trimmed lawn and the statue of the Virgin Mary. As we approached the driveway, moving within a few feet of Mr Hoffer's car, the car spoke to us.

'Please step away from the car,' it said, in Mr Hoffer's calm voice. 'Alarm will sound if you do not step away from the car.'

We both automatically stepped away from the car. Then Joan stopped, staring at the vehicle. She took a step towards it and the car spoke again. 'Please step away from the car.' She stepped back, then stepped forward again. 'Please step away . . .' She did.

'Careful,' I said. 'When the alarm sounds, the car starts honking its horn and switching its lights on and off.'

'What a strange thing,' Joan said, stepping towards the car. 'Please,' the car said. She stepped back, then forward again. 'Please . . . Please . . . Please . . .'

'Mr Hoffer had it installed a few weeks ago,' I said. 'He cares a lot about his car.'

Joan studied the shiny vehicle and nodded. 'I see. That's really an interesting device he's got there. I wonder . . .' She stopped in mid-sentence, then turned away and began walking towards her house. 'Yes,' she said quickly, her tone brightening. 'You're quite right about staying within the regulations. I think I can manage that.'

We took the flamingos down the next afternoon. While we worked, Joan told me about her days in Madagascar, studying lemurs in the forest and camping beside the lake where the flamingos nested. We put the flamingos in Joan's garage, and I thought that was that.

For a week, Joan's lawn was empty. Then, one afternoon, a truck arrived. Its cargo was wrapped in white canvas. I stared from my kitchen window, watching Joan chat with two burly men as they untied the ropes and unloaded the truck, setting up a new display on Joan's lawn: a garden gnome holding a lantern.

Only one gnome, no more. A traditional number for garden gnomes, I think. I didn't notice anything unusual in its appearance. It was a smiling, cheerful, innocent garden gnome. The only thing that seemed a little strange was the sign on the side of the truck. The delivery was from AAA Auto Alarms. Why would an automobile alarm company be delivering a garden gnome?

As I watched, a crowd of children gathered around the truck, around the gnome. They were behaving very oddly. One by one, they would approach the gnome then leap back, laughing. Mrs Johnson, who was walking her dog, had stopped and was chatting with Joan.

I went outside to find out what was going on. A girl in blue jeans and a red T-shirt stepped towards the gnome and I heard a gruff voice say, 'Please come close to the gnome. No alarm will sound. The gnome is not alarmed. I don't mind if you approach the gnome.' The child stepped away, giggling.

'I suppose you could think of it as an art installation,' Joan was saying to Mrs Johnson. 'I started thinking about it when Mr Hoffer's car told me to back off. It seems so sad, when even inanimate objects tell you to keep your distance.'

'I hate that car,' the woman said.

'It does seem rather unfriendly,' Joan said.

'Mr Hoffer is going to have something to say about this,' I said, gesturing towards the gnome, which was once again telling the children to approach.

Joan smiled. 'I don't see how he can object. There's nothing against it in the regulations. It's a traditional lawn ornament, in a traditional number.'

'I suspect the regulations will be changed again,' I said.

I was right, of course. Mr Hoffer didn't like the gnome. He called another emergency meeting of the Home Owners' Association to talk about amending the regulations. As before, we met in the Community Centre, but this time Mr Johnson had to set up extra folding chairs. Mrs Johnson was there. So was Mrs Scott, the woman who lived next door to Mr Hoffer.

Joan spoke first, talking about the importance of public art, about how it could provide us with a new perspective on our society. She talked about the isolation of modern life and the irony of lawn gnomes, which reflected our fantasy about and our yearning for a pastoral life. She discussed the sterility of modern life.

When she was done, Mrs Johnson spoke up in favour of Harold, the Talking Gnome, which is what the lawn ornament had come to be called in the neighbourhood. 'The kids like it,' she said. 'And I don't see that it's hurting anyone. It doesn't bother me, and I live right nearby.'

Then Mrs Scott directed a few remarks to Mr Hoffer. 'I don't like your car,' she told him. 'It's always yelling at me. If you make Joan get rid of the Talking Gnome, then you have to make your car shut up.'

Mr Hoffer turned red. Then he talked for almost an hour – about property values and about how the gnome was a public nuisance, encouraging children to gather in unruly groups. What would happen after the novelty of the Talking Gnome wore off? The children would be wandering around with idle hands, looking for something to fill their time. He talked about the crowds that would come to visit the gnome. In sombre tones, he described the consequences to Live Oak Estates – keep the gnome and there would be hordes of unchecked teenagers rampaging through the neighbourhood, tearing up mailboxes, painting graffiti on the walls, tossing garbage cans about; there would be crowds of curiosity seekers, trampling people's lawns and leaving litter behind.

'This is not an art gallery,' he concluded in an impassioned tone. 'This is our home. We can't have every Tom, Dick, and Harry trooping through, staring at our homes and leaving their litter behind.'

The discussion of how to change the regulations was more heated than before. Mr Hoffer's car, which had, apparently, annoyed everyone at the meeting at some time or other, drew fire. Mr Hoffer kept protesting that his car was not a permanent fixture of the development and was therefore exempt from regulation.

Mr Johnson, with an eye on his wife, defended the gnome. But Mr Hoffer maintained that lawn ornaments should not speak. In fact, he suggested that the board forestall future problems by dealing with other possibilities: lawn ornaments must not speak, light up, move, or otherwise interact with the passers-by.

Mrs Scott stuck to her guns. 'If we're going to make the gnome be quiet, then Mr Hoffer's car has to stop talking too.'

In the end, after much discussion, the regulations were amended to read: 'Homeowners may, at their discretion, install a traditional number of lawn ornaments depicting traditional subjects. Lawn ornaments, vehicles, and other objects must not be electronically embellished to speak, light up, move, or otherwise interact with passers-by.'

At the end of the meeting, Mr Hoffer was scowling, unhappy about his car alarm. But Joan did not seem at all upset. She thanked the two women who had spoken out on behalf of the gnome and left the meeting smiling.

'You seem to be taking this well,' I said as we walked home. 'I guess Mr Hoffer got his just deserts.'

'Oh, I suppose,' she said. 'But that isn't really the point.'

I frowned. 'What is the point, then?'

She strolled down the sidewalk, still smiling beatifically. The moon was full and it was a lovely autumn evening. 'Ripples in a pond,' she said at last. 'That's the point.'

'What do you mean?'

'Ripples, like the ones that spread out when you toss a pebble into a pond. I love watching what happens when you introduce a tiny perturbation into a system. You give a little push here – or there. And somehow, everything adjusts to accommodate that change. But you can't predict exactly how things will change.' Her smile grew broader. 'There's an element of chaos. I think that's what appeals to me.'

'I guess that's what Mr Hoffer is afraid of,' I said. 'Chaos. That's why you two will never get along. Chaos and order don't mix. Like oil and water.'

'Not at all,' she said. 'You've got it all wrong. Mr Hoffer and I belong together. In fact, we require each other. We're not like oil and water. We're more like yin and yang, two sides of the same coin, a cosmic balancing act. The world requires chaos as well as order.'

'If you say so,' I murmured.

A week later, the giant flamingos arrived. Two of them, in traditional lawn flamingo poses. I saw the truck and went out to watch the men set the birds up on Joan's lawn. The tall flamingo was over eight feet tall; the stooping one was easily six feet.

'Hello, Nancy,' Joan called. 'Aren't they wonderful?'

'Where did you get them?' I asked.

'I called around. A friend knew of a sign shop that had cast some flamingos for the Flamingo Hotel in Las Vegas. So I called them up and explained what I needed. I think they did a bang-up job.'

A boy riding past on his bicycle had stopped to watch. 'They're rad,' he said, nodding his approval. He called to some kids down the block, and they ran to see what was happening on the corner.

A woman in a turquoise blue jogging suit lingered on the corner, her eyes fixed on the flamingos. 'In the sixties, I had a dress just that colour,' she said, a trifle wistfully.

I gazed up at the taller flamingo. Against the blue of the sky, its head was an amazing shade of day-glo pink. Joan and the woman had started talking about the colour pink and their general hatred of pastels. 'But real pink is different,' Joan was saying. 'It doesn't have to be a pastel. A really intense pink is a fine colour.'

I listened to them chat as the men fixed the flamingos in place, sinking their legs deep into the sod. At last the woman jogged away, the boy pedalled off on his bicycle, and the other kids wandered off to tell their friends about the latest addition to the neighbourhood.

'Mr Hoffer won't have it,' I told Joan. 'You'll never get away with it.'

She shrugged, smiling. 'It's within the regulations,' she said. 'A traditional number of lawn ornaments, depicting a traditional subject. I don't see how he can object.' When I stared at her, she just laughed.

And so there was another meeting of the Home Owners' Association. This one was better attended than the last – Mrs Johnson and Mrs Scott had both brought friends. The kid on the bicycle was there. So was the woman who had been jogging.

Joan spoke about her flamingos very briefly. 'There are only two of them,' she said. 'They depict a traditional subject. And they aren't electronically embellished. There's nothing in the regulations against them.'

'They fall within the letter of the law – but not within its spirit,' Mr Hoffer protested. 'They're too big.'

Joan studied him calmly. 'I didn't think size was an issue,' she said. 'After all, the lovely statue on your lawn is at least eight feet tall, including the base.'

Mr Hoffer stared at Joan in horror. 'You're comparing those pink monstrosities to my statue of the Blessed Virgin?'

'Only as far as size goes,' Joan said. 'The flamingos come from a very different tradition, of course. But they are a bit smaller than your statue.'

The discussion of how to amend the regulations began at seven o'clock and ended at ten, but which time the members of the Board, with the exception of Mr Hoffer, looked exhausted. In the end, they added the phrase, 'of a traditional size' to the sentence about lawn ornaments. Mr Hoffer also insisted on adding a line that expressly permitted his beloved religious statue: 'Masonry figures of religious or cultural significance are exempted from regulations governing lawn ornaments.'

At the end of the meeting, as Mr Johnson wearily folded chairs and put them away, Mr Hoffer smiled at Joan grimly, certain he had won.

More than a month later, a truck pulled up by Joan's house and five burly men unloaded an enormous stone disk and stood it on edge in the middle of the lawn, like a giant wheel from some prehistoric monster truck. The disk was about eight feet tall and two feet thick, and it cast a long shadow across the lawn.

'Where did it come from?' I asked Joan. We stood in the shadow of the disk, gazing up at it.

'The island of Yap. On Yap, these disks have incredible cultural significance.'

'Of course,' I said. 'But how did you get it?'

She smiled. 'It wasn't easy. But I have friends who owe me favours and some of them work in museums. You have no idea the sorts of things that some museums have in storage.' She went off then on a story about the Smithsonian storage warehouse and what was in it. Apparently she had worked at the Smithsonian briefly, before being dismissed for 'irregular conduct'. I never did find out exactly how she had obtained the stone disk, but perhaps it was better not to know.

Of course, Mr Hoffer objected. He scheduled a meeting and Joan and I attended. So did all the people who had attended the meeting about the giant flamingos and all of their neighbours who had heard about it. The meeting had the air of a party. Mrs Johnson brought a cooler full of beer and Mrs Scott brought a couple of bags of potato chips. People set up folding chairs and filled the space with noise and chatter and the crunching of potato chips.

Mr Hoffer had to shout to call the meeting to order. The other members of the board seemed nervous. Mrs Michaels' knitting needles clicked along at twice their usual rate. Mr Johnson kept glancing around the room nervously.

'We are here to discuss that thing in front of Ms Egypt's house,' Mr Hoffer began. 'I don't think there's room for much discussion. The regulations permit traditional lawn ornaments of a traditional size in a traditional number. That chunk of concrete on Ms Egypt's lawn does not fit within the regulations. It's as simple as that.'

When Joan rose to speak, the room was quiet except for the crunching of potato chips. 'I'm afraid Mr Hoffer is mistaken about the artefact that decorates my lawn,' she began. And then she told us about the Micronesian island of Yap, where families display large stone disks, sometimes up to twelve feet in diameter, in front of their homes. The size and quality of each stone is an indication of the prestige and wealth of the family that owned it; the stones, anthropologists say, are a unique form of money. These masonry lawn ornaments are quarried on an island that lies some 250 miles from Yap. Each stone is transported to Yap at great trouble and expense.

The stone on Joan's lawn was, of course, a stone of great consequence, imported from Yap. 'I will,' Joan said, 'recite for you the credentials of this notable stone, in the language native to the island of Yap.' And there, in the Live Oak Estates Community Centre, Joan held out her arms like a high priestess about to perform a pagan ritual. She took a deep breath and she began to chant. Strange guttural sounds echoed from the white walls; long unintelligible polysyllables drowned out the sound of crunching chips. She turned as she chanted, her dark eyes scanning the crowd, as if inviting each of us to celebrate with her.

She paused to take a breath, then continued with the babble of unfamiliar sounds, ponderous and mysterious as the Latin of a high mass. Though I could not understand the words, her presentation was powerful.

She concluded the chant with familiar words that it took me a moment to interpret: 'Joan Egypt, Live Oak Estates.'

Then she took a deep breath. 'As any inhabitant of Yap could tell you, that list of the stone's owners includes many important warriors, chiefs, and religious dignitaries – whose company I am honoured to join. On the island of Yap, this stone disk is a traditional lawn ornament in a traditional size. So it quite clearly falls within the regulations. Unless, of course, you wish to amend the regulations to eliminate the provision that allows for masonry fixtures of cultural significance. Because this stone is an object of great religious and cultural significance, and its presence on my lawn brings prestige to our community.' She smiled at Mr Hoffer and sat down.

The crowd applauded and Mrs Johnson stood up to defend the stone as an example of freedom of expression. Then someone else stood to talk about the need for cultural diversity in the neighbourhood.

Through it all, I watched Mr Hoffer. His face had gone pale. He had, only now, recognised the trap. He could require Joan to remove the stone, but the change in regulations would necessitate the removal of his beloved statue.

The regulations did not change. The Stone from Yap stayed. At the end of the meeting, Mr Hoffer limped to his now-silent car, defeated at last. The neighbours remained in the Community Centre, drinking beer and eating chips and chatting about this and that. Joan circulated through the crowd, thanking people for their support.

Time passed. The grass grew thick around the base of the Stone from Yap. Every evening, Mr Hoffer walked through the development, just as he always had. But his attitude had changed. Before Joan's arrival, I would have said that he strolled through the development like a lord surveying his lands. Now his gaze was furtive. He glanced at each house as he walked past, a hint of fear in his eyes. What changes might he see? What new trouble was headed his way? He walked slowly, as if his old knee injury were giving him trouble.

Then Joan told me that she'd be moving away. 'It's been lovely here,' she said. 'The quiet has done me good. But one of my old friends has planned an expedition up the Amazon by hovercraft. It's a wonderful opportunity. I can't pass it up.'

'But what about the Stone from Yap?' I protested. 'What about the balance of yin and yang?'

She shrugged. 'I think I've done my part on behalf of chaos. But I was thinking – perhaps you'd like the Stone from Yap on your lawn?'

The evening before Joan left for the Amazon, she and I – with the help of half a dozen neighbours – rolled the Stone from Yap from her yard to mine, leaving a patch of bare dirt surrounded by green grass in the centre of Joan's lawn. After the others left, Joan and I sat by the Stone, drinking beer. She wrote down the chant that she had recited at the meeting of the Home Owners' Association. Even though I couldn't understand a word of it, she made me recite it over and over, correcting my pronunciation of the rolling polysyllables. 'There's a glottal stop there,' she said, pointing at the paper. 'Don't run the syllables together like that.'

At last, after much practice, she nodded. 'Close enough,' she said. 'Now just add on the last two owners and their villages. That's Joan Egypt and Nancy Dell of Live Oak Estates. And you're done.' She twisted the cap off another beer and leaned back against the Stone from Yap.

'I'm looking forward to this expedition,' she murmured. 'It's a great opportunity.'

'You're all packed?' I said.

'Pretty much,' she said. 'Except for the lawn flamingos.'

'The lawn flamingos?'

'I've still got all fifty of them. Goodwill didn't want them, so they're still in the garage.'

'I know what to do,' I said.

That was how we ended up strolling through the development at one in the morning, putting pairs of lawn flamingos on the lawns of twenty-five deserving neighbours. And the next day, I took Joan to the airport. 'Keep the balance,' she told me, and she flew away.

It's been almost a year since Joan left. I think about her every day. She gave me, as a going-away present, a pickled head from New Zealand. It's on my kitchen windowsill and I look at it every time I do the dishes.

I got a letter from Joan the other day. The envelope was grimy and tattered and covered with stamps that pictured exotic birds. 'I hope this letter reaches you,' she began. 'I'm entrusting it to the local trader and he doesn't seem like the most reliable sort.' She was staying in a small village somewhere in the rainforest. 'I'm getting to know the villagers,' she wrote, 'and I'm learning the local customs. It's a lovely place. So very peaceful.'

I thought about ripples in a pond and I wondered how long that would last.

TOUCH ME EVERYPLACE

by

Michael Cadnum

Michael Cadnum lives in northern California and is a poet and novelist. He is the author of eleven novels including *St Peter's Wolf, Ghostwright, Calling Home, Skyscape, The Judas Glass* and *Zero at the Bone,* and an illustrated book based on Cinderella called *Ella and the Canary Prince* (Cobblestone Press). He has also published several collections of poetry, most recently *The Cities We Will Never See.*

Cadnum is terrific at capturing in his short fiction the character of disturbed and displaced persons. As in this tale.

TOUCH ME EVERYPLACE

What it was like was, they put me in a big scoop like a detergent powder spoon, bright blue, and when I tried to climb out they put a giant strip of sticky tape over me. And then it was like a ride in a helicopter, which I have never been in, except higher. Way higher, up where you have to breathe air through a tube.

Which is what I did while my sweat got all frosty. They carried me into a bright room like a bowling alley, and I was terrified. The whole spaceship started to vibrate and I could tell we were going somewhere, and then they carried me still in the big plastic scoop all the way down a corridor to a room. And there it started, the ordeal.

Some of it I already told the proper authorities, some of it not. They undid the big sticky tape and then they lifted me out. I already told investigators about their hands and what they used for fingers, little pliers. Cold, too. What I didn't tell was what everybody probably already figured out on their own. They took off all my clothes and touched me everyplace.

Not only my private parts, which is what people expect. Naturally the creatures would take off clothes to touch the places clothes usually cover. My penis they looked at, and all the other parts, and my muscles – which I have a lot of – they felt those too. And also they touched under my tongue and my nose holes and in my ear.

You might think, well an ear isn't so bad, but an ear is an orifice. Imagine if you were sitting on a bus and someone put a breast nipple in your ear, for example. Even if it was a pleasant breast, if you weren't asked you would think *wait a minute*.

Ever since the elevator accident I have seen what is going on. You might have heard elevators can't fall nineteen storeys, they have brakes. And I would explain that they do have brakes, that the brakes slow the falling box of people – or in my case one person, yelling – from about sixty-five miles per hour to about ten. And I would argue that the impact is still unpleasant and damaging, not taking into consideration the fall, which doesn't do the human nervous system any good.

Which is why the court was going to award me punitive damages. The elevator company, a very famous one I agreed not to mention out of court, compensated me handsomely.

But to go back to the spaceship: when they were done they took me back to the Wendy's parking lot where they found me in the first place. I was dishevelled, but if you saw me you would think, this is a man who is always not quite tucked in, so you wouldn't give me a second glance. I went to the proper authorities and I was on television and in the newspaper. I didn't want to talk about it except to say they came and got me and felt me and went away. I could have talked about every little detail, but I didn't.

But then I woke up one morning and decided to make my life better. I vacuumed and I dusted. I washed out the tuna cans before I squashed them. People in my position don't think why me, they think: I know why me. I was conspicuous in some way, and I didn't want to be any more. I bought new shirts and new pants. I decided to dress my age, which is not so old, but still. I wore a necktie to Safeway sometimes, and you could tell the women in the deli section thought it was an improvement. I still have the limp, but I improved.

Friends would see me in the library and ask, and I would say I was OK, thanks for inquiring.

For a while I was recovering from what happened, and didn't take showers three times a day so I could feel myself. It took courage but I could eat and excrete and think about resuming normal relationships with people, even women. I have some personal qualities, although I always thought talking about your virtues automatically reduces them by half.

I called in for the new software, which is what I do. Companies send me the beta versions and I run them and I say they work and they make a funny noise. But after a while I noticed.

The UPS people stand in the lobby and they push buttons on an electronic clipboard, and they leave yellow UPS Post-its on the outside of the mailbox doors. And you think they do this because they are lazy or in a hurry and have to pretend they used the lobby phone to call up people and tell them there is a package.

But I knew there weren't any packages, that there were real UPS people, and then there were these pretend deliverers who were out to make sure I could still function, if you call getting dressed and using a mailbox key functioning, which I do. They were probably doing this all the time I lived in this apartment building, ever since the one on Shattuck Avenue burned down with me barely making it out alive. Maybe before. Maybe some of those tar-brown vans with no doors were totally empty, without drivers, even, motoring around on telepathic control.

If you stop to use your eyes you see there are way many more people than there have to be. In Safeway there is the guy shaking out the string bag full of russets and there is the guy in the back room checking off *potatoes* on a list, and then there is another guy, in a green apron like the others, not really doing anything, watching people.

So I decided I would let them know what it was like. I didn't plan. I just decided to act. I grabbed one in the lobby just standing there looking at a list of names we keep in a metal frame behind glass because sometimes someone wants to deface a name or add a drawing. I went up nineteen floors and carried the person down the hallway. I say *carried* and *person* because these are useful words people understand. But I have pains in my lower and middle back, and also this UPS-oid was stabbing me with a ballpoint pen.

I got him into my apartment. He was a very muscular one, like a male person, and hairy. He shouted and wrestled. I was very patient because I did not want to cause any terrible repercussions between far-away galaxies and my own planet. What I said was, 'How would you like it if I did this?' probing his belly button with my finger.

That was just an example, and the muscular one hit me a lot on the head and on the upper part of my shoulders so I got a pair of pliers out and said, 'Or for example if I did this?' taking hold of that dangling thing in his throat, what I always called the *gilly-woggle*, just as a sample of the outrage.

Because by now I was mad. I had repressed a lot of the anger, got way out of touch with it. They say 'repressed', and they mean like when you press all your clothes with an iron and fold them, and press the folds, like with hankies, so they will stack up neatly in the top drawer. I had done that with my feelings, and shut the drawers really tight.

After a while he lay still, not because I stood on him so much, which I did, but also because I told him he was just going to partake of more reciprocal treatment and see how he liked it. He was tired or frightened, or both.

Naturally, after it was all over and I wasn't all that satisfied, major misunderstandings took place. For one thing they came again and took me to a large facility on Earth, this time, and they were really lost about what to do with me. You could see the extent of the problem. Doctors were confused, if they were human physicians, knowing there was nothing wrong with me, or not confused, just wanting to make me watch television, if they were not human psychiatrists but the other kind.

This is why I was patient so long, wanting to avoid hurting feelings, and being polite, too, because there isn't enough courtesy; you hear *butt* and *ass* on the radio, and I say why bother turning on the AM/FM if people are on there talking like your friends.

I used to not care that progress had stopped. Germs don't die when you take a pill. Even bullets don't work that well, policemen having to shoot every bullet in the gun before the robber falls down. You paint a wall and after a short while you have to paint it again. I don't like to be dramatic, but the only thing that works sometimes is common sense.

So I have taken over this facility until delegations are formed or committees and investigators arrive and the authorities start to exert some authority. When was the last time you felt there was someone in charge?

This won't be a help, generally. Here I am in one small office, with a very obsolete computer and a grip exerciser I found in a drawer, and what can I do to help the situation worldwide? People pound on the door. Some of these are actual, genuine people, and earnest. I have these syringes of a colourless chemical, a very strong tranquilliser, judging from the effect on various personnel earlier in the day. If anyone needs calming, I am ready.

But if we show these curious visitors how to act they will stop probing and sneaking. When I fell nineteen storeys I was yelling. What I was yelling was not a word, just a noise. Now I am ashamed at the memory. So I turn on the mike and speak slowly. I enunciate.

And I say: Sit down and be quiet. I know what you like to do, so line up and stop talking. One at a time. If you want to, you can touch me everyplace.

SCREAMING MAN

By

Richard Christian Matheson

Richard Christian Matheson is a novelist, short-story writer, and screenwriter/producer. He has written and produced more than five hundred episodes of television for over thirty prime-time series. He is now the record holder in Hollywood for the sale of 'spec' screenplays. His latest sale is *Midvale*, co-written with his father, Richard Matheson. His short stories have been published in such diverse magazines as *Penthouse*, *Twilight Zone*, and *Omni*, and in anthologies including *Alien Sex*, *Off Limits: Tales of Alien Sex*, *Millennium* and *Dark Terrors*. His stories are collected in *Scars and Other Distinguishing Marks* and *Dystopia*. Matheson has published one novel, *Created By* and recently finished a second, *Idol*. He lives in Southern California.

Matheson is an acknowleged master of the short sharp shock. Here, an unusual haunting of an average kind of guy.

THE SCREAMING MAN

Bob froze in mid-bite.

He heard helpless moans drifting up his throat. A man inside him was crying.

It went on for an hour and wouldn't stop.

Bob was unnerved and went to his doctor. The doctor placed a stethoscope to Bob's chest and heard the man thrashing about inside, voice muffled by muscle and skin. Yelling like some trapped animal, within Bob's ribcage.

'Bizarre,' said the doctor, moving the stethoscope; a chrome checker, slowly hopping.

'What is it?' sked Bob, hearing the man's voice becoming angry; a faint echo of rage rising.

The doctor said he didn't know.

He listened a bit more, had the nurse come in, place her ear to Bob's mouth. He parted his lips. The man inside was screaming at the top of his lungs, and she pulled back, startled.

The doctor recommended further study.

Bob left the medical building and began to hear another voice. A woman's, pleading for mercy; tortured by something. He tried to ignore it, found it impossible. The man and the woman within almost sounded as if they were arguing with each other, snarling back and forth.

The hospital. Specialists. Tests.

No one could say.

They all gathered around him, suggesting he remain for observation, but he hated the gloom and loss of the huge ward.

On the way home, in the car, he noticed new voices and began to count; six, possibly seven. Children. Old people. All calling out with desperate fear or warring fury.

A friend suggested a psychiatrist.

*

'I think it's your imagination,' said the psychiatrist.

'Then why do others hear it?' asked Bob.

'Maybe they only believe they do.'

'My doctor recorded it. Listen.'

Bob played the cassette he'd brought and the reassuring office became a torture chamber; sounds of pain, dread and horror filling it.

The psychiatrist thought it over. Shrugged with vacant theory.

'It's extraordinary. The imagination is powerful. Perhaps you're literally creating these voices.'

A kind of nightmare ventriloquism was the implication; merely a subconscious trick.

Bob knew that wasn't it.

The psychiatrist could tell. Shifted focus.

'Or,' suggested the psychiatrist, 'we are simply hearing the voices in you that are in all of us. It's the power of suggestion.'

'That's crazy,' said Bob, unconvinced.

'Depends on how you look at it,' said the psychiatrist.

For the next twenty-four hours, Bob remained in bed, listening to the voices multiply, feeling their suffering sounds vibrate his ribs.

He tried to drown them by drinking large amounts of water. It didn't work. He tried to crush them with food. It only seemed to make them stronger.

'Perhaps you are nurturing them,' suggested his wife. 'Making them feel you care.'

After restless night, Bob decided to get up and go about his business. To do otherwise would be giving in to the chorus of pain.

Over the next few days, he began to realise that though the voices remained, they would settle down when he'd had a good day. On a very good day, they would stop altogether.

On bad days they all screamed.

He began to imagine they were only his emotions. The various shades of himself. The many beings within, calling out in pain. Needing his attention. Hurt by the people and experiences he'd come into contact with over a lifetime. Feelings in reply; the death knell of an endangered species.

He began to consider them a kind of hidden family.

Forgotten selves.

At night, as they howled their emptiness and despair, fighting among themselves in deafening dispute, he would struggle to calm himself. Sometimes it took hours. But as he did, gradually each voice would still. Slowly relax and become silent.

Bob would try to breathe evenly, allow only good thoughts.

Finally, the screaming, pleading voices would stop altogether and he thought they might be sleeping. He would be afraid to think about anything upsetting, not wishing to disrupt or wake them.

At times, he wondered if he'd been born guilty; done something unforgivable. If this was his punishment for unknown sins; necessary revenge.

But after a while, he mostly lost interest in the search for an explanation.

He realised, in some unnameable way, that there was none. Or none he was supposed to know. He came to see that curses and blessings were often interchangeable.

And he lived like this for the rest of his life. Forcing himself to see the good, managing to subdue the zoo of horror within.

Despite occasional consultations, no one ever came up with a reasonable explanation. In time it lost all importance to him. He slept better, felt better.

It seemed the voices had come to save him; that deliverance and vengeance had merged.

When he died, the autopsy revealed nothing unusual.

Except for the deep scratches and tooth marks that covered his bones.

RARE PROMISE

by

M. M. O'Driscoll

Mike O'Driscoll's stories have appeared in the magazines *Interzone, Far Point, Fear, BBR, The Third Alternative, Works* and *Albedo One,* and in the anthologies *Off Limits, Darklands 2, The Sun Rises Red, Last Rites & Resurrections,* and in all three volumes of *Cold Cuts.*

He is currently working on a series of loosely connected stories set in what he calls an 'alternative Ireland', of which 'Rare Promise' is one. In it, a childhood friendship has the power to change the lives of three people.

RARE PROMISE

Vincent lies face down in the sluggish water but he is not dead. He is slowing time the way Bear taught him to. 'You lie still,' Bear said, 'like you're dead, then hold your breath and count as high as you can.' One night, Vincent reached a hundred and seventy-five: the seconds slowed and coagulated, till it seemed he had dammed the flow of time. 'A real dedicated practitioner,' Bear said, 'could add at least five years to his life.' Having dreamed of immortality, Vincent felt cheated. The other thing about slowing time was the way it made the whole world sound different; you could hear things nobody else had ever heard, the susurrations that slip between sounds.

. . . Like whispers of the past, of days when the world seemed full of promise, when summer was a place of magic and secrets. Laragh Wood was such a place; a small, three acre gathering of ash and elm trees, bordered by a line of alders that ran beside the Graney. Here, he and Bear built a network of hidden dens where they acted out the rituals of adolescence unhindered by adult fears. It was a world in which they held no secrets from each other. Until, one fine spring morning, with the wood glistening in the after-rain sun, he asked his friend, 'What do you really think of me?' Bear replied, 'Think of you how?' Vincent laughed to hide his purpose: 'As a friend.' 'Why're you asking?' Bear wanted to know. 'I was wondering, when we're older if we'll still be pals.' 'I can't see the future, Vinnie, but me and you, we'll always be friends.' 'You promise, Bear?' ''Course I do.' But Vincent wasn't satisfied; already, at fourteen, he was beginning to sense all that might come between them. And though the wood remained a haven, he could never tell Bear the real fear, the real secret that ached inside him. There were some things, he began to realise, that you could never reveal, not in a place like Drumassan, not without cost.

. . . Like the brooding shadows that sometimes stalked his dreams, a hint of eyes, a murmuring, an earthen smell, the shape of a person he'd known long ago, the space that someone had filled. He'd wake suddenly, troubled by feelings of shame and a love, and a desperate need to please. He'd lie there, apart from the world, trying to focus on the remnants of his dreams. But when he'd get too close, they would disappear like those indecipherable shapes that linger on the edge of vision.

. . . Like the premonitions he'd had of Greta months before she came back to Drumassan. Alone one autumn evening sitting among the falling leaves, he felt the cold touch of rumours sifting through the jetsam of his past, and creating unease about the future. It made listening to his father's plans for him seem more intolerable than ever. 'You're still palling with that Sheehan fella,' his father said. Sheehan was Bear: two years previously, at sixteen, he'd pronounced himself educated and promptly quit school. 'He'll never be anything but a small farmer,' Mr Fitzroy went on. 'He hasn't got your potential at all. Can't you find some fellas you've something in common with?' Mrs Fitzroy added, 'You'll never fulfil your promise mixing with the likes of him.' They droned on, apprising him of all he had to live up to, unconscious, it seemed, of the malice which seeded their thoughts. 'You're looking at seven or eight honours next summer,' his mother went on. 'At least that if we're going for law.' Now it was law; once, she'd harboured a wish that he'd take Holy Orders – like her elder brother, Dan, who'd died last winter of a stroke, and whom Vincent could hardly remember – but Vincent being an only child, she'd grown reluctant to give him up to God. Then, as if she'd only just recalled it, she said, 'Your aunt and Greta are coming to live in Drumassan.' The shock that drove him from the room was the shock of recognition. Greta, he was sure, was the one the voices had spoken of. That night, as he lay restless in bed, he fought the memory of those muted whispers, whispers that filled him with shame and at the same time, enticed him with the lure of something forbidden. So that by the time she returned to the village in the winter – red-haired, green-eyed and possessed of a strange allure, so different to the quiet, sullen girl he barely remembered from childhood – he had cultivated an immunity to her charm. Not so Bear; whatever exotic magic she possessed made him putty in her hands, and in no time at all, much to Vincent's disgust, Bear was doing a line with Greta, and he was out on a limb.

. . . And now, like the hollow moans that begin as subtle ripplings of the subterranean silence and become echoes of distant memories not necessarily his own. Not dead at all but floating, holding his breath, blocking out the world, catching single words and snatched phrases, the sighs and murmurs of the past ebbing and flowing against the shore of his mind; memories, absences, premonitions, resentments. Counting the minute-long seconds and the hour-long minutes. Yet a breath can only contain so much time, and when he clears the surface there is only the chittering of insects and a soft breeze rustling through the trees.

Which doesn't explain the sudden fear which makes him strain to hear what is no longer there. In a world made up of voids, those you have loved are signified only by their absence. Even memories can't be trusted. He grasps the reeds at the water's edge and lets his body stretch out in the gentle current. He wonders if he has imagined the voices. But did he imagine, too, the tone of frightened pleading or of kindly, treacherous reassurance? And was it imagination that spoke of good and bad behaviour? Of how best behaviour got you sweets, like pear drops and blackjacks, and maybe a place in Heaven? And who had promised to never, ever say a word?

An awful scream tears the silence asunder, withering his heart, immobilising him in the water. He grips the reeds tightly to keep from going under, while the cry echoes horribly throughout the wood. It's not real, he tells himself, but there's no escape in imagination: this happens now. And as the sound of hurt dies somewhere deep among the trees, a profound shame settles on him, a feeling of complicity in a sin he cannot recall. For one moment he wonders what a backwards step in time might reveal but a dark and irresistible dread has spiked his nerve. He hauls himself up on to the bank, pulls on his clothes and then, like a child with a guilty secret, he steals furtively from the wood.

This is what Vincent understands about power: when you love someone, you cede them the right to cause you pain. It's not even a matter of intention; a hurt caused in ignorance hurts nonetheless. So when Bear calls round after Mass on Sunday morning, he is entirely unaware of the pain that fills Vincent's heart. But Bear's troubles are written on his face and, seeing them, Vincent melts.

This is power. Another example:

Once, in the teeth of his thirteenth winter, when snow settled in heavy drifts against the outhouses and in the ditches, Nancy Kelly took Vincent to her father's milking shed to show him something she had learned. There, in the cow-smelling gloom, he stood in awkward silence watching his frosty breath commune with hers. She took his right hand and placed it inside her coat where he felt her small breasts through an Aran sweater. 'D'you like 'em?' she asked, but he couldn't speak. Then her hands were at his trousers, unzipping, unbelting with silent purpose.

Afraid, Vincent's eyes beseeched the patient cattle, but they were content to yield their milk to the machines. He whispered, 'What are you doing?'

But she just pulled down his trousers and underpants and said, 'It's not very big, is it?' and took hold of his flaccid prick in her cold, pale hand. 'I thought it'd be bigger.'

'Jesus, would you let me go?' he cried, trying to pull away, but she held on to him and, despite his fear, he felt it grow in her fist.

'Ah now,' Nancy said. 'Something's stirring.' She pulled back the foreskin as if for inspection, said, 'Hmmm,' and began to masturbate him with quiet intensity.

'Christ,' he said. 'Go easy.'

'It's like milking,' she said, maintaining the rhythm of her stroke. 'I saw me brother doing it once.' Afterwards, she wiped her hand on a cow's back and said, 'D'you love me now, Vincent?'

To which he had replied, 'What for?'

Because back then he hadn't understood the subtleties of power or the implications of Nancy's unspoken contract. In rejecting her he drew her hatred; yet the sense of rejection he feels now is not enough to sustain a hatred for Bear.

'What do you want?' Vincent says, taking the proffered cigarette.

Bear says, 'Still looking to be excommunicated?'

'Why change the habit of a lifetime?' It's three years since Vincent last attended Mass, a fact of which his parents are unaware.

'I'm . . .' Bear begins, but falters. He takes a fierce drag on his cigarette, then mutters, 'I want to explain, 'bout me and Greta.'

'Forget it.'

'She's different to other girls.'

Vincent waves a hand, cutting him off. 'I don't want to hear.'

'I must talk to you about her.'

'Talk to someone else.'

Bear looks wounded; Vincent's moment of triumph is undermined by unsummoned compassion. 'Sure, who else can I talk to?' Bear says.

Vincent sighs and gets into the blue Ford Anglia that Bear inherited on his father's death. They drive east through the village where thirsty worshippers congregate outside the twin temples of O'Mahoney's and The Star, one on either side of the road. Strange omens fill Vincent's mind while he waits for Bear to talk, and the even stranger certainty that he will have heard it all before. When Bear finally says, 'I took Greta to the wood,' he's unprepared for the feeling of betrayal that wells up inside. He gulps air as if it were in short supply and finally manages to ask just, 'Why?'

'Jasus, why d'you think?'

But Vincent can hardly think at all, for he is remembering when all the world's secrets were hidden in the wood, and he and Bear were its custodians, sharing everything and keeping the world at bay. Now an inner voice prompts, *Everything*? Was the trust he'd shared with Bear any kind of trust at all? 'She's a child,' he barely whispers.

'She's sixteen, Vinnie, and we've been doing it for months. I know she's your cousin and everything, but don't think butter wouldn't fucking melt in her mouth. Sure, I wasn't the first she's been with.'

'Why there?' Vincent asks, too numb to feel pain.

'Why not there? I knew you'd be contrary about this.'

'It's the wood, Bear, you know what that means.'

'It's just a fucking wood, it's nothing special, it's just . . .' Bear's voice tails off. He tries again: 'Look, something happened up there.'

Vincent feels the world quiver with fatal instability. 'What?'

'She heard voices while we were going at it,' Bear continues. 'One minute everything's grand, the next she's lashing out, screaming so as you'd think I'd fucking raped her. But it wasn't like that.'

'What was it like?' Vincent asks, catching faint whispers that seem to come from a time when the world was more solid and real.

'I heard nothing,' Bear says sullenly. 'Nothing at all, only her going on about those voices, and some damn promise she made.'

'What promise?'

'How the fuck do I know? She just lost her head, I swear to God. She knelt in the dirt, crying how sorry she was she broke her promise. I cracked then and, God forgive me, I ran. When I came to my senses and went back to find her, she was gone.'

'This was when?' Vincent says, already knowing the answer.

'Yesterday afternoon.'

There's no moisture in Vincent's mouth. He feels an unbidden and profound pity for Greta. 'And you heard nothing?'

'Nothing at all,' Bear insists. 'I went to see her this morning before Mass but she wouldn't talk to me.'

'Why're you telling me this?' Vincent feels his pity turn to anger, and to something more.

'She's your cousin, I thought you might talk to her for me.'

'Why would I do that?' Something livid and hateful inside him.

But when Bear says, 'Because you're me friend,' Vincent is forced to acknowledge that that takes precedence over his sense of betrayal, and over the inexplicable sense of shame that has seeped into the hollow spaces of his heart.

For once, Vincent feels little pleasure in the slowness of time; he waits for something to happen without knowing what that something might be. He tries to study Yeats as the hours congeal around him, devoid of promise and fulfilment. Even sleep is no escape, for his dreams, too, have descended into fretful darkness. He takes his final exams on Wednesday morning, and afterwards he finds that his vague, indefinite tensions have coalesced into an awful dread of what Greta might have to say. But he has promised Bear and such a thing is sacred. No matter that his friend has let him down, he cannot afford such moments of weakness.

He gets off the school bus outside O'Mahoney's and walks the half mile east to the cottage that his aunt rents from an impoverished farmer. Mrs Scanlon, a widow, is still a young woman in her mid-thirties, and unlike her sister – Vincent's mother – she has to go out and earn a living. She works as a receptionist in the Drumassan Co-op, a position Vincent's father helped her obtain.

He knocks loudly at the front door, assuming a confidence he doesn't feel. The door opens inwards and Greta appears before him, green-eyed and pale-cheeked, wearing a yellow cotton dress from which her arms hang like the limbs of a sapling. The fiery lustre seems to have burnt itself out of her auburn hair but she nonetheless manages an awkward, unsteady smile that reveals a vulnerability he had not known she possessed. She raises a hand to shield her eyes from the sun and says, 'I knew you'd be coming.'

Vincent is unnerved by her certainty. 'How?'

She steps out into the bright sunlight. 'I remembered,' is all she offers by way of explanation, and then, 'Will you walk with me?'

'Sure,' Vincent says, and follows her to the boreen that runs behind the cottage and winds its way up the long, gentle slope of a hill. Apprehension fills the very cells of his being, preventing him from seeing clearly the child Greta in the Greta who walks beside him now. Has she changed that much, or is the change in him?

What he thinks are sly sideways glances become too obvious and Greta says, 'Would you ever stop gawping.' Then she climbs the ditch and runs off through a field of barley. Surprised, he follows her path till they come to a rocky outcrop that looms up out of the side of the hill. Greta skirts the base of the rock and picks out a path that leads them to the summit overlooking Drumassan lake.

She sits down, cross-legged, on the hard surface of the rock, 'God, it's quiet around here,' she says.

Despite himself, Vincent laughs and sits beside her. 'Takes a bit of getting used to, I 'spose, after Dublin.'

'It's like I remember, Vinnie.'

'Ye should never have left.'

Greta stares intently at him. 'We had to, remember?'

Vincent has no idea what she's talking about. 'It all seems a long time ago. Why did ye never come to visit?'

'Ma never said, but I understand now. Now it's safe.'

Vincent shrugs his shoulders. 'I wish I understood.'

'You will, Vinnie, when you remember.'

He feels that she's trying to read his mind and wonders if that would be so bad. Some animal swims through the ocean of barley below the rock, like a shark in search of prey. Calm settles on his mind.

'Have you a ciggie?' she says.

He lights one for her, then another for himself. 'I forgot what you looked like.'

She laughs. 'You really know how to flatter a girl.'

Neither mentions the wood, though the breath of cold murmurings clings to each of them. 'I don't get much practice,' Vincent says.

'Do you still have secrets, Vinnie?'

'Do you?'

I useta have a crush on you,' she says, her cheeks flushing red.

But there are holes in Vincent's memory, the deep darkness of which he cannot penetrate. Even peering over the edge requires a strength he doesn't have. Warily, he says, 'I saw Bear the other day.'

She stubs her cigarette out against the rock. Straggly curls fall across her face. He leans over and brushes them from her eyes and sees the sweat glistening on her forehead.

She says, 'Why did you do that?'

'To see if I can see what he sees in you.'

'And can you?'

'Tell me what happened, Greta.'

Suddenly she leans over and kisses him on the lips. Her mouth is sweet and warm but he is shocked. He pulls away, confused.

'What's the matter?' she says. 'Don't you fancy me?'

'Christ, Greta, it isn't that, it's . . .'

'Look at me, goddamnit!' She undoes the buttons at the top of her dress, exposing her small, white breasts. 'I'm no different to any other girl. No matter what they say. I'm as good as them.'

'Cover yourself up. I didn't come here for that.'

'Why? Is there something wrong with you?' Her bitterness stings, and so too does the accusation.

He stands up, feeling the situation slip beyond his control. She rises, too, saying, 'I'm sorry, I didn't mean anything by that.'

'Look,' Vincent says, 'I'm doing him a favour, that's all. He asked me to talk to you, to apologise for not understanding.'

'Do *you* understand?' she wants to know. 'The things I heard?'

Doubt and confusion fill him like some foul potion. He doesn't want to say anything but the question can't be ignored. 'I thought he might have hurt you.'

'He didn't.'·

'He said you imagined some things.'

'Not imagined,' she whispers, her gaze turned towards him but her eyes focused on some point beyond his head. Her words are soft but sure. 'Things that were real.'

It is as if she is speaking in a code no one has taught him how to decipher. 'He said you were frightened.'

'A 'secret for ever,' she continues, as if unaware of his presence. 'Mine and yours and his, eternal and sacred and never to be shared with anyone at all.'

'Dammit, Greta,' Vincent says, grabbing her arms. 'What the fuck are you talking about?'

'You remember, don't you?' Her voice is like a child's.

But he can't remember, or maybe it's that he doesn't want to. A long-forgotten fear undermines his few remaining certainties. He removes his hands from her and shouts, 'There's nothing at all to remember, not a fucking thing.'

'It isn't sacred after all,' she says, ignoring his rage. 'I understand that now. The promise was a lie.'

'Shut up,' he screams. 'Leave me the Hell alone.'

Before he can stop himself, he hits her across the face, knocking her down. 'Don't talk to me any more,' he warns. 'You're mad as fuck.' He turns away and quickly descends from the rock.

She cries out above him, 'I know you hear them.'

He presses on through the barley, closing his mind to her words, shutting her out before the world he thought he knew falls apart.

*

Vincent gets a summer job as a builder's labourer, mixing mortar and shifting concrete block for forty pounds a week. At night, his limbs aching, he listens to the soft murmur of his parents' voices downstairs, as they plan a future to which he feels no connection. He hates them for failing to see the amorphous nature of his reality, for not warning him that the forces that shape him lay beyond his, or their, control.

A week passes before Bear calls by. Vincent lies to him, saying he hasn't talked to Greta. If Bear suspects the lie, he doesn't say. There's no word from her, but her presence hangs heavy over Vincent's dreams, informing and elaborating them with the tissue of her being. The sickness he feels in the pit of his stomach is the sickness of certainty that she is waiting for him to remember.

And it is this sickness which drives him to Tallamount, to the Church of Our Lady, on the first afternoon of the summer rain. It is safer than Drumassan, he tells himself as he climbs the steps to the porch, for no priest will know him here. In the musty shadows of the entrance he tries to recall how long it has been since the rituals of this place have had the power to frighten him.

He peers through the stained glass and sees a woman with flowers walking up the central aisle of the nave. She genuflects before the altar then begins to arrange her blooms on either side of the chancel. Warily, Vincent steps into the aisle and takes a pew at the rear. Two flies buzz around his head, their entomological sacrilege disturbing the hushed gloom. A low, musical sound pervades the warm, still air: the woman humming while she works. The scent of flowers is cloying, shrouding his thoughts. A door opens somewhere in the church and crisp footsteps sound on the mosaic floor. From the sacristy a priest appears behind the altar and greets the flower woman, then kneels to say a prayer. Vincent finds the nerve to proceed towards the altar. Something creaks in the almost silence, but he keeps on till he sees a dozen sinners waiting in the west transept. Solemn faces cast shameful glances in his direction, as if somehow he reminds them of their own sins. He takes his place among them as the priest, middle-aged and ruddy-cheeked, comes from the altar, and, nodding at the penitents, steps into the confessional. An old woman enters one side, a young boy the other. And as the recitation of sin begins, Vincent's mind slips back through time to bear witness to the nature of evil.

A gaunt priest stalked the classroom, a leather strap dangling from his long, thin fingers. 'It isn't enough simply to turn a blind eye,' he spoke softly. 'A better man than me once said, "ignorance is no excuse".' He stared at the boys in turn, as if peering into their very souls. 'What's needed is a willingness to confront sin wherever you find it.' He stopped in front of Vincent and the strap whipped through the air, hitting the desk inches from the boy's hands. The priest's face broke into a bitter smile. 'But sometimes, cowardice will get the better of you and you'll think you can hide the truth from the Lord. I know that there isn't one among you who hasn't got something festering on his conscience. Am I right?' Vincent wanted to argue the point, but some despotic glint in the priest's eyes made him hold back; some hint of potential violence ready to confront the slightest doubt. Vincent dropped his gaze and the priest moved on.

Even now, after three years, he still has an irrational dread of priests. As if in confirmation, he feels the dead taste of guilt on his lips like ash. It is as if he has wandered from his own, familiar world into a place of blame and retribution, a place where all the hurt in the world is his. And now it is his turn to enter the box.

In the dark he whispers, 'Bless me, Father, for I have sinned.' He has come to find out what that sin might be. 'It's a while since my last confession.'

The scent of ripe, whiskey breath leaks through the curtain and he senses the bored irritation beyond it. Nervously, he recites a list of minor sins, some real, some invented. But when they are all used up he knows he is no nearer to discovering the truth. 'I useta have a friend,' he says. 'Someone took him from me.'

'And who was this friend?' the priest asks.

'The best friend anyone could have – but no longer.'

'What do you mean, boy?'

'It's the truth.'

'I doubt that.'

Vincent detects a note of sullen brutality in the voice, and all the fear he's been holding back comes closing in. 'There are things I can't remember,' he says. 'Bad things.'

'Ah yes, bad thoughts,' the priest suggests, as if on familiar ground. 'Tell me about them.'

'I can't.'

'You touched yourself down there, yes?'

'I promised to never tell.'

'We've no promises or secrets in here, so out with it.'

'I tried to tell her the voices weren't real.'

'*Her* now, is it?' Something lascivious in the words.

Vincent tries to express what he feels. 'She took him from – '

'Him now again?' A movement beyond the curtain.

'I hate her for it.'

'You're telling me you had impure thoughts about another boy? Is that it?' The priest's voice has risen noticeably. Vincent hears the almost imperceptible groan of a seat relieved of weight.

'You don't understand,' Vincent says, 'what he meant to me.'

And a shadow passes from the curtain as the priest says, 'By Jesus, you're right I don't understand.' But Vincent is already up and running down the aisle, even as the priest emerges and roars his pitiless rage.

'Promise me one thing,' Bear says. 'Just one thing.'

But inside Vincent's head his dreams are putting substance to something that was lost; he presses harder on the accelerator as if it might be possible to outrun the truth. And Bear says, 'Just tell me none of it was real, that it was just the wind in the trees, her mind playing tricks.'

And Vincent wants to, he really does, but right now he's hurtling foward through time, thinking he might just be able to escape the sense of unease that clots his days. This is not the first time he has driven Bear's car, but he has never driven so fast. Through the windscreen the world slips by in a blur; it's an epiphanic moment, one that reminds him of the first time he saw Bear naked, his lithe body striding out of the trees and diving into the cool water of the Graney. So unexpected a sight; so thrilling that Vincent had left his trunks in the towel and followed Bear into the stream. It was as if, at the age of eleven, he'd been shown a glimpse of a life he'd never imagined, one that erased the patterns encoded on his mind.

'I never hurt her, Vinnie,' Bear says. 'I'd never force her to do anything she didn't want. I love the girl.'

Which is exactly what Vincent doesn't want to hear.

'I don't understand how things could change so suddenly,' Bear continues. Vincent wonders how it would have been if he hadn't lied when Bear had once asked him, who, if he had the chance, he'd most like to fuck in the world. He's never forgotten that lie, not like his promise which – hidden for so long – is now coming home to roost.

'She saw a kid,' Bear says, heeding neither the speed of the car nor Vincent's numb detachment. 'But there was no one there.'

Vincent understands this: empty spaces once filled by people he had loved and trusted, silhouettes whose faces he can't even recall.

'She wanted me to help the kid, but what could I do?'

What did she tell? Vincent wonders. Her promise? Is that why light bleeds into the darkness, because of things she said that were better left unspoken? 'I never heard them, Bear.'

Bear is puzzled. 'I never said you did.'

'I'll look after you.'

But Bear doesn't note the pledge, only callously reiterates his need for Greta. 'I must help her, Vinnie, no matter what's happened, I want to be with her.'

Vincent's hands grasp the wheel tightly, not letting it move, and he can feel Bear – the essence of Bear – extricating himself, cutting unseen bonds and wrenching himself out of his world into some other.

A sudden bend in the road causes Vincent to lose control of the car. It slams into the ditch and Vincent, unrestrained by a safety belt, whips forward, his face smashing into the steering wheel. Dazed, he's vaguely aware of the blood dripping on to his shirt, and is pleased at how unreal it all seems.

'You've got it in you, laddie, to be whatever you want,' his father once said. It wasn't the wide vista of possibilities that most impressed Vincent then, but the realisation of how seldom his father called him by name. They should have christened him *Laddie*. A feeling that had long been latent in him crystallised then: the realisation that he was not who he had always thought he had been.

He remembers that now as he sits in a chair in the back garden, looking towards the sun with his fingers entwined over his eyes, allowing him to see the red beneath his skin that makes him real. Last night he dreamed he was a spirit returned to witness his own funeral, and like Tom Sawyer observing those who had wronged him, he felt both comforted and vindicated. Hearing a voice in the house behind him, he lowers his hand to his knees where they tremble visibly. Is it the way we see ourselves, he wonders, or the way we are perceived by others that makes us real? Or is it the past alone that shapes us? And is that past immutable? If so, then when Greta comes out into the garden, she will say, 'I came by to say I forgive you for hitting me. I had no right to go on at you like that.'

And he will reply, 'I was afraid of what you might say.'

Laughing, she'll muss his hair and sing:

> We made a promise, to keep silent and still
> So the past won't hurt us, and it never will.

It is a beautiful song but one she doesn't sing. She steps out into the garden and banishes the possibility of change. 'Vinnie,' she says. 'I heard about your accident.'

His heart begins to beat a little faster. He wonders how much of the world might be listening. 'It was nothing,' he says.

'Sure look at the state of you,' she says, kneeling in front of him. She touches his bruised face but such devices don't work with Vincent.

'I'm grand,' he says. 'I never felt a thing.'

'And Bear? He's OK too?'

The name makes him feel cold. He can't speak it, not now. So many shadows in the world, dark, hollow spaces that echo with the sounds of torment and shame. Darkness flickering in her eyes; he wants her to close them but he's worried she might think him weak, that she might think he'd be the one to tell.

'I was right, you know,' she continues. 'What I said before; we have to tell someone.'

'Please,' Vincent says. 'Don't talk about that.'

But she persists. She speaks of pain and suffering and guilt, and though he recognises these feelings, he can't acknowledge that they were ever his own. She speaks of trust and lies, and of a promise that has sealed their tongues for years. On and on, relentless in her need to make him recall the time they both grew old.

'I can't do it on my own,' she says. 'I need you to help me.'

'Jesus Christ,' Vincent cries in anguish. 'Would you just leave me be, Greta. You need to — '

'It needs to be both of us, together. No one will listen otherwise, no one will believe us.'

'They won't believe you anyway – they don't want to know these sorts of things. They'll just fucking hate you for it.'

'They'll believe the truth, Vinnie, someone has to.'

Hot, bitter tears well up in Vincent's eyes. He has little strength to resist her will. 'The truth? What is that? Fucking delusions, Greta, that's all. Yours, not mine. I don't see what you see, or hear what you hear. For all I know you've lost your mind.'

Then she's on her feet, pouring all her anger on him in one final effort to make him understand. 'You're lying, Vinnie. I know you, remember? It won't ever go away again, not for either of us.'

'You need help, so you do.'

'You're thinking you're a dirty little bastard and you can't bear to feel that way. But it's not our fault, for God's sake, we're not to blame. We trusted – '

Vincent claps his hands over his ears. 'I'm not listening any more,' he screams. And at the core of his being, a dark revulsion has taken root. It taps into his mind and soul, offering glimpses, not of the past but of the future; he sees himself slinking through the village, past knots of people who whisper behind cupped hands and surreptitiously point him out to strangers; alone and friendless, shunned by all except the dark, insubstantial creatures who wait to gather him in their cold embrace. This is the world that Greta would have him accept. She would rob him of the power to choose whatever he wants to be, strip him of all his bright and shining futures.

He stands up, dazed, waiting to see which way the world will turn. But it's his own mind that starts to spin, furious and

uncertain, fuelled by childhood demons, and dreams that once
set the world to rights. The love and fear that bind him to the
past tighten further around him while he spins faster and faster,
with voices whispering inside his head: *You are ours, you
always were*, taunting, warning, loving and pleading, burdening
him with intolerable demands, getting the measure of him,
sensing his weakness, sketching in the blanks, putting a face on
the absence, warm and familiar, reassuring and safe, so that here
and now he reaches out to make a connection, one that offers
him a salvation, or at the very least, a return to the way that
things once were.

A touch of light falls on him, illuminating his rare promise.

And Greta is there, standing before him shouting, 'We can do
it together, Vinnie, we can make him pay.'

But that sort of power is beyond him. He turns and runs from
the garden, out to the road. He speeds towards the place of
secrets, her treacherous screams ringing in his ears, knowing
that only the past can silence her lies.

A scent of rumour and complicity hangs heavy in the drowsy air,
a tang of corruption rising up from generations of dead vegetation, imprinting its dizzying fragrance on bark and moss and
flesh. The soft pink of twilight begins to fall through the
watchful trees, stilling his troubled soul. He sits with his back
against the rough bark of a broad-crowned ash, naked, a cigarette
in one hand, his cock in the other. He tries to masturbate but it's
a desultory attempt to capture a feeling that is gone; he is unable
to give substance to the fantasy.

The reason he is here, he admits, isn't Bear; nor was it simply
to escape Greta's insistence that he accept what she calls the
truth. Truth hides in a secret place far from prying eyes. The
strong secrets that bind lovers thrive in the dark spaces on the
fringe of reality: the tight spaces beneath beds, under-stairs
cupboards, cellars, dusty attics, the ruins of a stone cottage, a
wood. You have to be in such places to understand what they
mean. That's why he is here, letting cool shadows embrace him
like an old friend.

A large, brown moth hovers in front of his face, then lands on
his knee. He reaches slowly forward and catches one wing
between his fingers. The other beats frenetically against his

palm but it can't escape. He holds the cigarette in front of his face and blows on it till the point tip is burning red. He brings it down on the moth, incinerating its head, then tosses the dead thing away. He has come here to put flesh on the bones of a forgotten promise. He closes his eyes and starts to breathe deep and slow. After an indeterminate time, a fragment of awareness slips loose from his consciousness. He takes one final huge breath and holds it, five seconds, ten, and he becomes aware of the gentle thrum of persuasion against his mind.

And in the trees, a murmuring begins . . .

. . . *Promise me now,* a voice like treacle implores above a muted weeping. *On the Bible, on Jesus's life. This is our secret, yours and hers and mine, nobody else's.*

I promise, a solemn-eyed boy weeps. *If Jesus says.*

Oh, he does, he does . . .

See the cold, shamefaced sun cast speckled shadows on fragile limbs where goosebumps rise but not with cold. And listen as the girl pleads, reluctantly, as if afraid to plead, *Please don't hurt me.*

A heavy groan, burdened by a tender, weighty love. *It's OK, my doughty, he won't hurt you at all. . .*

Vincent is trying his very best to pierce the veil of time but somewhere a skittish heart is racing, like the heart of some dumb beast snared in incoherent dread.

Up on her now, boy, that's the way. The watching man's words caught on the wind of his breath, urging him on. *She's a fine one, isn't she, boy? A pure thoroughbred.*

The tremoring off the girl's body, the cold sweat on her flesh, the terror in her eyes. Seeing black garments being strewn on the ground. *Off her now.* A rhythm of brute need punctuates the words. *My turn, boy.*

Light falls among the shadows, pouring into the silhouettes, filling them with identity. See the arms and face and ruddy, quivering flesh of someone who was gone.

Bear witness, my boy, and never share this secret with another soul, lest the Devil come and carry you off to some bad place.

Please not there, the boy cries, plaintive notes rising and falling on a wind that sighs regret among the trees.

I'll save ye from the fire, the quickening voice assures. *Long as ye both shall tell no lies.*

No lies, one child promises. *No lies*, another echoes.

That part of Vincent which has slipped outside time fills with cold understanding: in this world of secrets, there is one more terrible than all the others, one that triggers a madness that threatens to disrupt the bonds between Vincent here and Vincent there. He siphons the air from his lungs and fills them anew till he feels the blood pounding in his head, and senses the backwards reach of time, coiling away from him, drawing him towards one who whispers . . .

Promise me . . .

And despite the fatigue that saps his strength he struggles to his feet, wanting to know, more than anything, who it was who had forced him on the girl, forced him to mimic what the man had done, and then made him watch as he did it to her again. And afterwards, the way he'd extracted a promise from them, as he'd extracted it so many times before. He stumbles forward in the failing light, groping towards the pain of understanding. And sees two children and the man, kneeling and praying together. *So ye must ask God to forgive ye for tempting me. Ye want his forgiveness, don't ye?*

Bless me Father, the children recite, while their uncle begins the litany of absolution, words that ring hollowly down the years.

And Vincent flails through the spiteful vegetation that wraps him in tissues of unreality. Reaching out his fingers, he can almost grasp the truth; just a little further, beating a path through reassured undergrowth, ignoring the heart that threatens to burst inside him, driven on awful fear and numbing shame which in the end is not enough, never will suffice. He touches something, just for one moment, just long enough to feel the searing pain of truth. Then he falls among the musty leaves and the breath roars from his lungs like something foul.

And time snaps back . . .

Seconds slip by at their normal pace and in the here and now he sees a slight and graceful figure moving towards him through the trees, full of hope and reassurance. A soft voice calls out his name and for a moment, he thinks perhaps he is back in an earlier time, a time before secrets and promises, but when her eyes alight on his naked flesh, the memory of that earlier time fills him with shame.

'I followed you here,' she says, not seeming to notice his nakedness. 'To tell you it's a promise not worth keeping.'

Vincent nods for he finally comprehends the cruel lie of love that's been hidden for years. On his knees he waits to accept the balm of truth. Her arms enfold him and her breath roars in his ears. 'It's OK, it's over now.' And he knows how right she is as he feels the burden fall from his soul. She holds his face in her palms and kisses the tears from his cheeks, from his lips. 'We'll tell the truth, Vinnie, they'll see we were innocent. Even Bear, even he'll love me again.' The words sink into his brain and with them, the knowledge of what he has lost. They hold each other tight, kneeling in the soft earth. He can't breathe because he is holding his breath; she, because he is holding her throat, holding tight and counting, reaching out, trying to recapture the ecstasy of forgetting.

The land slips away like a puzzled acquaintance, failing to understand the reasons for his leaving. It is not enough to say that Laragh Wood and the memories it contains belongs to the past, so he doesn't. He decides that what he feels is not loneliness, but anticipation. In fact, he feels very little at all. Ringaskiddy is soon left behind, swallowed up in the pale mists of morning and presently Vincent sees the tall, coloured buildings of Cobh sailing by the port side of the ferry.

He left home yesterday, hitching a ride to Cork and spending the night in the docks, not wanting to waste any of what little money he has. He reads the story in yesterday's paper one more time, thinking they might have used a more recent picture of his dead cousin. Bear was arrested the same day the body was discovered in the Graney. He's pleading his innocence, not understanding his own complicity in Greta's death, that he should never have taken her to the wood. In time they'll let him go and conclude suicide, or more probably a tragic accident, for you can't bury suicides in consecrated ground.

Years from now, when a general contentment settles again on the village, and parents recall her name only to warn children against hidden currents, no one will thank Vincent for sparing Drumassan the shadow cast by the monstrosities of childhood.

For they will never know of his promise, and the manner in which it was extracted from him. They both were innocent, she'd said; their uncle was to blame. But Vincent understands now that innocence, like truth, no longer has any meaning, not even for children.

And, accepting the shadow into his heart, he steps up to the rail and lets the newspaper fall over the side where it is snatched up by the wind and borne backwards and down into the engine-foaming sea.